PLAYING THE HAND
YOU'RE DEALT

Also by Trice Hickman

Unexpected Interruptions

Keeping Secrets & Telling Lies

Breaking All My Rules

Looking for Trouble

Published by Dafina Books

PLAYING THE HAND YOU'RE DEALT

Trice Hickman

Kensington Publishing Corp.
http://www.kensingtonbooks.com

DAFINA BOOKS are published by

Kensington Publishing Corp.
119 West 40th Street
New York, NY 10018

All Kensington Titles, Imprints, and Distributed Lines are available at special quantity discounts for bulk purchases for sales promotions, premiums, fund-raising, and educational or institutional use. Special book excerpts or customized printings can also be created to fit specific needs. For details, write or phone the office of the Kensington special sales manager: Kensington Publishing Corp., 119 West 40th Street, New York, NY 10018, attn: Special Sales Department, Phone: 1-800-221-2647.

Dafina and the Dafina logo Reg. U.S. Pat. & TM Off.

ISBN-13: 978-0-7582-9411-1
ISBN-10: 0-7582-9411-5
First Kensington Trade Paperback Edition: December 2012
First Kensington Mass Market Edition: July 2014

eISBN-13: 978-0-7582-9412-8
eISBN-10: 0-7582-9412-3
Kensington Electronic Edition: July 2014

10 9 8 7 6 5 4 3 2 1

Printed in the United States of America

Chapter 1

Emily . . .

What My Heart Desired

What do you do when you know right from wrong, and you know that what you're about to do is dead wrong, but you decide to do it anyway?

That was my predicament. My name is Emily Eloise Snow. It's an old-fashioned name for a young woman, and I guess that's the way my life had always been . . . something that wasn't quite what it seemed.

Actually, I wasn't surprised that I was stuck in this conundrum because Ms. Marabelle had predicted it several months ago, before I set out on this journey.

"Emily, you been waitin' a mighty long spell, and now it's time fo' you to follow yo heart," Ms. Marabelle had said to me in her low, raspy voice. "It ain't gon' be easy, and the road ahead's gon' be rough in some spots, but you got to ride it out 'cause love is waitin' on you. You finally gon' be happy, chile."

Marabelle Jackson, by my estimation, was at least

ninety years old, and the tiny, gray-haired woman's mystical powers were well known and trusted in my small, tight-knit community. Ms. Marabelle had what people called *the gift.* She foretold things that eventually would come to pass. She forecasted floods, tornados, and other natural disasters months and sometimes years before they happened, and accurately predicted prosperity as well as devastation for those who sought her out for personal readings. I had always tried to stay as far away from Ms. Marabelle as was humanly possible. She scared me with her haunting prophecies and cryptic visions, not because they were astonishingly accurate, but more so because they were usually full of gloom and doom—at least for me.

Now that Ms. Marabelle had finally told me that something good would unfold in my life, her prediction was tainted by the promise of hardship on the horizon, a rough road ahead, and I knew exactly what that meant. Her words sent me into a free fall of emotions that haven't stopped since they rang in my ears.

As I pondered my fate, I tried to concentrate on the road ahead because I was driving in unfamiliar territory, knowing that my final destination could very well be a place somewhere between virtual happiness and a living hell.

All my life, I had always tried to do the right things.

She's so nice. You can always count on Emily. She's a good girl. That was how people in my neighborhood, school, church, and hometown of Atlanta, Georgia, described me. Growing up, my mother used to say I was the kind of child that every parent wished for, smart, kind, obedient, and loving. As I matured, I grew into the kind of young woman who men wanted to take home to meet their mothers, and who mothers wanted their sons to marry. And as more years passed I became a responsible, levelheaded adult, dependable and solid in character—qualities that had been part blessing, part curse.

I tried to treat people with the same respect and courtesy I'd want in return because that was how I was raised. I put careful thought and consideration into my choices before I made them, and I pretty much played by the rules. But therein was my problem, presenting the troubling quandary that held me in its grip for the last few months. It was the delicate balance between exercising good judgment and throwing caution to the wind so I could finally have what I wanted, however risky it might be.

As I eased off the gas pedal, making a sharp right turn onto another busy street, my car sputtered and ambled along, just like my state of mind. I wasn't good at city driving, but like many things in my life, it was something I'd have to get used to. So I continued my course, navigating through the congested streets of northwest Washington, DC, my stomach rumbling and turning with the thought of what awaited me once I reached the red brick colonial on Sixteenth Street.

I kept telling myself that I couldn't give in to the warm sensation that had been keeping me up late at night because it was much too dangerous a proposition. But I couldn't help it. With each mile I traveled, I inched closer and closer to the man who'd been holding my heart hostage for the past eleven years. He was what I both passionately loved and desperately feared.

It had been seven months since I'd last seen him, and unfortunately, that occasion had been one of great sorrow. I'd been in a haze, barely able to enjoy the sweetness his presence usually brought when he was near. I had searched for him among the small gathering of friends and visitors who surrounded me that sad, dreary weekend.

"God will see you through this, Emily," mourners

whispered to me in somber tones, offering hugs of condolence for the loss of my mother. I appreciated the kind words and genuine show of affection that friends and church members had offered, but I'd been much too numb to really absorb them. Those days whizzed by like blank flash cards. But when I looked up and saw him through the sea of faces gathered at the church, it was the first time in a week that I hadn't felt dead, too. And even though our encounter was brief, as most of them had been over the years, it was, as always, meaningful.

After my mother's funeral, my world moved slowly, limping along in a crooked groove. Losing her devastated me. I lost my father when I was ten years old. One evening he went to the corner store for a carton of milk, despite my mother repeatedly urging him not to go. "It's too late to be out this time of night," she had said. She told him that she and I could have toast and fruit for breakfast instead of the corn flakes we both loved to eat every morning.

But my father wouldn't hear of it. "I'm gonna get my two favorite girls what they want," he told my mother before heading out the door. He was standing at the counter, ready to make his purchase when two thugs shot and killed him for the $21.34 in his pocket. It was my indoctrination into shattered hopes and stolen dreams.

I was an only child, and both my parents had been as well. Mom and I were all each other had left. Even though I was blessed with a small but close circle of friends, nothing could replace the inviolable bond of maternal flesh and blood. To lose your mother, your first connection to the world, is a hard thing to wrap your mind around.

I thought about Mom and sighed as I came to a stoplight at yet another confusing intersection. "Where in the world am I?" I mumbled aloud, glancing down at my iPhone's screen. The GPS app I'd downloaded had frozen yet again. I tried to gather my bearings as I recalled what my mother used to say whenever she got turned around in an unfamiliar part of town. "I'm not lost, I'm just exploring," she would announce with conviction. I smiled, remembering her remarkable optimism. I could really use her help right now.

Although it had been seven months since I buried my mother, I still couldn't believe she was gone. I had braced myself for her death because she'd been sick for so long, and because like other sad things in my life, Ms. Marabelle had predicted it. Mom battled multiple sclerosis until the degenerative disease eventually won the long war it had raged against her body. But when death finally came to claim her, I hadn't expected the magnitude of grief and emptiness that followed.

Thank goodness I had my ace, my best friend, Samantha Baldwin. Samantha was the sister I'd never had, and she was a lifesaver. She comforted me and helped me to cope with the heartache and pain I suffered after Mom's funeral. Samantha was also part of the reason why I was driving through a maze of Friday-afternoon rush-hour traffic, headed straight toward what could either make me whole or tear me into tiny pieces.

Samantha had talked me into moving here to DC, which was her hometown; Chocolate City, as she affectionately called it. She said that DC would be good for me, that it was the perfect elixir I needed to help me get on with my life and make a new start. "DC will bring you your heart's desires," she told me just a week ago when I was packing boxes.

I literally shook in my sandals when I heard my best friend's words. I was petrified of what my new start could possibly bring, and I felt that way because I knew what Samantha didn't. I knew deep down that if I got what I wanted, what my heart truly desired, it could not only change the course of my life as I had known it, it stood to disrupt the foundation of loyalty and trust on which we had built our rock-solid friendship and sisterhood.

The raw, naked truth was simple. What my heart truly desired was the man I had been in love with for the better part of my adult life—and that man just happened to be Samantha's father.

Chapter 2

Samantha . . .

The Pleasure Palace

I looked at my watch for what had to have been the one hundredth time in the last hour. Normally, I wasn't a time-conscious person—far from it. But I was anxiously awaiting the arrival of my best friend, Emily. I was busy all day, running errands and making sure I had everything in place to welcome her to her temporary home.

Emily was staying here with my parents until her contractor finished renovating her new home, which I prayed, for her sake, wouldn't take much longer. Living under the same roof with my mother could make you want to slit your wrists. Let me tell you, that woman's a certified trip! A little bit of her went a hell of a long way, and trust me, that was a generous assessment. But if anyone could put up with my mother's bullshit, it was Emily. She had the patience of Job.

Actually, Mother probably won't give Emily as hard a

time as she gives everyone else, and that's because Emily was one of the few people who just barely met her impossibly high standards—something I'd never be able to do. Mother was always telling me, "Emily is so responsible. Why can't you be more like your friend?" When she made comments like that, I'd just laugh and tell her it was because I was too much like her. That usually pissed her off because deep down, she knew there was a little truth in my words. Ironically, we were more alike than either of us cared to admit; she was just more refined about her shit than I was. But honestly, the real difference between my mother and me was that she was a genuine phony, and I wasn't. As you can tell, I've got issues with my mother, Brenda Justine Baldwin.

My mother and father married young, practically the day after they both graduated from Howard University. She claimed it was because they were so much in love that they didn't want to wait. Puh-leeze! She could save that lie for someone who'd believe it. I did the math, and my brother's birthday and their anniversary fell within five months of each other . . . and my brother wasn't a preemie, okay?

Even though Mother had never worked at anybody's job a single day of her life, she had the nerve to tell me about my "unacceptable" work habits. She volunteered at every museum in town, was a member of every bourgeois black women's organization you could think of, and she acted like the elaborate parties she threw were the second coming of Christ. Oh, and did I mention that she was a drama queen for your ass? Some of the stunts she pulled could win her a Daytime Emmy. Seriously!

I was much closer to my father, Edward Curtis Baldwin. He was a great man, and I would say that even if he wasn't my daddy. He was handsome, smart as hell, understanding, and fair. He was also a well-respected attorney who made a shitload of money. But it wasn't about the paper for Daddy. The reward for him was going up against big corporations who didn't give a damn about the little guy, and frying their asses in court. My father was cool as hell, too. Even though I had disappointed him on many occasions, he still had faith in me.

Emily had faith in me, too. That was one of the many reasons why I loved her like she was my blood, and why I had gotten up early this morning, which was a major feat for me, and driven all over the city buying special treats to make a customized gift basket to properly welcome her to town.

I started out at Whole Foods, filling my small shopping cart with some of Emily's favorite herbal teas, fresh fruit, and snack bars. She was an avid reader, so after I checked off all the items on my shopping list, I headed across town to the bookstore and picked up a few novels by some of her favorite authors. And last but certainly not least on my agenda was my most important stop of the day—the Pleasure Palace, in Georgetown. That was my spot! You can never go wrong with gifts from a sex shop; after all, everybody's got to get their freak on, right? I hand-picked an assortment of special goodies that I hoped Emily would be able to put to good use, 'cause truth be told, my friend needed a little spice in her life!

After I returned home, I took my time putting together the huge wicker basket, filling it with treats. I reached into the box that arrived from California yesterday and removed the Drippin' Nectar all-natural bath and body products I had ordered, which were Emily's favorites, and added the sweet-smelling jars of whipped shea body butter and sugar body scrub to the hefty basket. I wrapped it all in clear cellophane and topped it off with a silk turquoise bow, Emily's favorite color. I walked down the hall and placed her welcome gift atop the large dresser in the guest room where she'll be staying.

I returned to my old bedroom where I stayed when I was in town. I lived and worked in New York City, but the minute that Emily finally decided to move here to DC, I put in my paperwork for a transfer. Right now, she needed a good friend by her side, and hey, I was the best. I was also Lancôme's best senior account manager in the area, and that's why my regional director eagerly approved my request. In thirty days I'd be back in my city, Chocolate City, moving into my new condo. And the ironic part was that even though we hadn't planned it, Emily and I would be living just ten minutes from each other.

As I stood in front of the mirror of my old dresser, lightly dabbing my forehead, nose, and chin with the honey-colored makeup in my compact, I thought about how much fun Emily and I were going to have now that we'd be in the same city again. We hadn't lived near each other since we graduated from Spelman College eight years ago. And even though we talked on the phone nearly every day, it didn't replace having the comfort of a best friend nearby.

I checked my watch again. It was nearly six o'clock, and Emily would be arriving any minute. Unlike me, the girl was a stickler for time. She was so damn punctual it was ridiculous, and if she said she was going to be somewhere at a certain time, you could bet cash money she'd be there.

Beep, beep, beep, my cell phone rang. I knew it had to be Emily, calling to let me know that she was on her way. I smiled with excitement, but when I looked at the caller ID, the corners of my mouth faded into a deep frown. There were only two people who could cause me to scowl in frustration: my mother, and the man on the other end of the line. "What the hell does he want?" I huffed aloud as I stared at the digits, which seemed to jump out at me.

I hesitated for a few seconds, trying to decide if I should pick up. *Beep, beep, beep,* my phone chimed again. "Dammit!" I moaned. I knew I couldn't keep avoiding him, so I pressed the Talk button. "What do you want?" I said to Carl, hoping I sounded as pissed as I was at the moment.

"Why you always gotta step to a brothah wit' a attitude?" Carl snapped back at me.

I rolled my eyes so hard he probably felt it through the phone. I didn't have much patience for his drama. "Carl, I don't have time to fool with you today. I've got a ton of stuff to do before Emily gets here."

"First off, watch your tone," he piped up. "You always so hyper and shit. I was just callin' to check on you and see how you been."

"I'm fine," I responded in a flat tone.

"You been in town three days, why you ain't call a brothah?"

My eyebrows rose a notch. "How do you know how long I've been in town?"

" 'Cause I just know."

I didn't like this one bit. I knew the type of things that Carl was capable of, and having me followed was just one of them. I was about to give him a piece of my mind when my son walked into the room. "Hold on," I said to Carl, quickly putting my phone on mute.

"Is Auntie Emee here yet?" CJ asked.

I looked into my son's hopeful eyes. He was so excited about seeing Emily. "No, CJ, but she's on her way. Why don't you go to your room and play until she gets here."

CJ looked disappointed and anxious at the same time. He'd been asking about Emily's arrival every ten minutes, and it was beginning to drive me crazy. But I couldn't get too frustrated with him because I understood how much he loved my best friend. In many ways, Emily was more of a mother to him than I was and probably ever would be.

CJ looked down at his feet, then back up at me. "I'm going downstairs with Gerti," he said. "She's cooking good food for Auntie Emee!"

I watched my five-year-old son as he bolted downstairs, disregarding the fact that I'd just asked him to play in his room. Hell, I guess if I were him I'd rather be downstairs licking batter from the bowls of whatever Gerti was cooking than being stuck in my room.

Gerti Taylor wasn't just our housekeeper, she was family. And right now, she was busy preparing a small feast in honor of Emily's arrival. Gerti loved my friend to death and was just as anxious to see her as CJ and I were. Hell, my whole family was psyched about Emily coming to town. Speaking of which, I didn't have time to deal with Carl at the moment. Reluctantly, I unmuted my phone. "I have to go," I huffed.

"You gonna call me later?" he asked in a slightly demanding tone.

"I'm going to be busy tonight, but I'll see." *Where the hell did that come from?* As soon as the words came out of my mouth, I regretted them. I couldn't believe I had actually opened up the door to the possibility of calling Carl back. I had to break free of him, and this wasn't the way to do it.

"A'ight. Later," he said, and then hung up.

I couldn't see him, but I knew from the sound of Carl's voice that his slick ass had been smiling on the other end. He knew he'd gotten to me.

I prayed that he wasn't up to his old tricks again. I

was trying to end our dysfunctional relationship once and for all, but he refused to let go. Carl was a master at creating headaches and drama, but I had no idea how crazy he could be until four hours later . . . when he showed me face-to-face.

Chapter 3

Emily . . .

The Real Reason I Had Waited Up

According to my GPS, I was only a couple of miles away. I glanced at the ancient clock on my car's dashboard and smiled. It was close to six o'clock, and I was right on target to reach my destination on time.

As I drove through the city, I looked up at the houses and apartment buildings that were stacked so closely together that I could barely tell one from the other. Urban living was going to be a new challenge for me. I was born and raised in Atlanta, and until yesterday, I had lived there since the day I emerged naked and screaming into this world. Samantha had been trying to get me to move here for years, but relocating wasn't an option because my mother needed me. We'd always been there for each other. But after her funeral, and with no family left, I couldn't think of any good reason to stay in the Peach State. And ironically, my move to "the city" was part of a reading that Ms. Marabelle had prophesied to me many years ago, when I was just a little girl.

At six on the dot, I finally reached my destination. As I parked in front of the beautifully manicured driveway, an intense feeling hugged my stomach that I couldn't explain. Surprisingly, it wasn't nerves or anxiety, but it made my hands shake just the same. And even though my rickety air conditioner was pumping full blast, tiny beads of sweat dotted my forehead. I took a deep breath, turned off the engine, and prepared myself.

Looking at the impressive brick colonial in front of me, the house seemed much bigger than I remembered. I wondered if it was just my imagination or if they had built an addition to the five-thousand-square-foot dwelling. Then I realized that my mind had only made it seem larger because for the first time, I was keenly aware of the mountainous troubles that lay behind the stately walls.

"Auntie Emee! Auntie Emee!" CJ shouted as he rushed out the front door, running toward me like a hurricane on two legs. I hopped out of my car and leaned down to pick him up as he ran into my arms. I smiled so hard my cheeks started to hurt. This five-year-old little boy was the absolute apple of my eye. We squeezed and hugged each other as he wrapped his arms and legs around me, hanging on like a life preserver.

I missed CJ terribly. It had been a year since he left my care to come and live here with his grandparents. And even though it had torn me up inside to deliver him into the hands of Samantha's mother and father, I knew it was for the best. My mother's condition had deteriorated badly, and migraines had begun to take a toll on my own health. That, coupled with long work days, constant fights with the insurance company over Mom's medical claims, trying to maintain a sinking relationship with my boyfriend, and juggling all of life's other balls had left me with little time to care for an active, young child.

I didn't want to deprive CJ of the care and attention that he needed and deserved. After all, it was the reason why Samantha had given me legal guardianship of her son in the first place. Plus, I knew it was time for CJ to have a strong male figure in his life, and it was a role that Samantha's father was more than happy to step up and claim.

"Hey, Sweet Pea," I cooed after giving CJ a million small kisses on his softly dimpled cheeks. "Where's your mother?"

"Here I am!" Samantha shouted, strutting over to greet me with her hands perched on her imaginary hips.

I had predicted what her reaction to my new appearance would be, and judging from her wide-eyed expression, I'd been right.

"Oh my God!" Samantha screamed as she came closer. "Girl, I can't believe what you've done to your hair!"

Hair was to black women what weight was to our white counterparts, and my hair had always been a topic of discussion. It had been the only bone of contention between my mother and me . . . well, that and the fact that she thought I should've been married a long time ago.

My hair was a wild mixture of kinky, curly tendrils, in its natural state. When I was a little girl, my mother used to press my hair until it was bone straight. Every Saturday night, like clockwork, she'd separate my thick mane into tiny sections and then divide those into even smaller, more manageable pieces before coating my thick strands with coconut-scented pomade. Then she'd run the sizzling hot comb's steel teeth through each curly clump until my unruly hair submitted into long sheets of black silk that gleamed down my back. The next day at church my mother would smile proudly, enjoying the compliments that her painstaking handiwork garnered. And I, too, benefitted from her diligence, as I became known as the pretty girl with the great hair.

During my teenage years I rebelled against the hot comb and my much-coveted straight hair. It wasn't just the unrelenting hours of heat-emblazoned misery that I rebuked, it was the notion that my thick, unapologetically wild hair wasn't beautiful in its natural state. At the time, I wasn't aiming for any kind of militant social statement, I just knew what I liked, and what made me feel most comfortable in my own skin.

But my mother was old school, and she wasn't having it. "At least let me take you to Ms. Emma's shop so she can put a relaxer in your hair," my mother had said during one of our knock-down-drag-outs one weekend. "It'll look just like you had a good pressing, and it'll even last longer," she sighed, hoping I'd have the good sense to give in.

Finally, she gave up, not having the energy to argue because her disease had started to progress. I went natural my junior year of high school, and it wasn't until last week, sitting in Ms. Emma's chair in Heavenly Hair Salon, that my mother got her long-held wish. I had enjoyed my natural hair, but now it was time for a change. I wanted a new look to go along with my new life, in a new city. The large bush of hair that had once rested at the bottom of my shoulders now hung down to the middle of my back. It had taken a little getting used to at first, but now I loved my new hairdo.

"Well, I'll be damned!" Samantha gasped. "I can't believe you finally relaxed your hair!"

She circled around me while CJ began to examine

my hair, too, as if he'd just seen me for the first time. When he grinned, showing me one of his adorable dimples, I knew he approved. "Your son likes it." I smiled.

"And I love it!" she shouted. "Girl, your shit is fly!"

I bristled at the sound of Samantha cursing in front of her son, but I let the uncomfortable feeling go because I didn't want to spoil the happy moment. So instead of gently cautioning her about the importance of watching her language around an impressionable five-year-old, I reached one arm out and embraced her while I held on tight to CJ with the other. I saw that he liked the group hug because he started grinning even harder. As I watched CJ's face light up, it struck me that men, even in their early stages of development, loved the company of more than one woman at a time. But for now, I appreciated that my little Sweet Pea's enthusiasm was purely innocent. I constantly marveled at how Samantha and Carl could have created such a perfect little person.

Don't get me wrong, I loved Samantha dearly, and there was no one on this earth who could hold a candle to her as a loyal and trusted friend, but her life was filled with the kind of drama that could make the police officers on *Cops* take a pause. And Carl, her on-again, off-again boyfriend who happened to be CJ's father . . . well, let's just say he wasn't the type of guy one would ever mistake for being a good catch.

For someone who'd been raised around all the "right kind of people," I never quite understood why Samantha always gravitated toward the lowest common denominator when it came to men. I could only assume it was a rebellion thing.

It killed Samantha's parents, especially her mother, that she made such poor relationship choices. But Samantha seemed to almost delight in it. We'd been best friends since our freshman year of college—that was eleven years and running—and in all that time I had never known her to date a man who was worth the breath it took to call his name. Well, there had been one, but it was years ago, and she'd messed up that relationship in a disastrous way.

Samantha and I first met on move-in day at Spelman College. We were roommates and quickly became inseparable best friends, to the bewilderment of everyone around us, because with the exception of sharing the same birthday, and the same middle initial—my *E* was for Eloise, and her *E* was for Elise—we were polar opposites in almost every way.

Samantha was born into a family of old money and privilege, raised in the prominent Gold Coast section of DC—the right side of the tracks. Her father, Ed, the love of my life, was a well-known plaintiff attorney whose courtroom victories were legendary in the DC metro area. Her mother, Brenda, docent and socialite extraordinaire, was a beautifully elegant drama queen whose antics could easily rival those of a soap opera diva. Together, they had raised Samantha and her older, estranged brother, Jeffery, to be cultured members of the Talented Tenth.

I, on the other hand, was born into a lower-middle-class lot. My father, Roosevelt, was a janitor who took pride in a job well done. He was a strong, hardworking, God-fearing man with a gentle heart. My mother, Lucille, was a soft-spoken, but fiercely independent elementary school teacher who ran our home with the same efficiency and care that she demonstrated in her classroom. They'd met at the school where they both worked, and as my father had once said, "It was love at first sight." They were the salt of the earth, truly two of the finest human beings I'd ever known. I missed them dearly.

As I looked at Samantha, her face beaming with relief that I was finally here, I didn't have the heart to tell her what I was really feeling—that I was scared out of my mind knowing I'd be sleeping under the same roof as her father.

"Let's go inside. I know you want to relax after your long drive," Samantha said.

"Are your parents home?" I didn't know if their vehicles were parked out back in their three-car garage.

"No," she said, swatting a pesky fly that had invaded her space. "Mother's over at the Corcoran Gallery, and Daddy's probably knee-deep in paperwork at the office, as usual."

That information gave me the temporary relief I needed. We grabbed my bags out of the trunk of my beat-up but trusty 1985 Volvo, ready to head inside. Samantha stopped and looked at my car as if I'd driven up in a horse and buggy. "Emily, you need to get a new ride. I'm surprised you didn't break down on your way up here. City driving is gonna beat the last bit of life out of ol' Hazel."

Samantha was right, but there was a deep sentimental value attached to my four wheels. Hazel was the first brand-new vehicle that my father had ever owned. He'd always driven used contraptions that barely passed the lemon law. He bought Hazel when I was five years old, and was so proud that he'd worked hard enough to afford a fancy car for his family, especially on a janitor's salary. He loved this car, and after he died my mother drove her. When I graduated from high school she handed Hazel down to me. This old car was one of my few material possessions that had been shared by the two people who meant everything to me.

I looked at Samantha, and then toward Hazel. "I know, but she's all I've got left."

Samantha nodded with understanding and rubbed my shoulder. "Let's go inside."

* * *

When we walked into the house, I found it largely unchanged from the last time I'd visited, a year ago when I brought CJ here to live. The living room was gorgeous; not my taste, but still beautiful. Samantha's mother had many talents, and decorating was one of them. The color scheme was soft pastels and gentle neutrals, and the furniture was large and upscale. Everything went so well together, every piece in its proper place. It was so perfect, it was almost scary.

"*Mmm,* something smells like heaven," I said, breathing in the delicious aroma wafting through the air.

"Gerti's throwin' down, making all of your favorites." Samantha smiled.

Just then, Gerti Taylor came out from the kitchen to greet us. At five feet eight inches and nearly two hundred pounds, she was a force of nature. "Well, ain't you a sight! Come give Gerti some sugar." She grinned as she walked toward me with outstretched arms.

I loved Ms. Gerti. She was a good woman. She reminded me a lot of my mother. Only Ms. Gerti would curse you out quicker than a heartbeat and worse than a sailor. She lived in the guesthouse off the flower garden behind the main house. She had been a loyal employee, nursemaid, babysitter, chef, housekeeper, chauffeur, confidante, and psychologist to the Baldwin family for over thirty years.

"Hey, Ms. Gerti!" I beamed as we embraced in a big hug.

"Let me take a look at you!" Ms. Gerti exclaimed as she stared at my hair. "Well, I'll be." She smiled, pausing to inspect me as Samantha and CJ had just done. "Emily, you're just beautiful, I tell ya."

I smiled appreciatively, giving my thanks for her approval. "Don't tell me you're cooking fried chicken?" I asked, inhaling the mouthwatering scent that could put KFC to utter shame.

"Sure am, with collard greens, macaroni and cheese, cornbread, and sweet potato pie for dessert."

"Southern staples, my favorites!" I tossed my healthy eating habit out the window and gave her a kiss on her cheek for throwing in the sweet potato pie.

"I'm so sorry to hear about your mother," Ms. Gerti said as she patted my shoulder. "I know you two were really close. There's no hurt in this world like the kind that comes when you lose your mama. You just keep your head up, you hear?"

I nodded because her words were so true. The hurt was indescribable. She could see the sadness in my eyes, so she cut the conversation short, giving me a small reprieve. "You all go on upstairs and clean up, dinner will be ready in a minute."

Samantha, CJ, and I lugged my bags up the stairs and headed to the end of the long hallway, entering my temporary living quarters. I walked over to the other side of the room and looked out of the window, admiring the backyard. It was nothing less than spectacular, especially for the city. Brenda had done an amazing job of turning it into a miniature Garden of Eden. I glanced toward the other side of the room, where I spotted a large wicker basket sitting atop the mahogany dresser. "For me?" I smiled as I looked back at Samantha, walking over to inspect it.

"It's your welcome gift. I put it together myself," she said with a devilish grin before turning to her son. "CJ, go to your room and play while I catch up with Emily."

"But I wanna stay with Auntie Emee, too . . . *pleeeaaase*," he begged as he walked over and latched on around my leg.

"Sweet Pea, listen to your mother," I told him gently but firmly. I had to be direct with him, reestablishing our rules of behavior, otherwise he'd end up running all over me like he did Samantha. CJ looked at me with doubting eyes at first, but then decided to obey. "I'll read you a new bedtime story tonight," I said, blowing him a kiss before he ran off to his room.

Samantha flopped down on the bed. "My son loves him some Emily Snow. You should've heard him before you got here. Every five minutes it was, 'When is Auntie Emee gonna be here? Is she here yet? How much longer till she gets here?' I'm telling you, he almost drove me crazy."

"Well, I love my godson, too. I'll start grammar lessons with him first thing next week," I said, taking the basket of goodies from the dresser as I headed over to join Samantha on the other side of the queen-sized bed.

"Damn, give yourself a break," she said. "Just chill. You need to relax and unwind."

I shrugged my shoulders and untied the turquoise bow on my custom made gift. "Teaching helps me to relax and unwind."

"I don't know how you can sit in a classroom full of screaming kids every day and say that it relaxes you. You're weird, you know that, right?"

I laughed. "Speaking of work, when are you headed back to New York? I know your customers must be in desperate need of lipstick and moisturizer," I teased.

Samantha had taken so much time off from her job, I was surprised she still had one. She was a senior account manager for Lancôme, and even though a career in sales afforded her flexibility, she stretched the boundaries worse than a rubber band.

I remembered when she showed up at my door the morning after I called with the news that my mother had slipped away during the middle of the night. She must have packed her things and rushed straight to the airport at the crack of dawn.

"You just got back from a two-week vacation last month," I'd told her. "Are you sure they're going to let you take more time off?"

She held my hand in hers. "I left a voice message for my director and told her that I had a family emergency. If she can't deal, then she can kiss my ass."

That was my best friend. She made decisions on a whim, consequences to the wind. But truthfully, I wished I was more like her in that regard—having an air of daring and unpredictability. Samantha was fearless and bold, and I loved that about her.

"I've gotta check into the office this Monday," Samantha said. "But I'll try to make it back here again next weekend. I know by then you'll be ready to get up out of here, 'cause, girl, my mother is a damn trip!"

"Oh, Samantha, don't say that," I said softly. Samantha's mother was a very touchy subject.

"Hmph, it's the truth," she said with a roll of her eyes. "Hey, I have a better idea. Instead of me coming back here, why don't you join me in New York next Friday? We can have a girls' weekend out on the town!"

Part of me wanted to urge Samantha to come home and spend time with her precious little boy, or better yet, take him back to New York with her instead of planning a weekend of partying with me. But truthfully, CJ was better off with the arrangement here.

Samantha lived in a tiny but fabulous apartment in Manhattan, and CJ lived here in this big, beautiful home with his grandparents. Samantha said it was because the city was no place to raise a child, but I knew that wasn't really it. I loved Samantha to death, but honestly, she was about as equipped to raise a child as Lil' Kim was to sing in a gospel choir—she'd even admit to that. And Carl . . . oh my goodness! I wouldn't trust him to raise a pack of wolves for fear he might corrupt them. Samantha referred to him as her "baby daddy" just to get on her mother's nerves.

She and Carl were constantly involved in what her mother reviled as uncivilized ghetto drama. Regretfully, I had to agree. And even though Samantha was moving back here next month, she had no plans for CJ to live with her.

"I think I'll pass," I said. "I'm not really up for painting the Big Apple a new shade of red."

"Come on, Emily. You need to have a little fun."

"Exploring the city and hanging out with CJ and Ms. Gerti is all the fun I need."

"You call that fun?" Samantha said, shaking her head like I was pathetic. Then her eyes began to glow with mischief. "Take a look inside your gift basket."

I appreciated my best friend's thoughtfulness. "Samantha, this was so sweet of you." I smiled as I examined the goodies inside. She had gotten me two books by my favorite authors, a box of herbal tea, my favorite body-care products, snack bars, and fruit. As I dug deeper into the basket I discovered what had been at the root of her devilish grin. I held up a large vibrator. "Good Lord!" I gasped. The thing had to be twelve inches long and three inches in width. It looked like a weapon!

Samantha laughed. "That should tide you over for a while. And when you're ready, I know some fine brothers I can introduce you to."

I put the foot-long monster back inside the basket, letting it reclaim its place among the flavored condoms, nipple clips, and Ben Wa balls she'd included as part of my gift. "Samantha," I sighed, "at least let me unpack before you start trying to hook me up."

"Girl, don't front, 'cause I know your coochie is suffering from a serious drought." She laughed.

I had to laugh right along with her because she was right. "That may be true, but I'm not bringing men into your parents' home. Especially since they're being gracious enough to let me stay here until my place is ready."

"How long will it be before you can move in?"

"Well, my contractor should've finished last month. When I talked to him two weeks ago, he said it would take another month or so. Now he's not returning my phone calls," I said with mild frustration. "I'm going by my house first thing Monday morning to inspect the progress for myself."

Samantha shook her head. "These shady-ass contractors will tell you anything. As much as you're paying him, you should already be in there by now."

"Tell me about it."

"I know what you can do to speed things up."

"What's that?" I asked, eager to hear any suggestion that might help.

"Take Daddy with you and tell the contractor that your attorney wants to see if they're doing the work according to the timeline in your contract. That'll get his attention."

The thought made me so uncomfortable I began to sweat. "Excuse me for a minute," I said. I got up and made my way over to the bathroom on the other side of the room. I picked up a face cloth from the chrome towel bar by the sink, ran it under cold water, and patted my face with it. The cool dampness felt good against my warm skin. A minute later I walked out, feeling like I could breathe again.

At that moment, I realized just how difficult this was going to be. In the past, I could get away with my secret desires because I knew I'd never be in a situation that would test me on a daily basis. But now the safe rules I'd lived by for so long were about to change.

Samantha looked at me with concern. "How're you doing? I mean, how're you holding up? I know you still miss your mom."

"I'm okay. I have my moments, though. Sometimes I wake up in the middle of the night, panicking because I think I've forgotten to give her medicine, but then I remember that she's gone."

Samantha leaned over and gave me a long, comforting hug. "It's gonna be all right. It'll take time, but everything's gonna be all right."

I hugged her back tightly, praying that her words would ring true.

Dinner was outstanding. Brenda briefly breezed through as we finished up our small feast. She gave me two impeccable air-kisses and raved about my hair. "Emily, this look is so much more becoming on you. You were long overdue to let your real beauty shine," she told me as she ran her hand over my head as though I were a show pony. She gave CJ an apple-shaped eraser that she'd picked up from the museum and then chatted with us for ten minutes before heading off to her sorority's board meeting. Ed was still at the office, or as Brenda had said, and I quote, "Out doing only God knows what." I wondered about the meaning behind her comment.

After we ate, I gave CJ a bath, read him a bedtime story, and had him tucked in by eight-thirty. I turned out his light and then headed back downstairs to join Samantha and Ms. Gerti. The three of us sat around the kitchen table. They drank coffee and I sipped tea as we reminisced about the good old days. We were in mid-laughter when the doorbell rang.

"Who could that be?" Ms. Gerti asked, looking at her watch.

Samantha rushed off to the door to see who it was. When we heard a deep voice and the sound of huffing and bickering, Ms. Gerti looked at me and rolled her eyes. A minute later Samantha came back into the kitchen with Carl in tow.

Ms. Gerti didn't crack her mouth to speak. She simply stood up, walked over to the sink, and started washing out her coffee cup. Samantha and Carl looked mismatched standing next to each other. She was elegant in her yellow linen sundress and gorgeous designer sandals, while he was thugged out in his oversized Lakers jersey and sagging jeans that were in danger of falling to the floor at any minute. I knew that as hot as it was outside, his feet were probably roasting in his loosely laced Timberlands.

"Hello, Carl," I said, trying to sound pleasant.

"What up, ma?" He nodded in my direction.

Ms. Gerti sucked her teeth loudly and continued to rinse her cup. She and Carl didn't even try to pretend to be cordial to one another. I attempted to counter the tension. "How've you been?" I asked him.

"A brothah's just tryin' to hold on . . . nahmean? Just tryin' to hold on."

It amazed me that Carl had the nerve to say some of the things that came out of his mouth. The victims of natural disasters around the world were just trying to hold on. Our soldiers deployed in foreign lands and the families they'd left behind were just trying to hold on. Families who'd lost their homes due to layoffs and the economic downturn were just trying to hold on. Carl, on the other hand, was just trying to stay one step ahead of the law!

"Carl and I are going to step out for a minute," Samantha said, trepidation lacing her voice. "I'll be back in a little while."

They turned to walk away, but then Carl stopped and looked back at me, stuck his hands deep into his pockets, and said, "Yo, Emily. I'm sorry to hear 'bout yo moms."

His condolence was short and simple, but I could tell it was genuinely sincere. "Thanks, Carl." I was touched . . . a little.

They'd barely gotten out of earshot before Ms. Gerti started speaking her mind. "Now see, they're supposed to be broken up. At least that's what she claimed last month. I don't know why that child is always messing with men who ain't no damn good. She was raised better than that." She sighed. "That boy can't even keep his pants up around his damn waist. And he don't work a lick, but he drives a fancy car and wears more jewelry than you and me put together. Now how the hell you figure that?"

Ms. Gerti brought up a point that was a bone of contention and embarrassment for Samantha's parents—Carl's *questionable* career. He claimed he was a rapper, excuse me, a musical artist. But we all knew the truth. His real line of work was selling drugs.

"Ms. Gerti, you know as well as I do what that's all about," I said.

"Yeah, child, I know. And it burns me up. The only good thing that Carl can claim in his sorry-ass life is that precious little angel sleeping upstairs." She sighed again.

"Samantha doesn't talk much about it, but has Carl been spending time with CJ?"

"No, thank God," she said, raising her hands in the air as if in praise. "The only time he comes slithering around here is when Sam blows into town on the weekends every other month. I think he can smell her drawers as soon as she hits the city limits." She frowned. "Plus, you know he's not too welcome around here anyway. Ed made that clear years ago, and Brenda, shoot, she nearly shits in her britches when you mention his name."

"Well, at least CJ's got his grandparents, and you."

"And you, too." Ms. Gerti smiled. "CJ loves the ground you walk on. You're the only real mother that child's ever known, taking him in and raising him like your own. You're a good friend, Emily. Not many people would do that," she said as she put her hand on her hip. "So when're you gonna get married and have some babies of your own?"

I shrugged. "It's hard to find a good man, Ms. Gerti."

"Yeah, but you're a beautiful girl. You're smart, educated, and just as sweet as you can be. With all that going for you, you should be married by now. Didn't you leave a boyfriend behind in Atlanta?"

"Um, yes, I did." I blinked as I thought about my failed relationship with Bradley. "He just wasn't the right one for me."

I dreaded when people asked me that question. My mother, God rest her soul, used to ask me all the time. "Emily, when are you going to settle down and get married? I don't want you to end up alone," she'd said more times than I cared to remember.

I'd dated quite a few men, most of whom had been very nice and intelligent, and treated me well. But none of them had ever ignited a spark in me, and that was because the flame had been lit eleven years ago and had never gone out. Over the years I tried desperately to make my relationships work. The last man I dated, Bradley Johnson, had been a really sweet guy. He was an architect with a large firm in downtown Atlanta. We were together for a year and a half, my longest relationship to date. He was handsome and kind, and we even had a decent sex life.

My mother loved Bradley and had visions of wedding cake and baby booties in our future. Samantha thought I had temporarily lost my mind when I broke up with him. "That man is fine, and he's paid. Don't fuck it up," she'd said in her classic, no-frills wisdom. Bradley had been ready to propose, but I couldn't let that happen. I knew it wouldn't have been fair to him because my heart rested in a place he would never be able to reach.

Ms. Gerti looked squarely at me. "I hope you're not waiting for a perfect man, 'cause, sugar, there ain't no such thing."

"I know. I just want someone who . . . who moves me."

"Moves you?" She chuckled, shaking her head. "You young girls kill me with all that crazy talk. Just get you a man who respects you, pays the bills, and gives you what you're looking for under the sheets and you'll be all right."

"That'll work, too," I said, joining her for a laugh.

We chatted a little longer before Ms. Gerti's eyelids started to flutter. She walked over to the coffeemaker. "You still an early riser?"

"Like the sun."

"Want a cup of coffee in the morning?"

"No thanks. I've cut out coffee. I'm drinking tea these days." I smiled, raising my cup of lukewarm green tea that I'd made from the basket Samantha gave me.

Ms. Gerti reached into the cabinet above her head, pulled out a box of Earl Grey, and sat it by the sink. "If you ask me, nothing beats a strong cup of joe in the morning." She nodded, scooping out a precise measure of gourmet coffee from a bag she'd taken out of the refrigerator. She pushed a few buttons to program the machine and then opened the breadbox and split a bagel down the middle, placing it in the toaster. I could see that this was a nightly routine that no doubt helped her to prepare for the next day.

"Good night, sugar." Ms. Gerti smiled. She gave me a hug and then headed out the back door.

I wondered how she liked living so close to the people she worked for. I loved teaching, but when I left school in the afternoon it took an all-points bulletin for anyone on staff to find me. But it was different for Ms. Gerti. The Baldwins were like her family. Even though Samantha frustrated her no end, Ms. Gerti felt like she was her own child. She had raised Samantha and her brother Jeffery with the same love she now showered on CJ. It didn't seem fair that a woman full of so much goodness had never had a husband and children of her own. I wondered if I'd end up like her some day.

I was sitting in the den watching the local news, waiting up for Samantha, even though I knew it was pointless. Brenda returned from her board meeting and chatted me up for a few minutes. "I'm so glad you're staying with us in the comfort of our home," she said before gliding upstairs to her bedroom.

As I flipped between MSNBC and the local news, I thought about the fact that the only attractive features of living in the Baldwin home for the next couple of weeks were going to be Ms. Gerti's cooking, and spending time with CJ. These walls didn't hold the comfort for me that Brenda thought. And if she knew how I felt about her husband, I was sure she'd tell me to vacate the premises.

I walked over to the mantel above the fireplace and looked at the display of family pictures. Birthdays, Christmases, and family vacations, all captured by electronic photos and the miracle of God. I couldn't wait to put my family photos up in my new house. We didn't have exciting vacations to Hawaii or the south of France like the Baldwins. Ours had been more like Busch Gardens and Six Flags, but they'd been filled with love and happy memories.

I looked closely at a picture of the Baldwin clan on vacation circa the mid-1990s. Samantha and Jeffery had the look of defiant teenagers plastered on their faces, Brenda looked like a mother who was tired of dealing with defiant teenagers, and Ed . . . Ed had the look of clear water, and springtime, and shooting stars, and all of life's other wonders. I was temporarily drawn back to reality when I heard a familiar voice fill the room . . . the *real* reason I had waited up.

"I see you made it," he said.

I turned around and there he was, Edward Curtis Baldwin. My best friend's father. My Sweet Pea's *Papa*. And my heart's one true desire. I had loved this man for the better part of my adult life.

I remember the first day I met him, standing in my dorm room my freshman year at Spelman. My vivacious new roommate ushered her truckload of Louis Vuitton luggage and her enchanting father into my life, changing me forever. I was instantly struck by his gentle nature, handsome face, and indelible smile. At eighteen years old, I had fallen in love. A warm sensation flooded my body that day, but it was like giving birth to a stillborn infant—knowing I'd always carry the love in my heart, but that the precious life which could've been would never be realized because it was dead before ever having a chance to breathe. So I tucked those feelings away and buried them in a shallow grave next to the loss I felt for my father.

Over the years I was always polite, but distant. Courteous, but never engaging. Kind, but never overly so. I couldn't afford to be. I didn't want him to discover my true feelings. So I kept my distance, measured my words, and hoped that my love for him would dissipate over time. Sadly, it never has.

"Welcome to DC," he said, smiling at me in a way that made me feel warm inside.

"Thanks," I replied softly.

He held his jacket in one hand, his briefcase in the other. His impeccable silk tie was loose at the neck and his crisp white shirt sleeves were rolled up, giving him a casual air. At a little over six feet tall, with deep brown eyes, curly black hair sprinkled with a faint touch of salt, and skin the color of creamy caramel, he was the only man who'd ever made me lose my breath. I had to remind myself to exhale before I spoke again. "Thanks for letting me stay with you and Brenda. I'm not sure when my place will be ready, but . . ."

"Take your time," he interjected. "There's no rush here, unless you don't think you'll be able to stand us after a few days." He laughed.

"Oh, no, that's not what I meant at all. I just don't want to be a bother."

"Emily," he smiled, causing my knees to slightly buckle as the sound of my name escaped his lips, "it's no bother. We're glad to have you, and please know that you're welcome to stay for as long as you need to. Besides, that grandson of mine is crazy about you. This morning he came up to me, all excited, and said, 'Papa, Auntie Emee is coming to live with us today!' "

I smiled, genuinely touched. "CJ is very special to me, too."

We stood in awkward silence for a moment. Ed looked at me with inspecting eyes. He was the kind of person who noticed everything. Suddenly, I felt terribly inadequate in my denim shorts and cropped cotton shirt that showed a hint of my navel. His stare made me self-consciously aware of my exposed skin.

"So . . . you're up by yourself?" he asked, looking around as if he hoped to find more company in the room.

"Um, yeah. Samantha stepped out a little while ago." I dared not tell him that she left with Carl. "I was waiting up for her," I half lied.

"That daughter of mine. I can't believe she left you alone on your first night in town." He looked at his watch and shook his head. "Don't wait up for Sam. If you do, you'll be standing in this same spot tomorrow morning."

We both laughed because he was right. I nodded, trying to shake the warm feeling that was running through my body.

"Well, if there's anything we can do for you, just let us know," Ed smiled.

I wanted to melt when I saw his lips curve upward and his teeth shine through like the sun. His smile was so beautiful. "Thank you. You and Brenda have done so much for me already. Letting me stay here, helping me to find a job."

Ed had put in a good word for me at CJ's private school, where he also happened to be a member of the board of directors. Shortly after that, the headmaster called and offered me a position for the upcoming school year.

Ed stepped toward me and I could smell the intoxicating scent of his cologne mixed with natural perspiration, the result of the summer heat and his fourteen-hour workday. "Emily, it's no problem. I know the last few months have been difficult for you," he said, then paused. "The loss of your mother, moving to a new city, buying a new home, and starting a new job. It must be overwhelming."

"I'm managing," I said, trying to sound strong and convincing. The last thing I wanted was for Ed to feel sorry for me.

He breathed in deeply, "I, um, uh . . ." He stumbled. He looked as though he was forcing himself to continue. "Well, if you need to talk to someone, professionally I mean, I have the name of a great therapist I can refer you to . . ."

"No, I'm fine. But thanks for the offer," I said, injecting a little more edge into my voice than I'd intended. All of a sudden a thought occurred to me. There I was, fantasizing about Ed, and he was offering me referrals for psychiatric care. And not only that, he hadn't even noticed the dramatic change in my appearance. I'd gone from my trademark bush of wild, black spirals to my new silky-straight hairdo, and he hadn't said a word. I felt like such a fool. I quickly said good night and headed upstairs, rushing by him like wind blowing through the air. I left him standing alone, looking like a man who'd just stumbled upon a mystery. For someone so astute, he didn't have a clue.

After an intensely long lukewarm shower, I lay under the soft, 900-thread-count bedsheets, thinking about my day, trying to block out the last ten minutes, and quietly repeating Samantha's words aloud: "Everything's gonna be all right."

Chapter 4

Samantha . . .

No Longer What I Need

I should've had the title *Judge* in front of my name, because I was about to lay down the law to Carl Tyrone Thomas, otherwise known as my should-be-ex-boyfriend, father of my child, and as I had come to realize, a real pain in the ass!

"You look good," he said, roaming me with his eyes.

"Thanks," I responded in a flat tone. I was ready for him to talk to me about whatever had made him come over to see me in the first place. Carl never came by my parents' house, but tonight he'd showed up at the front door, unannounced, like it was no big deal. Trust me, it was a big freakin' deal.

I shouldn't be out with Carl, and I felt terrible for leaving Emily. But I knew it was better to step out rather than argue with him in front of her and Gerti. I couldn't pull my girl into whatever nonsense Carl planned to start tonight, because she'd been through so much.

I remembered the night Emily called me with the news that her mother had passed. I was sad, but also a little relieved. You see, Ms. Lucille had been sick for a long time. She'd battled multiple sclerosis for years, and the disease had left her a shell of her former self. Her death ended the pain and suffering the disease had caused, but it also left poor Emily all alone. I knew my friend didn't need to be by herself, that's why I pushed so hard until I finally convinced her to move here to DC. And now that I'd be here, too, it was like the icing on top of a fabulous cake.

This was the first time in Emily's entire life that she'd made a decision with herself in mind instead of someone else. She was always thinking of others first: her mother, her kids at school, CJ, me, and anyone else who she thought needed her help. And she did it without complaining. I admired her fierce loyalty and quiet strength. I used to tease her all the time about playing it safe and being so damn predictable, but the truth was, sometimes I wished that I was more like her, dependable and all.

I first met Emily on move-in day our freshman year at Spelman College. She and her mother had been waiting patiently when I walked into my dorm room with arms full of boxes and luggage. All of Emily's things were stacked in a neat pile against the wall. She hadn't unpacked a thing because she was waiting until I arrived to see which side of the room I wanted. That was the kind of selfless person she was. We hit it off right away. She made the dean's list while I made the rounds with a few upperclassmen over at neighboring Morehouse College before moving on to the local stock in town, who were more my flavor.

Emily's my very best friend in the world. She was right there in the delivery room when CJ was born, holding my hand, reminding me to breathe. But even before he took his first breath, we both knew that motherhood wasn't my thing. I remember thinking that she should've had him, not me. She cradled him with love while I looked on, too scared to hold my own child because I thought I'd do something wrong. When CJ was six months old, my job transferred me to New York, and that's when we decided that CJ would be better left in her care. So Emily raised my son for the first four years of his life. See, I told you she was a selfless person.

I knew I'd never find anyone who accepted me the way she did. And it was funny because we were as different as caviar and catfish, with one exception—we were born on the exact same day. But here's the rub, she was born in the wee hours of the morning, and I was born in the late hours of the night . . . interesting, huh? Even though she was technically older than me, I always referred to her as my younger sister.

Emily and I even looked like complete opposites. I stood at five feet ten inches tall, while she hovered at five feet five. She had one of those bodies that brothers loved—tiny waist, shapely thighs, curvaceous hips, and the proverbial onion . . . an ass that could bring tears to the eyes. Her bone structure was incredible and her flawless nut-brown skin was as smooth as silk. Hell, the girl didn't even have to wear makeup! She had natural good looks. And now she was sporting long, shiny hair that looked so fierce it could land her a spot on the cover of *Sophisticate's Black Hair* magazine. I paid top dollar at my salon to get what she had all on her own.

Natural good looks were something that I didn't have. I wasn't bad to look at, but I was realistic about my physical attributes. Now, don't get it twisted, my shit was always correct, but I was aware that there were things a girl could do to give herself that extra *oomph!* For instance, I was tall and thin as a rail, and my ass was as flat as drywall, but I rocked sexy skirts and fly heels that high-lighted my long legs. My face was all right, but I didn't have any striking features that made me stand out, so I ap-plied my makeup with the precision of an artist, creating a seductive illusion. And my hair, hell, my mother's al-ways been disappointed that I didn't have *good hair* . . . yeah, she's one of those Negroes! My coarse, sandy blond hair matched my skin tone and barely touched the bottom of my chin. But with the help of a high-quality human hair weave and Gwen, my fabulous stylist at Hair by NEWG, it flowed down my back like a graceful waterfall.

"I wish I had your curves and natural beauty," I'd told Emily thousands of times.

"I wish I had your long legs and stylish flair," she'd often said to me.

Funny how life was. Everybody wanted what they couldn't or didn't have. Speaking of which, I knew I needed to make better choices in the men I dated. I liked brothers with an edge—roughnecks. But let me be clear, that didn't mean I wanted someone who carried a Glock and beat my ass. I wasn't having that. I just liked brothers with that sexy ride-or-die appeal. My parents didn't understand my attraction, but I had to do me. You have to know who you are, and baby, I knew exactly who I was. Just like I knew I should've been home right now, sitting on the couch be-side Emily, who was probably waiting up for me.

As Carl and I sat at an outdoor table at Kramerbooks & Afterwords, a combination bookstore and café in the trendy Dupont Circle neighborhood, I noticed how un-comfortable he looked. This wasn't his scene; too many yuppies, buppies, and gay couples for his taste. He was uncomfortable in the northwest section of the city. If the territory wasn't his turf over in southeast, he wasn't down for it. But he agreed to come here because he didn't have a choice. I told him that I'd only leave the house with him under two conditions: one, that we drive in separate vehicles because if shit got funky I'd have a way to get back home; and two, that I choose where we were going. We ended up here because not only could I get a glass of wine to relax from whatever drama he was up to, I could also pick up a book for CJ at the same time. Emily loved reading him bedtime stories.

Carl sat slouched down in his seat, sipping lemonade and talking shit. "Now that you movin' back here, we can make this thing permanent. You know I'll take care of you. Besides, CJ needs to have his mothah and fathah with him on a regular basis. We need to be a family," he said as he ran his hand over his neatly braided cornrows.

"Carl, we're toxic when we're together."

"You listenin' to too many talk shows." He smirked. "Shit, you know I gotcho back. I told you I'll take care of you. Don't I keep you laced?"

"That's not the point," I snapped. I couldn't help but roll my eyes, a habit I'd picked up from Gerti when I was just three years old. "As I was saying," I continued, "CJ is just fine right where he is. And let's be honest, neither of us is parent material and you know it."

"Why you always gotta be talkin' shit 'bout my parentin' skills? Yo bourgeois-ass parents won't even let me come around the house and spend time with my own son. Tell me how I'm s'posed to be a good fathah and shit when I can't see my own flesh and blood!" he said, raising his voice.

I cut my eyes toward the people sitting at the surrounding tables who had started to stare. Little did they know that I didn't give a damn about their raised brows. I ignored them and proceeded to tell Carl exactly what was on my mind. "If you acted like you had some damn sense, you'd be welcome at the house. But listen, it's not even about that," I said, leaning forward, pressing my elbows against the table. "Until you get your shit together, and you *know* what I'm talking about, and I get myself together, CJ is staying where he is, with my parents."

Looking at Carl, I wondered why the hell I even dealt with him. Then I remembered the load he was packing between his legs, and the reason came back to me in vivid detail. But sometimes, even a big dick couldn't compensate for the madness he brought into my life. Although, to be completely fair, if you peeled back all of his layers, Carl wasn't the horribly bad person that everyone thought he was. He was just misguided and too slick for his own good.

I'd met Carl six years ago. We were at a club, eyeing each other when he walked over and asked if he could buy me a drink. I was instantly attracted to his ripped body and thugged-out good looks. I gave up the goodies that first night. Carl could fuck like a prize-winning stallion, and that went a long way in my book. Plus, he came into my life during a time when I was going through some serious changes.

I was dating a wonderful man at the time, Tyler Jacobs, the only man who had ever made me feel as happy as a kid and scared as hell at the same time. Ironically, he lived in Atlanta, and his best friend's daughter was one of Emily's students at the school where she taught. I met Tyler one weekend when I was visiting Emily and attending another friend's wedding, where he happened to be one of the guests. I wasn't a relationship girl, but Tyler was a relationship guy, and before I knew it I was swimming in an ocean of new feelings that I couldn't handle. Long story short, I fucked it up so that I wouldn't have to deal with the emotions that had started to build. I slept with Carl, basically sabotaging what I had with Tyler.

A month after Carl and I met, I found out that I was pregnant. But I was straight up with him from the jump.

He knew that he wasn't the only guy I was seeing. I'd already told him about Tyler, and that I wasn't sure which one of them was the father, although based on the calendar I had a pretty good idea that it was Carl. To my surprise, he didn't flinch. Actually, I think he wanted the baby to be his. A paternity test proved it was.

Tyler, on the other hand, didn't play that. And in all fairness, how could I have blamed him for being mad, pissed, angry, and hurt? Let me tell you, he was all of those things and more. After CJ was born and it was confirmed that Tyler wasn't the father, I never heard from him again. My failed relationship with him was something I truly regretted. Once things ended, I practically clung to Carl like a junkie. I guess that's why it was so hard for me to break free of him. But I knew it was time to let our relationship go.

When I told Carl that he needed to get himself together, he knew exactly what I meant, and until he could produce a W-2 form and explain where he got his money, his son was off-limits. I wasn't much of a mother, but I could at least try to protect my child from his father, and truth be told, from me, too.

I looked at my watch and saw that it was getting late. I needed to bring the evening with Carl to a close. "So, Carl, was this why you wanted to talk to me?" I asked, clearly irritated. "Because if it was, you wasted both our time. I need to get back home."

"Hol' up," he grunted. "Damn, can't we just spend some quality time together?"

I knew exactly what he was up to and I knew what *quality time* meant in his vocabulary. He had that look in his eyes that said he wanted to get a whiff of the kitty tonight. I had to shut him down. "No, we can't," I replied in a deadpan voice.

"So, whassup? You ain't got time fo' a brothah?"

"I told you last month, we're not a couple anymore. I'm dating other people, so . . ."

"Why you always gotta be dissin' me?"

"How is telling you the truth and being an adult about this dissing you?"

"Oh, so now you a model citizen and shit?"

I rolled my eyes again. "You know what, this conversation is over. I'm going to get CJ a book and then I'm going home." Carl just looked at me like I was crazy, so I stood up and started to walk away.

"I know yo skinny ass ain't walkin' away from me?" he said, entirely too loud.

Now why the hell did he have to go and do that? Carl was used to crazy hood drama and talking shit to everyone around him because most people feared him, but I didn't. You see, Carl forgot who I was from time to time. When he looked at me he saw my quality designer clothes, sophisticated air, and Gold Coast upbringing, but I wasn't the one to fuck with! I didn't carry a weapon or get into fights or any of the other mayhem he was used to, but I could still show my ass with the best of them.

"I know your punk ass ain't talkin' about nobody else's ass!" I said, in a pitch loud enough to match his own.

Carl hated when people raised their voice to him, especially in public. I had absolutely no doubt that had I been anyone else, man, woman, or child, no matter where we were, Carl would've knocked me out. But Carl had tolerance for my shit. Almost as if he liked it. That's messed up, right? But that was how we were. And that was why I knew I had to distance myself from him.

"You need to calm the fuck down," he said in a more hushed tone, trying to take control of something that he knew could quickly escalate. "Why you always trippin' and shit?" he huffed as he reached into his pocket for his wallet.

" 'Cause you're always trippin' and shit!"

I turned on my heels and headed inside, leaving Carl where he sat as he paid for our drinks. When I looked up again, he was standing next to me as I browsed for children's books. "Carl, it's late and I don't have time for your nonsense."

He leaned in close to me and pressed his huge dick against the side of my hip. "You sure you don't want none'a this?" he asked, licking his full lips.

Carl can sex you up like nobody's business. And I won't even lie, the thought of gettin' down with him was tempting. But sex would only cause our already warped relationship to drag on, and that was something I couldn't be a part of anymore. "The only kind of ride I'm up for tonight is the one that leads back to the house."

"Come on, baby, you know you want it."

"Carl, I'm not playing with you. Move out of my way so I can get these books for CJ and head back home."

"You don't mean that."

"Yes, I do."

"I know what you want, and what you need."

I looked at him and shook my head. "What I used to want is no longer what I need. Give it a rest, Carl," I said as I waved him off with my right hand.

What happened next was completely crazy. All of a sudden, this fool decided to lose his damn mind. From out of nowhere, Carl got a weird look in his eyes that I'd never seen before. He reached up and knocked several books off the shelf next to where I stood.

"You gonna have enough of fuckin' wit' my feelins'," he growled, standing so close I could smell the tart lemonade that lingered on his breath. "I'm steppin' so I won't have to hurt yo ass," he said directly into my ear, through clenched teeth, so low that only I could hear him. Then he calmly walked away.

I stood in the middle of the aisle with books lying at my feet and scared customers looking on, but trying not to *really* look too hard. I felt unnerved. This was the first time that Carl had ever threatened me in all the years I'd known him. I had yelled at him many times before, and one time I even shoved him in public. But not once had he ever been aggressive with me or uttered anything that remotely translated into a threat. *Maybe he's on something?* I thought. I had never known him to use the drugs that I knew he sold, but just like his threat, there was a first time for everything.

I was shaken, but I knew I didn't have time to dwell on Carl. I had to ignore the people who were still staring, resist the urge to curse them out, and get my behind back home so I could comfort my best friend. I hoped Emily was still awake.

Carl had ruined my mood, so I left the book section without making a purchase. I was headed out the door when I passed a group of brothers coming into the café. There were three of them, so I casually scanned each one from head to toe. When I came to the last guy I smiled, and he did, too. His friends slowed momentarily, but when they saw that we were making a connection, they nodded and kept walking.

"I don't mean to stare, but don't I know you?" he asked.

Although he was fine as hell, after further inspection I could see that he wasn't my type. He was wearing a white T-shirt, faded jeans, and brown flip-flops. His thick dreadlocks framed his beautifully squared jawline, which looked almost Romanesque. He smiled at me through pearls of white teeth with a face so handsome he could easily be a male supermodel. I could tell by his tight diction that he was highly educated and probably from somewhere in the northeast, judging by his accent. And looking at his choice of clothing and hairstyle, I surmised that he was one of those granola-eating, earthy kind of guys, and I wasn't into that. "I don't think so," I said, answering his question, ready to glide out the door.

"Yes, I think we've met," he said, taking a moment to reappraise me. "Aren't you Jeffery Baldwin's sister?"

His comment made me come to a complete stop. First of all, I knew for a fact that I'd never met this brother before tonight. How did I know? Because I always remembered fine, chocolate-dipped men draped in good-smelling cologne. But if he knew my brother, it brought a few other things into question—namely, his sexual orientation.

My brother Jeffery was gay, even though my mother refused to openly acknowledge or address the truth. As a matter of fact, his partner was a tall, dark, and handsome specimen, much like the man in front of me. They'd been living together in Paris, France, for the last eight years, and that was how long it had been since Jeffery was last home. He stayed away because of mother. He couldn't stand her. He once confided to me that she'd nearly driven him to the point of suicide. He basically excommunicated himself from our entire family, including me, all so he could break free of everything associated with her.

"Yeah, I'm Jeffery's sister. How do you know my brother?" I asked, raising my brow.

"We went to school together, at Howard."

"Oh . . . so you and Jeffery were *friends?*" I said, giving him a curious stare. The more I checked him out, the harder it was for me to believe that this man was gay. But then again, down-low brothers were hard to detect. Not only could they look you dead in your eyes like they were feelin' you, they could kiss you with passion, sex you up, and then go get their freak on with one of their boys after they left you. That wasn't down-low, that was just low-down!

He smiled, catching my drift. "Not exactly. We were both pre-med. I remember meeting you when you were with him during homecoming one year, at a mixer."

As I thought back to my college days, I remembered hanging out with my brother during Howard's homecoming one year. "That was a long time ago," I replied.

"Yeah, it was. That's been what . . . eleven, twelve years?"

"At least. But even so, I think I would remember if we'd met," I demurred, softening my eyes with a smile. I got a kick out of flirting with men.

"Trust me, we've met," he said. "You probably don't remember because I wore a close fade back in the day. Dreads can change one's appearance." He motioned as he raked his hand through his thick, shoulder-length locks.

"Oh, is that it?" I leaned in close to him, pretending to get a better look at his face, but I was really checking out his sexy scent. He smelled like the exotic oils that the African street vendors sold.

"Yes, I think so. You should see my before and after shots."

"Well, I look different, too, so how did you recognize me?"

"I never forget an intriguing woman, or a beautiful face," he said in a sexy voice.

We were briefly distracted when the hostess walked up to seat a couple next to where we were standing. I took that as a sign for me to get up out of there and head back home . . . fine, smooth-talking man or not! "I guess I better be on my way."

"Are you waiting for your boyfriend to bring the car around?"

I smiled and simply said, "No."

"You're headed over to his place?"

"You ask a lot of questions."

"I have a curious mind." He smiled, then extended his hand. "I'd like to reintroduce myself. I'm Tyme Alexander."

I stretched my hand out to greet his. His palm was soft and warm. "Samantha," I smiled back, "and you know the last name."

"I wasn't sure if it had changed. I guess it's my good fortune that it hasn't. It's nice meeting you again, Samantha Baldwin."

"Likewise, and I hope you and your friends have a good evening," I said, turning toward the door.

"Wait, do you have a card?"

I put my hand on my hip and raised my brow. "You tryin' to call me?" I said in my sistah girl voice.

"Call you, e-mail you, fax you, text you, Tweet you, Facebook you, whatever it takes to reach you."

I thought my little attitude would discourage him, but I thought wrong. There might be something to this guy after all. "Why don't you give me your card?" I smiled.

He dug into his back pocket and pulled out a Gucci embossed brown leather wallet. That was a very good sign for someone with my expensive taste. He was an interesting mix. A bohemian brother with couture flair. He removed a business card and handed it to me. "Do you have a pen?" He smiled, looking at the pastel-colored bag on my shoulder.

"Sure." I reached in and fished around for my Mont-blanc.

"While you're at it, why don't you give me your card, too," he said, slow and smooth. "I don't want to run the risk of you misplacing mine."

Normally, I'd be all over a handsome man like Tyme from the word go, even with the earthy look he had going on. But there was something about him that made me a little hesitant. Not that he was creepy or anything. It was just a vibe I got. But against my instincts, and in favor of my curiosity, I handed him my pen and then pulled out my sterling silver business card case. We exchanged information, and when he read mine he smiled before putting it in his wallet. I slid his card down into my bag without even looking at it.

"I'll call you," he said, extending his hand again.

I shook his warm palm one last time before saying good-bye. When I walked back out into the humid night air I felt a strange chill on my arms. I replayed my evening as I drove back home. Carl had really thrown me for a loop, and the way he acted tonight was a sure sign that I needed to stay the hell away from him. If he was using, I didn't even want to know. I just wanted to put as much space between us as possible.

Blocking Carl out of my mind, I thought about the man I had just met. There was something about him that I couldn't quite put my finger on, and it held a strange appeal for me.

As I turned into the driveway around the back of the house, I looked up to the second-story window and saw that Emily's light was still on. I felt like shit for having left her alone. I should've told Carl to leave as soon as I answered the door. But you better believe I wasn't going anywhere with him again. I was serious this time. No more bullshitting around. Right now I needed to concentrate on helping my best friend and making sure that I was there for her.

After all the things Emily had done for me over the years, and the countless times she'd stood by my side—from drunken skirmishes she helped me to avoid at wild college parties, to nursing me back to health our junior year after an abortion that had gone terribly wrong, Emily's always been there for me. Now I was finally in a position to repay her for her generosity, kindness, and love . . . and I needed to get this right.

I messed up tonight, but this was the last time. I was going to help Emily through her grief. I planned to give her the scoop on the city—where to shop, where to hang out, which areas to avoid, and last but not least, I was going to help her find a man. She needed someone to comfort her during times of loneliness. And hey, if it was one thing that I knew a little something about, it was men!

Chapter 5

Ed . . .

Careful Caution

I sat in my study, polishing off the last drop of vintage brandy in my snifter. It was the extra-good stuff I reserved to celebrate special occasions, but tonight it was helping me to temporarily escape the complications brewing under my roof.

I had a hell of a grueling day that began with depositions for a wrongful death case and ended with a last-minute request for a continuance on another. But that wasn't why I felt drained, like I'd been carrying five-hundred-pound weights on each shoulder, uphill. I felt this way because it had been almost a half hour since Emily retreated upstairs to her room, and I was still trying to figure out what the hell I was going to do.

I'd been thinking about how I would handle this situation since the day my wife informed me that she had invited our daughter's best friend to stay with us until her contractor finished renovating her new home.

"Ed, Emily will be staying with us until she can move into her house," Brenda said a month ago, not asking, but telling me that we'd have a houseguest for an undetermined amount of time.

The news caught me completely off guard. To know that Emily was moving to DC was one thing, but to know that she'd be sleeping in a bed down the hall from me was another. I couldn't let that happen. "Why did you tell her she could stay here before talking it over with me?" I asked.

"I didn't think I needed to check with you about helping Emily," she answered with indignation. "She's practically like our daughter, and she's in need right now, especially after everything she's been through."

Even though it pissed me off that Brenda had made a unilateral decision about something that stood to test me more than she could ever know, I was puzzled because generosity had never been my wife's strong suit, unless there was something she could gain for the effort. And although I wanted to help Emily, I knew that having her under my roof wasn't a good idea. So I tried to get out of it. "She can't stay with Sam?"

"Samantha won't be closing on her condo until sometime next month." Brenda grunted. "Besides, Emily's great with CJ and I could really use her help around here. Taking him to camp so early every morning is beginning to wear on me."

I knew it, and I wasn't surprised by Brenda's self-serving angle. Her real motivation had nothing to do with helping a vulnerable young woman make a smooth transition into a new city. It was all about how Emily's presence in our home could relieve her of her responsibilities to her own grandson. I wanted to call her out on her hypocrisy, but I held my tongue for a better time. After being married for so many years, I knew how to deal with my wife.

But right now, sitting here sipping my brandy, I had no idea how I was going to handle the situation with Emily.

I had prayed that by some small miracle Emily's house would be ready by now, thus freeing me from a potentially sticky situation. But then I thought, hell, I prepared for tough cases all the time, how hard could it be? Turns out it was going to be much harder than I thought.

My profession was the law—I was a plaintiff attorney, to be exact. And frankly, I was one of the best on the East Coast. That wasn't bragging, it was just a fact. I was blessed to have a very successful career, even by my profession's standards, which were quite high. I was a senior partner in a prestigious and well-connected firm on K Street in downtown Washington, DC—where the big boys played. I lived in a beautiful home, was father to two college-educated adult children and grandfather to a very smart and energetic grandchild who was just like me. And even though I was languishing in a loveless marriage, my wife and I had weathered the storm for thirty-two years, and that meant something to me. By all accounts I had a pretty damn good life.

That little piece of background information was very important because it spoke to my present state, which was a vast contradiction from the confident, self-assured man I was. Right now I felt unsure and anxious, and it was all because of Emily's presence. "Damn!" I whispered aloud. She still had a strong effect on me, even after all these years.

I remembered the first time we met. Brenda and I were helping Sam move into her dorm room her freshman year at Spelman. It was a hundred degrees that August day. The heat was oppressive, and amidst the flurry of intense estrogen at the all-girls school, the only thing on my mind was how quickly we could move Sam in so we could check into the hotel, get some rest, and then head back to DC the next day. I had been working nonstop on an upcoming trial, and it was imperative that I returned as soon as possible.

Sam and Brenda headed up to find her room while I grabbed two large boxes from the minivan we'd rented. I took the stairs because the elevator was too slow and too crowded. Sam, Brenda, and I arrived at the room at the same time, and the first thing I noticed was a neat stack of luggage and a few plastic crates lined up against the wall. A frail-looking, middle-aged woman with gray hair and a pleasant smile greeted us when we walked through the door. I smiled back, and then caught the image of someone standing near the window, and that's when it hit me. For the first time in my life I understood what people meant when they said that someone had taken their breath away.

I felt it the instant Emily looked up to say hello. She was delicate, innocent, and beautiful. She looked like a princess waiting to be rescued from something. I know it sounds corny as hell, and I, above anyone else, was surprised by my reaction to an eighteen-year-old girl who could've been my own daughter. But she was exquisite.

Her posture was erect and regal for someone so young, and her velvety smooth skin was a rich brown, like soft suede. She smiled as she swept her right hand through the wild mass of hair covering her head. I got the impression that she was nervous because she began to fidget with one of the large hoop earrings that dangled from her lobe. When she walked toward me I savored the way her curves filled out her faded jeans, which were torn at the knee, while her perky breasts seemed to tease me through her fitted T-shirt that boasted a multicolored peace sign. I was captivated.

We made introductions as handshakes and hugs were spread among us. I was glad for the commotion in the room; otherwise, I was sure it would've been obvious that I was taken by my daughter's new roommate. I went out on a limb and tried to start up a conversation with Emily.

"So, what do you plan to major in?" I asked.

"Um, I'm not sure, Mr. Baldwin. I'm leaning toward elementary education."

"Emily, please." I smiled, trying to put her at ease. "It's just Ed . . . okay?"

She smiled back, then quickly looked away, as though she was searching for something she'd lost. While her mother, Brenda, and Sam discussed the room setup, I took the opportunity to probe her. I wanted to find out everything I could about her. But instead of engaging me, she hesitated, offering polite yet guarded responses to my questions. Hell, I didn't know why I thought a young woman like Emily would be interested in shooting the breeze with an old man like me, which was no doubt how she perceived me through her youthful mind's eyes. But the more I talked to her, the more I felt a strained yet intense energy pass between us.

After my failed attempt at conversation, I made myself useful bringing up the rest of Sam's luggage, crates, and boxes, which were full of an assortment of supplies that Brenda said our daughter *had* to have. My wife always went overboard with everything. She had registered for Sam's graduation gifts at Saks Fifth Avenue, Neiman Marcus, and Williams-Sonoma. I thought it was much too extravagant, especially for someone just finishing the twelfth grade. Brenda single-handedly turned the simple task of housing a college freshman in a small dorm room into what looked like setting up house for a family of four. Between the new temptation in front of me and the old frustration staring me in the face, I prayed I'd make it through the day.

That evening after Brenda and I checked into the

hotel, I turned in early, citing an achy back. "I just need a good night's sleep," I'd said. What I really needed was to rest my mind because I felt like a damn pervert for the thoughts that had invaded my head since meeting Emily. The simple truth was that I wanted her. I wanted an eighteen-year-old girl more than I had ever wanted any woman in my life. To be frank, I was used to getting what I wanted. Whatever I set my mind to, I got it. But I knew this was going to be very different.

At the time, I honestly thought it was just a phase I was going through. A lustful attraction to a pretty face and a firm, young body. But when I found myself driving down to Atlanta to pick Sam up during school breaks and holidays, rather than sending her a plane ticket to come home, I couldn't fool myself any longer. I took those long road trips because I wanted to see Emily. I wanted a chance to be in the same room with her and inhale the sweet scent of her perfumed skin. I wanted to see her look at me with her beautiful brown eyes that made me feel alive. Even though our conversations were usually brief and a bit awkward, I looked forward to them like a kid waiting for his allowance. That's what she'd reduced me to. And although I was inwardly embarrassed by the thought, I still went back for more.

Over the years, Emily always kept her distance from me. I wanted to believe that it was because she felt the same way I did, but knew it was too dangerous to cross the line. However, my rational mind forced me to accept the probable reality that she was simply uncomfortable around me. Whatever the reason, she had put up a wall that gave us clearly defined boundaries.

I also had to admit that another reason why I was still sitting in my study was because I felt like such an ass. Even though therapy was a reasonable option to offer someone coping with a devastating loss, the look on

Emily's face told me that I had offended her. Actually, what I had really wanted to tell her was that I'd be here for her if she needed anything. But instead I played it safe because I had no other choice.

I was also sure that she took notice of the fact that I didn't comment on her hair. She'd always worn it loose, wild, and free, a stark contradiction to her disciplined and controlled manner. But now her thick mass of wiry hair was straight down her back, giving her a sleek, alluring aura. I couldn't tell her how beautiful I thought she looked tonight because the next thing to follow would've been the kiss I have wanted to devour her with for the past eleven years. That was out of the question, so I offered her a psych referral instead.

Everything inside me wanted to go upstairs to the guest room where Emily was sleeping and hold her close to me. But there was no way I could make a move like that, especially not in the house I shared with my wife. That would be like inviting hell to break loose, and we had been down that road before.

Brenda and I didn't have a loving relationship. We never had. She always thought I was having some sort of torrid affair. The truth was, yes, I had dipped my spoon in the past. They'd been meaningless affairs, quick thrills and simple indulgences. Brenda even caught me once and she never let me live it down. We went to counseling, but when the real issues of our marriage boiled to the surface, she told me that she'd had enough therapy. That was a long time ago, and now I was harmless and downright saintly, especially compared to a lot of the men I knew.

Brenda and I had been together since college, and that was a long time to spend with the same person. I cared about her, but I couldn't truthfully say that I'd ever been in love with her. We'd known each other practically all our lives. Our families vacationed together on the

Vineyard every summer. Her older sister was married to my first cousin. We were connected and intertwined. But we didn't start dating until our junior year at Howard University. I was president of our class and had been giving a speech for a peace rally in front of the student union when she approached me. I knew that political and social causes weren't Brenda's thing, but she volunteered to help me post flyers around campus after the event. I asked her out that evening and we've been together ever since. It may sound like a fairy tale, but it's far from it.

She was the sensible choice—attractive, smart, cultured, and respectable. Our families had both breathed a collective sigh of relief when we started dating, but I felt nuptial pressure almost from the very beginning of our relationship. We were in our senior year when she got pregnant, even though she'd been on the Pill. Three months passed before she told me that she'd missed her period. When I asked her why she had waited so long to tell me, she said it was because she didn't know how to break the news to me. My best friend, Ross Morgan, still swears to this day that she set a trap for me. Whether Brenda stopped taking her pills on purpose or not had been a moot point back then. The bottom line was that I had a responsibility to own up to. I was raised to honor family, and that was what I planned to do.

A month later we had a rushed but elaborate wedding with all the bells and whistles. Our son, Jeffery, was born five months after we married, and then Sam followed. Things happened so fast we really didn't have time to examine our relationship. The span between the births of our children and my law school graduation was a blur. In the years that followed, there were ballet recitals for Sam, softball practices for Jeffery, volunteer activities for Brenda, and career climbing for me. We were so busy with "things" that Brenda and I never had time to focus on the two of us. Once we did, neither of us really liked what we saw.

In Brenda's view, I was too practical and analytical, as well as too stubborn, abrupt, and frugal. Essentially, what that meant was that I didn't believe in putting on a show, and I didn't act impulsively. I didn't give in easily, and I didn't have patience for pretension. And my crowning vice, the painful thorn in her side, was what she considered to be my frugality—translation—I lived well, but didn't go overboard just because I possessed the material means to do so.

On the other hand, my wife was a free spirit, as she described herself. Translation—she was full of drama, and she acted as if the flowers she grew in our backyard bloomed hundred-dollar bills every spring. She spent money like she was the one making it! But make no mistake, I was no penny pincher and I didn't begrudge Brenda anything she wanted. But her extravagance and sense of entitlement have worn thin on me over the years.

She was the baby of her family and was always taken care of by her parents and older siblings. When she became an adult, it was engrained into her that she would marry well and be kept up in the fashion to which she was accustomed. It wasn't a second thought to Brenda that she'd have a husband who provided financially, and live-in help to take care of the kids and me. It was how she was brought up, so she simply followed the path that had been laid out in front of her.

I guess that was why I gave my daughter a pass. Even though Sam and Brenda were like night and day, they shared the same blood, and being motherly wasn't a component on their DNA strand. I loved Sam, but it bothered me that she was irresponsible as hell when it came to CJ. At one point I thought that having a child would force her to finally get her act together, but it didn't.

Sam's got one of the best hearts of anyone you could ever meet—honest and sincere, loving and genuine. She was the kind of person who fought passionately for the people she loved. She tried to act hard-core, but underneath all the hardships that she created for herself, she was just a sweet kid who wanted validation—ironically from Brenda.

During her teenage years, Sam was constantly in trouble. Most of her antics were deliberate, a result of her rebellious, defiant behavior. But her actions weren't directed at me, or at herself. She acted out to get back at Brenda. The two of them had a contentious relationship, a push-pull kind of coexistence.

But I had to accept some of the blame because I wasn't around as much as I should have been during my kids' early years. Working seventy hours a week didn't leave much time to bond. But when I did spend time with Jeffery and Sam, I tried to make it count. We'd go on picnics in the park, or just throw a blanket down in the backyard and eat peanut butter and jelly sandwiches. Brenda thought I should've done something more culturally enriching with them. But after Jack and Jill, Boy Scouts, Girl Scouts, museum tours, and every other type of social activity Brenda squeezed into their hectic little schedules, I figured they needed a break to just be kids and hang out with their dad.

Looking back, I wish I had spent more time with them, especially my son. Maybe if I'd been around for Jeffery he wouldn't have turned into the angry, bitter person he is today. Sam said that he confided in her right before he moved to Paris eight years ago that he was distancing himself from the family because of Brenda. But again, some of the blame rested on my shoulders as well. I felt a lot of regret when I thought about my son, but I was a man who knew that I couldn't change what had already been done. I just had to move on and deal with the here and now.

Dealing with the here and now meant that I needed to accept my current situation. Emily would be under my roof for what could be several weeks, and that meant I had to obey the rules I'd always followed with her, the two Cs . . . careful caution.

Chapter 6

Brenda . . .

He Should Appreciate Her More

Brenda propped her head up on one of her fluffy pillows and adjusted her body under the comfort of her luxurious sateen bed sheets. With carefree ease, she flipped the channel with the remote until she landed on HGTV. She nestled in, preparing to watch one of her favorite interior designers dispense decorating tips, when she heard the thud of her husband's footsteps coming up the stairs. She sighed, slightly annoyed because she knew that once Ed entered the room he would ask her to turn the channel to MSNBC. She hated MSNBC!

Brenda watched her husband as he walked toward the bed, noticing that he looked more preoccupied than usual. The last few weeks had been hectic for him, leading up to a big trial he'd been working on for months.

"How was your day?" she asked, not bothering to turn down the volume on the TV or miss a single word of the designer's presentation. She was ever the multitasker.

Ed looked down at his watch. "Long, and tiring."

"Mine, too," Brenda sighed, thinking about the exhausting day she'd had. After rising at eleven that morning, she read the Style section of the previous day's newspaper, then took a long shower before getting dressed. She lunched at Clyde's with her sister, Dorothy, then headed down the street to the Elizabeth Arden Red Door Spa for her weekly hair appointment, facial, manicure, and full body massage. After that, she whisked over to Saks Jandel and picked up a dress she'd special ordered before jetting off to the Corcoran Gallery, arriving in just enough time to conduct a docent tour. Afterward, she briefly dropped by the house to welcome her daughter's best friend to town, then she was off to an evening board meeting for her sorority.

No one knows all the things I do in the course of a day, Brenda thought as she looked at her husband. Keeping her beautiful house in perfect order, making sure that Ed was well cared for, maintaining her personal appearance through well-managed care, and being a social butterfly, volunteer, and organizer were no small feats! "It takes talent to hold this fabulous life together while making it all look so effortless," she'd told Porscha, her skilled massage therapist at the Red Door Spa, during her session earlier that day. "That's why I need these weekly treatments," she sighed as Porscha kneaded her back, trying to block out the song and dance that Brenda complained about every week.

Of course, Gerti and others were there to help, but still, Brenda knew that things would fall apart without her careful instruction and guidance. It was *work* keeping everyone in line, and she felt that she'd had a long and tiring day, too, just like Ed.

Brenda wanted to tell her husband that her schedule was just as busy and demanding as his, and that even though she didn't rise at the crack of dawn every morning like he did, she still worked hard. She didn't manage legal cases, but she knew how to manage the hell out of people. She was vigilant about making sure that the landscaper, water deliveryman, and even the mailman all provided their services on time, and she took meticulous care to ensure that she and Ed responded to social invitations and attended important events around the city that she carefully synchronized on both their calendars. Ensuring that all the fine details of their lives were attended to was what Brenda considered quite a heavy load.

It frustrated her that Ed didn't seem to grasp the magnitude of her many skills. Just because she didn't litigate high-profile cases or fight to preserve the civil justice system didn't mean that her activities were any less important—in her opinion. She wished Ed could trade places with her for just one day so he could see all the balls she juggled. If he did, she knew it would show him that he should appreciate her more.

Brenda took a long look at her husband, who was now sitting on the edge of their bed. She noticed that his shoulders were hunched over like he'd been doing hard labor. Even though he was sitting with his back to her, she could see that he was worried about something. "Ed, what's wrong with you?"

"Nothing, I just had a long day, that's all."

She strained to hear him over the TV, wishing he'd speak up louder. "What did you say?"

"Long day . . . I said I've had a long day," Ed repeated, turning toward her.

Brenda looked down at his hand and saw that he was still holding his brandy snifter. She thought that was very odd. Every night, like clockwork, Ed would unwind in his study by drinking a small snifter of his favorite brandy before heading up to bed. It had been his nightly ritual for as long as she could remember. But he never brought his glass upstairs. He always left it sitting on his large mahogany desk, and in the morning Gerti would retrieve it, clean it, and sit it back in the same spot for the cycle to begin anew.

Brenda watched as her husband held the empty snifter in his hand. "Why did you bring that upstairs?" she asked, pointing to his glass.

Ed looked down at his hand as though he'd just realized what he was holding. "I don't know," he responded in a faraway voice, shrugging his shoulders.

Brenda knew that from time to time Ed could become a little distant when he was working on a major case, but his detachment was usually mixed with excitement from the sheer thrill of the hunt because he loved his work. However, she noticed that his energy was very different tonight, evidenced by the distinct melancholy clouding his mood. She hoped he wasn't coming down with something because they had a very important event to attend tomorrow night. "Ed, you're not getting sick, are you?"

"No, like I said, it's been a long day."

Brenda looked at him as he sat the empty snifter on the antique sitting bench at the foot of their bed before heading over to their large walk-in closet. A few minutes later he emerged in his T-shirt and boxers, then climbed into bed with a stack of documents in his hand. No matter how much he frustrated her, Brenda had to admit that she loved seeing her husband crawl in between the sheets. Even though their love life was nearly nonexistent, she still liked the fact that Ed was damn good to look at.

She admired his smooth, caramel-colored skin, soft-looking dimples, and piercing brown eyes. Over the years he'd kept himself in astonishingly good shape by adhering to a disciplined workout regimen, from which he never wavered. Ed's looks were like the vintage wines she savored, they got better and more robust with each passing year. For Brenda, outward appearances rated high on her scale of requirements and made up for their lack of physical intimacy and emotional affection.

Brenda blocked out the designer on TV and watched Ed more closely. His reading glasses were perched on the bridge of his nose, but he didn't seem to be reading at all. More than ten minutes had passed and he hadn't moved beyond the first page in his pile of papers. She thought that was strange because by this time he would have normally gone through half the stack. And what was even more unsettling to her was that since he'd entered the room, he had yet to ask her to turn the channel to MSNBC. She knew that something was amiss.

"Ed?" Brenda glared. "What's wrong with you? You're acting strange tonight."

"No, I'm not."

"Yes, you are. You're walking around, looking like you just lost a case. You brought your brandy snifter upstairs, and you haven't even asked me to turn the channel to your beloved MSNBC. Something must be wrong."

Ed let out a frustrated sigh, put his documents to the side, and turned to his wife. "Damn, Brenda, if I come home happy or excited, you say it's because I must be up to something. If I ask you to turn the channel while you're watching your shows, you say that I'm not being considerate. Just because I forgot to leave an empty glass downstairs, it doesn't mean that something's wrong, it simply means I had a hard day," he said, agitation filling his voice. "Can you just give it a rest?"

Brenda ran her fingers through her silky, shoulder-length hair as she sat up in bed. She crossed her arms and returned her husband's stare. She couldn't remember the last time they'd had a real argument. One of the things she'd grown to appreciate about their relationship was that she and Ed were at the stage in their marriage where they just let things go. But tonight she sensed a strange tension in the air. "You can save your analysis for the courtroom," she snapped. "Don't try and make me out to be the demanding, nagging wife. I've known you long enough to see when there's something wrong. I'm just trying to get to the bottom of whatever has you in such a disagreeable mood."

Ed took a deep breath. "I had a rough day and I have to head back to the office bright and early tomorrow morning. We go to trial soon, so I've got to focus," he said, then returned to his papers.

"I hope you're not planning to work all day and then come home in another bad mood."

Ed didn't respond.

"Well, if you must work, you must work. Just make sure that you're up to going to the party."

"What party?"

Brenda looked at her husband as if he'd just told her that he had forgotten his own birthday. She hit the power button on the remote, transforming the plasma screen into a silent, black slate. "Joe and Juanita Presley's party!" she nearly gasped. "Don't tell me you've forgotten? It's been all the talk for the last month."

Ed glanced down at his wife over the rim of his glasses. "All what talk?"

"Ugghh," Brenda grunted, shaking her head. For the life of her, she couldn't understand why a man who was as well connected and as socially sought after as Ed didn't have a clue or desire about the details of important happenings. She knew that it was up to her to keep him on his toes. She tried to control her tone as she spoke. "Other than Samantha and Emily's birthday celebration next month, Joe and Juanita Presley's party will be *the event* to

attend this summer. All anyone could talk about this evening at the sorority meeting was Juanita's party tomorrow night, especially Juanita herself," she huffed. "It starts at seven, so be home by six."

"Fine," Ed agreed in a tone that let Brenda know he was shutting down.

She wanted to reiterate to Ed how important this party was, but she knew he wasn't in the mood to continue another word of the conversation. Although she would rather bathe in ice water than show up at an important social affair unescorted, she was determined to go to this party with or without her husband. This was an event she had to attend.

Juanita Presley was Brenda's archnemesis. Her sister, Dorothy, and Juanita were peers, and it stood to reason that the two of them would be natural rivals, but that wasn't the case. Juanita and Dorothy were actually the best of friends, and at one time they had hoped their children would marry and make them in-laws. To Brenda's relief, but to Dorothy's disappointment, that hadn't happened, yet.

To say that Brenda and Juanita didn't care for each other was a grand understatement. They'd been in competition with each other for years. They were both married to wealthy, successful men. They each possessed elegant good looks, exceptional taste, and membership in the right social organizations and clubs. The two competed on every level, even where their children were concerned—and that was the one area where Brenda felt woefully inadequate.

Juanita's son, Joe Jr., was a dentist with a lucrative suburban practice. He was married to a former beauty queen who'd given him three adorable children. Her daughter, Pamela, was general counsel for one of the most powerful lobbying firms in Atlanta. Several years ago, Brenda thought she'd finally get a chance to throw venom at Juanita when Pamela had a child out of wed-lock. But her temporary gloating was spoiled when she learned that the father of Pamela's baby was not only a prominent heart surgeon, he was her sister Dorothy's most beloved son, Parker.

Brenda, on the other hand, didn't boast about her children the way Juanita did. Even though she wanted to brag about the fact that Jeffery was a successful physician living in Paris, she refused to breathe a word because she'd have to explain why such a handsome, intelligent young man as Jeffery wasn't married—and she wasn't about to reveal that it was because same-sex marriage wasn't legal in Paris. She'd had high hopes for her first-born, but he had turned out to be one of her most upsetting disappointments.

And then there was Samantha. Although she thought her daughter was witty and mildly charming when she wanted to be, Brenda had so many issues with Samantha that she didn't know where to begin. She was heartbroken that despite all the piano, ballet, and etiquette lessons she'd lavished on her, Samantha had always chosen to stray to the wrong side of the tracks, preferring the seamier side of life.

Over the years, Samantha had run the gamut in men from would-be thugs to outright criminals, giving Brenda mild heart attacks along the way. It greatly disappointed her that Samantha had blown her one chance for happiness when she ruined her relationship with Tyler Jacobs. Samantha had purposely sabotaged their six-month courtship, and Brenda knew that her daughter had done it just to spite her. And for that reason she was determined to make Samantha's upcoming birthday party a success.

Samantha would turn thirty next month, and Brenda vowed to get her daughter married off before she became an old maid, as if she weren't already dangerously close.

A lavish summer garden party was the perfect way to invite a host of eligible bachelors into Samantha's life and properly announce that she was in the market for a husband.

Brenda thought it was high time that Samantha started acting like an adult and get her life together, if not for her sake, then for the reputation of the Baldwin name. She was embarrassed to no end that Samantha had a child but no husband to round out a traditional family. Come hell or high water, she was going to make sure that she remedied the situation. And as an added bonus, she would be able to throw a party that would have people talking.

Just as she was thinking over the details for the lavish event, Ed turned to her with a quizzical look stretched across his face. "What's this about Sam and Emily having a birthday party next month? This is the first I've heard about it."

Brenda pursed her lips. "I'm throwing a thirtieth celebration party for the girls," she said matter-of-factly.

Ed removed his reading glasses, giving his wife a questioning stare. "Do they know you're throwing them a party? Sam hasn't mentioned it."

"It's going to be, um . . . sort of a surprise," Brenda replied.

"You better check with Sam, and Emily, too, before you start planning one of your extravagant parties," Ed cautioned. "They've spent every birthday together since they were nineteen, and they probably have big plans for this one."

"And that's exactly why I'm going to help them celebrate this milestone. Turning thirty, being in the same city again, and starting fresh new lives . . . they will appreciate this, you'll see."

Ed stared at Brenda with skeptical eyes. "What's in it for you?"

"I beg your pardon?"

"Don't play innocent. Everything you do has a motive that's usually tied to a self-serving gain, just like having Emily as our houseguest. It works out nicely that you'll have someone around to pick up the slack with CJ."

Brenda wanted to feign outrage, but she remained silent because Ed was exactly right—she had her motives. In addition to helping with CJ, and her quest to make a respectable woman of Samantha, Brenda had her sites set on another mission that would yield her the treasure she'd been coveting for over a year, and she needed Emily's help to get it. Yes, she was going to remain silent and she was going to make sure that she accomplished her goal. "Good night, Ed." Brenda smiled, then turned out the light, thinking about her strategy.

Chapter 7

Emily . . .

I Need to Move Now!

I loved Mondays. It was my favorite day of the week because it represented a new beginning. My mother used to say that everyone needed a fresh start because you never knew what was waiting around the corner. As I began my day, I hoped that her truism would stand as my moniker for the weeks to come.

I was an early riser, a trait I inherited from both my parents. I was up before the sun rose this morning so I could drive Samantha to Union Station. She had decided to leave her car here until she moved in a few weeks, relieving her of the tremendous hassle of parking it in New York City. On our way to the train station we talked about her lunch date yesterday with the new man she'd met last Friday night. He sounded like a great guy, but Samantha seemed hesitant about him. He was opposite from the type of man she usually went for, which was probably a good thing. Even though Samantha made poor choices, she was a good person, and she deserved good things in her life. I hoped she would realize that before it was too late. She had so much to offer and didn't even know it.

After I dropped Samantha off, I miraculously found my way back to the house without getting lost. I was sitting at the kitchen table drinking hibiscus tea when Ed walked into the room.

"Good morning. I see that I'm not the only early bird around here." He smiled as he dropped the morning paper on the breakfast table.

"Good morning." I smiled back, but couldn't look him in the eye. I still felt embarrassed by the way I practically ran out of the room last Friday night. I had every intention of apologizing, but we kept missing each other over the last two days. Now that we were alone and finally had a chance to talk, I couldn't seem to push out the words.

I discreetly scanned Ed as he walked over to the coffeemaker and poured himself a freshly brewed cup. He reached over and pushed a button to warm the bagel that had already been split the night before and was waiting for him to toast. It amazed me how Ms. Gerti attended to the smallest of details that kept this family running.

When Ed slid down into his seat, my breathing became shallow. Sitting across from him, I felt more nervous than Rush Limbaugh at an NAACP convention. "May I see the Metro section, please?" I asked. I needed something to do, a distraction to take my mind off the seductive scent of his cologne.

He looked at me for what seemed like a long time before handing me the paper. He opened the Business section and read it as he ate his bagel. We exchanged sections as we finished them, like it was a morning routine we shared every day. We read through the entire

Washington Post together, and I was surprised by how comfortable it felt.

"Do you have a busy day ahead?" he asked, rising from the table to place his empty cup and crumb-splattered plate in the sink.

"After I drop off CJ at camp later this morning I'm going to swing by my house and check on the progress."

"When did your contractor say they'll be finished?"

"Last month," I half joked.

"If you need any help, I'll be happy to make a phone call because—"

"Thanks," I said, cutting him off, "but that's okay. I know you're busy. I don't want to impose on your time."

"Helping you isn't an imposition at all."

His offer made me smile. "Thank you. I'll let you know."

I watched as Ed pulled on his dark blue jacket and grabbed his briefcase and gym bag from the floor. He was off to start his day, and a part of me wished I could join him. He walked toward the back door and stopped. This was my chance. I took a deep breath. "Ed, I want to apologize for leaving so abruptly the other night. I had a long day on the road and I was tired. It had nothing to do with you," I lied.

I hated this—making up excuses and telling him things that weren't true. Lying to someone you love really sucks, but the truth wasn't a proposition I could afford to exercise with him. As paradoxical as it was, my truth could cause more problems and pain than any lie I could ever choose to tell.

Ed squinted his eyes. "Emily?"

"Yes?"

I watched as he hesitated. Ed was a very decisive man who didn't second-guess himself, let alone hesitate about any action he was about to take. I couldn't imagine what he was thinking. I prayed that he wasn't going to revisit his suggestion that I seek psychiatric help. But as I studied him more closely, I realized that he was looking at me in a way that made me feel warm inside. My hands began to tremble and I wondered if he could sense my inner thoughts. Our eyes locked, and for a split second I felt something intense.

Just then, Ms. Gerti came through the door. "Good morning," she said, walking slowly toward the kitchen sink. She apparently picked up on the vibe surging through the room because she stared back and forth from Ed to me as if to say, *Let me in on your secret.* I was inclined to ask the same thing . . . of him.

"Have a good one, Gerti." Ed smiled and then nodded toward me. He closed the door behind him so fast it made Ms. Gerti's skirt whip around her legs.

After I got CJ up and dressed—something for which Ms. Gerti was truly grateful because like his mother, our little CJ was *not* a morning person—she made us a delicious breakfast of scrambled eggs, homemade waffles, and freshly squeezed orange juice. Brenda was still asleep as we began our day. According to Ms. Gerti, she didn't stir until well after eleven most mornings.

"Auntie Emee's gonna take me to camp," CJ announced to Ms. Gerti with a big grin, biting into his syrup-drenched waffle.

"Well, I know you're gonna love that." She smiled.

After we finished breakfast, CJ threw his Transformers backpack over his small shoulders and we headed out the door. We laughed and talked on the drive to his summer camp out in Bethesda, a Maryland suburb right outside the District line. The directions that Ms. Gerti gave me were excellent, and I only got turned around once. I smothered CJ with a hug and a kiss and told him I'd be back to pick him up this afternoon.

DC wasn't a particularly driver-friendly city, and I discovered that when I ventured out to find my new home. I had only been there a few times several months ago, so it was difficult for me to gather my bearings. After getting turned around four times and nearly rear-ended twice, I finally found it.

My block was beautiful with its lovely old Victorians and begonia-covered tree boxes. But it was also crowded. Cars were lined up on both sides of the street. If it was like this during the day when everyone was supposed to be at work, I could only imagine what it was like in the evenings and on weekends. Yet another thing about city living I would have to get used to. Thankfully, I loved this neighborhood! It wasn't far from the U Street Corridor, where everything was happening. There were lots of neat shops, cool restaurants, trendy cafés, hip lofts and condos, eclectic young urbanites, and access to the citywide Metro train system, which was priceless.

My Victorian row house was originally built in 1910, and had been in the same family for four generations. Luckily, they'd taken meticulous care of the place over the years. However, it hadn't been updated since the 1970s. Needless to say, a major renovation was necessary.

After my offer was accepted back in February, Bradley flew down with me the following weekend to sketch the schematic drawings for the interior redesign. It had been a kind gesture on his part. And even though I had reiterated that his visit wouldn't change the direction of our relationship, he still insisted on making the trip. "I want to help you," he'd told me. He was a really great guy, and he was going to make someone a good husband. But as I said before, he just wasn't the one for me.

With drawings in hand, the following week my Realtor put me in touch with a contractor who promised that he and his crew could complete the scope of work in four months, permits and all. The time line sounded perfect because my house would have been finished a full month before I planned to move. I closed on my new home in record time and two weeks later, Emmanuel Santiago and his crew began their work. I had been tracking their progress by phone and e-mail since they started, but for the last few weeks Emmanuel hadn't responded to any of my messages.

Because the parking pad for the garage out back hadn't been poured, I found an empty space on the street and parked Hazel as close to my house as I could get. When I turned off the engine she coughed and hiccuped like she was fighting for air. I was going to have to find a reliable mechanic in the area.

I was walking up the steps to my house when I spied someone two doors down.

"Good morning! How are you!" the flamboyant man called out as he watered an array of colorful potted plants gracing his stoop. He was dressed in a pair of linen capri pants and a white cotton shirt that was tied in a knot at the waist. He adjusted his stylish sunglasses and peered at me, resting his weight on his right foot, which was adorned with a pair of cute hot pink flip-flops.

"I'm well, how are you?" I smiled. I instantly liked him.

"I'm *fab-u-lous.*" He smiled back, waving his hand for emphasis. "You must be our new neighbor!"

"Yes, I guess I am."

He put down his green watering can, clapped his hands together, and then crossed them over his heart. "Oh, it's so good to finally meet you," he beamed, revealing a beautiful set of glow-in-the-dark teeth, so white they couldn't have been natural. He walked past the small wrought-iron railings that separated our tiny front yards. "My name is Ruben Rodriguez." He extended his hand, shaking mine with gentle pressure.

"Hi, Ruben, I'm Emily Snow. It's nice to meet you, too." A strange sensation went through me as his palm rested in mine. There was something familiar in his touch. I think he felt it, too, because he paused for a second before regaining his composure.

"*E-mi-leee*, you're a doll!" he sang. Ruben looked me up and down like he was sizing me up, but not in a nasty way. It was more like he was eyeing me with approval.

"Looks like I won't be the only beauty on the block anymore." He smiled as he toyed with his long, glossy black hair. "I love the look you've got goin' on. The whole bohemian meets chic thing is very hot!"

I giggled, looking down at my ankle-length gauze skirt. The three large bangles I wore on my right arm clanked together as I tugged slightly at my brown Lycra tank top. "Thanks." I blushed.

"And the hair is fierce," he appraised. "Have you found a stylist in the area yet?"

"No, I haven't. Can you recommend someone? Whoever does your hair really knows what they're doing," I said. Ruben's hair looked like he could shoot a Pantene commercial right here on the street.

"That would be *moi*." He smiled from ear to ear. "Honey, I'm a master stylist with one of the top salons in the city, and I can hook you up." He leaned over, taking the liberty to run his fingers through my hair. "Nice, healthy texture and great condition," he said. "Oh, yes. I can definitely work with this."

"I think I'll need a trim in another month or so."

"Lovely! I'll put you down in my book. And by the way . . . love those slingbacks." He winked, glancing down at my canvas covered shoes.

I could see that Ruben and I were going to be good friends.

"We were wondering when our new neighbor would appear. Last night I was telling Roger, he's my partner," Ruben winked again, "that I couldn't wait to meet you. When Emmanuel told us that our new neighbor was from Atlanta, I was so excited to hear that another Southern belle would be living on the block."

I chuckled. Ruben was a mess. "Where're you from?"

"The beautiful state of North Carolina."

"Yes, it's lovely down there." I nodded.

After a few more minutes of nice chitchat, I looked in the direction of my first-floor window and could see the partially completed drywall. "Want to come inside with me and take a look?" I asked, knowing this would make Ruben's day.

"I thought you'd never ask. I've been dying for a look around, but Emmanuel hasn't let me have a peek inside in over a month."

I made a mental note—I needed to find out what Ruben's relationship was to Emmanuel because this was the second time he'd mentioned my contractor.

When I inserted my key into the door and we walked inside, I had to catch my breath. I'd fallen in love with this old house when I first saw it, but I had no idea it would look this beautiful once the renovation was under way. Ruben hooked his arm around mine and pulled me close to him. "I'm *soooo* jealous," he gushed. "Sweetie, this place is *in-cre-di-ble!*"

"I know!" I beamed with excitement.

As Ruben and I walked arm-in-arm through the first

floor, we oohed and aahed over the fine work that had been done. Although my house wasn't in move-in condition, it was coming together nicely. The kitchen and powder room still needed the finishing touches of paint, fixtures, and lighting, and the spacious basement still needed quite a bit of work. But I could see that it was all going to be beautiful once it was completed.

Moving on to the upstairs, we discovered that it was just as lovely as the first floor and that mostly everything was finished, save for the two bathrooms. Even in its present state it was clear that my house was shaping up into something out of a magazine. I planned to send Bradley some pictures and a big fruit basket this week. His design turned out better than I could ever have imagined.

Ruben and I headed back downstairs, dodging piles of discarded wood, nails, and sawdust. "I hope it won't be too long before I can move in. It should've been finished a month ago."

"Was that in your contract?"

"Sure was."

"Since Emmanuel hasn't delivered on his end, you should try to get something out of it." He winked conspiratorially.

I noticed that winking was like breathing to Ruben. He was hilarious without even trying to be. "You seem to know Emmanuel pretty well. Are you two friends?" I ventured to ask.

Ruben let out a small laugh and shook his head. "No, honey. When Emmanuel started work on your house, I introduced myself and became the dreaded pain-in-the-ass, nosy next-door neighbor from hell, so now he knows who I am. Plus, we have the Latino thing in common, ya know?" He winked with a flip of his hand and a toss of his perfect hair.

"Oh." I nodded. "Well, I'm going to contact him because he needs to get his crew back to work. I've got to move in soon," I said, looking at my empty living room. "I have so many things to do this week, I'll see if Emmanuel can meet me this Friday." After only one weekend, I knew that I couldn't last much longer under Ed's roof.

"If I see any activity between now and then I'll let you know," Ruben said, placing his hand on his hip. "And I'll meet with you this Friday, too, if you like. No need in you having to go through this process alone, there's power in numbers. Besides, I can act as your interpreter in case Emmanuel feeds you the old *no hablo Inglés* routine."

I smiled wide. "Thanks, Ruben. I really appreciate that."

After Ruben and I walked outside we exchanged cell phone numbers and agreed to meet here at noon this Friday.

"Auntie Emee!" CJ squealed when he saw me enter the playground area.

He abandoned his playmates and ran up to me, giving me a big hug. I loved this little boy with all my heart. "Hey, Sweet Pea. Did you have fun today?" I asked.

"Yes. I played with my friends and we had Popsicles!" He grinned.

"Oh, boy, you did have a good day."

"And I drew pictures and I learned a new song!"

Later that evening, CJ rummaged through his toy box for his favorite dinosaur magnet and affixed the picture of me that he'd drawn today onto the refrigerator. Although I got the feeling that Brenda didn't want her stainless steel Sub-Zero cluttered with elementary school art, she held her breath and allowed it.

She appeared to be in a particularly good mood

tonight. I'd never seen her so relaxed, and it seemed a little odd. She was usually very high-strung. I think it came from her insatiable drive to do all things well. She wanted everything to be just so, and at times she could develop a bit of tunnel vision, causing her to lose perspective of other people's feelings. She didn't mean any harm, that was just who she was.

Samantha said I gave her mother too much credit and that Brenda was simply selfish. They had a strained relationship at best, so I remained largely silent on topics that concerned her. On the other hand, she loved her father and was always singing Ed's praises. Samantha was the ultimate daddy's girl if there ever was one, and for obvious reasons I remained largely silent on my thoughts about him, too.

An hour later, we sat at the dining room table, eating as a family. I knew this kind of gathering was rare in the Baldwin house because CJ loudly announced, "Papa and Nana are eating with us tonight!" as if it only happened on rare occasions, like the holidays.

This was supposed to be my official welcome-to-town dinner, and after seeing that my house still needed lots of work and not hearing from my contractor all day, Ms. Gerti's cooking was a much appreciated treat. After a fantastic meal of herb roasted chicken, garlic mashed potatoes, and sautéed vegetables, I was devouring Ms. Gerti's pineapple upside-down cake when Brenda hit me with something that made me lose my appetite.

"Emily, dear, I have delightful news," She smiled as she pushed her dessert aside. "You're going to love what I have planned for you."

I wiped my mouth with my napkin. "Please don't go through any additional trouble for me. I appreciate that you're letting me stay here, and I promise I'll be out of your hair as soon as my contractor gives me the word."

Brenda shook her head. "You must stop with that nonsense, my dear, you're a joy to have."

"Amen to that," Ms. Gerti chimed in.

"Auntie Emee, I want you to stay with us forever!" CJ cheered, cake spilling from his mouth.

I noticed that Ed seemed uncomfortable. He hadn't said a word throughout the entire meal.

"So, back to my good news," Brenda said, handing me a greeting card size envelope. "The invitations just arrived from the printer today."

Brenda smiled like she had just announced that I'd won the lottery. When I pulled out the invitation, it read like wedding script: *Mr. and Mrs. Edward Curtis Baldwin, Esquire, Cordially Invite You to Share in the Thirtieth Birthday Celebration of . . .*

I tried to act like I was happy about the party they were throwing for Samantha and me because I could see how much it meant to Brenda. She had obviously put a lot of time into planning it. "Wow, this is, um, really nice of you Brenda . . . but you shouldn't have."

"Wait until you see the birthday cake the caterer has designed. It's simply gorgeous," Brenda said with excitement.

Samantha and I always celebrated our birthday together, it was our ritual. When we turned twenty we made a pact that we would celebrate our thirtieth in grand style, maybe even go to the motherland, Africa, the birthplace of all civilization. Thirty was supposed to be momentous, or at least we thought so back then. But now, after all we'd both been through, we agreed that we felt like we hit the thirty mark a few years ago.

With our birthday only one month away, Samantha and I knew we'd be right in the middle of moving into our new homes and adjusting to our new jobs, so we decided to keep things simple. We planned to celebrate by going to a nice restaurant, eating a good meal, drinking lots of wine, and laughing our way into the big 3-0, just the two of us.

I suspected that Samantha didn't have a clue about this party. For one, she would've mentioned it to me before now; and two, she tried to stay as far away as possible from anything that involved her mother. "I guess Samantha's just as surprised as I am." I smiled. I looked around the table for a reaction. CJ was excited; Ms. Gerti looked irritated; and for the first time since he sat down, Ed looked engaged in what was happening.

Brenda cleared her throat. "Well, you could say that. But I know once she sees how excited you are about the party, she'll be excited, too."

CJ clapped his hands together. *"Yeaaaaah,* we're gonna have a party!"

Ed narrowed his eyes at Brenda while Ms. Gerti rolled hers. I knew that something was up, but there were too many dynamics going on for me to accurately discern what had caused the sudden shift in the room. Still, one thing was for sure, the only people happy about the party were an unknowing five-year-old, and Brenda.

A few uncomfortable minutes passed in silence, so I felt obligated to try to lighten the mood. I made small talk until everyone started to feel a bit more at ease. After dinner I went up to my room and gobbled four extra-strength Tylenol. I had a headache just thinking about the party. I was grateful that Brenda thought enough of me to want to include me in a party that she was throwing for her daughter, but elaborate affairs weren't my cup of tea. After a quick shower, I crawled into bed and called Samantha.

"The party's just a ruse," she said. "Mother's planning this shit just so she can show off and get me hooked up with some straitlaced, weak-ass brother who she thinks is *appropriate,*" she ranted. "And I know for a fact that she wants to throw a party that will top the one Mrs. Presley had last weekend."

"Couldn't it just be that your mother wants to do something nice for you, for both of us?"

"Hell, no! This party has nothing to do with us. It's all about her, you'll see."

Brenda may have a heavy-handed way of doing things, but I wanted to believe that her intentions were good. I had to. Acknowledging her redeeming qualities and believing that she was essentially a good person was one of the things that kept me from making a big mistake—after all, how could I justify not only lusting after my best friend's father, but also a good woman's husband?

I couldn't believe today was Friday. The week had flown by in a whirlwind of activities, and luckily I'd managed to accomplish a lot. From standing in a ridiculously long line at the DMV to register my car and secure a DC driver's license, to dropping off and picking up CJ from summer camp each day, to taking care of utility connections, I'd been on the go. I was glad to have a list of things to occupy my time because it served to keep my mind busy.

Ever since my intense eye contact with Ed on Monday morning, and the news about my birthday party later that evening, I'd been on edge. I had kept my distance from him all week. I would leave my room only when I was sure he had already left for the day, and I made certain that I was out of sight when he returned in the evening.

But this morning as I sat at the kitchen table waiting for him, I had to push my uneasiness aside because I needed his help. Emmanuel hadn't returned any of my phone calls or responded to my texts or e-mails all week.

I planned to meet Ruben at my house at noon. And in the last message I'd left for Emmanuel, I told him as forcefully as I could that he'd better be there, too. I hoped that Ed could pressure him into showing up. Samantha was right, having *Esquire* at the end of your name could make people change their tune.

I pressed my back against the soft fabric of the chair, listening, as I heard the soles of Ed's expensive leather shoes click against the hardwood floors down the hall. He was surprised to see me when he entered the kitchen. "Ah, the early riser is back." He smiled, placing the newspaper on the table. He walked over and poured himself a cup of coffee.

"Good morning," I said. I watched him as he reached over and pushed the button on the toaster, allowing the bagel to slide into place. He leaned against the counter and adjusted his silver cuff links, but he didn't move when the two round discs popped up. By that time he could see that I was staring at him . . . intently. Before I could stop myself, the question that had been on my mind since Monday suddenly slipped out. "Do you eat the same thing every morning? Coffee and a bagel?"

"Yes, I do." Ed smiled, sliding into the chair across from me.

"Every morning?"

He raised his brow as he spread a generous amount of cream cheese over the warmly toasted dough. "Every morning."

"Oh . . ."

"Why? Is there something wrong with what I eat?" he asked, taking a bite of his bagel.

"No, I was just curious. I mean, why have a bagel when Ms. Gerti's around? Obviously you haven't had her omelets or Belgian waffles." It was an attempt to make a joke.

Why had I opened my big mouth? If I noticed things about him, I was supposed to keep them to myself. Asking questions would only lead to awkward moments like this, revealing my desire to know all I could about the man I loved. This was exhausting and frustrating, which brought me to the reason why I needed to talk to him this morning. I had to get out of this house. So before Ed could ask the question that was poised on the tip of his tongue, I interrupted him. "I have a favor to ask you."

He paused and leaned forward in his chair. "Sure, what is it?"

I explained that Emmanuel had been MIA and that Ruben and I were supposed to meet at my house at noon to see if any new work had been done. "I've asked Emmanuel to be there, too, but it's very doubtful that he'll show. However, I think a call from an attorney might spur him into action."

"No problem. Just give me his number and I'll be happy to contact him. Do you have a copy of your contract handy?"

"Yes, I do."

"Fax it to my office. You can use the machine in my study."

I finally found the courage to look directly into Ed's beautiful brown eyes. "Thank you, I really appreciate this."

"You don't have to thank me." He leaned back in his chair, and with the lightning-quick memory that was his nature, he asked the question that I'd interrupted. "Do you think it's odd that I eat the same thing every morning?"

Just as I was about to try to explain my way out of the situation I'd created, Ms. Gerti came through the back door. She managed to always save the day.

"Morning." She smiled, scooping up Ed's coffee cup

and empty plate. "What's got you looking so puzzled?" she asked, staring at him with curious eyes.

"Well, Emily thinks I'm a boring old man who's stuck in his ways."

"She catches on quick." Ms. Gerti chuckled.

Ed laughed, too, but I didn't. I wanted to correct my error. "I didn't mean it that way," I spoke up.

He smiled. "She's referring to my obligatory coffee and bagel."

Ms. Gerti thought for a moment. "Shoot, that's been the routine for what, thirty years now?" She placed the dishes in the sink, then turned around and faced us. "I guess when you get used to certain things over the years it's hard to break away from them," she said, peering at Ed. "Even if you do want to try something new," she added, this time looking directly at me.

I felt hot and nervous, like I'd been exposed. I wanted to leave the room. Ed looked away from Ms. Gerti and down to the unread newspaper in front of him. He stood, reached for his briefcase and gym bag, and headed toward the door. "Emily, don't forget to fax over your contract this morning. The office fax number is on the business card at the edge of my desk." He opened the door, then smiled at Ms. Gerti before saying good-bye.

After Ruben and I finished our inspection, it was apparent that no work had been done since we'd been here last Monday. I was so upset I wanted to scream. I needed to move in as quickly as possible. This morning's breakfast conversation was proof of that. I sighed and looked around my living room at the dried putty on the Sheetrock. "Ruben, I can't believe this."

"I know you're frustrated, but just think, things could be worse."

"I need to move in now. I'm tempted to get a hammer and start working myself."

"Sweetie," Ruben said, putting his hand on my shoulder. "You're much too beautiful to be covered in paint and sawdust. Let's just wait for Emmanuel to get here."

"That's just it, I don't think he's going to show up."

No sooner had I spoken than the doorbell rang. When I opened it, I was shocked to see Ed standing in front of me. He was talking on his BlackBerry and holding a large folder under his arm. "Very good, I'll see you shortly," he said to the person on the other end before disconnecting the call. "May I come in?" he asked with a smile.

I moved aside to let him enter, taking secret pleasure in the feel of his suit coat as he brushed against my bare arm. He looked around and I could see that he was impressed with the work that had been done. When he spotted Ruben he walked over and introduced himself, extending his hand. "I'm Ed Baldwin. You must be Ruben. Emily has spoken very highly of you."

"Thank you, and I've heard wonderful things about your family."

Ruben glanced at me and raised a perfectly arched brow. I had told him about Samantha and her parents, and that I was staying with the Baldwins until my place was ready. He was obviously taken by Ed's good looks, evidenced in his broad smile.

"What brings you by?" I asked Ed.

"I'm here to serve as your legal counsel for your meeting with Mr. Santiago. I just got off the phone with him. He should be here any minute."

As if on cue, Emmanuel rang the doorbell. After I ushered him inside, the four of us stood in the middle of my living room. Emmanuel started with a sob story about why the work had not been completed. As he continued with a litany of lame excuses, Ed opened his folder and handed him a document.

"Noted are the portions of the contract under which you are legally obligated, and because Ms. Snow," Ed nodded toward me, "has honored her obligations under the contract by meeting the financial responsibilities as stated, you, Mr. Santiago, are in breach of said contract." He went on to tell Emmanuel that because of the hardship he'd caused me by not being able to move into my house on time, he had one of two options. He could work out an appropriate form of compensation with me that included home improvement upgrades, or he could see me in court. "If you choose the latter, I'll make sure a processor serves you with the appropriate papers before the close of business," Ed spoke with finality.

Listening to Ed take control, telling this man what he needed to do to make things right for me, made me tingle. His power and cool command stirred my entire body. He was taking care of me, and it made me want him even more.

Emmanuel didn't have to think long on the proposal. He gladly, and smartly, chose the first option. Before he stepped out of the door he agreed to meet with me first thing Monday morning to work out a plan that would make me happy and have me in my house within the next few weeks. I was already thinking about the upgrades I planned to have him install.

"Sweetie, I've got to get going," Ruben said as he looked at his pink leather watch with its large, diamond-studded face. "I'm running late and I have a bitchy client who's in dire need of some color and a trim. I'll call you later, okay?" He gave me an air-kiss and a curious smile, then shook Ed's hand before he floated out the door.

I knew that Ed wanted to say something about

Ruben's black cropped pants and bejeweled three-inch thong sandals, but his good manners prevented him. He was very diplomatic in that way, and that was one of the reasons I loved him so. He was a good man, and I couldn't believe what he'd just done for me. "Ed, thank you so much."

"I told you, it's no problem," he said.

"Well, I know it's an inconvenience of your time. Samantha told me that you're very busy, working on a big case."

"Emily, really, it's nothing."

"I don't know how I can repay you." I wanted to hug him, draw him close to me and feel his body next to mine, but instead I looked down at the floor and kicked at the sawdust lying in a small pile near my foot.

He smiled at me with a tender expression. "No need for that."

We stood alone, facing each other for a slightly uncomfortable moment before he said he had to get back to his office. We stepped out together into the bright afternoon sun, and being the gentleman he is, he walked me to my car, which was parked in front of his shiny Range Rover. I slid my key into the lock of my old standby, and opened Hazel's door.

Ed paused, looking at me with a serious stare. "On second thought, there is a way you can repay me."

"How?" I held my breath.

He leaned slightly against my door. "I'll take my payment in the form of a large, thirty-two-teeth-revealing smile."

"A smile?"

"Yeah, you know, when you curl your lips upward like this." He demonstrated, letting a silly grin slide across his face.

I broke into a big smile, followed by a burst of laughter. He joined me and we both enjoyed the moment. "Thank you, Ed. I needed that."

"Me too," he said in a soft whisper. "Maybe I'll see you later tonight?"

I rubbed my hand across my collarbone, trying to sweep away the heated sensation that the suggestion in his words left upon my skin. I looked down at the shiny band of gold on his ring finger and cleared my throat. "Maybe."

I climbed into Hazel and drove away, watching Ed in my rearview mirror as he headed off in a different direction. I thought about the laugh we'd just shared, and I couldn't shake the feeling that Ed liked me, and not just in a friendly way. I thought this because of the way he looked at me, the way his voice softened when he spoke to me, and the complicated chemistry that swarmed around us. His comment about seeing me tonight sounded like an invitation.

But wait. That would be absolutely crazy! Ed wouldn't come on to me. What was I thinking? I was letting his smile and his kindness go to my head. "Maybe I do need to seek professional help," I whispered to myself as I headed across town.

Chapter 8

Samantha . . .

Excitement, Not Complications

It was the middle of the week and I was sitting on my couch in my apartment, looking at more than a dozen empty boxes scattered across the floor. I didn't know where to begin. I had approximately two weeks before I was supposed to move and I hadn't thrown out, organized, or packed a thing.

Even though the moving company would do all the heavy work for me, I still needed to take care of my valuables and personal items that I didn't want them to touch. I knew I had to get started so I walked over to my entertainment center, grabbed a handful of CDs, and began packing them into a box. I wished Emily was here to help me because she was the queen of having-your-shit-together. She could pack up my entire apartment in one day. She was moving into her new house next weekend and she already had everything lined up.

I had just taped up the box of CDs when my cell

phone rang. It was Carl, again! It had been three weeks since our incident at the restaurant, and I'd been avoiding his calls. He had left several messages, apologizing for the way he showed out that night. It startled me because that was very uncharacteristic of him—to apologize, that is. Normally after we had a run-in, he'd just buy me an expensive piece of jewelry or send me a nice chunk of money as a peace offering. But ever since he showed his ass at the café, I was completely through with him and he knew it. Threatening me was the final straw. But he kept calling, and right now with everything I had going on in my life, he was one headache I didn't need. Even though I didn't want to, I picked up the phone.

"I'm outside your building, buzz me up," Carl said.

I never popped up on people, and I didn't like it when people did it to me. This was the second time he'd done this shit. It was times like this that I wondered why my fancy building didn't have a doorman. Thank goodness I was moving soon. "Why are you showing up at my door like this?" I asked.

" 'Cause you won't call me back."

"I don't want to see you, Carl."

"Look, we need to talk . . . about me, you, and CJ."

I shook my head. "There's nothing to talk about. Don't you get it?"

Carl said he wasn't going away until I let him in. I knew he would do it, too, and he'd probably bang on the access door and cause another scene if I didn't buzz him up and let him in. See, that was the thing about Carl, once he seared something into his mind, he wouldn't stop until he got what he wanted. *Damn!* I thought to myself. I felt like I had no other choice but to let him up. Yeah, I could've called the police, but that would open up another can of messy worms that I wanted to keep closed. "Come on up," I said.

We sat on my couch and he apologized, again, for losing his head at the café. He said he'd been in a bad mood because one of his boys, Big Johnny, had been shot earlier that afternoon. I wanted to roll my eyes. Not because a sister was insensitive or anything, but because his boys were always getting shot, jacked, or stabbed. Hell, Carl had taken four bullets himself. So I listened with my arms folded, trying to figure out what the hell Big Johnny gettin' shot had to do with Carl's sudden desire to spend more time with CJ and me.

"Sam, I'm tellin' you," he sighed, "shit like that make a brothah put things in perspective, nahmean? I gots ta handle my business, and you and CJ . . . y'all my heart."

"Carl, I'm sorry about Big Johnny, really I am. And you're right, there are things that help us put life into perspective, like the way you threatened me. It made me realize once and for all that we both need to move on. I mean it this time." I got up and walked toward the door. I was ready for him to go.

"Hol' up. I just got here, and now you gonna put me out and make me drive all the way back to DC? It's almost midnight."

I let out a deep breath. "Carl, most of your activities are done after dark, driving late at night should be a piece of cake."

He stood up and walked over to me, planting himself only inches away from my face. When he put his arm around my waist and drew me into him, I tried to pull back but my attempt was weak, and he sensed it. I hated to admit it, but Carl's strong, forceful grip felt good. Slowly, he leaned forward and kissed me, whispering tantalizing words into my ear. He told me how much he wanted me and all the ways he'd please me if I let him spend the night.

Okay, I'm not even gonna lie. He turned me on like a

fluorescent lightbulb. The next thing I knew I was letting him rub his rock-hard erection into me while he slipped his hand down my shorts. He kissed me on my lips and then on my neck. I threw my head back as he slid down to his knees and knelt in front of me, pulling my shorts and panties to the floor. "Spread yo legs," he said in a forceful tone.

I like a man who takes charge! I assumed the familiar position that I'd enjoyed countless times, ready to be licked like an ice cream cone. I held on to the back of his head and tried not to lose my balance as I felt Carl's hungry mouth between my thighs. His long, warm tongue worked its magic in a circular motion that made me moan. He held one hand around my waist as he rubbed my behind with the other, all the while continuing to eat me like a meal. When he finally came up for air I was ready to do anything he wanted.

We walked through the maze of clutter and boxes and made our way to my bedroom. I undressed him in less than twenty seconds and laid him across my bed. Carl had one of those Mandingo stud bodies that could drive you wild. I looked at his sculpted thighs, chiseled abs, and strong biceps, which distracted from the dark round marks that decorated his upper body, compliments of a rival's trigger finger. I took in his chocolate perfection as I reached into my nightstand for a condom.

"We ain't gotta use that," he breathed heavily.

I stopped cold and looked him in the eye. "If you want some of this," I motioned, pointing to my goodies, "you gotta cover that up." I glared, staring at his large, pulsating dick.

Carl let out a big sigh like he was trying to stress, but when he saw me shrug like I didn't care and then lean back like I was getting ready to rise from his lap, he snatched the condom out of my hand and quickly suited up. Once he got it on he held me by my hips, eased me down on top of him, and slid into me using just the right amount of force. We both moaned as we bucked frantically against each other, enjoying what we did best together.

Carl fucked me like he was on a mission. He wanted to win me back and he was prepared to do what it took to make that happen. We did it every way you can imagine: cowgirl, missionary, doggy, reverse piggy-back, spooning, kneeling, lotus, T-square. You name it, we were on it. We dozed off around two in the morning, after eating some left over Chinese from my fridge.

When I awoke this morning I felt like I was hungover. My head throbbed and my stomach felt uneasy. I sat up in bed and looked at the faint, three inch scar on the left side of Carl's cheek. He looked so calm and peaceful as he slept—a huge contrast to who he was in his waking hours. The more I studied him, the more I realized what another big mistake I'd made. I eased out of bed and went to my bathroom. I looked in the mirror and wanted to scream, but instead I reached for my shower cap, turned on the hot water, and attempted to wash last night down the drain.

I was dressed when Carl finally awoke. I told him that I still wanted to end our relationship. "Last night was a mistake," I said.

Carl sat up in bed and swung his bare legs around to the edge. "You wasn't sayin' that when I was hittin' it." He grinned.

I shook my head and tossed him his shirt. "All we've got is what's between our legs and under those sheets." I sighed. "At this point in my life I need more than that."

"You always trippin'," he grunted in a dismissive tone.

After twenty minutes of going back and forth about a topic that was dead in my mind, I ushered Carl out of my apartment so fast he barely had time to put on his shoes. After he was gone, I started gathering my things because I was running late for a morning meeting.

As I headed to the subway, I thought about the mixed blessing that moving back home would bring. I was excited about returning to the city I had always loved, but I knew that Carl was going to try to stir up some shit. I had to be strong and put my foot down. He needed to know that I was serious and that there would be no more backsliding like last night. As a matter of fact, I was going back home in two days, and I had plans to have lunch with Tyme when I arrived.

Tyme was an interesting man. We had been talking on the phone several times a week since we met, and last Saturday he took the train to New York to spend the day with me. He was a good guy and a perfect gentleman; however, there was something about him that still made me a little hesitant. But in comparison to Carl, he definitely won hands down, so I'd just have to jump in and take my chances.

I should've been enjoying my delicious lunch, but I wasn't. I was at one of my favorite restaurants in DC, Lauriol Plaza, with a fine man, Tyme Alexander. And to top it off I looked fly in my tan Calvin Klein business suit. Tyme had picked me up from Union Station when my train arrived an hour ago, then we headed to the restaurant for a quick lunch before my afternoon sales call to one of my new customers. But instead of feeling great, all I could think was damn, men will take you there if you let them!

The worst part about the shitty feeling that rested at the bottom of my stomach was the fact that I had no one to blame but myself. The bottom line was that I knew bet-

ter than to sleep with Carl. I know, I know, you don't even
have to say it, I fucked up . . . again. The last forty-eight
hours had been hell. I'd been working double duty, trying
to confirm dates with the moving company and trying to
avoid Carl's repeated phone calls. But I knew I had to
stop myself from thinking about him and what we did the
other night because at the moment, Tyme was sitting
across from me, staring into my eyes.

Tyme had called me the very next day after we met. I
was a little surprised, but not overly so because I sensed
from our brief interaction that he was the kind of person
who followed through with what he said he'd do. He
asked me out to dinner that night, but I declined. "I need
to spend time with my best friend who just came to town,"
I told him. He was understanding, but persistent, so we
agreed to meet for lunch the next day. Besides, how could
a girl turn down a meal at Café Milano? His expensive
wallet apparently wasn't just for show.

Throughout our meal I was surprised by how easy it was
to talk to him. He asked me lots of questions. He wasn't nosy
or intrusive, just inquisitive. He acted like he was genuinely
interested in getting to know me, as opposed to just getting
with me.

During our conversation I learned that Tyme was a
doctor, excuse me, a surgeon. And let me tell you, there
was a difference. Doctors are highly respected, but surgeons, baby, they're rock stars! As I stared at him, I realized that Tyme's calm, laid-back demeanor was more in
line with that of a social worker rather than someone who
had the power to reach inside another person's body and
wield life or death with his hands. I knew a few surgeons,
and most of them were arrogant assholes with inflated
egos and unapproachable attitudes. But Tyme was different.

Back in the present, I was trying to maintain a happy

exterior even though I didn't feel cheerful. My cell phone rang, and against my better judgment I pulled it out. I cringed when I saw Carl's number appear across the screen, and I could feel my mood begin to slip down the rabbit hole.

"Everything okay?" Tyme asked with concern. "You look a little upset."

It was hard to hide my frustration. This was the third time today that Carl had called. I was pissed that I had allowed him to take advantage of my weakness. He knew my vulnerability when it came to our sexual chemistry—and he preyed upon it. He was so damn cunning; when he smelled blood he stalked the vein like a vampire. I looked at my phone again before switching it to vibrate and dropping it down into my bag. "I'm okay," I replied as I smiled at Tyme.

Even though I had ended things with Carl, I couldn't tell Tyme that my ex was blowing up my phone like a bill collector. If I did, I'd have to explain that I slept with him again, and trust me, I wasn't owning up to that. Normally, I didn't have a problem telling a brother straight up that he wasn't the only one, that I had dick on standby. But with Tyme, I didn't feel right disclosing that to him. And I didn't know why because it wasn't like we were in a committed relationship. Hell, we'd just started seeing each other. Yet there was a part of me that wanted to guard myself.

Right in the middle of my complicated thoughts, Tyme's pager buzzed. "That's the hospital. Please excuse me for a minute," he said as he dialed his phone.

I looked around the restaurant, trying to keep myself busy while he made his call. Just then I heard the vibrating buzz of my cell phone calling out from my bag. This was getting ridiculous. If it was Carl again, so help me I was going to march straight over to the fourth district police station after lunch and file a harassment complaint. I was sick of his shit. I retrieved my phone and looked at the caller ID. Thank goodness it was Emily. "Hey girl, what's up?" I asked with a relieved smile.

"Not much, I'm on my break and I wanted to call and make sure you got into town all right. Are you having lunch with Tyme?"

"Yeah, I am."

"You better hold on to him." She grinned through the phone. "And please thank him again for agreeing to help with my move."

I had told Tyme that Emily was going to move into her new house next weekend, and he graciously offered his assistance. He even said he'd get a few friends to help so we could complete the job in half the time. "Make sure they're single. I'm trying to hook Emily up," I told him.

"Samantha, he seems like a really nice guy," Emily continued. "Give him a chance."

I had also told her about my reservations, which I knew sounded crazy. Maybe I was trying to sabotage a good thing again? The last time I did that I lost the only man I'd ever loved.

"What's next on your docket for today?" Emily asked, breaking my thoughts of Tyler.

"I have to pay a sales call to a new customer, but after that I'm free. You still want to meet up at the house this afternoon?"

"Sure, but I won't get there until a little later. After I leave school I'm going to drop CJ off at Ray's."

"Drop him off at Ray's . . . for what?" I asked.

There was a brief silence on the other end.

"CJ is sleeping over at Ray's tonight, remember?"

I didn't remember at all. I knew I needed to be more involved in my son's life, but honestly, he was better off with Gerti, my parents, and Emily. The only thing I could add to his world was confusion. I quickly wrapped up our call and slid my phone back into my bag. When I looked up, Tyme was staring at me, smiling. "What?" I asked.

"I like you, Samantha," he said in a soft, romantic voice.

I didn't know how to respond so I didn't say a word.

Tyme reached across the small table and put his hand over mine. "I hate to run, but I've got to get over to the hospital."

"I've got to run, too. Customers I need to see." I suddenly felt anxious to leave.

"I know you'll be hanging with your girlfriend this weekend and spending time with your son, but I'd like to see you again before you go back to New York. Do you think you can carve out a little time?"

Part of me wanted to run away from Tyme and the other part wanted to kiss his soft-looking lips. I told him that I'd call him later tonight so we could make plans. Even though I wasn't sure about where things were going, I knew the only way to quiet my reservations was to get to know him better.

After we finished our lunch, Tyme hailed me a cab. I gave the driver the address to where I was going, while Tyme handed him a crisp twenty. I tried to figure out why I was tripping so hard. This man was into me, so why was I stressing like this? I should be happy . . . right? Tyme could see the slightly confused look on my face.

"Don't worry, Sam. I feel it, too, and it's all right." He smiled gently, then kissed me softly on my lips before shutting the door.

I looked at him through the window as my cab pulled away. I knew he couldn't have been feeling the same emotions that were running through my body and my mind; otherwise, he wouldn't have been standing on the curb, smiling.

*   *   *

My visit to the Lancôme counter at Bloomingdale's
was quick. Sasha and Carmen were no muss, no fuss.
After giving them several bags of samples and some information about the launch party for a new product we
were introducing this December, I hailed a cab and
headed to my parents' house.

When I walked through the door I knew I was in for
some bullshit. Mother was there. She was usually out
shopping, lunching, or giving someone a headache, but
she was rarely ever home this time of day.

"Samantha, is that you?" she called out from the
kitchen, of all places. "Come here, please, I need to speak
with you."

I sighed, then sat my bag down at the edge of the
staircase and walked into the kitchen. The aroma of
Gerti's homemade brownies made my stomach jump, but
as soon as I saw Mother sitting at the table the sensation
turned to nausea. "Hey, Gerti," I said. I walked over and
gave her a quick kiss on her cheek. "Hello, Mother," I
forced myself to say. "What do you want to talk to me
about?"

She wrinkled her nose and looked down at my feet.
"Are those Chanel?" she asked with a frown.

I couldn't believe she was turning her nose up at my
red patent leather Chanel pumps. My shoes were fierce
and she knew it. I immediately got an attitude. "Yes," I
said, putting my hands on my hips. "And they're fly. Why
you askin'?"

Mother bristled because she hated bad grammar. *"I
am asking,"* she enunciated to make her point, "because I
just bought the same pair in black last week."

Now see, why couldn't she just say, "Sam, nice shoes.
I bought a pair just like them." But *noooooo*, she had to act
like I'd just walked in with shit smeared on the bottom of

my feet. That was the reason why she didn't have any friends, because of petty bullshit like this. People tolerated her, but they didn't like her. Some people were even afraid of my mother and only dealt with her because they had to, or out of respect for Daddy.

My mother was a bitch. It's a terrible thing to say about your own mother, but it was true. She'd been this way all my life. I was ten years old when I came to that realization. We had been shopping at Nordstrom one Saturday afternoon, looking for shoes . . . for her, of course. As we browsed, several sales associates came over to help us. I remember noticing that even though Mother had hardly spoken a word to those ladies, they were extremely nice and friendly to her. They went to the stockroom several times to check on different items of her choosing, all done with happy smiles and enthusiasm. But when I went to the back of the department to inspect a shiny pendant that had caught my eye, I found out what the real deal was.

"Mrs. Baldwin is such a bitch. She's going to make me scream," the plump blonde who'd been helping my mother said to her coworker. "She's rude and insufferable. If it weren't for the fact that she spends a small fortune every time she comes in here, I would walk away from her right now. She's so nerve-wracking!"

"Yeah," the other woman said. "But a big spender equals a big commission."

Those women didn't like my mother because she was notorious for coming in and treating people like shit. Before that day, I thought she only treated our family that way, but standing in the back of the department store that afternoon, I learned that my mother cast her darkness on everyone around her, unless she wanted something from them.

I didn't have time for her bullshit today, so again, I asked her, "What did you want to talk to me about?"

"I need to know when you'll be available to go to Saks Jandel with me."

Saks Jandel was one of Mother's favorite boutiques. I was starting to smell a rat. "Why do you want me to go there with you?"

She looked at me like I'd just asked her how to spell my own name, like I was asking her a stupid question or something. *"Because,"* she paused, "we have to pick out your outfit for the party. It's only two weeks away."

I let out a big huff and rolled my eyes.

Gerti looked at me. "You better get those eyes straight," she warned. "Don't look at your mother like that."

Even though I learned how to roll my eyes by watching her, I knew better than to disobey Gerti, so I looked away. I had a lot on my plate, and Mother's demands were the least of my concerns. "I already have an outfit for the party, so don't stress me. I know how to dress," I said in a hostile tone.

Mother sat in silence. She knew I was right and that there was no point in arguing. She and I had similar taste in fashion, hence the Chanel shoes. Brenda Baldwin was a fashion tour de force, and even though she was in her fifties, she didn't look it. I gave credit when it was due, and the truth was that my mother was a good-looking woman. And sadly, that was another reason why she had always been disappointed in me. I wasn't pretty enough by her standards. I knew how to spruce myself up, but I definitely wasn't a natural beauty like she was. Physical looks were very important to her.

As I stood near the counter looking at her and thinking about what she'd just said, I started to get angry. Mother knew I had great taste, yet she wanted to take me shopping, as if I couldn't pick out my own clothes. She had called me in here just to mess with my head because she knew I wasn't thrilled about the birthday party in the first place. She was also probably afraid that I'd show up in something ridiculous just to make her look bad, which I had to admit was something I'd done in the past. But that was when I was in high school. I was an adult now, and I didn't play childish games anymore. I left that foolishness to her.

"If you think what you're going to wear will be appropriate, I guess that's that." Mother sighed, then planted her eyes squarely on mine. "But, Samantha, I do hope you'll be on your best behavior. This is a very important party. Try not to mess it up, for Emily's sake."

I wanted to curse her out so badly. Gerti knew it, too, and she gave me a *calm the hell down* look. I hated that I felt this way about the woman who gave birth to me, but I couldn't help it. She was such a hypocrite. She had the nerve to sit there and tell me how important this birthday party was for Emily, when she knew that she didn't give a damn about Emily or me, for that matter. It was our birthday, but it was her party.

I knew I shouldn't let her stress me out. I reminded myself to chill, "for Emily's sake," as Mother had just said. I looked at her and smiled. "Don't worry, Mother. I'll be on such good behavior, it'll blow your muthafuckin' mind."

Before she or Gerti could say a word I turned on my Chanel heels and marched upstairs.

"She burns me up," I said to Emily as I reached for another Q-Tip to dab off the excess color that had settled on the side of my pinky. We were lying across my bed, polishing our nails. Emily's looked good, but mine looked terrible. I was used to having someone else do the dirty work for me. I had made appointments for us at my salon, but Emily convinced me to cancel. She said it would be fun to stay in, do our nails, order pizza, and talk all night like we used to when we were roommates in college. She was right, as usual. CJ was at his sleepover, mother was out with Aunt Dorothy, thank God, Gerti had turned in early, and Daddy was still at the office, so we had the house all to ourselves.

"She's so damn phony and evil," I snarled, still talking about Mother.

Emily shook her head. "Samantha, don't you think you're being a little harsh? She's not *that* bad. I mean, she's your mom."

Poor thing. I knew she was still mourning Ms. Lucille's death, and probably thought I was a disrespectful ingrate for talking about my mother the way I did. But she didn't know the real Brenda Baldwin. For some reason, Mother had always put on a good face in front of Emily. I could tell my friend some stories that would make her want to curse, too. But Emily didn't need to hear all that garbage, so I decided to change the subject. "Tell me how your first week of school went."

Emily perked up with a big smile. "The other teachers are friendly and the kids are so bright!"

I was happy to hear the joy in my best friend's voice. Things were finally falling into place for her. She talked for nearly a half hour as we moved on to polishing our toes. She told me all about her students, the friends she'd made at her school, her flamboyant neighbor with the perfect teeth and hair, and the fabulous new upgrades that her contractor had added to her house.

After the pizza arrived we headed to the kitchen to continue our girl talk. But as I listened to Emily, one thing became very clear. She'd been here for nearly a month and she hadn't gone out on a single date in all that time.

"Emily," I said, sitting my pepperoni slice on my plate. "Why haven't you met a man yet? What's up?"

She waved me off. "There you go again."

"Listen, I know the dating scene is rough, but you're gorgeous and you have a lot to offer. I can't believe you haven't met anyone who piques your interest?"

She took a sip of her sparkling water and lowered her eyes. "I've been way too busy trying to get my life together. I don't need a man to complicate things."

"Wow, now, that's a good attitude to have."

"I'm serious. Between school and the house, I haven't had time to think about dating. Right now my focus is on lesson plans and my move next Saturday."

"Have you ever thought that meeting a new man could add excitement, not complications, to your life?"

"Maybe."

"Girl, at this rate, CJ will be dating before you," I teased as I took a bite of my pizza. We both had to laugh on that one.

Just then, we looked up when we heard a key rattle in the back door. I hoped it wasn't Mother, and to my relief it wasn't. It was Daddy, and even though he was visibly tired, he still managed to give us a big smile. Unlike Mother, who was out socializing over apple martinis, Daddy had been grinding it out at the office. I knew he would be glad when his big trial was over. He was in serious warrior mode. We talked several times a week, and he had mentioned how intense things were right now. But I'd never heard him sound as stressed as he had lately. I was a little worried about him.

"Hello, ladies." He nodded toward Emily, and then to me. "Did I interrupt a joke?"

"I was just teasing Emily about her love life."

"Samantha!" Emily hissed, seeming embarrassed.

She looked at me like I'd just told Daddy her cup

size. She'd always been shy around him, but damn, we were family. Daddy looked at her as his second daughter and couldn't care less about her boring-ass love life. The trial was all he was focused on.

"You've met someone?" Daddy asked Emily, raising his brow. I guess he was thinking that it was about time.

"No," I interrupted, "and that's the problem. But don't worry, I'm gonna hook my girl up and introduce her to some men in this city." I grinned as Emily looked on like she was still embarrassed. "Anyway, how was your day, Daddy?"

"Long, but good. I'll leave you two alone to enjoy the rest of your evening." He gave us a smile, said good night, and then headed into his study.

Emily looked at me with slight annoyance. "Why did you tell him that?"

"Chill, it's just Daddy."

"But you didn't have to tell him . . ."

"Daddy's so involved with his case, he's not even thinking about you. His mind is on the courtroom and that expensive brandy he's about to drink. Besides, there's nothing to tell about your love life because you don't have one."

Emily folded her arms across her chest. "I guess you have a point."

We were silent for a moment before she spoke again. "Samantha, does your father drink brandy every night?"

"Yep, ever since I can remember. It's his one guilty pleasure. Why?"

"Just curious."

"Girl, living with my mother for thirty-two years, can you blame him? I'm surprised he doesn't do more than that."

At the very mention of her, Emily and I looked up in unison as the door opened and Mother appeared. I held my breath and braced myself for some mess. She walked in and stopped in front of the table. She stared at our plates, mine covered with two pepperoni slices and Emily's with her vegetarian slice.

"Eating food like *that* at this late hour will wreak havoc on your waistlines," she said as she wrinkled her nose.

Well, I'll be damned! No hello, kiss my ass, or nothing. She couldn't even greet people nicely. Since she was being so nasty, I decided to return the favor. "Kind of like that Grey Goose you've been throwing back tonight. Alcohol can do damage to the waistline, too." I glared. There, I shut her down like a club at dawn. She was embarrassed as hell, but only because I'd hit a nerve of truth. When she got together with my aunt Dorothy they mixed martinis all night. She drank a little too much and then had the nerve to get behind the wheel . . . and she called me careless and irresponsible!

Mother ignored my remark. "Good night," she said, smiling nicely in Emily's direction before leaving the room. I guess she had to spread her evil around because I heard her and Daddy exchange irritated words in his study before she went upstairs.

"See what I mean about my mother?"

Emily didn't say anything. "Hey, let's talk about *your* love life." She smiled. "Tell me about your lunch date with Tyme, how'd it go?"

"Hmm, I don't know how to feel about him."

"What do you mean? He sounds like a dream, and any man who'll offer up his weekend to do manual labor is worth giving a chance," she said.

"It's hard to explain. He's handsome, smart, considerate, and very nice. But there's something about him that makes me want to hold back."

Emily stared at me, chewing her veggie slice while

she listened with intense concern. I knew what she was thinking, so I addressed the question before she asked it. "And no, it's not because he's straitlaced. I'm older now, and I know I should look for other things in a man besides a good time."

"Do you have a good time with him?"

"Yeah."

"Does he make you laugh?"

I thought about Emily's question, and the answer I came up with threw me for a loop. "Actually no. I mean, he makes me smile, but he's never made me laugh."

"Drop him."

"What?"

"Drop him now," she repeated.

I was shocked. "I know you're not telling me to drop a decent, upstanding man just because he doesn't have jokes?" I hoped the hardness of the city hadn't already started to affect my friend.

Emily put down her pizza slice and wiped her mouth. She leaned forward in her chair and gave me the familiar, soft and sincere expression I had come to know over the years. "Samantha, I might not have much of a love life, but one thing I do know is that you need a man who can make you laugh. Laughter is medicine for the soul."

I thought about Emily's words as she continued. "Remember back to the times in your past relationships when a man made you laugh, and not because you were out partying." She paused. "I'm talking about laughter that came from a general conversation when he said something simple, yet so funny that it made you both crack up like you were sitting in a comedy club. That's the kind of laughter that comes from deep inside, and a man who can bring laughter from that place can reach your heart."

I reflected back, knowing I had experienced that feeling only once—with Tyler. That man could have me rolling so hard I had tears in my eyes. "Did Bradley ever make you feel that way?" I asked.

"No."

"Has any man ever made you feel that way?"

Emily looked off to the corner, like she was thinking about someone from her past just like I was. "Yes, but it was never meant to be."

I nodded and wondered who she was talking about. We shared everything, but as I knew all too well, some memories were better left alone and untouched. I lowered my head, trying to block out my past.

Ever since Mother walked through the door, the mood in the room had shifted from fun and lighthearted to bleak and dreary. We were laughing and having a good time until she killed it with her wicked aura. But I refused to let her funk up my groove. "Back to your love life." I grinned. "Have you had a chance to test any of the goodies I got you?"

Emily smiled wide and put her hand up to her mouth as she blushed. "I have to thank you, girl! You know how to hook a sister up!"

"See, I knew you were a closet freak!"

We giggled like schoolgirls, carrying on so loudly that Daddy jokingly yelled from his study down the hall, "Don't you two get into any trouble."

After our laughter and sex talk, I decided to tell Emily about the dumb mistake I made—sleeping with Carl. She didn't look surprised, and as usual, she didn't judge me. The thing I loved about my friendship with Emily was that she accepted me as I was. She was the only person in whom I'd ever felt that level of trust. I didn't even tell Daddy all of my business.

"Samantha," Emily said in her soft but solidly firm voice that let you know she was dead serious. "Please stay away from Carl. I have a bad feeling about where he's headed, and I don't want him to take you there with him. Promise me you're going to leave him alone?"

"Emily, you ain't said nothin' but a word."

I really meant it this time. I was going to stay away from Carl. He had called me right before I got home this afternoon and this time I picked up. I told him that if he didn't leave me alone I'd file a stalking complaint and get a stay-away order issued for his ass. That seemed to defuse him because no matter how bold Carl was, he didn't want any trouble from the police. It was amazing, that with all the shit he pulled and his criminal activities, he had never served a single day behind bars in his thirty-three years on earth. He was just that slick.

I planned to heed Emily's advice and my own gut feelings because I could smell the trouble that was brewing. I made up my mind. I would go out with Tyme again and see where it led because I needed a change in my life.

Chapter 9

Ed . . .

You Looking for a Change?

I was trying to block out the sounds coming from the kitchen as Emily's delicate hiccup-like laughter pounded in my ear. She and Sam were having a good time talking about all the men that my daughter was lining up for her. I knew I shouldn't be so sardonic, but I couldn't help myself. When Sam made the remark about playing matchmaker, I wanted to probe but I couldn't. This kind of thing was maddening for me.

As I sat in my study enjoying the smooth taste of my brandy, its pleasure drew me back to the encounter I'd shared with Emily several weeks ago when I surprised her by showing up at her new house unannounced. She was having problems with her contractor, so I thought that rather than draft a threatening letter, a face-to-face showdown with the man would be more effective. Plus, I was dying for an opportunity to be in a space with Emily other than in this house.

She thanked me, and then insisted on repaying me for my efforts. I told her that a simple smile was all I needed. Man, she lit up and gave me more than I'd expected. Her smile gave me hope. When I looked into her eyes that day, something told me that she knew what I was thinking, and I believe she was thinking the same thing, too. I was a good judge of human behavior, and I was rarely if ever wrong about people's intentions or motivations. That smile sparked something, and it led to more intense moments, like last week.

As usual, I had been in my study having a nightcap, going over case documents for the coming week. Brenda was out at a volunteer function for her sorority, and Emily was reading CJ a bedtime story. After Emily finished, I heard her quietly tiptoe down the stairs. She increased her pace as she passed by my study, avoiding me. She walked through the kitchen and headed out the back door on her way to visit with Gerti, as she did from time to time.

After an hour or so, I heard the soft sound of the door open and close. Emily tried to creep past my door again without being noticed, but this time I stopped her. I needed to talk to her. "How are things coming with the house?" I called out from behind my desk. I knew this would be a safe opening.

She stopped in the middle of my doorway and hesitated for a moment. "Everything's working out well. Emmanuel says they'll be finished very soon, finally."

She said the last part with relief. I knew she was ready to have her own place, but I hated that she was so eager to leave. I'd miss seeing her around the house, even if it was only for a glimpse. I walked over to her and stood close. I could tell by her body language that she was nervous because she leaned back against the door frame. It was a move meant to put distance between us, but I could still feel her heat.

"Do you need help with your move? I can lend a hand."

She shook her head. "That's okay. I know you're busy with your big case. Samantha's going to help and—"

I had to interrupt. "Emily, I believe that women are every bit as capable as men, but I'm also an old-fashioned gentleman, and I'd never let two ladies move a houseload of furniture by themselves."

"Oh, we won't be." She smiled, clearing her throat. "Samantha's new friend and a few of his buddies are going to help us."

My head involuntarily jerked back. I knew I had to intervene in the situation. I loved my daughter dearly, but she made terrible choices in men. I didn't know much about the new guy she was seeing because she'd barely mentioned him in our conversations, which wasn't a good sign. Knowing that, I could only imagine what his buddies were like. "You're moving on a Saturday, right?" I asked.

"Yes."

"Court's not in session during the weekend."

She looked around the room, avoiding my eyes. Finally, she spoke. "I'm sure you have more important things to do with your weekend than move furniture."

"I can't think of anything I'd rather do more, especially since it would mean helping you."

I watched her closely as a slight smile came to her face. She still wouldn't look at me, but she nodded and told me that she appreciated my offer. We stood close to each other as the room became warm. It was a noticeable heat that could only be explained by the chemistry building between us. I took a deep breath and leaned against the other side of the door, inhaling the soft floral notes of her perfume. We were close enough to reach out and touch each other. Just as I was feeling dangerously comfortable, Emily broke the trance.

"I guess I should head to bed now. Good night," she said, making a quick exit.

I stood in my doorway and watched as she walked down the hall toward the stairs. Her slow, sexy strut made the front of my trousers come to life and I wondered what it would be like to make love to her. When she reached the banister she looked back and caught me staring. Our eyes locked. I should've looked away, but I didn't, so she did.

Now, as I sat in my study reflecting on that moment along with a few others, I could see that my observations hadn't been wishful thinking. This was real, it was within my grasp, and I couldn't avoid it much longer.

Under different circumstances this wouldn't be a problem. I'd confess my feelings to the woman I loved and that would be that. But I was a married man, and the woman I loved was my daughter's best friend. It was the kind of situation that could hurt people, physically and emotionally. But Emily had given me hope, and a man with hope can weather anything if he thinks it's worth the fight.

I was glad it was Friday. The past five days had been professionally gratifying, but personally frustrating. I had a great week in court, working the witnesses and the jury as if they were under my spell. It soon became apparent that things were going downhill for the defense. First thing this morning, two hours before court was to be called to session, lead counsel for the opposing side called and offered my client our initial asking figure. I laughed and told him to keep dreaming. The stakes had risen, and I didn't hesitate to tell him how high. Twenty minutes later he called again and capitulated. My client accepted.

The trial that we all thought would last for two months was over in two weeks, and we were going to get a substantial amount above our initial request. You'd think this would've kicked off my weekend and that I'd be on top of the world. Well, I wasn't. I was happy for my client, of course, because now the big oil company that knowingly exposed her husband to cancer-causing agents was going to pay for its corruptness, and for his death. But ever since last Friday when Sam told me that she was playing matchmaker for Emily, I hadn't been able to get that thought out of my head.

Right now, it was almost ten o'clock and Emily wasn't home. She was out with Sam. Even though I knew that whatever they were doing, it probably involved Emily's house because she was moving in tomorrow, I still wondered if Sam had introduced her to someone new. I'd never been the jealous type, but lately I found myself thinking about Emily out on the dating scene. She was a beautiful woman, and I knew her attributes hadn't gone unnoticed, especially not here in DC.

As I polished off my brandy, I heard Gerti rustling around in the kitchen. She was getting my coffee and bagel ready for the morning. I needed a distraction from my thoughts, so I walked in and joined her, bringing my empty snifter with me. "Hey, Gerti." I smiled.

"Hey there."

"How's it going?"

"Goin' like it always goes." She chuckled. "How're you holding up?"

"I'm fine."

"You sure?"

"Of course I'm sure. Why? You don't think I am?"

She shook her head. "Didn't say that. You just seem real stressed lately."

"Well, you know, the trial and everything."

"Mmm-hmm." She sliced the bagel and put it in the toaster.

I studied Gerti as she performed the nightly task that she'd perfected over the years. She could do it with her eyes closed. "Do you ever get tired of getting my coffee and bagel ready every night, and washing out this damn brandy snifter?" I asked, sitting my glass on the counter.

She laughed, took my glass, and put it in the sink. "You ever get tired of it?"

"Sometimes."

"You looking for a change?"

I shrugged. "Maybe."

"Mmm-hmm," she mumbled again, this time looking at me as she folded her arms. "I'm sure gonna miss Emily. It's been real nice having her around."

I nodded. "CJ will miss her, too, but this move will be good for her."

"Mmm-hmm."

Gerti was mmm-hmming as if she had knowledge of something that no one else was privy to. She was a tried and trusted old friend. We didn't have a lot of in-depth conversations, but we knew each other well. In many ways, she knew me better than Brenda did. She knew little things, like exactly how much starch I liked in my shirts and how much salt I liked on my vegetables. She knew when I was tired and not just frustrated. She could sense when I wanted to talk and when I preferred to be left alone to think in silence. She knew my habits and quirks, good and bad. And just as she knew me, I knew her, and her mmm-hmms meant something.

Gerti smiled. "Guess I'll turn in now." She walked to the back door, then stopped and looked at me. "Funny thing about change." She sighed. "Most people don't change what they want, they change where they get it from."

And like that, I knew she understood. "Good night, Gerti."

"Good night, Ed."

I stood alone in the empty kitchen, staring at the coffeemaker and toaster.

The next morning CJ and I sat at the breakfast table. He lingered over his cereal and toast while I drank my coffee and ate my bagel. He was usually a bundle of energy on Saturday mornings and you could hardly tear him away from his cartoons. But he was sad today because Emily was moving out. He looked up at me with the most sincere expression and asked, "Papa, can I go over to Auntie Emee's new house and visit her?"

"Sure, sport," I said. I reminded him that he'd still see her at school every day, which brought a smile to his face and changed his mood. I smiled, too, because I suddenly realized that taking him over for visits would be a way for me to see Emily from time to time without suspicion.

After breakfast, I dropped off CJ at his friend Ray's house to play for the day, and then headed over to Emily's place. The sun was shining brightly and it was hot as hell outside. I didn't see Emily's car so I assumed Emmanuel had completed her garage in the back.

I found a space on the other side of her street and saw the large U-Haul double-parked in front of Emily's row house. Her door was ajar, so I walked inside. I didn't focus on the people in the room right away because I was admiring how nicely the completed renovations had turned out. I could see that Emily had made Emmanuel pay dearly for his malfeasance. But when I finally began to take in the sight in front of me, I had to force myself to stay calm. What stood out the most over the richly painted walls, high-end lighting fixtures, and shiny hardwood floors was the group of men I saw. There were six of them, sitting on the floor with Sam and Emily, eating danishes and drinking coffee.

I recognized one of them as her neighbor whom I'd met, and he was sitting close to who I assumed was his boyfriend, judging by their openly intimate demeanor. Sam was sitting on the other side of them, looking slightly uncomfortable. Next to her was a guy with dreadlocks who seemed to share her mood. There were two other men to my left, and a third was planted much too close to Emily for my comfort.

Damn! Leave it to my daughter to fill the room with testosterone. When I focused my stare on the guy who was sitting too close to Emily, his face registered in my memory. I had seen him several months ago at her mother's funeral. *He must be her ex,* I thought. I wondered what the hell he was doing here.

"Good morning." I nodded to everyone, trying hard not to sound irritated. Sam jumped up, came over, and gave me a tight hug.

"Hey, Daddy!" She smiled.

Sam was unusually happy to see me and after a minute I quickly understood why. Upon further inspection of the room, I realized that one of the men sitting to my left was none other than her ex-boyfriend, Tyler Jacobs. Now I was really confused. Was this some sort of reunion of the exes? Sam released my neck and gave me a nervous smile.

I scanned the room again, and I had to say that these young men weren't anything like what I'd expected from my daughter. I guess it was because they obviously had some association with Tyler. It was going to be interesting to see where he fit into the equation.

The guy with the dreadlocks stood up, came over to me, and offered an outstretched hand. "It's nice to meet you, sir." He nodded.

Sam swallowed hard like she was taking medicine. "Daddy, this is my, um . . . my friend, Tyme Alexander."

I shook Tyme's hand and appreciated his firm grip and that he looked me in the eye when he spoke. "It's nice to meet you, Tyme," I greeted him. He was counter to Sam's usual taste in men and I wondered why she hadn't said much about him.

"And this is Tyme's cousin, Jason." Sam motioned as she politely, but cautiously introduced us. She didn't introduce the guy who was sitting too close to Emily, and before I could go over and meet him for myself, Tyler approached me.

"Mr. Baldwin." Tyler smiled. "It's good to see you, sir."

"Good to see you, too," I said as Tyler and I greeted each other with a handshake that turned into a hug. Tyler was the only man my daughter had ever dated who I approved of. He was a stand-up guy. I respected him. He was the kind of young man I'd be proud to call my son-in-law. Sam stood beside us looking like she used to when she was a kid and had just done something wrong. When I glanced over to my left, I saw Emily walking up with the "close sitter" in tow.

"Hi, Ed." Emily smiled. "Thanks for coming. You really didn't have to."

"I wouldn't miss your big day." I nodded, turning my attention to the man standing beside her.

"I'm Bradley Johnson. Emily's friend." The strapping young man extended his hand.

I pumped his wrist with more force than necessary. He didn't pick up on my irritation, but Emily did because she cleared her throat and looked away.

"Daddy, I have a question I need to ask you," Sam said. She took me by my hand and led me out the front door. I watched her brow furrow as the sun beat down on her face. "I can't believe that Tyler's here. Daddy, what am I gonna do?"

Sam explained that Tyme had asked his cousin if he and a couple of his friends would help Emily with her move. His cousin agreed, and one of the friends he asked just happened to be Tyler, who was in town for a business conference. He'd flown in a few days early, and because he didn't have anything on his agenda for today he decided to help out. It was a small world.

I looked at my daughter, who was acting uncharacteristically nervous. "Sam, all you can do right now is help Emily. Concentrate on that and you'll get through the day."

"Then what?"

"You'll just have to see how things play out, kiddo. Just be calm and use your head." After I gave her a quick pep talk followed by a comforting hug, we went back inside.

I walked into the living room and studied Bradley. He was looking at Emily in a way that I could never allow myself to do in public. I scrutinized the two of them together, searching for signs of any romantic entanglement on her part. I wondered when he had arrived in town, where he was staying, and how long he'd be here. I didn't have those answers, but I was going to make damn sure that I got them before I left.

After another twenty minutes the work finally began. Emily and Sam cleared away the discarded cups, napkins, and paper plates while the rest of us started bringing in the furniture and boxes. When we opened the U-Haul truck it was packed from top to bottom and front to back. I learned that this was what Emily and Sam had been doing until late last night.

"It took us nearly six hours to pack this truck last night," Bradley said as he held the other end of the sofa we moved into the living room. His comment answered one of my questions. He had been in town since at least yesterday.

We lifted the heavy furniture in a steady stream, as though we were working on an assembly line. The ninety-degree temperature made our task hard, and sweat poured off us as if we'd run through a rain shower. I was glad I worked out every day; if I didn't, I'd be in serious trouble. I looked at the young bloods around me and felt good knowing that I could hold my own. As a matter of fact, my arms were more cut and my body was more defined than any of them, except for Bradley.

We had unloaded over half the truck when we decided to take a lunch break. Gerti came by and dropped off sandwiches, chips, cookies, and a bottle of champagne that Brenda had sent over as a housewarming gift. Brenda was in Manhattan this weekend with her sister. She claimed she wanted to buy gifts for Sam and Emily's party next weekend and that she could only find what she needed in the Big Apple. She could have easily found what she wanted right here in DC. She was really in New York to shop for herself.

After we started eating, a calm hush fell over the

room. Everyone seemed to mellow out and relax; thanks to the good food that Gerti had supplied. I was probably the only person who was still uncomfortable. I wasn't in the frame of mind to eat or socialize. Not after talking with Bradley.

While we were moving furniture, I'd asked him questions to get a better handle on the extent of his involvement with Emily. What I learned caused a small rise in my blood pressure. He flew into town yesterday afternoon and was staying with relatives who lived in the city. It was clear to me that this guy had no intention of remaining "just friends" with Emily.

I also learned that he and Emily maintained regular communication. He said he hoped that being in her new house would help her to relax because she had been going through a stressful time with two kids in her class. He even knew the names of some of her neighbors and coworkers. That kind of information came from nightly conversations on the phone, not a few hours of chitchat while packing a U-Haul late at night.

It was nearly five o'clock by the time we unloaded the last box from the truck. Ruben and Roger called it a day, and shortly after that, Jason took Tyler back to his hotel. Emily and Sam started unpacking the boxes downstairs while Tyme, Bradley, and I set up the furniture in Emily's second-floor rooms. She had very nice belongings, some of which had been in her home in Atlanta, but most of which she bought shortly before moving here. I knew this because I overheard her tell Sam that she wanted new things for her new life.

A short time later, Sam and Tyme announced they were leaving, and from the expression on their faces, I knew they were going their separate ways. A few minutes later, Bradley left, too. He had asked Emily out to dinner with him and his family, but she declined, citing all the unpacking she still needed to do. I volunteered to stay and finish setting up the furniture in her home office upstairs. That left only the two of us. Finally, we were alone.

It was dark when I finished my task. The entire time I worked, I could hear Emily downstairs, ripping boxes open and moving things around. When I came down I was beat. I stood in her living room and surveyed the space. It was the only room that was completely set up. She'd even put pictures on her mantel.

"You must be worn out," she said.

"Yeah, and I bet you are, too."

"A little, but there's still so much work to do."

"Can I help with anything?" Even though I was tired as hell, I wanted her to say yes.

"No, I can handle it from here. I know you're ready to get home so you can relax."

I wiped the sweat from my forehead. "As a matter of fact, I think I'll take a little breather before I get going, if you don't mind?"

"Of course not." She smiled.

I started to feel the heat that always rose between us when we were in the same room. I had stolen awkward glimpses of her all day, but now that we were alone I could take in her full view. She wore a blue T-shirt and denim shorts, the same ones she had worn the night she arrived in town. She did wonders for denim.

Emily looked around the room as she always did when she was nervous. I realized I was staring too hard, so I averted my eyes. "I'll sit on this," I said, moving a heavy box from the corner. "I don't want to ruin your nice new furniture."

"Excuse me," she said, then disappeared into the kitchen.

I watched her shapely brown thighs and perfectly round behind move like slow-motion footage as she walked out of the room. A minute later she returned with two glasses of lemonade. She pulled up a crate and joined me, surprising me by sitting so close I could touch her.

"Thanks," I said, accepting the ice-cold drink. "When did you have time to make lemonade?"

"When I poured it from the Minute Maid carton," she teased.

I laughed, and a warm comfort surrounded us. For the next hour we talked with more ease than we ever had in all the years I'd known her. I discovered that Emily was hilarious. She had a wonderful sense of humor. She was also witty and quick with a comeback.

She sat her glass down on the floor and put her hands on her knees. "Ed, thanks again for helping out today. I know you're busy with the trial and you could've spent the day preparing for the week ahead instead of breaking your back lifting furniture."

"The trial is over. The defense offered us a settlement yesterday."

"Really!" she said in an excited voice. She was genuinely happy for me.

"Yes, and my client is getting more than we originally asked for."

"That's great!" This time she clapped her hands.

"Thanks." I nodded. I put my glass down next to hers. "But even if the trial was still going on, it wouldn't have stopped me from being here today. Nothing could stop me from doing what I can to help you." I tried to look into her eyes, but she avoided mine, so I cleared my throat and plunged forward into new territory. "Bradley seems like a good guy." I said it because I wanted to know how she felt about him, but also because it was true. Emily deserved the best, and even if it couldn't be me, I wanted her to be happy, despite my jealousy.

"Yes, he's a very good man. I told him that he didn't have to make a trip here to help me move. But he surprised me by showing up yesterday. He's a good friend."

"He wants to be more than just your friend, you know that don't you?"

She fidgeted and then stood to her feet. "Wow, I can't believe how late it is. I'm really beat. Um, I think I'm going to call it a night."

I could've let the issue go and beat around the bush like we always did, but tonight I felt compelled to stop the denial. Our intimate conversation gave me the license to go further. I rose to my feet next to her. "Why are you avoiding my question?"

"Because I don't want to talk about it."

"Why not?"

"Because it's complicated."

"Are you in love with him?"

She folded her arms across her chest. "Ed, I'm not trying to be rude, but I think you should leave now."

"Why?"

She raised her brow and craned her neck like only a black woman could. "Because I said so. And the last time I checked, Emily Eloise Snow was the name on the deed to this house."

The minute the words came out of her sweet mouth we both started laughing. "Oh, so now you're breakin' bad, layin' down the law and kickin' brothers out!" I laughed.

"And I'm gettin' numbers and takin' names."

We rolled for a few minutes before we finally calmed our laughter. "Emily," I said in a soft, low tone, "I'm sorry if I was pushy. I only asked because I care about you."

She looked down at her feet, then lifted her gaze to meet my eyes. "I know."

We stood in silence for a minute. The heat between us reappeared, and this time I agreed with her, I needed to leave—before something happened. She walked me to the door and we said an awkward good-bye before I headed to my truck.

When I walked through the back door and into the kitchen, I found Gerti standing by the sink, taking food out of the refrigerator.

"I hope you don't feel as bad as you look," she said as she inspected me.

"Worse." I nodded, taking a seat at the kitchen table.

"Here, eat this." Gerti sat a small salad loaded with veggies and topped with chicken in front of me.

I hadn't eaten much today because Bradley's presence had stolen my appetite. But now it was back with a vengeance. I ate my delicious salad while Gerti went about gathering spices out of the cabinet and more food from the refrigerator. She was preparing a meal for tomorrow. I had nearly cleaned my plate when she turned to me and said, "You need to take a long soak in the tub to ease those bones."

"That's exactly what I intend to do, if I can make it up the stairs," I half joked.

"Lord have mercy. The ego of men. This is what you get for doing all that bending and lifting, trying to act like you're twenty-one," she said, shaking her head. "I'll run and get you some Epsom salt for your bath."

I had to smile because she was right. "Thanks, Gerti."

A minute after she left, Sam walked through the door and came into the kitchen wearing a big smile. She told me that she and Tyler were going to give their relationship another try. I was happy for my daughter because Tyler was forthright, principled, and above all, he had a good heart. I was enjoying our conversation until she told me that Bradley was going over to Emily's house tomorrow to help her finish settling in. It was news that I definitely didn't want to hear.

Sam went on to say there was a chance that Emily and Bradley might get back together. I felt a stab in my stomach, and she could see that there was something wrong with me, something that went beyond tired, achy muscles. She was about to ask, when Gerti returned with the salt for my bath, saving me from having to lie to my daughter. I made my exit so I could be alone to think.

I went to my study and took only a quick sip of brandy before heading upstairs for a long soak in the tub. I submerged myself in the deluxe Jacuzzi and turned on the power jets. The pressure felt good and was just what my tired body needed. After I managed to pull myself up out of the water, which had turned lukewarm, I toweled off and literally crawled over to my bed. Every inch of my body ached. Even my toenails hurt. My grandmother used to say that everybody wants to live a long time, but nobody wants to get old. She knew what she was talking about. Getting old was a bitch. I was in damn good shape for a fifty-four-year-old man, but no matter how many hours of cardio and strength training I did, Mother Nature had her own set of rules.

It dawned on me as I lay in my king-sized bed that I didn't miss Brenda's presence in it. But I also didn't want to be alone. What I wanted at the moment was to lie beside Emily. And I meant that—literally. I just wanted to *lie* beside her because God knows I couldn't do anything else. Then a heavy thought crossed my mind. I had fantasized about making love to Emily a million times, but the pain in my body suddenly made me aware that I might not be up to the challenge.

I crawled out of bed with the speed equivalent to a turtle and limped over to the full-length mirror in my walk-in closet. I pulled off my T-shirt and boxers and examined my naked body. I looked good, and I had plenty of equipment to get the job done. But the reality was that I didn't have much of a sex life. The only time I even got an erection anymore was when I thought about Emily. Brenda and I had sex once a quarter. It had been that way for years, and it was always routine. Vanilla sex was what I called it. I had resigned myself to the situation and let my career fill the void.

Damn, even if I did get the chance to make love to Emily, I wasn't sure that I could keep up with her. I remembered the way she whipped around today—bending, lunging, lifting; she was in great shape.

This was the first time in my life that I had ever felt inadequate about anything. I felt like an old fool. I shook my head as I stared at my reflection in the mirror. I was tired as hell, and I was getting more tired by the minute just thinking about the energy it would require to have sex. I had barely made it out of the bathtub, so what in the hell made me think that I could handle a night of love-making with a young, active woman like Emily?

I put my boxers and T-shirt back on, trudged over to the medicine cabinet, and swallowed two ibuprofen. When I finally reached the bed again I sank down onto the pillow-top mattress and it felt like heaven. I lay flat on my back, closed my eyes, and allowed visions of Emily to enter my head. I could see myself kissing her inviting lips, rubbing her soft skin, caressing her smooth thighs, and making passionate love to her. I got hard just thinking about her, and relieved myself with a hand job. After that, my worries went away.

The mind's a powerful thing. I had made the mistake of letting my current state of exhaustion tackle me with unfounded fear. I had always been a good lover, and I knew how to take care of a woman. I was completely confident that when the time came, I would please Emily in every way. I was going to make sure she felt the pleasure I'd been waiting to give her for the past eleven years.

Chapter 10

Brenda . . .

You Could Be a Girl's Best Friend

"What's taking so long!" Brenda huffed into the phone. She was on the line with the Four Seasons Hotel's room service manager, giving him a piece of her mind. "I placed my order an hour ago and I'm still waiting to be served. I expect better from a five-star hotel."

Brenda stood at the window with the phone to her ear, looking down at the people walking forty stories below. "This is completely unacceptable and far below the standards I'm used to. Maybe I should check out and take my business to the Waldorf-Astoria or the Ritz-Carlton," she threatened. She hated to be inconvenienced, and far worse, she detested substandard service.

"Mrs. Baldwin, you're a valued guest and we appreciate you staying with us. I apologize for the mix-up and I'll personally make sure that your meal arrives at your door within the next ten minutes," the deep-voiced manager assured her.

"I'll be counting," Brenda snapped before hanging up the phone. She stomped over to the high-back chair in the corner and kicked off her designer heels.

She'd elected to have dinner in her room rather than dine in the company of Juanita Presley. When she and her sister Dorothy arrived at the hotel that morning, to Brenda's shock and surprise, Juanita was standing at the registration desk, checking in. Dorothy and Juanita hugged while Brenda forced a reluctant smile through pursed lips.

"What a surprise to see you here, Juanita," Brenda said with suspicion as she looked around the richly decorated lobby. She couldn't help but notice that her archenemy was dressed to kill so early in the morning, wearing a sleek designer chemise. It was an outfit one would wear if she wanted to look good for someone special. Brenda wondered if they'd caught Juanita in a compromising situation; having an out of town secret rendezvous. "What brings you here, to this hotel?" she asked.

Juanita cleared her throat and gave Brenda a semicordial smile. "Actually, I'm here with Pamela. She's receiving an award today from the Association of Black Women Professionals."

"That's right!" Dorothy said. "I completely forgot that the ceremony was this weekend."

"Well, I know you've been very busy," Juanita said.

"You must be so proud," Dorothy praised.

The air fluttered from Brenda's sails as the two women chatted. Not only had Juanita's party last month been a grand hit in their social circle, now she had an award-winning daughter to brag about.

"Here's Pamela now." Juanita smiled.

Pamela strolled up to the group with the grace of a ballerina. Her gently relaxed pageboy highlighted the sparkle of her large, hazel eyes. The petite beauty was fashionably dressed in a power suit that managed to throw off an air of unmistakable femininity. Only a true diva could pull that off, and a true diva Pamela was. She greeted Dorothy and Brenda with delicate air-kisses, careful not to disturb her flawless makeup in the process. She was picture perfect and it made Brenda seethe with envy.

"Mrs. Baldwin, I'll be in town next week on business and I'd love to stop by Samantha's party to wish her happy birthday," Pamela said.

"Yes, dear. Please do," Brenda said. "It's going to be *the* event of the summer." She smiled in Juanita's direction. "The party planner I hired is amazing."

It was apparent that Brenda was trying to compete with Juanita, so apparent that her rival decided it was time to bury the hatchet. So in the spirit of conciliatory gestures, she invited Brenda and Dorothy to dinner that evening to help celebrate Pamela's prestigious award. Dorothy was delighted, but Brenda was less than enthused. In her mind she determined that Juanita had only extended the invitation as a means to gloat. Brenda had no intention of breaking bread with them, but she also didn't want to look like a poor sport. She knew she had to bow out gracefully, so an hour before dinner she came down with a migraine and said she needed to rest.

Now, sitting alone in her room, Brenda longed for her room service order to arrive, especially her bottle of chardonnay. She'd had a long, frustrating day of shopping and now she was ready to unwind. She was thinking about the boutiques she planned to visit the next morning, when a knock at the door drew her from her thoughts. "It's about time," she muttered aloud. She slipped her heels back on and walked to the door.

"Room service," the voice called out on the other end.

Brenda looked through the peephole and saw two men standing on the other side, one in a uniform and one behind him at an obstructed view. She opened the door and allowed the young man in the uniform to push the linen-draped cart into her room as the other man followed. She looked at the cart full of covered dishes and let out an exasperated huff. "I can already see that you brought the wrong order. This isn't the meal I requested. I need to speak to the room service manager immediately!"

"Excuse me, Mrs. Baldwin," the man standing next to the server spoke.

Brenda turned her attention to the deep voice that she remembered from the phone. The man was immaculately dressed in a tailored navy suit. His dazzling smile and smooth ebony-hued skin made her lose her train of thought. He extended his large hand, shaking hers with a gentle grip.

"My name is Harry Winston, and I'm the room service manager. This is the meal you ordered," the handsome man offered. "I took the liberty of enhancing your dining experience to amend for the inconvenience we may have caused with the initial mix-up." He motioned with his right hand, directing the server to remove the lids of the covered dishes for Brenda's inspection.

In addition to the salmon Dijon, wild rice, asparagus with hollandaise, and the bottle of chardonnay that Brenda had ordered, there was a platter of fresh fruit and imported cheeses, chocolate-covered strawberries, a bottle of champagne, and a small vase of beautifully arranged flowers.

"I hope this is to your liking," the manager said.

It took Brenda a second to respond. "Um, yes. This looks fine."

"We're glad you're pleased," the manager said. "This meal is on me."

After Brenda inspected the food, she escorted the two men to the door. As they were on their way out, the manager stopped and turned toward her, letting the server float out into the hallway. "Again, I apologize for the inconvenience and I hope you enjoy your dinner."

Brenda smiled. "Thank you, I'm sure I will." She didn't know what possessed her to say what came out of her mouth next, but before she could stop herself she purred in a playful tone, "With a name like Harry Winston, you could be a girl's best friend."

She shocked herself, and couldn't believe she had said something so flirtatious, and to the help of all people! She wondered if he had even caught the meaning behind her tease.

The manager nodded and smiled. "Yes, but even the rarest of jewels can't compare to the gift of meeting a new friend, especially one as beautiful as you," he said in a smooth, even tone.

His remark startled Brenda, but then she reminded herself that she should've known he would understand. Working in a luxury hotel, he was bound to know a little something about *Harry Winston,* one of the most exclusive jewelers of rare gemstones in the world. It was every hotel manager's job, regardless of their department, to understand the needs of their discriminating guests. "Thank you." Brenda blushed.

Harry looked deep into her eyes and gave Brenda a smile that made her body tingle. "Again, I hope you enjoy your meal, and please make sure to call and let me know if everything meets with your satisfaction." He bowed his head slightly before walking away.

After Brenda closed the door, she stood in place for a moment, feeling light and free. She wasn't sure what had come over her. She pulled the desk chair up to the cart and began to eat her meal. In no time she devoured her entire entrée and side dishes along with half the chocolate-covered strawberries. Brenda shook her head when she realized she'd just broken a rule that she'd adhered to for over thirty years—to never clean her plate. It was one of the practices that helped her maintain her slim figure. She always left food on her plate regardless of how tasty the dish, but tonight she'd eaten until the last drop of hollandaise sauce disappeared. She wondered where her ferocious appetite had come from.

Brenda walked over to the chair in the corner and sipped her chardonnay as she thought about Harry Winston. She hadn't been this excited about anything or anyone since she could remember, not even one of her parties.

She'd done her share of flirting over the years and had come close to taking it to the next level on a few occasions. But she ran in small circles and knew those trails could easily lead back to her doorstep. So she was always careful to stop things before they grew out of control, limiting her escapades to heavy fondling, and in exceptional cases, a quick romp of oral sex. In her book, that didn't qualify as *real* sex; even Bill Clinton had said so. Her discipline was one of the many qualities upon which she prided herself. Unlike her husband, who'd been weak to the flesh of others, actually committing full-fledged adultery, she had remained true to the vow of fidelity she'd taken thirty-two years ago—at least in her mind.

Brenda remembered the first time she learned of one of Ed's affairs. She was furious and couldn't believe that with her good looks, charm, and sophistication, Ed had been stupid enough to risk their marriage over a hot-to-trot tennis instructor. But her anger soon calmed because after seeing the woman, she realized that the only draw for Ed had been the easy convenience and well-toned body that the woman possessed. She was no real threat, so Brenda let it go, as she did one or two others she'd discovered. They may have had their fun with him, but she had his last name and his money.

But Brenda also knew she had to teach Ed a lesson. She forgave him, but he needed to pay for his infidelity, so they began counseling—her way of punishing him. They attended therapy sessions for three weeks before Brenda realized it had been a big mistake on her part. The therapist wasn't helpful at all, and had actually inflicted more damage on their marriage.

During one particular visit, the therapist asked them to trace their relationship back to the reasons why they had married in the first place. Brenda nearly had a stroke when the woman made pointed suggestions, alluding to the possibility that she'd gotten pregnant on purpose to coerce Ed into marrying her. After the session ended, Brenda stormed out of the office, never to return. She knew the homely, bifocaled therapist could never understand that sometimes a woman had to do what she had to do. It had nothing to do with entrapment, but everything to do with executing a strategy.

Satisfied from her full stomach and delicious meal, Brenda let out a small sigh, followed by a devilish grin as she thought about a new strategy formulating in her mind. She had a growing desire to see Harry Winston again.

Chapter 11

Emily . . .

Standing in My Friend's Shoes

Today was one of the most wonderful yet intensely exhausting days of my life, and it all started yesterday when Samantha came walking into my empty, newly renovated home and shouted, "Surprise!" as Bradley walked in behind her. I was unpacking a box and was so stunned that I had to blink to make sure I wasn't imagining things. Bradley was the last person I had expected to see.

Samantha had been trying to play matchmaker for me, and because her other efforts to hook me up hadn't worked out, she decided to contact Bradley. I couldn't believe she didn't warn me first, but instead of getting upset, I bit my lower lip and tried to be polite.

A part of me felt guilty about the constant communication I had been having with Bradley. After I sent him the card and fruit basket last month to thank him for the wonderful design work he'd done, he called and thanked me back, beginning a series of nightly phone conversations.

Talking to Bradley felt comfortable and allowed me to open up about things. I told him about the loneliness I felt without my mother, the adjustment of starting a new job, and the frustration of getting the house in order. Samantha and Ms. Gerti had been wonderful and supportive, but I didn't want to constantly unload my burdens on them, so I accepted Bradley's calls. It was something I now regretted. I knew it was selfish, and that was why I felt so guilty. Although I had made it clear to him that I wasn't interested in resuming a romantic relationship, I had used him as a sounding board, knowing deep down that he wanted more.

Earlier in the morning when Samantha and I walked around the corner to Starbucks to get coffee and danishes before everyone arrived, I told her where things stood. "Even if I wanted to be with Bradley, which I don't, I'm living here now and it wouldn't be fair to him because he doesn't like long-distance relationships."

"Girl, if you took him back he'd quit his job, sell his house, pack his shit, and move straight up I-395 in a heartbeat," she said. "He even told me that he's looking at jobs up here. When are you gonna realize that you got it like that?"

Having it like that with Bradley wasn't what I wanted. What I wanted was right in front of me. What I wanted was exhilarating, if not exceptional. What I wanted was the only man who had ever been able to stir the intoxicating blend of love and lust deep inside me that made me feel whole each time the sound of my name escaped his lips. What I wanted was her father. But how in the world would I ever be able to look Samantha in the eye and tell her the truth?

When we returned to my house with breakfast goodies in hand, it was Samantha's turn to experience shock. We walked through the door to find her ex-boyfriend, Tyler Jacobs, shaking hands with her new man, Tyme Alexander! Samantha looked as if she'd seen a ghost. It was one of the very few times she'd ever been rendered speechless. I had to admit I was shocked, too. Samantha's face went pale and I had to remind her to breathe.

After tense introductions were made, it became obvious to Tyme that his new woman had a past with Tyler. I pulled Samantha into the kitchen so she could gather herself. "Just relax, it's going to be all right."

"It's not that easy," she sighed with anxiety. "How would you feel if you were in the same room with one man who you'd slept with and another who you planned to sleep with?"

I had no idea that ten minutes later I'd be standing in my friend's shoes.

Half of me had hoped that Ed would come by today, and the other half prayed he wouldn't. When he walked in I could see his eyes search the room as he scanned all the men until he landed on Bradley. He was trying to place him, and when he did, I saw the memory register in his steel-trap mind. Although they'd never met, I knew Ed recognized him as the man who'd held my hand as I cried on his shoulder during my mother's funeral. Ed noticed everything.

When the guys began to unload my furniture from the rented U-Haul, my mouth went dry when I saw Ed and Bradley bringing in my sofa, chitchatting like old friends. I could see that Ed was questioning him like a witness on the stand because Bradley was doing most of the talking, responding to what I knew were carefully crafted questions on Ed's part. He was like that. He could get you to talk about things without you ever realizing you were giving him information. He had done the same thing to me a few times.

Bradley must have given him an earful because Ed kept glancing at me all day with an expression that I couldn't quite place. It was unnerving. My only relief was that I had a house full of people to distract from the effect that he always had on me. At one point, Ruben asked if I was okay. I made up an excuse, telling him I was a little tired from all the moving.

After a full day of sweaty, back-breaking labor, we finally emptied the entire truck of all my things. Slowly, the room cleared as everyone began to head out, tired from hours of rigorous lifting. Bradley asked me to join him and his relatives for dinner, but I declined. Although he was disappointed he took it in stride, understanding that I had lots of work left to do. I invited him over tomorrow, and that seemed to lift his spirits. But I knew his enthusiasm would be short-lived because I planned to reiterate that while I appreciated his friendship, that was all we would ever have.

Finally, my house was empty, except for Ed and me. He offered to stay and put together my new computer desk in my home office. After he finished he came downstairs looking slightly tired but still devastatingly handsome. I stopped the work I was doing and offered him my thanks along with a cool drink. I thought I'd be nervous with just the two of us in the house, but to my surprise I wasn't. Just as I had welcomed Bradley's unsolicited calls, I welcomed Ed's company.

We sat on crates beside each other and laughed and talked for an hour. It was the first time we'd ever engaged so much and for so long without me feeling uneasy. Generally, being around him had always carried a strained and tiring fatigue, having to keep up a veil of pretense that hid my longing. But last night I felt like I could be myself—my goofy, silly, dry witted self. I showed Ed the real me and he liked it.

But suddenly our conversation took a serious turn, on his prompting. He brought up Bradley and his suspicion that my ex wanted more than just friendship. He said he'd only mentioned it because he cared about me. I smiled inside and told him that I knew he did. Our words echoed in my ear because they were revealing.

All the doubts and questions I had concerning the way Ed felt about me were erased. We confirmed our feelings without being specific. We didn't have to spell it out because it was already there—on my face, in his eyes, lying on our tongues ready to leap forward. After eleven years, we finally acknowledged what had been hanging over us. But very quickly our moment returned to the undeniable heat that always managed to rise between us, pulling us back to the sensible side of ourselves that protected us from making a mistake.

When Ed told me he had to leave, I knew that he didn't really want to go. I didn't want him to leave either, but we both knew it was for the best. I closed the door and watched from my window as he drove away, all the while my heart still pounding as if he were standing next to me. A half hour later my phone rang.

"Girl, I'm in love!" Samantha yelled into my ear.

"With who?"

"Who do you think?" She laughed. "Tyler and I are back together, just like that," she sang through the phone.

"I knew it, I knew it! I could see something brewing between you two the minute you laid eyes on each other, and so could everyone else, for that matter." Then a thought occurred to me. "What about Tyme?"

"Like you said, everyone saw it, and he did, too. I'll call him tomorrow."

"Wow," was all I could say.

Samantha went on to tell me how she and Tyler had rekindled their flame, and she was going to see where it would lead. After we ended our call, I opened the lone bottle of wine that I'd stored in my refrigerator, poured a glass, and then went upstairs to relax in my tub. I drew a hot bath and soaked. The welcoming water felt good to my skin. I was happy for my best friend, but I was also excited for myself. I smiled at the thought of Ed, and how much I wanted him to hold me, how good it would feel to rest in his arms. Now that we'd all but verbally confirmed our attraction, I didn't have a clue about our next move, or if there would even be one. I knew he cared about me, he'd said that, but it didn't necessarily mean love. And I certainly couldn't speculate on how it translated to his marriage.

Ed's marriage was the colorful elephant I'd danced around for years. Rather than think about Brenda, I concerned myself with how Samantha would react if she found out that I was in love with her father. Focusing on Samantha's feelings helped to absolve me from my guilt of wanting to engage in a relationship with a married man. Either way, I knew I was caught in a no-win situation.

After what seemed like hours, I rose from the tub and wrapped a big, soft towel around my tired body. I walked over to my suitcase, rummaged through the pile of clothes inside, and pulled out a pair of panties and a T-shirt. I slipped them on, secured my hair into a ponytail, and then crawled into bed.

As I relaxed under my fresh-smelling sheets, all I could think about was Ed, and what I would do the next time I saw him. Then a thought crossed my mind. Besides the birthday party next weekend, when would I see him again? Now that I was no longer living in his house, our interaction would be limited. When I was under his roof I had avoided him, but now that I was in my own place I wanted to see him. I'd been so preoccupied with moving out that I hadn't thought about the trade-off—not seeing Ed on a daily basis. The relief I thought I'd feel was replaced by a sudden sadness. I couldn't win for losing.

As I closed my eyes and settled into sleep, I let my worries drift away with the rest of my tired muscles. And like that, I stopped worrying about the future of my relationship with Ed and what it might hold. After the moment we shared tonight, anything was possible. My dreams could come true or my nightmares could spring to life. Today was over and tomorrow was a new beginning.

Chapter 12

Samantha . . .

That Was All I Needed to Hear

I was like my father, in the sense that not too much could throw me off my game. But when I looked dead into the eyes of the only man besides my daddy whom I had ever loved, respected, and admired, I felt as if I was going to lose my balance. There in front of me stood Tyler Jacobs. Over the years, I wondered from time to time if I would ever see him again, but I tried not to dwell on the thought because of the hurt and pain I had caused him.

Emily and I had just returned from a Starbucks run when we walked into her living room and saw Tyme shaking my ex-boyfriend's hand. "There's my girl," Tyme called out to me as Emily and I hesitated for a moment, completely at a loss for words. Tyme introduced me to his cousin, Jason, but when he attempted to do the same with Tyler, that's when things got funky.

"No need for intros." Tyler smiled as he looked into

my eyes and extended his hand. "Samantha and I are old friends."

Even though Tyler's statement was casual, it was loaded with meaning, and Tyme could sense it along with everyone else in the room. When I shook Tyler's hand I felt a strong, liquid heat spread through my body . . . and I hadn't even touched my coffee! At that moment I knew it was going to be a long day. Thank goodness for Emily. She carted me off to the kitchen, calmed me down, and gave me the encouragement I needed to go back out and face the music and the men.

A minute later we heard the doorbell ring and I sprang forward, glad to have a distraction. I greeted Emily's flaming next-door neighbor and his fine-ass boyfriend as they breezed into the room. Another round of introductions was made, but it did nothing to cut the tension that filled the air. I decided to focus on the brazen Latin lover and his man, who looked like a dead ringer for Tyson Beckford.

"Samantha, it's so nice to finally meet you," Ruben said to me with a smile.

Ruben fiddled with something in his hand, and when I looked to see what it was, it turned out to be a beautiful crystal hairpin. Next thing I knew, Ms. Thang whipped his silky shoulder-length tresses up into a perfect chignon in one quick swoop. I couldn't have replicated his move if my life depended on it. This queen was one bad bitch! After a few minutes of conversation I fell in love with Ruben. He was a straight-up trip, in a very good way.

I chatted with Ruben while trying to avoid the stares of both Tyler and Tyme. Tyler was as cool as an ice cube, glancing at me with a slight smile as he talked with Emily and Bradley. But Tyme was more than a little put off because of the obvious vibe I had with Tyler.

We all settled on the floor and dug into the coffee and

danishes. Tyme sat close to me, an attempt to stake his claim, while everyone else tried to ignore our strained body language. When Daddy walked into the room I felt myself jump for joy. He seemed mildly out of sorts, but then I realized it was probably because he was bewildered to see Tyler in the room. So after I introduced him to everyone I ushered him outside. I gave him the lowdown on the situation with Tyler, and as Emily had done, he imparted some good advice that helped me suck up my emotions and walk back into the room with a more level head.

After we finished eating, we went to work moving Emily's furniture off the large truck and into the house. An hour or two later I asked Tyme to make a beverage run for water, beer, and soda. He looked at me with suspicion, but then decided to go. Two seconds after he walked out the door, I approached Tyler. "What's goin' on?" I smiled.

"It's been a long time. You look good, Sam."

Damn, I wanted to melt. "So do you."

Our chemistry was instant. Tyler stood in front of me, inspecting me from head to toe while I did the same to him. He hadn't changed a bit. His café au lait skin still held the same boyish good looks that framed his sexy goatee when I last saw him six years ago. His modest dimples and large brown eyes made me want to crawl into his arms. Everything about this man turned me on. Even the few small blemishes that teenage acne had left behind on his cheeks managed to look like pure bliss on him.

Tyler was the perfect mix between smooth sophistication and the rugged streets. He was a clean-cut "good guy" with an edge. He was born in Brooklyn, on the good side of the borough. His father had been a prominent pediatrician, and his mother a tenured professor at NYU. His family was similar to mine—educated, well-to-do black folks who took pride in being educated and well-to-do. But his parents were a bit different from the rest of their social milieu. They were down for the cause, the kind of people who volunteered at soup kitchens and shelters. They used to take Tyler with them because they wanted to teach their son about life outside the walls of their luxury brownstone.

After his parents were killed in a car accident, he moved down to Virginia where he was raised by his mother's sister. His parents had left him a sizeable trust fund that had matured when he turned twenty-one, and even though I had no idea of his exact net worth, I knew he was quite comfortable and didn't have to work if he chose not to. But he loved what he did and wouldn't give it up for the world. He'd founded his nonprofit organization, Youths First Initiative, after graduating from Morehouse so he could continue what his parents had instilled in him before they died. Today, YFI was one of the most highly respected youth organizations in the country.

Tyler wasn't your average guy, he was special. He was intelligent, compassionate, and giving. And that was part of what had attracted me to him in the first place— that and his six-foot frame and tight, lean body. Standing in front of me, he looked fine as hell in his worn, loose-fitting cargo shorts and white *I Love New York* T-shirt.

I was sweating like a field hand from lifting boxes, and my makeup and hair had taken a slight beating from the hot sun and humidity, but I still looked cute in my pink shorts and matching tank with silk appliqué. You know I gotta bring it! Although I had to admit, I should've taken Emily's cue and slipped on some comfortable sneakers instead of my wedge-heel sandals because my feet throbbed like they were on fire. But like I said, I looked good, and I could tell that Tyler thought so, too.

When our eyes finally locked and I concentrated on his, I couldn't believe what I saw . . . a smile! This man who I'd hurt so badly in the past and hadn't seen in years was looking at me like a long-lost friend. I tried to compose myself. "So," I began as I put my hand on my hip, "you came to town just to help your friend move furniture?" I already knew the background story because Tyme had told me, but I asked anyway because it was a start to a conversation that had ended six years ago.

Tyler shook his head and smiled. "Not entirely. I'm in town for a national youth conference that starts this Monday. I decided to fly in a few days early and just chill for a minute, so I let my boy, Jason, know that I was coming up. That's when he asked if I'd help his cousin," he paused, clearing his throat, "because his girl needed a favor." He said the last part with a smirk.

"I see," I replied.

Tyler and I chatted as we lifted boxes and moved furniture. I found out enough to know that he was still single and that he'd be in town until the end of next week. He was curious about me, too, but he didn't ask a lot of questions. There were too many ears milling around. I told him I was moving back to DC in a few days, and for some reason he smiled in response. We continued talking and exchanged looks filled with a combination of comfort and caution, but after Tyme returned we kept our distance.

It was late afternoon when we finally finished unloading the truck. Emily had spent the last few months buying just the right furniture to decorate her new home. She had eclectic taste, and I could see that everything was going to be beautiful once she set it up. As we brought in the last of the boxes, I was already plotting my next move—how I could ditch Tyme and hook up with Tyler later tonight.

Now I knew exactly why things had never felt right

with Tyme. Normally, I would've slept with a man like him on the first date, or shortly thereafter. But I'd known him for weeks and we hadn't done jack. The vibe had never hit me, and that's because without me even knowing it, his connection to Tyler, though it was distant, made it feel wrong. I usually made terrible decisions when it came to men, but thank God I had trusted my gut in this situation.

Tyme walked over to me. "Want to go out to dinner or catch a movie later?"

My first inclination was to tell him the truth. But Tyme was a decent guy, and I wanted to be mindful of his feelings. I would have the opportunity to tell him the real deal at a more appropriate time. So I looked at him and said, "I'm wiped out. I think I'll just head home and call it a night." I threw in a little yawn even though I wasn't the least bit sleepy. Tyler cut me a quick glance and nodded like he knew what was up.

A slight air of tension filled the room again, as it had earlier this morning, and sensing that things were a little too close for comfort, Ruben and Roger left, but not before giving me two air-kisses and warm hugs. They were a great couple. Then Jason announced that he was taking Tyler back to his hotel, and why did he have the nerve to look directly at me when he said it? Tyme was pissed.

Nearly an hour later, I was beyond tired as I walked outside and opened the door to my little red convertible. I sat behind the wheel and was about to put my key in the ignition when my cell phone started chirping *The Godfather* ringtone that I'd set last night for Carl's number. "Shit!" I mumbled. I sat back in my seat and listened to the music before his call rolled into voice mail. I took a deep breath, then leaned forward to start my engine when my phone rang again. This time it wasn't the ringtone from hell. I looked at the caller ID and smiled. "Hello," I answered in my best "sexy" voice. Tyler's number hadn't changed, and I was so glad I'd never deleted it from my contact list.

"Can you talk?" he asked.

"I wouldn't have answered if I couldn't."

"What're you doing right now?"

"Sitting in my car in front of Emily's house, getting ready to head home." I was smiling into the phone and I knew Tyler could hear it in each word I spoke.

"Instead of driving home, why don't you come over to my hotel room like I know you want to. You already know where I'm staying."

Yes, I knew where he was staying because I'd over-heard him mention it loudly to Daddy when they were talking earlier this afternoon. And he was right again, his hotel room was exactly where I wanted to be! "You want me to come over now?"

"Sam, I just want to talk."

"I'm sweaty and I need to take a shower."

"They have running water over here."

That was all I needed to hear. I turned on the engine, put my car into drive, and headed straight for the Palomar hotel.

When Tyler answered the door I was taken aback be-cause he was still wearing his dirty clothes from this after-noon. Before I could censor myself, my thoughts flew from my mouth. "You left Emily's house over an hour ago. Why haven't you cleaned up?" I could smell his sweaty man-scent from where I stood.

Tyler chuckled. "Sam, you haven't changed a bit."

"Sorry," I said as I looked around his room, "but I heard they have running water up in this joint."

We both laughed, and it calmed me. Tyler walked

over to the edge of the bed and took a seat while I joined him. He leaned forward and rested his elbows on his knees. "Jason had to make a few stops before he dropped me off and it took longer than he thought. I just got back here when I called you, and I didn't want to jump in the shower because I thought I might miss your knock on the door."

I nodded.

"So, why aren't you out with your boy?" he asked, looking at me through seductive eyes.

"Because I wanted to be here with you."

We sat in silence. I was dying for him to say something, but because I was the one who'd fucked things up between us, I knew I needed to be the one who took the first step. I tried to look into Tyler's eyes the same way he was looking into mine, but I couldn't, so I focused on the lamp sitting on the nightstand as I struggled to speak. "Tyler, I'm so sorry for the way I hurt you," I began. "There were so many times when I wanted to call you and apologize for what I did, and just ask for your forgiveness. Besides my father, you're the only man I've ever loved."

I couldn't believe I just told him that I loved him. But hey, what did I have to lose? I had already lost him once due to fear and stupidity, and I knew I couldn't let that happen again. This was my chance to make things right, so I continued. "Yes, Tyler, I loved you. And as messed up as it sounds, that's why I did what I did. I knew with my track record that I'd eventually find a way to ruin things, so before we went any further I saved us both the trouble."

We sat in more silence. I hated the quiet because it was so freakin' uncomfortable. I shifted in my chair. "Are you going to say anything?"

He let out a long, heavy sigh and rubbed his hands over his nicely trimmed goatee. "I know, Sam."

"You do?"

"I know your story because it was my story, too. A long time ago when I was young and foolish, I sabotaged a meaningful relationship because I felt I needed to end it before I got hurt. After losing my parents, hurt and loss were something I ran from," he said as he positioned himself closer to me. "After you and I broke up I tried to figure out what had gone wrong between us, then it hit me like a slap on my face. You played the same game that I'd played in my past. So I understood it."

He was talking about his late wife, Juliet. They had been through trials and tribulations before they finally married, only for him to lose her to kidney disease just a few years later. Tyler had suffered many losses, and now my actions made me feel even worse. "I'm so sorry," I said softly.

"Me too. But look at us now. We grew from our experiences, and actually, you, our breakup, made me see myself more clearly. Ever since then I've been living my life without fear."

He paused, reached for my hands, and held them in his. It was a move that startled me. "Sam, you freed me, and that's why I can look at you and smile. I know you didn't mean to hurt me. Sometimes we have to go through pain so we can find joy."

I didn't cry easily, but Tyler's words nearly caused me to burst into tears. I could feel the drops coming, but I fought them back. I knew I didn't deserve the understanding or kindness this man was giving me, and I let him know. "I don't deserve you," I said with my head held low.

Tyler placed his finger under my chin and lifted my face so he could meet my eyes. "You're a better person than you think you are, and you deserve a lot more than you limit yourself to."

This wasn't the way I thought our evening would flow. I knew I needed to apologize to him and that there might be some tense moments in our conversation, but I never bargained for this. The emotions building inside me were overwhelming, almost frightening. I was never good at handling things in a mature, responsible, or adult manner, but that was the way Tyler operated, and I knew that if I wanted to be with him, that was how I needed to start living my life. So I sucked up my fear, stopped feeling sorry for myself, and smiled back at the man I loved.

"That's what I'm talkin' about." He grinned. "Now, no more talk about the past or apologies. Let's bury that baggage where it belongs and move forward, starting this very minute."

I smiled with a lightheartedness that I hadn't felt in years. "Sounds like a plan."

I drove to my parents' house on a mission, making it there in record time. I needed to take a shower, get dressed, and head back over to Tyler's hotel so we could have a late dinner. I was thinking about which outfit I should wear when I saw the light on in the kitchen. Daddy was sitting at the breakfast table having a meal. I walked in and jumped straight into my good news about Tyler and me. But after a few minutes I could see that something was wrong. "Daddy, how're you feeling?" I asked.

"Your old man is beat."

I took a seat across from him and studied his tired eyes, slumped shoulders, and five o'clock shadow. I knew my daddy well, and his mood seemed much deeper than sore muscles. It couldn't be work because when we talked yesterday, he told me that he'd won his big case. Something else had to be wrong. "Is she back?" I asked, referring to Mother. She was the only person I knew who could kill the joy of a multi-million-dollar settlement.

"No, she's not getting in until tomorrow morning," he said with a little relief.

"Then what's wrong?"

"Like I said, I'm beat. You're still young, but wait until you get my age."

"I'm not your age and I'm tired. Emily is, too. As a matter of fact, she's probably soaking in the tub right now."

"Oh, yeah?"

"Yeah, I just talked to her on my way over here and she's worn out. She finished unpacking most of her things downstairs and she plans to work on the upstairs when Bradley comes over there tomorrow afternoon."

"Hmmm . . ." he said in a questioning tone.

I read his mind. "Yeah, I know. I'm thinking the same thing, too." I nodded. "It's just a matter of time before they get back together. He's crazy about her."

"Is she crazy about him?"

"Emily's so emotional right now, she doesn't know what she wants. Hopefully she'll come to her senses."

Daddy let out a deep sigh.

"Are you sure you're okay?" I questioned again.

I was about to grill him when Gerti walked through the back door. "Hey, baby girl." She smiled and bent over to give me a kiss on my cheek. "Here you go," she said to Daddy, handing him a box of Epsom salt.

He stood up slowly. "Gerti, you're a lifesaver."

"Tell me something I don't know." She grinned.

Daddy walked over to me and patted my head like he used to when I was a little girl. "Don't worry about me, I'm fine. Now, if you ladies will excuse me, I'm going upstairs to take a long soak in the tub."

Gerti and I looked at Daddy as he dragged himself

down the hall. "Have you noticed anything strange about Daddy lately?" I asked.

"Strange like what?"

"His behavior. It seems like something's really bothering him. He said he's just tired, but I think there's more to it. He's never like this after a big court victory."

Gerti picked up her knife and started chopping vegetables at the sink. "He's all right. Just going through a little adjustment."

"Adjustment to what?"

"Change." She sighed. "Your father's a good man, and right now he's trying to do the right thing and it's wearing on him."

I knew she was talking about Mother. She put Daddy through changes every couple of years, trying to make his life a living hell. One year she made him go to marriage counseling. Ironically, I thought the only thing that could fix their marriage was divorce. If Gerti was right, which she usually was, he might finally make that leap. Thinking about change and making leaps drew my mind back to Tyler, and a smile covered my face when I thought about him.

"What has you grinning so hard?" Gerti asked.

I twisted in my seat with excitement as I told her about my visit to Tyler's hotel room.

"I always did like Tyler. He's a fine young man," Gerti said. "And he's cute, too."

"Gerti, I love him." When I said it, she stopped cutting up the vegetables and looked at me. She had never heard me make that kind of declaration.

Gerti wiped her hands on her dish towel and came over to me. She sat down beside me and gave me a warm hug, filling me with emotion as I spoke. "A lot of men have told me that they loved me, but I knew that none of them ever really meant it, and I definitely never told any of them that I loved them back. But I *love* Tyler. I always have, and I hope he loves me, too."

Gerti tilted her head. "The question is, do you love yourself?"

Leave it to Gerti to flip the script on me right in the middle of a soul-stirring confession. I knew what she was getting at—if I didn't love myself, how could anyone else love me? But it wasn't that easy, and at the moment I didn't feel like exploring those emotions, so I brushed off her question with a joke. "Gerti, you know I love me some me." I laughed, trying to lighten the mood.

Gerti stared at me, not blinking her eyes. "Sam, I'm gonna tell you something, and I want you to listen up and listen good. There's more to loving yourself than having confidence and a kiss-my-ass attitude. Loving yourself means taking care of yourself and honoring who you are by not allowing just any and everything into your life. It means honoring your body and your mind. And it means being a bigger person by making amends to those who might not deserve it, and showing love to those who do. If you want that man to love you, you better start working on yourself and the choices you make."

I knew that Gerti was right and that she was talking about the two people who I loved and hated most—my son and my mother.

Chapter 13

Emily . . .

The Gift

"Thanks, Ms. Gerti. I don't know what I'd do without you." I smiled. We were sitting at my dining room table eating the baked chicken and steamed vegetables she had brought over. After we finished our delicious meal I gave her a quick tour of my house, carefully dodging the empty boxes that remained from yesterday's move.

She raved about how much she loved the rich colors I'd chosen for the walls both upstairs and on the main floor, and the detailed fixtures in the kitchen and bathrooms. I had to say that my house was absolutely beautiful. I had decorated with a mixture of African, Middle Eastern, and Mediterranean influences. It was eclectic, but it was also soothing because everything flowed in harmony.

After I finished showing Ms. Gerti around, I poured us two glasses of iced tea and we settled comfortably onto my soft living room sofa.

"You've got a really nice place here, Emily. Your mama would be so proud."

"Thanks, Ms. Gerti." I looked over at the picture of my parents on the antique fireplace mantel that Emmanuel had expertly restored.

"You're doing the right thing, sugar." She nodded. "A lot of people aren't strong enough to do what you've done."

"What do you mean?"

"You didn't give in to the feelings you've been carrying around for Ed."

We stared at each other—her with wisdom and knowing in her eyes, and me with bewilderment in mine. "How did you know?"

She smiled and shook her head. "I suspected for a long time. I've watched you two over the years, how you looked at each other, stealing glimpses when you thought no one was watching. Then after you moved up here I could see it as plain as daylight."

"I'm that obvious?"

"Humph, it ain't just you, sugar. Ed's got that look, too. Got it bad, worse than you. He thinks he's fooling somebody, trying to act like he's just asking me questions about you because he's concerned about how you're coping with things. He knows we talk." She winked. "But I knew the real reason why he would ask what time you were coming home in the afternoon, if you'd had a good day at work, and if you were going out and making friends."

Her words gave me the validation that Ed really did have strong feelings for me. But with that validation came the keen awareness that if Ms. Gerti saw the attraction between us, others probably had, too. "Ms. Gerti, do you think anyone else knows?"

I was fairly confident that Samantha didn't have a clue, otherwise she would've confronted me by now, so I held my breath as visions of Brenda flashed through my mind. "Do you think Brenda knows?"

When she shook her head no, I started breathing again.

"No, Brenda's too caught up in herself to pay attention to anyone else, and besides, she'd never even suspect you. And Sam, bless her heart, she can barely see what's in front of her own eyes. You know how your friend is."

I'd waited eleven years to feel this way, but now there was a strange weight hanging over the moment. So I did what I thought I needed to do. I let it all out. "I love him," I confessed. "I've loved Ed for so long, right from the beginning. But I couldn't do anything about it."

Ms. Gerti nodded slowly, listening as I continued.

"I've never loved anyone the way I love him. I've tried to have relationships and I've wanted to fall in love so many times, but my heart just wouldn't allow it because it already belonged to him." I felt emotionally drained, but I also felt free because for the first time I was able to release what had been bottled up inside me for years.

Ms. Gerti smiled. "Oh, Emily. Child, I know what it's like to love somebody you can't be with."

"You do?"

"Sure I do. I was young once, and in love." She sighed, nodding. "I loved a man who I knew I'd never be able to have. It was doomed from the start because we came from different worlds. He was a college student and I was a domestic. He came from one of the most prominent black families in this city, kinda like the Baldwins, only they were a whole lot snootier," she said, hunching her shoulders. "His people didn't like the notion of him taking up with a housekeeper from Alabama. But it was good while it lasted, and those sweet memories are still with me to this day."

Ms. Gerti smiled, but there was a sadness swimming behind her eyes that made me feel even more pitiful. Was she saying that I was going to end up like her, with nothing but crushed dreams and the bittersweet memories of something that could never be? As if sensing my fear, Ms. Gerti answered my thoughts.

"I've known Ed a long, long time, and I've seen him and Brenda fall away from each other over the years, some of it her fault, some of it his. Yeah, she's stuck-up, selfish, and a pain in the ass. But, sugar, at the end of the day she's still that man's wife."

"What if he comes to me? What if he doesn't want that life anymore?"

"Well, I know that whatever I sit here and tell you, your mind is already made up, right?"

"I think so," I sighed. "I love him so much. I just want to be happy. I want to experience real love."

"If he comes to you, be prepared for what comes with him."

I looked at her, knowing exactly what she meant.

"You're gonna gain something, but you're gonna lose something, too, and once you start down that road, sugar, there ain't no turning back. You understand me?"

I thought about the consequences. The wounded feelings and sense of betrayal that were sure to follow. Not just from Brenda, but more importantly, from Samantha. Sleeping with Ed would be a breach of our sisterhood, yet being with him was something I wanted so badly it hurt.

Ms. Gerti and I both looked up when the doorbell rang. "That's Bradley," I said. I had invited him over because I needed to tell him once and for all, face-to-face, that there was no future for us.

Ms. Gerti shook her head as she stood and gathered her things to leave. "Emily, what you're about to do is like trying to catch a falling knife." She sighed. "You sure you don't want to give it another try with Bradley? He's such a nice young man."

I rose to my feet and walked her to the door. "Yes, he is, but he's not the one for me."

Ruben and I were having dinner at Woodmont Grill. Roger was out of town on business, and Samantha and Tyler were spending the evening together, so the two of us decided we'd hang out. This was one of Ruben's and Roger's favorite restaurants, and I could see why. Not only was the food absolutely delicious and the service top-notch, but the low lighting, dark wood-paneled walls, and luminous candles on the tables created an atmosphere ripe for a romantic dining experience. I'd love to have dinner here with Ed.

"So, what are you going to do about Bradley?" Ruben asked.

"There's nothing *to do* about him," I responded, taking a bite of my couscous.

"Chica, that's one fine man. I can think of a lot of things I could do with him!"

I laughed. "I'm sure you could. But I told him in no uncertain words that I wasn't interested in anything beyond friendship."

Ruben chomped down on his steak. "You can't get any more to the point than that."

"I had to be honest with him because I'd want the same in return."

"Awww, listen to you. You're such a good girl."

I shook my head. "Not really." If Ruben knew the thoughts that had been running through my mind since last Saturday night, he'd eat those words right along with his succulent filet.

Ruben looked at me and tilted his head. "Don't even think that way," he said, waving his hand as he made a tsking sound.

"What way?"

"Emily, just because you want to get down with Samantha's father, that doesn't make you a bad person, just a little freaky." He smiled and winked.

Somehow I wasn't surprised that he knew, and it made me rethink what Ms. Gerti had said about no one else suspecting my true feelings for Ed. "It's a delicate situation," I said softly.

I was normally very private about my personal life, but because Ruben already knew my secret I decided to share my feelings with him as I had with Ms. Gerti, opening up about my long-held love for Ed. Don't ask me why, but my gut told me that I could trust him. After I finished, Ruben stopped eating his food and gave me a look so serious it made me put down my roasted garlic bread. He nodded, his glistening black hair swaying back and forth over his shoulders.

"Yes, it's time," he said, barely above a whisper, as if talking to himself.

"Time for what?"

"Emily, I want to tell you something, but I don't want you to become alarmed or dismiss what I'm about to share with you."

"Okay." I braced myself for the *Honey, you're headed for trouble if you get involved with a married man* speech.

"I have *the gift*," he said quietly. He looked into my eyes and held my stare without blinking as he continued. "I have the gift of prophecy. I was born with it. I have the ability to see things that have happened in the past and that will happen in the future. And the spirits speak to me, too."

I stared back at Ruben without the apparent alarm he'd expected. All Southerners that I knew had either heard of or knew someone with *the gift*. For me, that person was Ms. Marabelle.

When I was ten years old, shortly after my father died, Ms. Marabelle gave me my first reading. I was waiting for my mother after church while she collected canned goods for our youth ministry's food drive. Ms. Marabelle walked by me with slow, labored steps, then stopped and turned around. When I saw her mouth begin to open I panicked because I didn't want to hear what she had to say. I knew it wouldn't be good. She touched my hand with hers, and surprisingly, her heavy-looking fingers felt as light as a feather. "You a good girl, Emily, and you got a good spirit. But you got lots a' heartache waitin' on you down the road. You gon' have yo mama fo' a good lil spell, but then she gon' leave you befo' yo third decade in life . . . fo' you make yo way to the city."

I didn't know what the old lady's words meant at the time, but a year later my mother was diagnosed with MS, and I stayed as far away from Ms. Marabelle as I could.

Then there was the precious little girl I taught in my kindergarten class back in Atlanta. Her name was Alexandria Thornton, and she was the prettiest little thing I had ever seen. She was smart as a whip and was well advanced beyond her years. But sometimes she'd say and do strange things that made the hairs on my arms bristle. It was the same feeling I'd get whenever Ms. Marabelle was near. I suspected this little girl had *the gift*, too.

One afternoon when her parents came to pick her up from school, her father suffered a heart attack right there in the parking lot. He survived, but it had been a trau-

matic scene, and Alexandria took it hard. I gave her a little latitude over the next few weeks, allowing her extra
time to herself during nap and recess. On one particular
day as she sat alone at her desk, she drew a picture that I
found oddly curious. "This is my family," she said, pointing to the paper on which she had drawn a dark-skinned
black woman and a white man holding hands with a
cream-colored little girl and a dark-complexioned little
boy. Alexandria was biracial and had captured her family
perfectly. But I was intrigued because she was an only
child, so I wondered about the little boy she'd sketched
with chocolate-colored skin and eyes that looked like
blue marbles. "That's my brother, but he hasn't happened
yet," she told me with a straight face when I inquired.

Her answer didn't shock me because I was used to
her saying unusual things, but it did unnerve me. At the
end of that term she transferred to a different school, but
I never forgot her and I often wondered what became of
the beautiful little girl who I suspected had *the gift.* Then
last year I was at Lenox Mall doing my holiday shopping
when I ran into Alexandria and her family.

She and her parents remembered me and gave me
warm hugs. But what struck me like a bolt of lightning
was that her father was holding the hand of a handsome
little boy who looked to be about five years old, and
shared his same ocean-blue eyes, but was wrapped in the
same smooth, cocoa brown skin as his mother. "Christian
was born a year after Alexandria left Peachtree County
Day," her mother said. Alexandria had predicted what was
to come for her family, right down to the color of her
brother's eyes.

I never dismissed the supernatural, and I had seen
enough to know that I shouldn't discount what I couldn't
explain. And for that same reason, I knew that Ruben was

telling me this because he could see something on the horizon for me. "Something bad is going to happen to me, isn't it?" I asked, mild fear coating my voice.

He raised his neatly arched brow. "You're not surprised by what I just told you?"

"Ruben, you know I'm from the South."

"Yes, but, honey, not everyone is a believer."

"Believer or not, I know you wouldn't be telling me this unless you were serious. You must see something important that I need to know."

"Yes, Emily. I've sensed it from the moment I met you," he sighed. I had never seen Ruben this serious, and it made me even more nervous as he continued. "I knew there was a burden hanging over you, something you'd been struggling with for a long time. Then when I met Ed, the mystery was solved."

I nodded. "Go on . . ."

"May I?" he asked, gently motioning to put his hand on top of mine.

I extended my hand across the table so that we were within each other's reach. Ruben took a deep breath and gently put his soft hands over mine. I was calmed by the warmth and comfort of his smooth palms. "Yes." He nodded. "I see, and it's just as you told me. You've loved Ed for a very long time."

"Will we end up together?" I implored, sitting on the edge of my seat.

Ruben paused for a moment, squinting his eyes as if trying to see through fog. "Yes, Emily. You two will be together."

I tingled inside. I'd always been skittish about people who claimed to have supernatural powers. I didn't even read my horoscope because my future always seemed to hold some sort of devastating kink. But now I was overjoyed to know someone with *the gift*. I squeezed his hand. "Thank you, you've just given me the best news I've heard in years."

Suddenly, Ruben shuddered. Just as quickly as he had blanketed my hands with his, he pulled away. "What's wrong?" I asked.

Ruben looked at me like he'd seen a ghost. "I just got the strangest feeling when you squeezed my hand." He frowned, peering into my eyes. "Oh, no . . . Emily, danger is around you."

Hearing those words sent chills down my spine. I straightened my back against the cushioned leather booth. "What kind of danger?"

I knew there were risks involved with entering into a relationship with a married man. I'd even thought about the possibility of Brenda finding out and creating a scene. I didn't think she was a violent person, but if she were emotionally hurt and had been drinking, who knew what she was capable of. Over the last few weeks Samantha had told me some crazy stories about her mother's tirades that had left me shocked and made me finally see where my best friend got her penchant for drama. Ruminating over what Ruben had just told me, I knew I had to push ahead with the obvious question. "Will someone get hurt, physically?"

He reached for my hands again, holding them for a long pause. Finally, he said, "Yes, Emily. I'm afraid so."

I gulped hard. The tone in his voice put the familiar bristle on my arms that I always felt whenever I was about to hear bad news. He held my hands tightly as he prophesied my bad fate. "I see confusion, chaos, shouting, and bright lights," he rattled off, squinting again, closing his eyes so he could fully concentrate.

Our server came by the table to refill our water glasses, but when he saw Ruben straining and me looking frightened in his grip, he eased away and left us alone. "I see uniforms," Ruben continued, "I think it's the police. Yes, it's the police, Emily."

"Oh God."

Ruben gritted his teeth. "Someone's going to get hurt."

"How badly?"

He shook his head, concentrating harder. Slowly, he opened his eyes and looked at me. "I see death."

Sweet Jesus! My heart pounded and my ears rang. Our relaxed dinner had turned into a nightmare. I wanted to end the conversation, go home, and bury my head under the covers. But I had to know more. "Is it because of my involvement with Ed?"

He nodded. "Yes, Emily. I'm sensing that the danger is connected to him."

My heart dropped to my stomach. I felt cold and numb, like I did when I was a little girl and Ms. Marabelle told me that my mother would die before my thirtieth birthday. Just like I did years later when she told me that I would be a mother without giving birth to a child. And just like I did when she kissed my cheek before I left Atlanta, smiling at me in a way that had made me feel haunted.

If someone I loved was going to die, why hadn't Ms. Marabelle prophesied that to me? Why had she simply smiled and told me that it was time for me to follow my heart, that I was finally going to be happy? Before I could ask Ruben to concentrate harder so he could tell me who was in danger, he answered my question. "I'm not sure who it is, honey. I just know that the danger has something to do with Ed. You must be very careful and keep the ones you love close."

I was so beside myself I could barely speak, but as frightened as I was to learn more, I knew I had to ask him again. "Ruben, are you certain that someone I love is going to die?"

"Sometimes I can see things very clearly, and at other times the visions come to me in fragmented bits and pieces, kind of like a puzzle. I'm not sure about all the details, but I feel death hanging in the air around you."

"Ruben, I'm scared."

"I know, honey, and I'm sorry. I've felt strong vibes flowing from you from the first day we met, when I shook your hand. But until tonight I hadn't been led to say anything." He paused, letting out a heavy breath. "But the spirits said it was time. That means they're looking out for you. They're helping you, Emily. Don't be afraid."

Ruben and I skipped dessert and asked for the check. I was a bundle of nerves and he looked tired, as if he'd just run a marathon. During our drive home he told me that intense readings often drained him, and that mine had been one of the most exhausting he had had in a very long time.

An hour later I sat in my bed, a nervous wreck. I tried to review my lesson for the next day, but I couldn't focus. I kept thinking about my conversation with Ruben. I knew that danger meant drama, so my mind automatically landed on Samantha. I had to call her.

"Hey, Emily, what's goin' on?" Samantha answered.

"That's what I'm calling to ask you. I'm worried about you. Is everything okay?"

"You worry like an old woman." She laughed. "I'm over here at the house trying to pack all of this stuff so I can take it over to my place in the morning."

Her voice sounded upbeat and happy. I had expected her to be frazzled, not excited. Samantha was supposed to meet the movers early tomorrow morning, and as usual, she hadn't organized half of the things she needed in order to move into her new condo. "I'll try to leave school by noon so I'll have more time to help you," I told her.

"Scratch that. Tyler will be there and we've got everything covered."

"Are you sure?"

"I'm more than sure. Besides, I don't have nearly as much to move as you did."

Despite my offer, I was a bit relieved that Samantha didn't need my help. I was physically and emotionally worn out and I didn't think I could lift another box, especially because I was still recovering from my own move last weekend. But my true comfort came in knowing that Tyler would be with her. He was a good man, and he was a protector. I knew Samantha would be safe with him, so that calmed a small part of my worries.

"You're asking about me, but how are you? You sound strange. What's going on?" Samantha asked.

"Nothing. I'm just a little tired," I responded. "Samantha, you haven't heard from Carl, have you?" Danger was Carl's middle name, and I hoped he wouldn't drop by while Tyler was helping her move. That could be the vision that Ruben had seen.

"No, and I hope I don't see or hear from him anytime soon," she said, almost with a growl. "Why do you ask?"

"I just have a bad feeling about him, and I want to make sure you're safe."

"I'm fine. And like I said, Tyler will be there with me, so don't worry."

"I'm glad you two are back together."

"Me too. Emily, he's the best thing that's happened to me in a long time. He makes me so happy."

"Good. You deserve happiness."

"I don't know about all that, but I'll take it. And speaking of happiness, we've got to get you hooked up."

"Here you go with that again," I sighed.

"Yes, here I go with that again. You need a man!"

A part of me wanted to tell her that the man I wanted was her father, but I knew better, so I kept my mouth shut. "Please, let's drop it."

We chatted for a few more minutes before ending our call with Samantha sounding out of breath from packing boxes and me feeling a little better knowing that Tyler would be with her. Now my mind drifted to Ed. He was close to me, close to my heart. And again, with danger came drama, and drama was right up Brenda's alley. I knew that if I continued down the road I wanted to travel, Ed could possibly get hurt, or as Ruben had predicted, something even worse!

"What am I going to do?" I whispered aloud to the cozy rust-colored walls of my bedroom. I was frustrated and tired at the same time. Ruben had said that the danger and possible death was linked to Ed, but without knowing who, when, where, or how the tragedy would play out, I was at a loss for how to protect anyone. Then I remembered another thing that Ruben said, "Keep the ones you love close." I knew I had to call Ed in the morning. I had to warn him.

I put my notebook on the nightstand, turned off the light, and prayed for restful sleep that never came.

Chapter 14

Samantha . . .

Mmm, You Have a Good Memory

Last weekend I helped Emily move into her new house, and now I was doing the same, huffing and puffing as I walked up the stairs to the second floor of my brand-new condo. I was carrying a box marked *master bedroom closet* that felt as if it was loaded with cement blocks instead of clothes. Why the movers left it in the kitchen downstairs I'll never know. They arrived at the crack of dawn, and it only took them a few hours to unload my belongings from their huge truck. I had a beautiful sleigh bed, a gorgeous sofa, an elegant dining room set, and a nice entertainment center. Other than that, the majority of my things consisted of clothes, shoes, clothes, shoes, and more clothes.

Daddy stopped by to make sure things were going well, but he left in an unexpected rush after checking his office messages. An urgent matter had come up and he had to get back to take care of business. I hadn't mentioned too much about my move to Mother because I didn't want her anywhere around, and she didn't offer to come by.

"Damn, I'm not cut out for this kind of work," I panted as I struggled with another heavy box. I hadn't organized my things into any type of order, so there was chaos everywhere.

I felt frustration growing, but then I stopped because at that moment, I reminded myself of my mother, bitchy and ungrateful. Here I was, standing in the middle of a brand-new home that I owned. I had a beautiful son, a good man, and friends and family who I loved and who loved me back. I had a whole hell of a lot to be thankful for, and moving heavy boxes was a small price to pay. So I became determined not to let anything get me down, not even my aching back.

I had hoped I would be able to get most of my things unpacked today because I wanted to be settled in before the big birthday party this Saturday, which was only two days away. If it weren't for Emily not wanting to disappoint my mother, I wouldn't show up for it at all. But the good thing was that I would be celebrating another year of life, and I would do it with my best friend by my side. And oh yeah, did I mention that Tyler would be there, too?!

The last few days with him had been like a dream, one from which I didn't want to wake because it felt so good. I had seen Tyler every day since last Saturday. Each afternoon when his conference meetings ended, I would slip over to his hotel and we would hang out together. We laughed, talked, and caught up on the last six years of our lives.

I was ripping open another heavy box with a pair of scissors when I heard my doorbell ring. I looked at my watch and knew it was Tyler. He finished up early today so he could come over and help me. I forgot about my sore muscles and rushed downstairs like a cheetah. Hell, my back didn't even ache anymore.

"Hey, you," Tyler said as he greeted me with a smile. He held a big bouquet of freshly cut flowers that were tucked inside a small grocery bag under one arm, and a brown leather duffel under the other. "Just a lil somethin' to brighten your new home and fill your fridge, because I know it's empty." He laughed.

I hugged him long and hard as I welcomed him through the door. "You know I don't do the grocery-shopping thing." I winked, giving him a quick kiss on his lips. "Thanks."

Tyler took the flowers and groceries into the kitchen and sat them on the counter, then walked over toward the staircase and put his duffel on the floor. He decided to spend the night so he could help me unpack. He was considerate like that. He opened doors, held the umbrella over my head if it rained, and made sure that I was comfortable at all times. At first I thought our reunion was too good to be true, that things were moving way too fast. But now I just thanked God for him and this second chance. The last five days had been so wonderful, all except for one thing—we hadn't done the nasty yet!

I know, can you believe it? Me . . . fly ass, always horny as hell, Samantha Elise Baldwin, seriously involved with a man whom I wasn't sleeping with! That was like a cat sitting still while a mouse ran across the floor—it just didn't happen. Emily's mouth nearly dropped to the floor when I told her that Tyler and I hadn't had sex yet. She just assumed that I gave it up to him last Saturday night when I went over to his hotel room. And I couldn't say that I blamed her for coming to that conclusion because that was how I usually rolled. But aside from long, romantic kisses and some serious heavy petting, that was all we had done.

Tyler had been busy with his conference meetings during the day and I was busy visiting my new customers and preparing for my move. When the sun went down, we'd meet up at his hotel, go to a restaurant, eat, and then return to his room where we'd spend hours talking and revealing things to each other. And believe it or not, I was so into our conversations that I didn't think that much about sexing him. Really, I'm not kidding! While we talked he would rub my arm or hold my hand as he listened and asked questions. Just being in his presence was enough to satisfy me. I liked the fact that he saw the real Samantha and accepted me for who I was. But I had to admit, I was ready to get my freak on right about now, and I knew he was, too.

As I looked at Tyler, I wondered if sex with him would be as good as it was in the past. Sometimes things change, but I hoped that particular detail had not. I think he was flowing on my same vibe because when I bent over to pick up a box that was sitting on the dining room floor, he looked at me, licked his lips, and said, "Mmm, I like that position."

I got so turned on I dropped the box back to the floor. I was sprung and we hadn't even done anything. This man made me weak, yet surprisingly strong. I could see the change he'd already made in my life, and it was definitely for the better. Just yesterday Daddy told me that he was happy for me. In the past, I had kept the men I dated as far away from my father as possible, but last weekend I couldn't wait to tell him that Tyler and I were seeing each other again. Daddy really liked Tyler and he was overjoyed that I was with someone whom he considered worthy. I had finally made a good choice, and I was going about things the right way.

As each minute passed, my desire for Tyler grew stronger and stronger. I watched his lean muscles shine with perspiration as he lifted box after box that the movers had carelessly misplaced and carried them to the right room. Looking at him, I knew the time had arrived for us to take care of grown folks' business.

It was approaching dinnertime when the Chinese take-out I ordered finally arrived. We had both worked up an appetite and a serious sweat. Tyler stretched his neck, arched his back, and groaned like he had just fallen down and couldn't get up.

"Sore?" I asked.

"You know it. Between last weekend and today, I'm whupped."

"I can give you a back rub after we eat." I smiled seductively.

His eyes lit up. "That sounds nice."

"But you need to get cleaned up first, you're grungy and funky." I laughed. His shorts were smudged and his T-shirt looked as though he had been playing outside.

Tyler pulled me in close and kissed me on my lips. "As I recall, you like it nice and dirty."

"Mmm, you have a good memory," I purred. I kissed him back, loving the way his lips felt on mine. "I'll just have to hold my nose."

"Okay, I get the hint. I'll get cleaned up before we eat."

I smiled. "I think I'll freshen up, too."

Tyler walked over to the stairs where he had left his overnight bag, then headed up to the guest bathroom as I followed close behind. I strolled down the hall to my spacious master bedroom suite and began to peel off my clothes. I stepped into the shower and turned on the water. The warm stream felt good against my skin. I turned away from the showerhead, closed my eyes, and let the water beat down on my tired shoulders and sore back. I tried not to get my hair wet since I had forgotten to unpack my shower cap. Even though my weave could stand the rain, I knew I'd be too tired to fuss with it tonight. But then again, if I was lucky, maybe I'd be sweating it out with Tyler anyway.

I was about to lather up my netted sponge when I heard a knock on my bathroom door.

"Can I join you?" Tyler called out over the rush of water and foggy steam.

I smiled and slid open the frosted glass shower door, exposing my naked body for him to see. He was naked, too, and the first thing I did was inspect the goods. I'd almost forgotten how scrumptious he looked without clothes. And it was funny because I was used to brothers who were hung, packing a serious load. Tyler wasn't small, but he wasn't large either—and baby, I'm not a fan of the average. But I remembered that he had given me pleasure, and I prayed that my recollection of the past wouldn't fail me in the present.

He stepped into the shower, stood behind me, and poured a handful of my body gel into his palm. He rubbed the sweet-smelling lather over my back, bathing me, massaging me, relaxing me like a professional masseur. I eagerly returned the favor. It felt good to glide my hands over his skin, which was soft and electric to the touch. Our communal bath turned me on so much I didn't even care that my hair had gotten wet. Our erotic shower was complemented by plenty of slow caresses and soft kisses as the water drenched us. We quickly toweled off and headed into my bedroom.

Tyler reached into his bag and took out a box of condoms. He guided me over to the bed and gently laid me down across the fresh sheets that I had put on earlier. "Sam," he whispered into my ear, "I missed you, baby."

He kissed me softly, pressing his body into mine, moving and grinding against me with a smooth rhythm that made me moan with anticipation. His tongue lingered in my mouth, tasting mine as he held me close. "Mmm, you feel good," he moaned. After some intense kissing and sensuous fondling that made me throb between my legs, Tyler slipped on a condom and looked deep into my eyes. I could tell this was going to be some mind-blowing sex and I was ready for it.

Slowly and delicately, Tyler inched his way inside me. His warm body covered mine as he traveled within my inner walls. I lifted my pelvis as he placed his hand under my lower back, holding me in a position exactly where he wanted me to be, allowing me to feel the full brunt of his penetration. He knew how to work what he had.

He kissed my neck and the ball of my shoulder while he kept his stride steady, stroking me with a tenderness that was mixed with a tantalizing combination of hard yet gentle force. He swerved his hips in a sensual rhythm, plunging deeper inside me, pumping me harder as he breathed into my ear.

"Ooohhh, yeah," I panted loudly as he increased his speed. The sex-sweat we were creating made our bodies slick and moist. Nothing had ever felt like this, not even the lovemaking I experienced with him when we used to date. I bit my lower lip and screamed out like a woman in the wild. Tyler grunted with pleasure as he moved in and out of me, filling me with a passion and hunger that made me melt into my mattress.

Then he slowed his rhythm, holding me close to his body as he continued to glide in and out of me, his warm breath teasing my ear, coating the side of my neck. He adjusted his stride and stroked my middle with deep, deliberate, and oh-so-tender thrusts. My lower body shivered when he landed on my magic spot. "That's it," I purred.

"Right here?"

"Yeah, baby. Right there."

Tyler hammered home, making sure to stay in the right zone so he could bring me to orgasm. He moaned softly above my head, enjoying the pleasure just as much as I was. We were in sync. I had been with a lot of men, but none of them had ever made love to me like this. That's what this was—not screwing, not fucking. This was making love.

Afterward, we lay together with me resting my wet head on his chest. I knew I was completely whipped when I let him run his fingers through the tracks of my weave, giving me a scalp massage.

"Sam, can I ask you something?"

"Yes." I could sense that it was going to be a tough question because of his tone. But at the moment I felt so good I was prepared to answer anything he wanted to know.

"Why don't you like being a mother?"

I expected him to ask something like this. Tyler was a smart man and he could read between the lines. He knew that I had had an abortion when I was in college. He knew that my parents had legal guardianship of my son, and before them, Emily had shouldered that responsibility. And he'd also observed that over the last five days I had spent more time with him and Emily than I had with CJ. He didn't judge me for it, but I knew it was something he would eventually question. And frankly, any man would, especially a man like Tyler. Ironically, I was dating someone whose life was dedicated to working with kids.

I thought about his question as I played with the soft, curly hairs on his chest. I had to be honest. "I'm not a good mother," I said.

He stopped massaging my scalp and unhooked his right arm from around me. He turned onto his side and faced me. "Sam, why are you so afraid of connecting with your son?"

"Who says I'm afraid?"

"Your face lights up when you talk about CJ, yet you make excuses not to spend time with him. The other afternoon you made an offhanded comment, something like, 'I'm trying to protect him from me.' I know that your relationship with your mother is messed up, but . . ."

I sat straight up in bed and pointed my finger at him. "Hold on one freakin' minute. You don't know shit about my relationship with my mother or my son. Not everyone grew up with a loving mother like Clair Huxtable, okay!"

"Not everyone grew up with a mother at all," he replied.

I was sorry that I had made such an insensitive comment and I regretted it as soon as it flew out of my big mouth. I was still working on my impulsive tendencies, and I knew that Tyler didn't deserve the bad attitude I was dishing out. He allowed me to be myself and not feel ashamed of my past. But now that he was talking to me about motherhood, I was freaking out. It was a subject I didn't like to discuss for a variety of reasons. But truthfully, what really lit my fuse was the mention of my mother. I'll be damned if she couldn't spoil everything, even a night of great sex.

Tyler sat up in bed beside me. "Sam, I love you. But I'm tellin' you straight up, I'm not gonna let you go off on me and talk shit to me like I'm some kinda punk just because I ask you a tough question."

What? Wait a minute! Back up! Did this man just say that he loved me? Forget that he just called me out and that he was on point with everything he had said. What was more important was that he verbalized the three little words that made every woman's heart beat fast, and mine was racing. No, it was pounding inside my chest.

"If we're going to be together," he continued, "we need to be able to talk about things openly and honestly. I'm not going to judge you. All I want to do is understand you."

There was a pause filled with silence before I spoke. "You love me?" I whispered.

Tyler nodded his head and smiled. "Yes, Sam. I love you."

I threw my arms around him so hard we fell back onto the bed. We laughed and kissed and jostled around on my damp sheets. "Tyler, I love you, too."

He held me on top of him and looked deep into my eyes. "Sam, don't be afraid. You can do anything, and I won't let you fall."

When Tyler kissed me this time, it erased everything. If I had a dollar for every bad decision I'd ever made I'd be a millionaire, and half of that money would come from dealing with Carl alone. I had been involved with so many knuckleheads and, as Gerti would say, shady no-good scoundrels, that I couldn't remember them all. I had been in trouble with my parents, friends, employers, the law . . . you name it. But right now, all those transgressions were wiped clean from my record. I was finally making good choices and I was in as much shock about it as anyone. But there would be no more mistakes from this point forward, 'cause, baby, I was in love!

Chapter 15

Ed . . .

Let's Not Dance Around This

I was standing on the pristine hardwood floors of my daughter's spacious new living room as I watched the movers bring up the last of her boxes. I decided to check in at the office, so I dialed the number to the general line and punched in my passcode. I had already cleared nine calls out of my box an hour ago, most of them consisting of congratulatory praises for the big case I had won last week. I listened and hit Delete as I plowed through each message until I came to the last one.

"Um . . . hi, Ed. This is Emily. Um, can you please give me a call when you get this message . . . I need to talk to you. Thanks," she said before quickly rattling off her number.

I hit Replay three times and listened over and over to Emily's voice as I concentrated on the cadence and inflection of each word she spoke. Although she sounded hesitant and unsure, there was a definite urgency layered in

her softly delivered request. That she wanted to see me
was a thrilling proposition, that she hadn't said why was
an unnerving concern. Emily had never called me for any
reason, not even after the few times that I was bold
enough to extend the invitation in case she ever needed
anything. So I wondered why she was contacting me now.

I hadn't spoken to or seen her since last Saturday
when she moved into her new house. I wondered if the
reason behind her call had anything to do with the connection we made. Many thoughts rushed through my
mind, but I knew I wouldn't find the answers to my questions standing in Sam's living room. I was normally very
good at keeping my composure, but many things about
Emily could throw me off my game—like the simple
sound of her voice. Sam sensed that something was
wrong by the look on my face.

"Daddy, is everything okay?"

I put my BlackBerry back in its holster and tried to
appear casual. "Something came up at the office," I lied.
"Sorry, kiddo, I've got to get back down there so I can
handle a situation that just came up."

"It must be pretty serious."

"Nothing I can't handle."

I walked out of my daughter's door, wanting to believe my words.

I dialed Emily's number and listened as it rang into
my Bluetooth. I was behind the wheel of my truck, making a right onto Sixteenth Street, headed toward Springwood Preparatory School. I had a feeling that whatever
she wanted to discuss, it needed to be face-to-face. I was
convinced after the fourth ring that my call was going to
land in her mailbox, and just as I'd given up on a live
voice, she answered.

"Hello," she whispered.

"Good morning, Emily. It's Ed."

"Oh, um . . . hi, Ed. Thanks for calling me back."

She sounded tentative and her voice was so low I could barely hear her.

"I got your message, is everything okay?" I asked.

"Hold on for a minute, I'm going to get my teacher's aide to take over."

I could hear the chatter of students slowly fade into the background and the sound of her breathing pattern change as she walked down the hall for privacy. I tried to picture what she was wearing. Whatever it was, I knew she looked beautiful in it. "Is this a bad time?" I asked, hoping it wasn't. I needed to know what was going on.

"No, I just left my classroom. I can talk now."

I turned onto a side street and parked my truck so I could concentrate, anticipating what she was going to say next. I took a deep breath and remained silent. If you allow someone who's withholding information the opportunity to speak without interruption, they will eventually, and unknowingly, give you the answers you're looking for without you having to ask. So I listened as Emily struggled to speak.

"I know you're very busy, and I apologize for intruding upon your time," she began, "but I need to talk to you about something, and it's not exactly a phone conversation."

I felt a smile come to my lips as I spoke. "Is this about you and me?"

"Um, it's complicated." Her voice sounded low again.

I could see that I was going to have to work for the answers I wanted. "When and where can I meet you?"

"Hmm, uh . . ."

I knew that her trepidation came from the thought of

meeting with me in closed quarters. We'd have to meet on neutral ground, so I made a suggestion to put her at ease. "I can pick up CJ this afternoon and we can meet in one of the conference rooms."

"I have after-school duty, can you come a little early?" she said, sounding relieved.

"I can do whatever you like."

From that moment forward my day unfolded like mental torture. I couldn't get Emily or our brief conversation out of my mind. I was a fifty-four-year-old, grown-ass man, acting like a schoolkid toying with the question—she loves me, she loves me not. At one point around lunchtime I got so frustrated I couldn't even concentrate on the brief in front of me. I wanted so badly for three o'-clock to roll around so I could see Emily. Gerti always picked CJ up from school, but I called and let her know that today I was doing the honors.

At a little after two, I told my secretary that I was leaving. I arrived at the school in record time and could have probably driven here with my eyes closed. Both Jeffery and Sam had attended Springwood, and I had been on its board of directors for the last few years. My long association made me intimately familiar with the school and its layout, so I parked my truck in the lot around back that was reserved for the head administrators.

I had called Emily when I left my office and told her to meet me in the Lowery Conference Room, which was the smallest and least used meeting room in the building. It would give us the privacy we needed. When I opened the door to the stately, wood-paneled room, she was already there.

I had hoped to arrive early enough to gather myself before we met, but my ten-minute cushion couldn't match her promptness. Emily was more time-conscious than anyone I knew. Over the years, I often heard Sam speak of Emily's money-in-the-bank punctuality, and how if it hadn't been for her best friend, Sam would have slept through nearly every exam she had when they were in college.

Slowly, I closed the door behind me and took a moment to appraise her. Even though I could only see her from the waist up, she was so beautiful the rest didn't matter. No woman should possess the ability to completely capture a man the way she did me, but she had that power. And the irony was that she didn't even know it, but if she did, I knew she wouldn't abuse it.

Emily was sitting in a high-back chair near the head of the conference table, sifting through a small stack of papers. She looked up at me and smiled nervously. I smiled back, but no words were exchanged between us as I entered the room. Instead of taking a seat opposite her, or at the head of the conference table where she cleared her papers and motioned for me to sit, I pulled out the chair directly beside her, unbuttoned my jacket, and settled in close. She didn't move her chair to put distance between us, which surprised me. She simply sat there, darting her eyes from me to the wall and then back to me again. I knew I needed to start slow and then ease my way toward getting to the bottom of what had prompted her message. "It's good to see you," I said, smiling to let her know how much I meant it.

She blushed, and it made me want to kiss her. "It's good to see you, too."

We engulfed the silence in the room, waiting to see who would speak first. I took the lead. "So . . . what you wanted to talk about is complicated?"

She took a deep breath and ran her delicate, clear-painted nails through her shiny black hair. My eyes zeroed in on her, watching her every movement as she returned her hands to her lap, resting her palms on top of her skirt. "Why are you doing that?" she asked.

"What? Staring at you?" I knew I'd been caught.

"Yes, why are you staring at me like that?"

"Why are you answering my question with a question?"

There was silence again.

"Emily, let's not dance around this." I moved my chair closer to hers and hoped she wouldn't move away and that no one would come in and interrupt us. The angels were smiling down on me because neither happened, so I proceeded. "Did you want to talk about the feelings we obviously have for each other?"

She looked at me for a long moment. "No," she said. "I want to warn you."

For the next ten minutes I listened as Emily told me the most harebrained story I'd ever heard. Something about spirits and soothsayers. She was such a trusting and good-hearted person, but her naïveté startled me. She rambled on for a few more minutes about a mysterious friend of hers with *the gift* who had warned her about impending danger.

"My friend told me to keep the ones I love close," Emily said in a whisper. Suddenly, her eyes flashed with panic as they landed on mine before darting back down to her papers. She fidgeted in her seat.

I could see from her sudden nervousness that she hadn't meant to say that last part. "You want to keep the ones you love close to you, that's why you wanted to talk to me?"

"I needed to warn you to be careful."

"Emily . . ."

"Ed, I can see by your expression that you don't believe in premonitions." She sighed, gathering her papers as she placed them into the tote bag beside her chair. "I know you think this is all so silly. I apologize for my hasty call, but it was prompted out of concern. I'm sorry that I intruded upon your valuable time with this," she said, sounding deeply remorseful in her always warm and gentle tone.

I cleared my throat. "You're right, I don't give much credence to psychics."

"People who have the gift of prophecy aren't psychics."

"Excuse me." I nodded. "I don't give much credence to that kind of thinking, but that's not really the point. And the warning that your friend gave you isn't the point either, nor is the fact that you said you called me in haste. The point is that you want to keep the people you love close to you." I paused, lowering my voice to a slow and soft whisper. "You want to keep me close." I leaned back in my chair and hoped she wouldn't leave me hanging.

Emily's back stiffened. "Um, I have to go," she said abruptly, looking down at her watch. "I should've been in my classroom five minutes ago."

I put my hand on the arm of her chair and leaned forward, sitting so close I could smell her sweet skin and feel her warm breath. If I bent my head at an angle our lips would touch. She didn't move and I didn't back down. I could feel the heat rising between our bodies. When she breathed out, I breathed in, exchanging the air between us. Her heart was racing, and I could see it through the rise and fall of her breasts beneath her cotton blouse. "Emily, I know this is difficult for you, it's difficult for me, too. But we can't keep dodging the obvious."

"CJ's waiting for you and I need to go to my classroom," she said, pushing her chair back, disengaging from the intensity of the moment as she rose to her feet.

I could see the anxiety on her face. I took a deep

breath as I rose from my chair, following suit. "Emily, I'm sorry if I've made you uncomfortable."

She bit down on her lower lip. "You're an honest and good man, Ed. You have nothing to be sorry about. In a perfect world things would be different. But we're in this . . . this situation."

"We don't have to be."

"But we are."

"Things could be different."

"There are rules," she whispered.

"Rules? Whose rules?"

"Unspoken rules that we live by. Rules that have kept us from making a mistake."

I took a step forward, moving even closer to her so that our bodies slightly touched. "Rules are broken every day," I said.

"And so are people's lives, and it's usually at the hands of those who break the rules."

I was beginning to wonder who was the litigator here, Emily or me. She was good, and she made a hell of an argument. But I knew what I wanted, and now I knew without a doubt that she wanted the same thing, too. This breakthrough, albeit not the way I had pictured it, was worth the cost of laboring through her story about spirits and prophecies.

This was what I had been waiting eleven years for, so I relaxed my body and reminded my big head to look at the larger picture. I knew that patience was a virtue, and lucky for me, I was a patient man. I knew this wasn't the time or place for revelations beyond what we had just shared. There would be another opportunity, of this I was sure, so I let it go. Again, I could feel Emily's relief.

We walked toward the door, our bodies close, still lightly touching, and it felt better than any courtroom victory. We headed down the long hallway to Emily's class as several students ran up to her.

"Bye, Ms. Snow. See you tomorrow," a freckled face little boy said as he grinned like Emily had just given him a year's worth of allowance. I smiled because it was the way CJ grinned at her, too, and so did I. But unlike the young boys, I had mastered the art of hiding it.

"How's Samantha's move going?" Emily asked out of the blue. She had changed the subject, returning to her safe world of structured rules.

"Just fine. Tyler's over there helping her. And because she doesn't have much furniture she'll be settled in fairly quickly."

"Hey, Papa!" CJ yelled as he ran up to me from his classroom down the hall.

I bent down and rubbed the top of his head the way I did his mother's when she was his age. "What'cha know good, sport? How was your day?"

"Good!"

Emily smiled. "I guess it was. I heard that someone got a gold star for his perfect handwriting today. I wonder who that was?"

"Me!" CJ shouted, smiling with pride. "Auntie Emee, are you coming home with us?"

I looked at Emily as she answered. "No, CJ. I'm staying here for the after-school program, and then I'm going home to my house."

"Can I come to your house, too?" CJ asked, then turned to me. "Papa, you promised I could go to Auntie Emee's new house."

"Yes, I did. But you have to be invited first. Once you receive a proper invitation, I'll take you over anytime your aunt Emily says it's okay." I smiled.

CJ turned and looked at Emily as if to say, *Hey, where's my E-vite?*

Emily paused for a moment, then looked directly at me as she spoke to CJ. "It's not that I haven't wanted to extend the invitation, it's just that the timing hasn't been right. But now that it's out there, you're welcome to come over anytime."

CJ and I both smiled, but for vastly different reasons.

Chapter 16

Brenda . . .

NY Jewelry Store

Brenda smiled with satisfaction as she looked down at her feet. She was at Saks Fifth Avenue, trying on a bronze-colored pair of Valentino pumps. She loved the way the shoe enhanced the curve of her slender legs. "I think I'll take these," she said to the young salesgirl, not bothering to look in her direction. She stepped out of the beautiful $1,200 pair of shoes and back into her own equally stylish ones. "I'll meet you at the counter," she instructed before strutting away to make her purchase.

Brenda was delighted that after several weeks of shopping she had finally found the perfect pair of shoes to complement the one-of-a-kind dress she planned to wear to the party she was throwing tomorrow night. Initially, she was worried that Samantha might turn the elegant affair she was planning into a giant mockery. But from the moment she managed to persuade Emily to stay with them while her house was being renovated, all her worries were put to rest.

Emily was going to share top billing in the birthday celebration, which would make Samantha behave because she wouldn't want to spoil things for her best friend. Brenda knew that as determined to humiliate her as Samantha seemed to be, she was equally determined to do whatever it took to make Emily happy, especially after the pain she had suffered since her mother's death.

Brenda desperately wished that Samantha could be more like her best friend. Emily was responsible, exercised good judgment, and displayed perfect manners. She was hardworking and carried herself in a way that commanded respect. She never used foul language or raised her voice above an acceptable volume in public. She always adhered to the principles of time, never arriving late as Samantha always did. And even though her sense of style drifted toward the bohemian flavor, it was forgivable because she managed to pull it off with a hint of elegance. Unlike Samantha, Emily possessed a natural beauty that didn't require artificial enhancement.

Emily was the kind of daughter that Brenda had always longed for. She often thought about the cruel hand that life had dealt her. If circumstances had been different and had the stars been aligned just right, Emily would be her child instead of Samantha. Because as fate would have it, both girls were born on the same day. But Brenda knew that she couldn't lament over what could have been, which was why she was determined to guide Samantha toward a lifestyle more befitting a daughter of hers.

Brenda smiled to herself when she thought about the party, which was going to help her accomplish her goals. The first and most daunting goal was to usher Samantha back into the DC social scene and hopefully nab her a suitable husband in the process. Her second goal was to win a coveted position on the executive board of the Rock Creek Family Support Collaborative, one of the city's most notable charities. Brenda knew she possessed all the criteria that the board required. However, she needed to show her giving, selfless side beyond the sizeable donations that she and Ed made each year. And yet again, that was where Emily came in.

Brenda planned to demonstrate her generosity by the fact that she had opened up her home to a grief-stricken young woman who had just lost her mother to a debilitating disease and needed a place to stay. And going a step further, she had been instrumental in helping the poor girl find a good job. And if that weren't enough, she was making her a guest of honor at a birthday celebration that would also serve as an event to raise money for charity. Brenda knew those acts of kindness would surely impress the organization's board chair.

And Brenda's last but certainly not least important goal was to one-up Juanita Presley. She was apoplectic that the success of Juanita's party had netted another feather in her enemy's cap. Brenda thought that Juanita was the most egotistical, self-centered, and disingenuous person she knew. She flaunted her unearned good fortune as though it were her supreme entitlement. It made Brenda furious that everyone seemed to gravitate toward Juanita's fake charm instead of seeing the woman for who she really was—a social-climbing shrew!

But it wasn't just their rivalry that made Brenda determined to rise above her nemesis, it was a matter of family. Brenda was livid about the fact that Dorothy, her own sister and only true friend in the world, acted as though she and Juanita shared the same bloodline. Even though Juanita had managed to sucker Dorothy, Brenda refused to let her win in any other area.

For Brenda, everything was about style and competition. She learned at an early age that in order to get what she wanted, she had to devise a strategy. In society's pecking order there were always people at the top who made the rules, and people at the bottom who followed them. She had plotted all her life to make sure that she was one of the people standing at the top, and that she stayed there.

Although birth order had relegated her to the bottom ranking in her household growing up, Brenda had used it as an advantage to get what she wanted. Before she could even crawl, she had figured out that a small pout of her dainty lips or a perfectly executed quiver of her adorable chin could elicit oohs and aahs that caused her parents, siblings, and other relatives to give her whatever her little heart desired. As she grew older and lost her cuddly baby appeal, she mastered the next stage of development in the art of manipulation. During her teenage years she embraced her picture-perfect, girl-next-door good looks and tastefully developed sense of style to influence and persuade people to give her what she wanted.

Brenda prided herself on being clever and resourceful, efficient and calculating. In addition to her natural physical beauty, it was those qualities that she attributed to her landing a husband like Ed. Ed was the prized catch in their social set, and from the time they were small children in Jack and Jill, she had set her sights on becoming his wife. There were other boys in their circle who were poised to be successful professionals with prominent careers, but Brenda saw early on that Ed's potential far surpassed the rest, and she was determined to land him.

She sat back, watched, and waited as Ed had his fill of the young beauties who clamored for his attention. They were much like she was, well-cultured girls from some of the best families in the city. But she wasn't concerned because she possessed something they didn't—a strategic plan.

During their senior year of college, after Ed had run through as many coeds as she cared to tolerate, Brenda decided that it was time to settle him down and stake her claim. She studied his ways, took her time learning about the things that were important to him, and paid close attention to the causes he championed. And even though none of his interests seemed to mirror her own, she aligned herself with them for the sake of winning his heart.

The final stage in her well-orchestrated plan was sex. Brenda withheld physical intimacy until Ed nearly begged her on bended knee. It was then that she knew she was going to be the one on top, literally. She'd cultivated an arsenal of sexual skills through secret summer rendezvous on Martha's Vineyard. She picked boys who came up to the resort for summer work because she knew they had no social standing, thus removing the threat of a trail which could lead back to her group and damage her reputation. After several summers of hot and heavy action, Brenda knew that she was skilled, and when the time was right she'd make Ed forget about all the other women he'd been with.

Finally, after months of dating and waiting, Brenda allowed Ed the privilege of sleeping with her. "You're my first. This is so special for me," she told him. She didn't show him all that she knew at once because her expertise would have been a dead giveaway. Instead, she rationed her abilities in small doses until she knew he was wrapped in her web.

But she soon discovered a problem she hadn't anticipated. The skills that she thought she owned were some of the same moves that Ed had experienced countless times with other women, and he told her as much one night during a heated confrontation. They had just finished making love in his off-campus apartment, and he was driving her back to her dorm room when the drama began.

"Brenda, I care about you, you know that. But I'm not ready to make a commitment of marriage," Ed told her as he parked his car in front of her dormitory. "After graduation I'm heading to law school this fall. There are things I need to do before I settle down and start a family."

Brenda sat in the passenger seat of Ed's brand-new red Mustang convertible, an early graduation gift from his parents, and seethed with anger at his reaction to the ultimatum she'd just issued—marry me or lose me! She knew she had to snag him before he entered law school, otherwise all bets were off. "You don't want to settle down because you want to sow your wild oats," she said above soft sobs. "You don't love me."

"Brenda, c'mon. We've been through this a thousand times."

"How could you, Ed?" Brenda sobbed harder. "I went against my upbringing and slept with you before marriage. You were my first and only, and now you want to just toss me to the side. And for what? Suzanne Jones?"

Suzanne Jones was a radical young feminist from San Francisco. The tall, dark, and lovely coed sported a perfectly coiffed six-inch afro and had managed to catch Ed's eye . . . and Brenda took notice.

"This has nothing to do with Suzanne," Ed sighed. "This is about me and what I want for my life."

"You're saying you don't want me?"

"I'm saying I don't want to get married right now."

"Same thing." Brenda pouted.

"Whatever."

"That's all you have to say to me?"

Ed gripped the steering wheel. "It's late and I've got an early-morning class. I'll walk you to the front door."

"Haven't I been a great girlfriend to you?" Brenda continued. "I've fulfilled every fantasy you could ever imagine, in and out of bed. You've never had it so good!"

Ed let out a smirk followed by a small chuckle.

Now Brenda was pissed. "What're you laughing about?" she asked, raising her voice.

"Brenda, let's just drop it."

"No, I want to know what that little smirk was all about."

"No, you don't."

"Yes, I do!"

"Brenda, trust me. You really don't want to know what just crossed my mind, so why don't you let me walk you to your door and we'll call it a night."

Brenda was furious. "Be a *man,* Ed. Tell me the truth!" she spat out, knowing her challenge would spark a reaction—and it did.

Ed turned in his leather bucket seat and looked straight into Brenda's eyes. "The truth is that I've had all kinds of women, all kinds of ways. So when you sit there and tell me that I've never had it so good I have to laugh, because quite frankly I have, many times."

Brenda wanted to scream at the top of her lungs and slap Ed across his face, but there was a small group of underclassmen that had just gathered out front and she refused to let them know that she and her boyfriend were arguing. So instead of causing a scene, she let Ed walk her to the front door of her building, then gave him a small kiss on the cheek to make the onlookers jealous before bidding him good night. Once she was inside her room she burst into rage-filled tears, throwing every object on her dresser to the floor. "He just said those hurtful things to get back at me because I challenged his manhood," she reasoned aloud. "How could any other woman possibly compare to me!"

After she calmed down, she put Ed's foolish slip out of her mind and didn't spend another moment thinking about the other women who had come before her. She wasn't concerned about them because again, she had something they didn't—a strategy. And this time her plan was already in motion, thanks to the fetus growing inside her womb with Ed's name on it.

For the last thirty-two years her plan had worked. Now, as Brenda admired her newly purchased designer shoes, she was confident that her next set of goals would come to fruition.

She smiled to herself as she watched the sales associate tuck her expensive purchase into the black-and-white shopping bag. "And to think that I wasted my time in New York looking for the perfect pair of shoes when they were right here waiting for me all along," she said to the sales associate who swiped her platinum card. Then her mind turned to Harry Winston and the night they had shared during her stay in New York. He had given her a type of pleasure that she hadn't experienced in a very long time. Until now, only Ed had been able to truly satisfy her, but Harry had matched him.

As Brenda walked out of the store and into the hot summer sun with her new shoes in hand, she experienced a jolt of excitement just thinking about her next encounter with Harry. She slid into the seat of her freshly washed Mercedes, pulled out her cell phone, and hit *NY Jewelry Store* on her speed dial. "Well, hello," she purred in a low, seductive voice when Harry answered.

"Brenda, I'm glad you called. Are we still on for next weekend?"

Brenda's mind flashed back to the steamy passion they had shared during their night of wanton pleasure. She wouldn't miss another chance to be with him for all the Valentino pumps on Saks' shelves. "Of course," she chirped enthusiastically. "I'm looking forward to seeing you again."

"Are you sure you can't make it up this weekend? I'm off tomorrow and we could spend the entire day together."

The idea of lying in bed with Harry was deliciously appealing, but Brenda knew she had to stay focused on her goals. As good a lover as Harry was, he couldn't match the items on her list, which included a prestigious board position and further notoriety in her social circle. "I wish I could, but I have relatives coming into town that I haven't seen in years," Brenda lied, not wanting him to know all of her business. After all, even though he was handsome, kind, and amazing in bed, he was just a fling.

"I understand. Family is important and I'm glad you value that," Harry said in a sincere tone.

"Yes, family is all that matters."

They talked a few minutes longer, flirting and reminiscing about their passionate night together before they ended their call.

Brenda was glad that she had the good forethought to volunteer on the planning committee for her sorority's spring cotillion. It was the perfect excuse for staying out until the wee hours of the morning. And once she was confirmed on the board of directors for the Rock Creek Family Support Collaborative, she would have all the more reason to be absent from home with good cause. Harry was only a quick train ride away, and she intended to use that time for their secret trysts.

Brenda smiled as she steered her car into her garage and walked through her beautifully landscaped flower garden. In twenty-four hours her backyard would be the scene of one of the most lavish social events of the season, and she couldn't wait. All of her plans were working out, and she gave herself a pat on the back for orchestrating such a wonderful life.

Chapter 17

Emily . . .

Dangerously Sexy and Bold

It was naptime, and the kids were resting peacefully on their mats. This was the only quiet time I had during the course of my workday, so I usually tried to make the most of it. I charted out lesson plans, graded papers, and caught up on the e-mails I received from parents, other faculty, and staff. But today I did none of those things. I spent my quiet time daydreaming about Ed. I hadn't been able to get him off my mind since he showed up here yesterday afternoon.

We met in one of the small conference rooms that was rarely used. I made sure that I arrived early because I knew I'd need the extra time to gather my thoughts. I was determined not to make any slips and vowed that I would keep my composure. I was going to control my emotions and mask my wanting. I even practiced what I was going to say to him. But the brilliant pep talk I'd given myself had been useless because when Ed walked into the room I lost all train of thought.

Discreetly, I admired his polished navy suit, crisp white shirt, and pewter gray tie. His broad shoulders were impressive and perfectly squared, allowing his jacket to drape him as though he was born in it. Ed's sense of style was impeccable, and his aura was dangerously sexy and bold. I wanted and loved everything about him. And although I knew I shouldn't have, I allowed myself to relish in the wonderful scent of his Bulgari cologne as he settled into the chair beside me.

Ever since those intense moments we shared last weekend during my move, I knew we were inching closer toward the feelings that had been simmering for years. But I was still hesitant to embrace it because there was so much at stake. It was ironic that our happiness would ultimately result in someone else's pain, or as Ruben had foretold, something deadly.

After I told Ed the real reason for my call, I was almost sorry I shared it with him. Thank goodness I opted not to use Ruben's name because Ed lumped my story about people with *the gift,* and Ruben's premonition, into the category of nut jobs similar to the con artists on late-night infomercials. He didn't think much of the whole idea, and at one point it crossed my mind that he might once again suggest the name of a good therapist I could visit.

Nonetheless, I was glad I got it off my chest. I passed my test and was ready to leave the room, but Ed flipped things around, shifting the dynamics and the mood. He scooted his chair close to mine, leaned over, and started questioning me about why I wanted to warn *him* in particular. My motive was obvious and there was no denying my feelings.

"Those I love," I had said. I gave myself away when I

let those three little words slip from my tongue, and there was no secret tunnel that could lead me out of where I had gone. I knew it, he knew it, and the familiar heat that rose between our bodies confirmed it. We expressed our feelings for each other without using words. Our truth was suspended in the way I looked at him, the way he inhaled the air around me, and the way my chest pounded when he sat so close I could literally feel him. It was all around us, and it felt glorious and frightening all at once.

Sitting here in my classroom, I continued to daydream about Ed, somehow making it through until the last bell signaled the end of the school day. As one part of my life was about to end, another was set to begin. It was Friday afternoon, the beginning of the weekend. And not just any weekend, it was my birthday weekend. Tomorrow was the big day. At approximately five fourteen in the morning, I planned to kiss my twenties good-bye and welcome my thirties in with open arms.

Samantha and I had spent every birthday together since we were nineteen. No matter where we were or what we were doing, we made sure we were together on our shared day. And because we would be spending this year at a party that neither of us wanted to attend, we decided to celebrate tonight. But that was before Tyler came back on the scene. When Samantha called me earlier today to confirm our date, I told her that we could hang out at another time. I knew she wanted to spend as much time with Tyler as she could before he returned to Atlanta. But she insisted that we keep our dinner date.

"We can have dinner next week," I told her. "You and Tyler need to spend time together while you can. Besides, we'll see each other tomorrow night at our party."

"Emily, I don't know why you're trippin'," Samantha said. "Men can come and go, but a true girlfriend, a sister, can never be replaced. Tyler and I can spend time together after I get home. Tonight, you and I are gonna have some good drinks and a great time."

She was the best friend I could ever have. "Samantha, I love you! Thanks for sacrificing your evening with Tyler just to hang out with little ol' me."

"Girl, *no man* will ever come between us."

My palms sweated as my mind flashed to images of Ed. I hoped Samantha would remember those words because I had a feeling they would be tested sooner than she thought.

Chapter 18

Samantha . . .

A Big Mistake

I woke up this morning feeling as if I was on a cloud. But it wasn't because today was the start of the weekend, or because it was one day away from my birthday. I was floating because Tyler and I had confessed our love for each other and had spent the last six days making up for the last six years. He cooked me breakfast from the groceries he picked up yesterday. I tried to help, but ended up burning the toast. He said it was okay, scraped off the black crusty parts, and slathered on some jam. He was so sweet.

After we ate, Tyler headed over to the convention center for his final day of meetings and I called Emily to give her the skinny on my evening. She couldn't talk long because she had to start her class, but she was just as happy for me as I was for myself. She even wanted me to cancel our pre-birthday celebration tonight so I could spend time with Tyler. She was one of the most considerate people I knew. But I told her no way. As many times as she'd been there for me, I wouldn't dream of leaving her hanging. We had a true friendship. Even though her love life was in the toilet, she was ecstatic that I had finally reunited with the man of my dreams. It's hard to find people who want more for you than they have for themselves.

After we finished our conversation I got dressed and prepared to start my day. I was on my way out the door for a sales call to my new client at Bloomingdale's when I heard my cell phone ring. I usually ignored calls that came in unknown, but for some reason I decided to pick up. "Hello?" I said. I could hear the person breathing on the other end, but they didn't say anything. I was about to hang up just as I heard Carl's voice.

"You got everything moved in?" he asked.

I had blocked his number to avoid his calls, but now he'd circumvented that. It was something he was good at. He must have been calling on one of those pre-paid, nontraceable phones. Two years ago when he had to "get ghost" for a few months until some trouble blew over, his cousin, Ronnie, delivered one of those nondescript phones to me so Carl and I could communicate.

I prayed that Carl would just go away, but I knew that would never happen because even though we weren't good at it, we were parents, and our son would always keep us in each other's lives. But with all that said, I didn't have time for Carl's drama, especially since things had been going so well in my life without him. "Why do you keep calling me?" I asked.

"Why you got that chump all up in yo crib?"

I was silent for a moment.

"You fuckin' ol' boy or what?"

I put my handbag down, eased over to the window,

and peered through my miniblinds. My face grew hot with anger when I saw Carl's shiny black Escalade parked directly across the street. "What the hell are you doing? Spying on me?" I yelled through the phone.

"Answer my fuckin' question."

"I don't have to answer shit. This is my house and my life, and I'll have whoever I want in both!"

"You makin' a big mistake, Sam. A big mistake," he said calmly.

Just then it occurred to me that Carl hadn't raised his voice once, not even when he cursed at me. I knew him well, and this was very strange and very wrong, so I decided to come at him a different way. "Listen, Carl. I don't want any trouble with you. We had some good times while they lasted, but now it's over. All I want to do is be happy and get on with my life. Please let me do that."

As if from out of nowhere, Carl flew into a rage, just like he did last month at the restaurant. "That new crib you got and that new life you tryin' to lead can be over befo' yo ass can blink," he yelled into the phone.

Oh, hell no! This fool had the nerve to threaten me for a second time. I was so pissed I forgot about trying to play nice. I had to bring this nonsense to a stop. "If you think you can make idle threats and get away with it, you've got another think coming. How about I blink my ass right over to the police station and let them know that Carl Tyrone Thomas of 1003 South Place just communicated a verbal threat to me and—"

The next thing I heard was silence on my end of the phone and the sound of Carl's tires speeding away outside. I watched as his truck made a right turn at the end of my block before he disappeared from sight.

I sank down onto my coach, slightly shaken. Just when I thought my life was finally headed in the right direction, a monkey wrench was thrown into the mix. "Well, I can't do anything sitting here on this couch," I said aloud. I gathered my handbag, put on my game face, and hit the door.

After Carl's threatening phone call I went to see my clients like a good corporate employee, completed my paperwork, and sent e-mails to several new customers. Then, after I finished taking care of business, I headed to the police station. I was intent on getting Carl out of my life once and for all. But as I sat in my car, ready to go inside to file my complaint, a wave of second thoughts suddenly bombarded me. I knew that if I led the police to Carl's door he'd be furious and would retaliate in some way. The police were to Carl what doughnuts were to fashion models—the unthinkable! He was the only criminal I knew who'd never had the slightest brush with the law. It was an amazing feat, considering the fact that he was a black man who sold drugs for a living.

I wasn't sure what he would do to get back at me because he had been acting so strange and unpredictable lately. But what I did know was that Carl was very capable of starting some real shit, and he would probably try to drag Tyler into it. The thought made my stomach queasy. Then a more disturbing realization popped into my head, one that I had completely forgotten. Carl had a few officers in his pocket whom he paid to make his problems go away, one of the reasons why he'd never had trouble with the law. I remembered hearing his cousin, Ronnie, casually tell him that a few of their guys on the inside were going to need a little increase in order to keep looking the other way. At the time I pretended that I didn't understand what they meant. But growing up in a house that was ruled by the law, I knew the real deal.

I had to admit that I was a little worried because my initial theory was probably right. Carl might be using his own supply. What else could it be? Other than a woman, the only things that could make a man lose his mind, act irrational, and spin completely out of control were the loss of money or the use of drugs. And because Carl had plenty of loot and a few hoochies tucked away on the side to keep him happy, it had to be the drugs. If that was the case, this was a situation from which the police couldn't protect me. Being around Carl over the years had taught me that much. So I pulled out my phone and hit Emily on speed dial.

"Hey, Samantha, what's—"

"What time will you be home?" I asked, cutting her off.

"In about ten minutes. Why, what's wrong? Did you change your mind about going out tonight?"

I could hear the concern in Emily's voice, but I didn't want to go into too much over the phone. "I'm on my way to your place now and I'll tell you when I get there."

I hung up the phone, flipped on my turn signal, and headed straight to Emily's house.

"This is what I was worried about when we spoke the other night," Emily said to me. "Samantha, you've got to go to the authorities. Carl is dangerous, and the police can protect you from him."

We were sitting on Emily's cushiony soft sofa. The aromatic smell of patchouli-scented candles and the soothing effect of her sienna-colored walls made me almost forget about my troubles. I took a sip of my Coke and shook my head. My naïve best friend still didn't understand, even after I had explained everything to her.

"The police have been trying to pin something on Carl for years but nothing ever sticks, and you know why?" I said, pausing as Emily looked on with anxiety. "Because Carl has officers in his pocket. If I file a complaint against him they'll be dialing his cell before I walk out the door."

Emily sat her cup of green tea on the coffee table in front of us, shaking her head with worry. "There's got to be something you can do."

"There is, I just haven't figured it out yet."

"I knew it. This is the danger that Ruben spoke of. It's got to be."

"What're you talking about?"

Emily tucked her legs under her hips, adjusting into a more comfortable position as she began to tell me about the premonition that Ruben had shared with her. Before I met Emily, I'd never heard of people with *the gift*, but where she grew up it wasn't uncommon for people to claim to have the power to see into the future and talk with spirits. It must be a Southern thing. In the city we called them psychics or scam artists. I remembered during our freshmen year of college, Emily told me about an old woman in her neighborhood who possessed such powers. I thought it was a crock of shit, but you couldn't convince my girl that the woman wasn't legit.

I loved Emily to death, but right now I couldn't get sucked into her or Ruben's supernatural foolishness. I had real-life issues to deal with. "Emily, I know you believe in that crap, but I don't. Yes, Carl is dangerous, and yes, he's been acting strange lately. But I honestly don't think he'd bring physical harm to me."

"What makes you so sure? Samantha, he threatened you!"

"When it comes to me, Carl is all talk. If he really wanted to hurt me he would've done it this morning after Tyler left. But he didn't. Instead, he called me up and talked shit. He's just jealous and he's having a hard time dealing with the fact that I'm finally moving on for good this time."

Emily let out a deep breath. "This doesn't sound good. Carl could fly into a fit of rage and snap, then you'd be six feet under."

"He's not going to kill me."

"Didn't he tell you that your life could be over before you could blink?"

I sighed. "His threats are just that, threats. I know that Carl is capable of a lot of things, but he'd never physically harm me. His ego is bruised because I rejected him, but he'll eventually get over it. I just have to make sure that he doesn't start any drama in the meantime."

"I don't think you should take his threats lightly," Emily said.

I nodded, full of lukewarm confidence. "I understand your concern, but trust me on this. Besides, once I mentioned that I would file a police report, you should've seen how fast he made tracks trying to get as far away from me as he could. He's got a few officers on the take, but not all of them."

"Samantha, I warned you to be careful around Carl when I first got here, and now Ruben has predicted that someone I love is in serious danger and could lose their life. That someone has to be you, and I'm very afraid."

I patted Emily's arm, trying to calm her—and myself. "Don't worry about a thing. You've been through a lot this year and I don't want you upset at a time that we should both be celebrating. I'm sorry I even mentioned this nonsense."

"It's not nonsense, Samantha. I don't think you understand how serious this is."

"What I understand is that tomorrow we'll be entering into an exciting new phase of our lives, and we're going to celebrate with each other like we always do, in spite of my mother's ridiculous party. And I understand that you haven't been laid in months and I'm going to make sure that you meet somebody fine at the party who can rock your world!"

Slowly, I was able to get a smile out of Emily and then a laugh. I changed the subject, teasing her until we both howled. It felt good to laugh after having such a shitty day. I thought about how things had gone downhill since breakfast, and I hoped this evening would make up for it.

Chapter 19

Emily . . .

I Didn't Want to Test It

I changed into an outfit more appropriate for a night out on the town. I was usually the designated driver, but it was unanimous that both Samantha and I needed to drown our sorrows and continue our laughs over heavy doses of margaritas. We knew that after a night of drinking we would have to find alternate transportation, and because she lived closer to the Metro, we got in her car and headed to her place. When we walked through her door, Tyler was already there.

"Hey, hon, how did your last meeting go?" Samantha asked as she leaned over and gave Tyler a kiss on his lips.

I made a mental note that she must have given him a key. This was an unbelievable development because Samantha didn't go for that. I remembered she told me once, "Girl, giving a man a key to your place is like asking for trouble. No man will ever be able to unlock my door unless there's a ring on this finger." Funny how time could change things.

As I watched them, it occurred to me that no one would ever believe that Samantha and Tyler had reconnected just last week. They looked like your typical married couple who greeted each other at the end of a long day. Tyler was stretched out on the coach, typing on his laptop while eyeing ESPN on Samantha's large plasma TV.

"You ladies ready for your night out on the town?" Tyler asked.

"We sure are." Samantha smiled. "I'm gonna change and I'll be back in a sec."

Samantha walked upstairs to her bedroom and I made myself comfortable on the other end of the couch from where Tyler sat. I really liked him. I knew Tyler through the wonderful things that Samantha told me about him when they first dated, and also through his association with my former student, Alexandria, the little girl with *the gift*. Ironically, Tyler was Alexandria's godfather, and much like Samantha and me, he and Alexandria's mother had been best friends since college. After Alexandria's father's heart attack, Tyler had stepped in, dropping her off and picking her up from school for a solid month until her parents resumed their normal schedule. I knew then that he was the kind of man Samantha needed in her life.

"Emily, I'm really sorry to hear about your mother," Tyler said, transferring his laptop to the coffee table. "I know what it's like to lose your parents. So if you ever need to talk, just give me a ring. Sam can give you my number."

I smiled and nodded. "Thanks, Tyler. I really appreciate that."

My friend just might get that ring sooner than I

thought because Tyler looked and sounded like he planned to be around for the long haul this time. We chatted while I continued to wait for Samantha. Thirty minutes later she emerged downstairs, looking the picture of urbane style at its best in her hot pink miniskirt, multicolored silk top, and a pair of sexy stilettos. Her tall, thin frame coupled with designer clothes and designer styled hair made her look as though she'd just stepped off a runway.

"You look good, babe." Tyler smiled.

"You like?" Samantha asked as she spun around.

All Tyler could do was laugh and shake his head. We both knew that Samantha was a big ham and a huge flirt.

"Let's head out," Samantha said to me.

Tyler grabbed his keys, stood, and walked toward the door. "No need for you lovely ladies to walk down to the Metro when I can drive you to the restaurant."

As I rode in the backseat of Tyler's rental car and watched him and Samantha laugh and discuss their plans for the rest of the weekend, I suddenly realized that she was right. My love life was in the pits! It was September, and I hadn't had sex since January, and that was only because I'd been so distraught after mom's funeral that I had welcomed Bradley's physical comfort one cold, lonely night. But other than that, I'd been as dry as an empty well. And now that I didn't have to focus on grieving, moving, or starting a new job, I was acutely aware of my lack of, and longing for, physical companionship.

As much as I daydreamed about Ed, and in spite of what Ms. Marabelle and Ruben had told me, I knew deep down that a relationship with him could never be. To say nothing of the fact that he was my best friend's father, he was also a married man. I thought about the conversation I'd had with Ms. Gerti last weekend and I realized that she had been right, too. If I crossed the line, I had to be prepared for the consequences. As I watched Samantha smile with happiness, I knew that I couldn't live with her likely disapproval if I became involved with Ed.

Samantha talked about her mother with the annoyance of someone battling a toothache. But I knew my friend. For all her chutzpah and tough talk she really did want her mother's approval. I remember once in college we were talking about our futures and what we wanted to do with our lives. I told her that I wanted to be a teacher like my mother, and I never forgot the look on Samantha's face—like a little lost child—and her words that followed, "I wish I had a relationship with my mother like you have with Ms. Lucille."

Samantha's mouth said one thing but her heart spoke another. If Brenda discovered that Ed was having an affair she would be livid, and if she learned that it was with the young woman whom she had treated like a daughter and welcomed into her home for summers and holidays over the last eleven years, she'd be devastated. And if she would be hurt, Samantha would be, too. The saying that blood is thicker than water wasn't a cliché, and even if it were, I didn't want to test it.

I knew that I needed to work on getting Ed off of my mind and out of my heart. And the only way to do that was to start dating so I could have a chance at happiness. It was too late for Bradley and me, and it wouldn't be fair to yo-yo back to him after my declaration last weekend. I knew the dating scene was rough, but I had to have faith that there was someone in this world for me.

When Tyler double-parked in front of the restaurant, I hopped out and went inside to wait for Samantha while they kissed good-bye. The minute I walked through the door I knew I was going to have a good time. The interior was sleek with the perfect combination of bold colors and modern design. Its trendy location in the Verizon Center/Chinatown area made it a hotspot for people with an urban flair. I walked up to the hostess stand and stood to the side, trying to survey the crowd. It was packed like they were giving away food. A minute later Samantha joined me. "How long's the wait?" she asked the ultra thin hostess.

The Kate Moss look-alike studied her seating chart. "About an hour."

Just as the hostess was about to put our name on the waiting list, two prime spots opened up at the bar and we made a beeline in that direction. I noticed eyes following us as we glided across the room. I had to admit, Samantha and I looked good. I was sure they all thought she was a model, and as for me, well, I cleaned up pretty well. Because I was turning thirty in a few hours I decided to bring it in with a bang and shake things up a bit. My outfit of choice was a simple but ultra-sexy burnt orange halter dress that clung to the curves of my body. I accessorized my look with a pair of bronze-colored stilettos, and large gold and bronze bangles on my wrist.

E-mi-leee! I heard a familiar voice call out my name. I lit up when I saw Ruben and Roger as we approached the two empty seats. Ruben was smiling from ear to ear, happy to see us. Samantha and I exchanged hugs with them before settling atop our bar stools.

"You two are the hottest bitches in this place!" Ruben said as he snapped his fingers. Samantha ate up the adulation while I just smiled. Ruben pointed from Samantha to me. "*Vogue* model and beautiful temptress, that's what you two are. Absolutely fierce!"

I laughed. I had never thought of myself as a temptress, but I decided to embrace the compliment and go with the flow.

"Thank you, cutie. Love your outfit, too." Samantha smiled.

As always, Ruben was fashionably dressed in a stylish pair of dark denim jeans, white linen top, and leather sandals—men's sandals for a change! Roger sat beside him looking just as handsome in a similar outfit, which I was sure Ruben had coordinated. But instead of looking upbeat and happy like his partner, Roger looked bored, as though he were ready to go.

"You okay, Roger?" I asked.

He smiled. "I'm fine, just tired from so much travel with the job. It would be great if we could leave at, I don't know . . . before dawn," he hinted, nudging Ruben in his side.

"He's always tired. Don't mind him," Ruben said with a quick wave of his hand, his silver bracelets clanking together as he spoke. Roger just ignored him and smiled. They had been together for so long that they simply accepted each other's quirks and kept on moving.

"Well, we're having a little pre-birthday celebration," Samantha announced.

Ruben clasped his hands together with excitement. "Tomorrow's the big day, and I can't wait for the *faaaaabulous* party!"

Samantha rolled her eyes at the mention of the event.

"What's that look all about?" Ruben asked, raising his brow. "Do tell?"

"I need a drink first," Samantha said.

I was with her on that one. "Make that two."

Roger raised his hand for the bartender. "Give these ladies whatever they like. It's their birthday."

The bartender made a big deal of it, calling attention to the "two lovely ladies celebrating their birthdays," as he announced to everyone gathered near the bar. Before we knew it, Samantha and I had so many drinks coming our way we had to share them with Ruben and Roger, which elevated Roger's spirits considerably.

An hour and several appetizers and drinks later, I was officially buzzed. I was feeling so good I temporarily forgot about anxiety and forbidden love. But even in my hazy state I realized that something interesting was happening. This was the first time Samantha and I had ever gone out that she hadn't flirted with every man in sight. Instead, she was wrapped in conversation with Ruben and Roger, explaining the complicated mother/daughter dynamics that led her to roll her eyes. If I had questioned her feelings for Tyler before, she laid them to rest tonight. She wasn't thinking about any other man except the one who was back at her place, curled up on her couch, waiting for her to come home.

While the three of them drank and immersed themselves in Samantha's stories of family drama, I sipped and flirted with a few of the men who'd bought me drinks. I was feeling loose and free, but then my entire night changed when I saw Ed approach the bar.

"Well, look what we have here." He smiled.

Samantha leaped from her stool and gave her father a big hug. "Hey, Daddy!" She threw her arms around Ed's neck and then reached over toward a tall man standing by his side. "Hey, Uncle Ross!" she squealed like a kid. "When did you get into town?"

"Your old man picked me up from the airport this morning, and he's been running me ever since," her Uncle Ross said. "Matter of fact, I wanted to rest and relax in my hotel room, but Ed insisted on dragging me out tonight." His playful wink let us know that it was really the other way around.

I had heard many stories about Ross Morgan over the years. He was Ed's best friend. They had met in undergrad and became thick as thieves when they both entered Howard Law School. Samantha loved her Uncle Ross, who also happened to be her godfather, and a free spirit

just like she was. And from what I'd been able to glean
from listening to the stories she'd told me, Uncle Ross
had a bit of an edge, which made his stock rise further in
Samantha's eyes. But I think what bonded her to him even
more was that they both had contentious relationships
with Brenda.

Unlike Ed, Uncle Ross looked every bit a man in his
mid-fifties, but his magnetic smile and high energy balanced out the hands of time. He also had a sexy swagger
that could only come from self-assured confidence, which
he exuded, just like Ed.

"Good to see you again, Ed," Ruben sang out. He was
clearly tipsy, as were Samantha and I. Roger was the only
sober head in our group, despite devouring several cock-
tails.

Ed tipped an imaginary hat in Ruben and Roger's direction, then introduced them to Uncle Ross. In the meantime I sat on the edge of my seat, my heart beating fast,
my palms beginning to sweat.

Ed turned his attention to me. "Having a good time?"

I nodded. "Yes, I am."

His eyes found mine and locked into place. Over the
last few weeks I had become accustomed to catching Ed's
subtle stares that hinted of something more, but tonight it
was different. He looked at me the way I imagined he
would one of his clients, professional and solidly business. There was also a noticeable shift in his body language, which was surprisingly formal. He folded his
arms high across his chest and waited, like he was expecting more than the simple answer I had given him. I may
have been buzzed, but not so much that I didn't know
there was something strange about Ed's mood.

"And you must be Emily," Uncle Ross said with a
smile. He slid past Ed and took my hand into his. "It's a

pleasure to finally meet you. I've heard so many wonderful things about you."

"Likewise." I nodded, wondering if the words of praise had come from Samantha or her father.

Uncle Ross ordered a round of celebratory drinks in honor of Samantha and me, and then a short time later, Ruben and Roger bid us good night with hugs and air-kisses for everyone except Ed and Uncle Ross, who both received handshakes. "See you at the party tomorrow night," Ruben called out on their way to hail a cab.

As we sat at the bar laughing and talking, I was keenly aware of two things: Ed was completely sober and had not taken a sip of alcohol, and he was ignoring me on purpose. Beyond his initial greeting, he had not uttered another word to me or even looked in my direction, and I couldn't figure out why. Just the other day he practically seduced me with his stare, but tonight he barely had two words for me.

I grew annoyed, and my body filled with the same indignation I had experienced my first night in town when he failed to notice or mention my new hairdo. I wasn't one to brag about myself, but I looked hot tonight. Nearly every man in the restaurant had glanced my way, even Uncle Ross! And each time I went to the restroom I was handed a new business card to slip into my clutch on my way back. Men were salivating over me, but Ed merely looked at me as though I were wrapped in a burka.

I had told myself that I was going to move on, that I was going to do a little flirting tonight and maybe even set my sites on getting a date out of the evening. But now I was reduced back to the eighteen-year-old girl trying to free her heart from a coffin. I couldn't stay a minute longer without either exploding or crying. I looked at my watch and leaned over to Samantha. "I think I'm heading home."

Samantha looked tired and ready to go, too. "Girl, I'm right behind you." She yawned, checking her cell phone.

She'd been drinking her stress away in an attempt to forget about the threat that Carl had made earlier today. I watched as she scrolled through her phone, then a minute later she smiled, sensing my worry. "I'm good. No unknown calls," she assured me.

I breathed a sigh of relief. Now I just needed to get home so I could take a shower, lie down, and sort out my feelings.

"Daddy, can you and Uncle Ross give Emily and me a ride home?" Samantha asked.

What! I couldn't be confined inside a moving vehicle with Ed. "That's okay, I can take a cab," I said, hopping down from my bar stool.

Samantha shook her head. "Now, what kind of sense does that make? You're just a few blocks away from me, we can drop you off."

I was quiet as I rode in the backseat with Samantha, who was slumped over with her head on my shoulder, half-asleep. She was tired from work, worn out from her move, but most of all, she was exhausted from dealing with the weight that Carl had put on her mind. After this weekend, and when Tyler was safely back in Atlanta, I planned to have another long and more serious talk with my friend.

We reached Samantha's condo first. Ed double-parked, then walked her to her door, making sure she was safely inside. I watched as he walked back to the truck, but then looked away when his eyes caught mine. I shifted against the soft leather seat. A few minutes longer and I'd be free.

Finally, we turned onto my street. Ed double-parked again and put on his flashers. "You don't have to walk me to the door, I'm fine," I told him.

"Nonsense."

I thanked Uncle Ross again for the birthday drinks and told him that I would see him at the party tomorrow night, then I held my breath and quietly walked to my door with Ed by my side.

"Emily, about tonight . . . I need to explain my actions."

My alcohol-induced courage hijacked my sober mind. "You don't owe me any explanations. The only person you're accountable to for your actions is your wife."

He looked at me like he was genuinely hurt. As much as I wanted to be angry with him and not give a second thought to his feelings, I couldn't deny mine, which were still centered around a long-held love. I lowered my head, embarrassed by the saltiness of my words. "I'm sorry."

"No, I'm the one who's sorry." Ed took a deep breath, rubbing his hand against his neck. "Let me explain . . ."

"It's okay, really." The hot, muggy air, multiple margaritas, and hours of pent-up frustration all hit me like a tidal wave. It was one in the morning, and the only thing I wanted to do was lay my head on my pillow. "Good night, Ed. I'll see you tomorrow."

I turned my key in the lock, about to push open the door when Ed stopped me. "Happy birthday, Emily."

I smiled. "Actually, it's technically not my birthday until five fourteen."

"So that's when it's official?"

I smiled again and nodded.

"Listen, about tonight," he tried to continue again.

"Ed, I'm so tired I can't think straight, as you can see. Can we have this conversation later?"

He nodded. "Of course we can."

Once I was inside, I looked through my peephole and watched Ed walk to his truck. I was exhausted from my pre-birthday celebration, so I dragged myself up my stairs and fell into bed—sexy dress, stilettos and all. I drifted off to sleep as soon as my head hit the pillow.

Chapter 20

Ed . . .

Sucker Punch!

"**Y**ou got it bad, my man," Ross told me.

We were sitting in my truck under the portico in front of Ross's hotel, talking about our long day and the tense moments that had just unfolded. More specifically, how those uncomfortable moments involved the beautiful passenger we had dropped off just five minutes ago.

"Yeah, you can say that again," I agreed. I leaned back in my seat and thought about all that had transpired and led up to my encounter tonight with Emily.

After I picked up Ross from the airport earlier this afternoon, he checked into his hotel room before we zipped out for a quick round of golf. Other than women, golf was Ross's favorite pastime. While we shot holes, I revealed my true feelings for Emily. I had talked about her over the years, and he'd heard his fair share of Emily stories from Sam, but until now, I had never had the balls to completely admit the depths of my emotions for her.

"You're fucked," Ross said as he pulled out his nine iron and eyed the ball. "If you go there with this girl, there's no good way to recover from it. You'll have so many women up your ass you won't be able to take a shit in peace."

I frowned, listening to my friend as he continued. "First of all, Brenda will plot murder against you, maybe worse. Sam will definitely catch a case, and might even stop speaking to you for hookin' up with her best friend. And Emily . . . she'll want some kind of commitment. So you'll be jumping from one lockdown straight into another."

"But that's the thing. Being with Emily won't be like lockdown, it'll be the freedom I've been waiting for."

"You've been watching Oprah, haven't you?"

I hated to admit it, but Ross was right. I was in the middle of what had the potential of turning into a big mess. Still, I had to argue my point. "My marriage is a joke," I said. "And to be perfectly honest, Brenda would care more about how our divorce would affect her social standing than the actual demise of our relationship." Hearing myself admit that fact aloud was sobering, but it was true. "And I know that Sam is emotional and can be irrational at times, but she'll come around. Hell, she's made enough mistakes not to judge."

"Man, I know you don't really believe what you just said," Ross replied. "I'm with you on the Brenda thing, but baby girl, that's a different matter. It's one thing to tell Sam that you're screwing another woman and leaving her mother, which actually, I don't think she'd be too broken up over. But it's a whole other issue to tell her that you're doing it with her best friend."

"It's not like Emily and I would be a one-night stand."

"Ed, you're missing the point. What do you think it'll do to Sam and Emily's friendship? They're like you and me, they're like blood. And let me tell you, if you ever stepped to my mama," Ross said, sounding repulsed as he shook his head. "Enough said."

I simmered on Ross's words for the rest of the day and didn't bring up the subject again until hours later when we were eating dinner at Rosa Mexicano. I knew that Sam would be shocked and more than a little dismayed at the prospect of Emily and me together, but would she be so disappointed and angry that she'd stop speaking to me, and Emily as well? Then I thought about what Ross had said about me stepping to his mother. It made me cringe and forced me to ask myself the same question. If my mother were still alive, how would I feel if he became intimately involved with her?

The hard truth was that I would definitely have a problem. Ross has had more ass than a toilet seat, so I'd take issue if he became involved with anyone I cared about, let alone a relative. I loved him like a brother, but the truth was the truth. I, on the other hand, while not perfect, didn't qualify in the dog category like my man. I hoped my daughter knew me well enough to understand that I wouldn't become involved with Emily unless I was really serious. It wouldn't be some kind of fly-by-night fling.

"Ross," I said, wanting to drive my point home and solidly win my case. "Once Sam realizes that I have genuine feelings for Emily, she'll understand. We've always had a great relationship and we can talk about anything. I know it'll be awkward at first, but she'll come around."

Ross chewed slowly, thinking over what I'd just said. "Okay, let's take Sam, and for that matter, Brenda, too, completely off the table. Let's just deal with Emily."

I nodded, knowing that he was getting ready to hit me with a new angle. "All right."

"Going strictly by what you've told me, you and

Emily have never had a conversation about how you feel about each other, right?"

"Well, technically . . ."

"You've mutually confirmed and formally verbalized your feelings for each other, yes or no?"

"No," I answered.

"Does Emily know that you're willing to leave your wife for her?"

"I'm sure she does . . ." I wanted to make my case for that point, but I didn't have any concrete evidence to back up my assertion. "Um, no," I conceded.

"Can you say with complete certainty that Emily's willing to risk her friendship with Sam for a relationship with you?"

"No, I can't. But what's *complete?* Nothing in life is certain or guaranteed."

Ross sat back in his seat, smiling as he eyed an attractive woman who had just walked by our table. "Can you say with *moderate* confidence that Emily's not seeing anyone right now?"

Sucker punch! My mind flashed back to Bradley, and I wondered if Emily was still receiving his late-night phone calls. I didn't want to answer Ross's question, but I knew I had to. "No," I finally said.

"So you're willing to risk everything for a maybe? For what you *feel?*"

I was ready to launch a rebuttal when the expression on Ross's face changed. *"Mmm, mmm, mmm,"* he practically drooled.

There was only one thing that could elicit that kind of reaction from my friend—a woman. Ross sat forward in his seat, pressing his elbows to the table. "Man, you gotta check out the prime piece of real estate that just walked through the door."

I was trying to confide in my best friend what I'd never revealed to anyone, and there he was, lusting over another piece of ass. I wanted to be incredulous, but I couldn't because after thirty-four years, I knew it was just Ross being Ross. "Man, focus," I urged.

"Naw, man. Check her out," he said, licking his lips as he nodded his head toward the front of the restaurant.

I stuffed a forkful of plantains into my mouth and indulged him by taking a quick look so we could get back to our conversation. I turned in my seat and nearly choked on my food when I saw Emily. She was nothing less than breathtaking, striking from head to toe. Her hair was pulled away from her face and rested down her back, further exposing the beautiful symmetry of forehead, eyes, nose, and cheekbones. Her tiny waist and voluptuously round hips were molded into a dress that showed off her Coke-bottle figure. And her thighs and calves looked succulent as she leaned on one leg, looking around the room as if she owned the place.

"It makes no sense for a woman to be that fine," Ross declared, molesting Emily with his eyes.

"Man, that's *Emily.*"

Ross coughed like he'd swallowed too fast. "You're shittin' me."

Just then, Sam came walking up beside her. They nodded toward the waitress, then headed across the room. We watched them, as did every other man within gawking distance, while they sauntered over to the bar. Ross looked at me with serious concern. "Damn, man. You're fucked."

From the moment I saw Emily I didn't touch another morsel on my plate. I watched like a stalker as man after man came up to her. I tensed as she ran the palm of her hand over her silky black hair and threw her head back as

she smiled and accepted what I knew were well-deserved
compliments from hopeful admirers. Sam was engrossed
with Emily's neighbors, but Emily seemed to be en-
thralled with all the men coming her way. I had never
seen her interact in a social setting, and it made me think
about Ross's question. I honestly didn't know for sure if
she was seeing anyone, or if she was *trying* to see anyone.
After all, Sam had talked about introducing her to men.

The more I watched Emily, the angrier I became. I
was heated and jealous. Just the other day she had acted
as though she shared the same feelings that I did. But now
she was parading around like a candidate for Match.com.
Ross motioned toward the bar as he finished his dessert.
"You want to head on over, partner?"

Once we arrived at the bar, Emily looked wide-eyed,
like she'd been caught stealing money. I knew that look. I
saw it all the time in the eyes of men and women alike
when I tripped them up on the witness stand. Samantha
gave me a hug, and then I introduced Ross to Emily's
neighbors who were seated next to them. After a few minutes I started up a conversation with Emily, careful not to
let my feelings show because we were in a public place.
"Having a good time?" I asked.

"Yes, I am."

I bet you are, I thought. I couldn't help myself. I became mad all over again. *Damn, I'm too old for this shit!*
I screamed inside my head. Then I realized that I wasn't
upset with Emily, I was frustrated by how I had allowed
myself to feel. It was the same emotion that had overcome
me when I saw her head resting on Bradley's shoulder at
her mother's funeral and when I walked into her house
and saw him sitting on the floor beside her last weekend.
It was a crippling combination of ego, insecurity, and my
territorial male instincts kicking in. So I ignored her

rather than deal with the real issue running through my mind—the thought of her with another man.

Now, as Ross and I sat in front of his hotel, I had to agree with my friend's earlier assessment. "You're absolutely correct, I'm fucked."

Chapter 21

Samantha . . .

Rattle My Cage

Tonight was the big event. Emily and I were going to celebrate our thirtieth birthday with an elegant summer garden party in my parents' lavish backyard. Sounds good, right? Wrong! I was dreading it worse than a Pap smear.

I was glad that Emily and I had celebrated last night. We had a better time at the restaurant than we would ever have at the stuffy, pretentious affair that mother was planning for us this evening. We had genuine fun, and as an added bonus, we shared our good time with Emily's neighbors, who were real sweethearts. Daddy and my Uncle Ross had shown up, and the only thing that would've made the night even better was if Tyler had joined us. But it was all good because when I walked through my door at one this morning, I found him lying on my sofa, waiting for me. I knew I didn't deserve these blessings, but I was gonna take them.

Tyler and I made love and then fell asleep until my ringing cell phone awoke me at what felt like the crack of dawn. My back tensed as I reached down to the floor where I'd left it, and tentatively looked at the caller ID. Thank goodness, it was only Gerti. "Good morning, Gerti," I said in a groggy voice.

She was calling to tell me that the rental company had just finished putting up the gigantic tent in the back-yard and that the house had been buzzing with activity all morning. And of course, Mother was working everyone's last nerve.

"I just wanted to catch you before you got out this morning so I could say happy birthday, and tell you to brace yourself for this evening," Gerti said.

She was giving me a heads up, warning me that judging from the chaos Mother had caused already, she was going to be in rare form, meaning she would undoubtedly piss me off more than usual. "You know I'm not looking forward to tonight," I told her.

"I know," Gerti sighed. "I want you to come over early, though. Your son has a birthday gift he wants to give you."

I was quiet.

"He's staying over at Ray's house again." She paused. "I usually try to have him in bed no later than nine o'clock on the weekends, but because so much is going on at the house tonight he's going to stay with his friend. Get here around five, that way you can spend a little time with him."

I hung my head, glancing over at Tyler as he rustled in bed beside me. I was a terrible mother, and regardless of what he said, I knew he had to think so, too. How could he not? I knew that CJ probably hadn't given my birthday a second thought and that it was only at Gerti's urging that he even had a gift for me. I knew this because yesterday I had seen the *Happy Birthday Auntie Emee* hand-drawn card he'd made, prominently displayed on Emily's mantel. When she saw me staring at it she quickly made up an explanation as to why she'd gotten a card from CJ before his own mother. "I'm right there at school with him every day, you know?"

I waved it off, telling her that I understood, and I really did. We both knew that CJ thought of her as his real mother and that I was just the woman who delivered him. It was the basic truth. I could be accused of many things, but being a phony liar wasn't one of them.

Gerti could tell by the silence on my end that I was processing things. But she wasn't playing around. "No ifs, ands, or buts," she said. "Be here at five sharp, you hear me?"

"I'll be there," I said before hanging up.

Tyler yawned, then reached over and brought me to his chest, where I rested my head.

"That was Gerti," I said.

"Everything okay?"

"Yeah, everything's fine." I didn't know how to say what I'd been putting off, so I just blurted it out. "You'll get to meet my son today."

Tyler gently lifted me up by my shoulders so he could see my face. He knew this was a big deal for me. "You sure?"

I nodded. "I'm sure."

Over the last few days he had asked me lots of questions about my son, wanting to get a feel for him. Now I could see that he was excited about the opportunity to meet CJ. I should have been happy that the man I loved was eager to meet my son. But instead of feeling good, I just felt worse, knowing that Tyler was already a better parent than I was. "We need to get there early so we can see him before Gerti takes him to his sleepover," I said.

"Sounds good, babe." Tyler kissed my cheek and then hopped out of bed to take a shower.

I sat up with the sheet around my waist. It was a crying shame that until talking to Gerti this morning, if you'd put a gun to my head and asked me what my son's bedtime schedule was, I'd be a dead woman because I had no clue.

I knew I had to stop feeling sorry for myself and start actively working toward making a more pronounced change in my life. It was my fault that my son viewed me as a surrogate instead of as his *mom*. It was my fault that I didn't know his bedtime. It was my fault that I didn't know his teacher's name. And it was my fault that I felt guilty that a man whom I hadn't seen in six years showed more open concern for my child than I did. But starting today, I was going to turn things around.

I inhaled the spicy scent of Tyler's soap as he showered in my marble tiled bathroom a few feet away. I envisioned CJ growing up to be a good man, just like him. If I was lucky, Tyler and I would make sure that he did.

With a better frame of mind, I walked down the hall to my home office. I wanted to check my personal e-mail account and respond to the birthday well wishes I received before they piled up. I turned on my computer and looked out the window at the rain that had begun to pour. Once I logged on, I was shocked to see a message sitting in my inbox from Carl.

Based on our last disastrous conversation, I knew this message had to contain something bad. I held my breath and clicked on the e-mail marked *CTT*.

Date: Sat. September 20, 5:29 a.m.
To: diamondfox@mail.net

From: 1badboy@mail.net
Subject: Happy Birthday

Happy birthday boo. All I can say is I'm sorry. I don't
want to lose you.

C

I noticed right away that he had sent the e-mail very
early this morning, which was a big deal. Like me, Carl
wasn't a morning person. This was starting to get out of
hand. I knew that Carl could be obsessive, stubborn, and
of course, a jackass, but I saw that side of him mostly
when it related to something involving his *business* matters. I had never seen him act this way over a personal relationship. But then again, this was the first time since
we'd met six years ago that I had cut him off cold.

For Carl to actually say that he was sorry, and put it in
writing, told me he was genuinely hurt that our relationship was ending. But in my mind, it was already over. I
took a deep breath because I knew that kind of hurt. I felt
the same pain when my relationship with Tyler ended, in
spite of the fact that I was the one responsible for our
breakup.

I was deciding how to respond to Carl's message
when Tyler popped his head into my office. I smiled at the
sight of him. His skin was still wet from the shower and I
could see his curly black hairs peeking through the
loosely draped towel at the base of his waist.

"I forgot to tell you, happy birthday, babe." He smiled
and then unhooked his towel, letting it fall to the floor.
"Come here so I can give you your gift."

Mmm, I loved birthdays!

* * *

Tyler and I arrived at five o'clock sharp, just as Gerti asked. Even though it was raining outside I felt as though the sun was shining. I was on time, and that was a major accomplishment for me. I was already starting to turn things around.

Gerti smiled wide, greeting Tyler as he charmed her with a warm hug and a kiss on her cheek. "Sure is good to see you," Gerti told him, and then looked over at me. "CJ will be down in a minute. He's in his room getting your present together."

I didn't deserve a gift from my son, but I swept those feelings away. "Where's Mother?" I asked, looking around as if a black cat was lurking nearby.

"Upstairs getting ready. She's in a tizzy because her hair appointment ran too long."

Just as I was about to curse, CJ appeared. He looked adorable, like a little version of my father in his khaki shorts and polo shirt. "Happy birthday!" He grinned as he walked up to me, handing me a card much like the one I saw on Emily's mantel. "This is for you, too!" he said, placing a small, neatly wrapped box in my hand.

I hugged my son tightly. "Thank you, sweetie. I'm going to earn this by my next birthday, I promise," I said, holding my card and present close to my heart. CJ continued to grin, not understanding what I meant. But Tyler and Gerti knew, and they simply looked on, smiling. They could see that I was trying to do better and *be* better.

The four of us spent the next hour tucked away, talking and laughing as we watched a flurry of people dressed in black pants, white shirts, and black bow ties scurry around in preparation for the party. The event planner walked by and introduced herself. I knew right away why Mother had hired the woman—she was a bitch, too!

I put both of them out of my mind and concentrated on having a good time, until I heard Mother's voice. It had the same effect as a pair of fingernails sliding down a chalkboard. I had heard her say some really jacked-up things over the years, but what she said next made me want to spit.

"I can't afford to be awakened in the middle of the night, Ed," Mother sighed in an annoyed voice. "That's why my eyes are puffy now."

"Fine, Brenda."

"I'm serious. I can't be disturbed once I put on my night cream, otherwise it throws my entire beauty regimen off balance."

"Next time, I'll just stay out the entire night. That way I won't interrupt your precious beauty sleep," Daddy said.

I couldn't believe my ears. You'd think she'd be more concerned about her husband being out all night in the company of a known womanizer, Uncle Ross, than she would be about the cream she puts on her face at night. Unbelievable!

Tyler looked at me as if to say, *What the hell?* Gerti rolled her eyes like I did, and CJ, in his unknowing innocence, was the only person who smiled when Mother entered the room. "Hi, Nana!" He grinned.

She didn't even say hello to her grandson—so much for her much-touted etiquette. But hey, why exercise good manners when she had the opportunity to rattle my cage? So instead of acknowledging CJ, she zeroed in on me. She was ready to start some shit about why I wasn't running around and getting myself all worked up over the party like she was doing. But then she saw Tyler sitting beside me and paused.

"Hello, Mother. You remember Tyler, don't you?" I said it with sarcasm. It was the best I could muster without saying something rude. Gerti cut me a warning stare.

I could see that Mother was shocked at the sight of

him. She remembered Tyler right away because she liked him, a lot. She had snooped on him when we dated, and learned through her bourgeois grapevine that he came from money, had a fat trust fund, and was the founder of a nationally recognized organization. In her eyes, he was a prize worth winning.

I remembered when I announced that I was pregnant. I had gathered Daddy, Gerti, and her around the kitchen table to tell them. The only thing that had kept Mother from shitting a brick was that she thought it was Tyler's baby.

"Well, I guess there's a silver lining to the dark cloud you've cast," Mother had said, looking at me with disdain as she rose from her chair and left the room. A minute later she returned with a calendar in hand. "We must start planning the wedding, immediately," she said without looking at me. "Get Tyler on the phone so we can decide which weekend in June is best."

I balked and then swallowed my embarrassment. "I'm not sure it's his."

My relationship with my mother had always been strained, but from that moment on it was officially broken. After CJ was born and it was confirmed that he wasn't Tyler's child, my mother told me that I'd robbed her of parental joy. Can you believe that shit? So in her mind, seeing Tyler meant that maybe I had another shot at respectability.

Mother put her hands over her heart, shook her freshly styled hair from her left shoulder to her right, and opened her arms like Moses parting the Red Sea. She walked right by CJ without saying a word and went straight over to Tyler for a hug. "It's so good to see you after all these years."

Tyler rose to his feet and hugged her back. I could see that he was trying to gauge my attitude. "Good to see you, too, Mrs. Baldwin."

I glared at Mother. "You walked right past CJ without saying hello," I snapped.

Mother cast me a nasty look, released Tyler from her tentacles, and then turned on her heels to acknowledge her grandchild. "Hello, my love," she said, almost sounding sincere. She paused a second, then glanced at her Rolex. "It's time for someone to leave for their sleepover, isn't it?" she sang in a playful, kid-like voice, looking from CJ to Gerti. "Gerti, the guests will be arriving any time now, be a dear, would you?" She looked at CJ again as if to say, *Get this little boy out of here, can't you see I'm trying to throw a party!*

Gerti ignored Mother. "CJ, you want to go out back with me and put your mother's birthday card on the cake table so all the guests can see it tonight?"

CJ leaped up from the floor where he was sitting and bounced his head up and down with excitement. "Yeah, let's go!"

My son ran out the back door before Gerti could get up from her seat. After they left, the room fell silent. Just as things were starting to get uncomfortable, Daddy walked in. "Happy birthday, Sam!" He smiled as he came over and gave me a hug. "I love you, kiddo."

It hadn't dawned on me until that moment that Mother hadn't even wished me happy birthday. "Thanks, Daddy. I love you, too."

Dong, ding, dong, the doorbell chimed. The first guests were arriving. Mother forgot that she was pissed and manufactured an instant smile. She was about to walk out to the foyer to perform her hostess duties when she turned around and looked at me. "Where's Emily?"

I glanced at the big clock on the mantel as it chimed. Emily was always early, if not right on time. "Maybe that's her now," I replied.

"She's not here yet?" Daddy asked.

One of the bow tie–clad servers welcomed the couple who had just rung the bell and escorted them to the large tent in the backyard as Mother followed on cue. I pulled out my phone to call Emily, but just as I did, it started to ring in my hand. *UNKNOWN* flashed across the screen and I let out a hard sigh. It was Carl. He was probably calling to wish me happy birthday, his way of trying to smooth things over. Even though it was a kind gesture, I knew that I couldn't accept it. I had to break away from him. Tyler saw the expression on my face and looked at the phone in my hand.

"What's up, babe? You okay?" he asked.

I was saved by the bell when Emily walked into the room. I hit Ignore on my phone, dropped it to the bottom of my handbag, and went over to hug my best friend. "Happy birthday, sister! We're the big *three-oooohhhh,*" I cheered. We both screamed like excited little girls as we embraced.

Emily was the stabilizing force I could rely on, and now that she was here, I knew that everything was going to be all right. So I put Carl out of my mind and didn't think about him again until he showed up later that night . . . at the party!

Chapter 22

Emily . . .

Do You Love Me?

It was early morning. Saturday morning. My birthday morning. I was sitting on my couch drinking a cup of tea, thinking about my life and my future.

When I was a little girl, I loved Saturday mornings more than any other day of the week. I would get up bright and early to watch all my favorite cartoons. I loved anything that involved princesses and happy endings. I would sit glued to the television, devouring a massive bowl of corn flakes while I cheered for the heroine in the story. Sure enough, every week on every cartoon, the princess would find her prince, win her struggle, save her kingdom, or overcome whatever adversity life had thrown her way. No matter the situation, there was always a happily ever after. But once my father died, I stopped eating corn flakes and watching cartoons because I realized there was no such thing as happy endings.

I curled my feet under my hips, looking at my side table filled with pictures of my parents and me, Samantha and me, and CJ and me. My world was small, and revolved around an even smaller group of people. I was thirty years old, but I hadn't really lived. I'd always played it safe, taken precautions, and tried to do the right things. But what had it gotten me? I was single, childless, and in love with someone who was off-limits.

I was about to start feeling sad until my eyes landed on a picture of my parents. In the photo, they were young and in love, smiling with all the hope and idealism that made one think they could conquer the world. I knew that if either of them was sitting on the couch beside me, they would tell me to stop my moping and be thankful for what I had: good health, a great friend, a good job, a beautiful home, and another year of living under my belt with the promise of a new one in front of me. I took another sip of my tea, looked around my beautiful living room, and smiled. "Thanks, Mom and Dad. I needed that." Even though they were gone, they were never far away.

I got up, walked over to the front window, and watched the rain that had started to fall. The sun had been shining bright in the sky when I poured my tea ten minutes ago. In less time than it took my drink to cool, the clouds had moved in. But instead of looking at it with gloom, I saw the rain as a good sign. "The heavens have opened up, and the rain is going to wash away all the hurt and grief and replace it with new hope and new possibilities," I whispered to myself, claiming what I wanted.

I thought about the message I received early this morning when I woke up and saw the red light flashing on my cell phone. My heart immediately struck panic, wondering if something terrible had happened to Samantha, but when I pressed the green button I saw a simple text appear. It was from Ed.

5:14 a.m.
Happy Birthday, Beautiful!

He'd sent the message at the exact moment that I turned thirty. It felt good knowing that he was thinking about me. He called me beautiful, which made me smile.

My mind took me back to last night, and I wondered why he'd been in such a bad mood, and why he had ignored me. Hopefully, I'd find out at the party tonight.

I stood in front of my antique floor-length mirror and gave myself a thumbs-up. I glided my hand over the raw silk fabric of my one-shoulder, ankle-length dress and smiled, pleased with the purchase I made last week from an obscure boutique. The rich color and exotic print pattern made my outfit glow against my brown skin, and the plunging back gave it a hint of sexiness. I fastened the posts of my shimmering gold earrings and watched them dangle as they accented my slender neck. Carefully, I draped my antique turquoise necklace down my back, which added just the right amount of style and color contrast to my outfit. And to complete my look, I slipped on the bronze bangles I wore last night, before sliding my feet into a pair of high-heel sandals. My ensemble was exotic yet natural, simple yet alluring, and I looked pretty . . . beautiful, as Ed had said in his text.

I wanted to arrive at the party early so I could visit with CJ before he left for his sleepover. I walked out to the garage, put my key in the ignition, and listened to Hazel sputter. She coughed and then went flat. I tried turning the key again, but no dice. I sat for a few minutes to let the old girl settle before my next attempt. This time the engine didn't even make a sound. Hazel was on her last leg.

The clock was ticking so I went back inside, grabbed some money for a cab, and headed out the front door in search of one of the many taxis that always zipped up and down my street.

I arrived at the Baldwins' home in record time, thanks to my speed demon of a driver. After paying the fare, I raised my umbrella and dashed toward the front door. Just as I was about to ring the doorbell, a stone-faced woman greeted me.

"Welcome to Samantha and Emily's birthday party," the hostess said in a bland voice.

I told her who I was, and she walked me back to the family room where Samantha, Tyler, and Ed were gathered. Samantha jumped up and hugged me like I'd thrown her a lifeline. I knew that something was up, but I couldn't ask questions with everyone around, so I simply reciprocated her excitement, happy to be celebrating my thirtieth birthday with my best friend. Tyler walked over and hugged me, too, then gave me a small kiss on my cheek and wished me happy birthday.

When I looked over to Ed, he was smiling, standing by the end table with his hands in the pockets of his tan trousers. "Happy birthday, Emily."

I smiled at him. "Thank you."

"Emily, you look beautiful, and this outfit is fierce," Samantha said, admiring my dress. "Girl, you look so good I know you're bound to find a man tonight!"

I glanced over at Ed out of the corner of my eye. His expression remained unchanged after hearing Samantha's comment.

"You look gorgeous." I smiled at Samantha. She did look good in her little black dress and chic lizard-skin pumps.

Samantha smiled nervously, directing me toward the staircase. "Let's go upstairs so you can put your things away." Once I put my raincoat and purse on the bed in the guest room I used to occupy, Samantha told me about the e-mail from Carl and the phone call she had just received. Even though her caller ID registered an unknown number and no message had been left, she knew it was Carl. I had a bad feeling that he was going to show up here unexpectedly, just as he did my first night in town. I wished she had never mentioned this party to him the night they'd slept together last month. And now I knew she did, too. "Do you think he'll try to crash the party?" I asked.

"Girl, I sure hope not. I pray he'll stay away. He knows that my parents and all my family will be here, and he's uncomfortable around them," Samantha reasoned. "Plus, the event planner has her staff posted at the door. No invitation, no entrance to the party," she said.

I prayed for her sake that she was right.

As we headed downstairs we ran into CJ and Ms. Gerti, who were on their way up. "Happy Birthday, Auntie Emee!" CJ shouted. I gave him a big kiss, and Samantha and I promised to save him some birthday cake from the party.

"I love you, CJ, and I'll see you tomorrow when we go out for ice cream," Samantha said, hugging her son before Ms. Gerti carted him off to get his small overnight bag.

I was glad to see that Samantha was making an effort to become more involved in CJ's life. I squeezed her hand. "You're going to do great."

She smiled. "Finally."

When we returned downstairs, Ed, Uncle Ross, and Tyler were huddled together, talking sports. Then a minute later I heard the sliding glass door open as Brenda breezed into the room. She was beautiful, the picture of sophistication in her beige cocktail dress, accompanied by a pair of shoes that had to have cost almost as much as my mortgage payment. Her hair was perfectly coiffed with not a strand out of place. It was as if she had just stepped out of her stylist's chair instead of the stuffy humidity outside. And as always, her makeup was flawless.

I stood statue-still as she walked up to me and delivered one of her signature perfect air-kisses in the direction of my right cheek. I watched Ed over her shoulder, and not to my surprise, he met my stare. He paid close attention to our interaction, but his eyes were blank, and it made me wonder what he was thinking. Whatever his thoughts, he turned away.

"Emily, it's so good to see you, dear." Brenda smiled before she turned to Samantha, gesturing for her to join us. "Come, girls, it's time to greet your guests."

Ed continued to eye me as Brenda led us to the tent-covered garden. Once outside, I was amazed by the beautiful sight before me. The Baldwins' backyard looked like a magical place out of a fairy tale—like the faraway lands I used to lose myself in on Saturday mornings when I sat in front of the TV with my bowl of corn flakes, rooting for the princess.

Hundreds of bright, clear lights were strung loosely across the tent's ceiling, casting a soft glow over the lush flora and fauna that Brenda had cultivated. The wonderful smell of exotic flowers was enough to make you close your eyes and think you were in paradise, and the three-piece band playing smooth jazz had everyone swaying to the beat of their sound. The caterers had set up a huge food station with offerings that looked so delicious they were certain to satisfy even the most finicky of eaters.

In lieu of birthday gifts, I had asked that donations be made to charity. Samantha thought it was a good idea and agreed to follow suit. So, prominently displayed in the middle of the gift table was a big, mock-up check, like the kind you see on the sweepstakes commercials, made out to the local MS Society in the amount of $25,000. It was because of Brenda's vigorous fund-raising efforts that this was even possible. I was overwhelmed with emotion.

I turned to her. "Thank you. I appreciate your kindness and generosity more than you know. This donation will go a long way toward helping people so they won't have to suffer the way my mother did. You've truly made this a birthday I'll never forget," I said loudly. I normally spoke in a soft tone, but I wanted to deliver my thanks at a volume high enough to drown out my guilt. I had just lusted after her husband not two minutes ago, in spite of the fact that she'd thrown me the most extravagant party I would probably ever have. And on top of all that, she'd selflessly raised money to help eradicate a terrible disease. I felt lower than dirt.

"Emily, there's nothing I wouldn't do for the people I love. It's all about giving." Brenda smiled. She actually touched my cheek with hers, sacrificing her perfect makeup. It was a first, and it made me feel even lower.

Samantha stood over to the side and rolled her eyes. I could see that she wasn't touched or impressed. Tyler whispered into her ear, probably trying to calm her down before she said something inappropriate. Brenda ignored Samantha's glare, took my hand, and walked me over to meet some ladies from a local charity. By now, Samantha and Tyler were headed to the other side of the tent, straight for the bar.

I was relieved when I saw Ruben and Roger in the crowd. They had trudged through the rain to help me celebrate. *"Oh, E-mi-lee,* this party is to die for!" Ruben gushed as he twirled around under the lights with a champagne flute in his hand.

"Happy birthday." Roger smiled, planting a kiss on my cheek.

Samantha and I cut our cake, received a heartfelt birthday toast from Brenda and Ed, and then we each went up to the mic and thanked everyone for coming. An hour later the party was in high-octane mode. It was still raining hard, but the beautiful setting, bountiful food, and abundance of alcohol kept everyone's spirits high. As I surveyed the tent, I couldn't believe the large crowd of people flowing throughout. There were nearly a hundred people in the backyard and about thirty milling around the first floor inside.

I was trying to have a good time; after all, it was my birthday. And as Ruben had said, the party was to die for. But as I watched Brenda with Ed hovering close by her side, smiling and laughing with guests as they worked the crowd, I felt a sharp stab in the pit of my stomach. He was her husband, so it only seemed fitting that they socialize as a couple. I knew that. And I knew that I had no right to be upset. But when I looked up again and saw Ed holding his arm around Brenda's waist as they greeted another couple, I felt a part of me melt away. Then anger and resentment took over.

My mind went back to the way Ed had practically seduced me at school the other day, then to his strange behavior last night—ignoring me one minute and then sending me a thoughtful text message hours later. I felt like a fool being strung along on a back-and-forth ride to nowhere. When he glanced in my direction, I shot him a look that could've struck down lightning. "I've got to get out of here," I whispered to myself.

I headed inside to get my things and call a cab. I climbed the stairs and was on my way to the guest bedroom when halfway down the hall I heard the voice that made my heart beat fast.

"Why aren't you out there enjoying your party, birthday girl?" Ed asked.

I was upset with him and I was sure he knew, otherwise he wouldn't have taken the risk of following me here. I turned around to face him, trying to find a place for my eyes to rest other than on his. They settled on the John Biggers painting on the wall behind him. "I'm going home. I just need to get my things." I didn't want to give him an explanation beyond that.

"But the party's in full swing."

"All the more reason for you to go back so you can continue socializing with your wife." I knew it was a childish thing to say, but it was what I felt.

"Emily," he said softly. "What you saw down there was obligation, nothing more."

"If that's what you say." I turned and began to walk away.

"Wait," he said as he reached for my arm, stopping me in my tracks. His touch felt warm and inviting. "Why won't you look at me?"

Instead of answering him I turned away and focused my eyes on the guest bedroom at the end of the hall. I knew that if I could make it to safety on the other side of that door, I'd be able to gather my thoughts. I tried to walk away, but my feet felt as though they were stuck in cement. Ed faced me, still holding my arm, forcing me to look at him. This time I cast my eyes down to my feet.

"Emily, why won't you look at me?"

"I can't."

"Why not?"

"You know why."

"Do you love me?" he asked, softly.

I couldn't answer. I had to get away from him. Shaken, I walked toward the room I had slept in only weeks ago—he followed. After what seemed like a mile, I reached the door and put my hand on the chrome-plated knob. He stood close behind me, his body leaning into mine. I could feel his chest on my back and his cool lips on my bare shoulder as he bent his head and delivered a gentle kiss to my skin. "Ed, please don't." I trembled.

"I love you, Emily," he whispered into my ear.

He put his hand over mine, turned the knob, and pushed as he opened the door. I thought I'd find safety once I reached the other side, but now all I felt was panic. Ed closed the door behind us and repeated his question. "Do you love me?"

I thought about his dutiful wife socializing outside, about my loyal best friend partying in the backyard and the chain of events that would follow if I reached out and seized the moment. My rational mind said no, but everything else inside me said yes. My back was pressed against the door and Ed's body was close to mine. He took a step forward and leaned into me until I felt his strong chest against my breasts, and the intoxicating heat that arose from our bodies. I inhaled the robust scent of his cologne and the faint hint of wine on his breath. His hand moved toward my face, his fingers resting under my chin as he lifted my head toward his lips. "I said I love you, Emily," he whispered again, leaning in as I held my breath.

Suddenly, our mood was broken when we heard a loud crash from outside, and an even louder *Fuck you, ma'fucka!* coming from a deep, male voice. Ed pulled away and we both ran to the window in the direction of the sound, looking down on the backyard below. We couldn't see anything because of the tent, but we both recognized the man's voice. It was Carl!

"Shit!" Ed cursed. He turned, opened the door, and hurried down the hall as I followed close behind.

Chapter 23

Samantha . . .

You Better Slow Your Roll

Even though Mother grated on my last nerve with her phony pretense, I had to give her credit, she knew how to throw a hellafied party. The ambience was beautiful, the food was delicious, the band was excellent, and the alcohol was flowing. And despite the steady rain and oppressive humidity, people had come out in droves. The party was an official hit. Things were going well until I looked up and saw Carl walking through the crowd.

Oh, shit! I said to myself. Carl was headed in my direction with a look on his face that made sweat drip from my armpits. I wasn't sure how he got past the event planner and her team of pit bulls posing as servers, but I knew I had to act fast. "Excuse me one minute, baby," I said to Tyler. I left him in conversation with Uncle Ross as I rushed to cut Carl off before he found his way into the flow of the party. When I reached him he was already in the middle of the tent. "What're you doing here?" I asked in a low voice, trying to be civil.

Carl looked past me and saw Tyler standing in the corner. "What the fuck is that punk ma'fucka doin' here?"

His tone was nasty and his voice was loud enough to be heard over the soft jazz in the background. My mother and her snooty friends looked up with horrified stares. Carl didn't seem his usual self, and I could tell he was definitely on something. His eyes were glazed over and his face was twisted. He was wearing a black bandana tied around frizzy-looking cornrows, a white sports jersey, sagging jeans, and his signature Tims. To say he looked out of place among the Brooks Brothers and silk around us was an understatement.

"Carl," I said as gently as I could, trying to reason with him again. "It's not too late for you to turn around and leave, that way we won't have to get the police involved." I knew the mention of men in blue uniforms would snap him out of whatever trip he was on.

"Fuck the *po-lice*. I don't give a damn 'bout no *po-lice*," he growled, rocking his body back and forth in an animated gesture.

I rolled my eyes, unfazed, by his gangster pose that was meant to intimidate the bourgeois crowd. But my attitude quickly changed when I saw his cousin, Ronnie, standing behind him—there for backup! At that moment, I knew some real shit was about to go down.

If this had been any other function, with any other people, at any other time, I wouldn't have paid a second thought to Carl and his outrageous hood drama. But this was different. This wasn't just my party, it was Emily's, too, and it was actually more for her and her late mother than it was for me. Tyler was here, my father and Uncle Ross were here, Gerti was here, and above all else, this was the home where my son laid his head every night. Nobody messed with the people I loved, and I was furious that Carl had brought his bullshit to my parents' front door. I was trying to be good and make better choices, but now Carl had pissed me off. Before I knew it, the crazy, hot-headed, say-anything Samantha returned with a vengeance.

I came up on Carl so close I could reach out and touch his nose. I stepped out of my heels and started removing my Swarovski crystal earrings as I spoke. "All right muthafucker, you made your point. But I'll be damned if I'm gonna let you come up in here, uninvited, and fuck things up for my family. Now, if you don't get the hell outta here right now, I'ma start beatin' your ass right here in front of all these people!"

The music stopped, heads turned, and it was on.

I wasn't the least bit afraid because I knew that if I hit Carl, he only had one of two choices. He could either hit me back and face a serious beat down from every man under the tent, or he could walk away in shame. Either way, he was going to lose.

"What the hell's goin' on?" Tyler said, coming up from the back. He quickly took me by my arm and shielded me behind him, where Uncle Ross was now standing. "What's your damn problem, man?" he barked at Carl, unleashing his Brooklyn-born flavor.

I didn't want Tyler involved in my mess. But now that we were together, my mess was his mess, too. I felt terrible, but I didn't have time for regrets, I had to think fast before something deadly happened.

Crash!

Everyone under the tent except Uncle Ross, Tyler, and me hit the ground as if bullets were flying. Uncle Ross didn't flinch because he was tough like that. Tyler stayed firmly planted where he stood because he was fearless. And I didn't move because I was crazy.

I hadn't noticed before now, but Carl had a beer bottle in his right hand and had thrown it to the ground, causing a loud explosion that landed at his feet. "Fuck you, ma'fucka!" he yelled at Tyler.

They stood face-to-face, neither of them backing down. I heard my mother call out in the background, "Dear God in heaven, someone call the police!" I glanced over at her and she looked as though she were going to faint.

If anyone had told me that my party would end up like this, I would've stayed inside my condo with the door locked and the dead bolt on. I stood in the middle of a backyard full of people, feeling pissed, humiliated, and stunned all at the same time. It was my birthday, and it was a freakin' disaster.

Daddy came running into the backyard with Emily behind him. He looked directly at me. "Sam, are you all right?"

I was too disoriented to answer, so I simply nodded to show that I was okay.

"I thought I told you to never come around here again," Daddy said as he got up in Carl's face. His voice was as hard as concrete, and I could tell that he was ready to wipe the floor with Carl's ass.

Thank God I would never know what could've happened next because just as Tyler, Daddy, Carl, and Ronnie all stepped to each other, one of the party guests wearing a silk shirt and pants that were way too tight came rushing over, holding up a badge. "Everyone step back!" he said. Then from out of nowhere, sirens started blaring and uniformed officers rushed in.

Less than twenty minutes later it was all over. Carl and Ronnie were in the back of a squad car headed downtown. The event planner had dialed 911 as soon as Carl and Ronnie pushed past her and one of her servers on their way to the backyard. The police knew who Daddy was, and because the off-duty officer had witnessed the entire scene, it was pretty much a wrap.

At first I thought I might be going downtown along with Carl and Ronnie because technically, I was the only person who had communicated a verbal threat. But I had the best trial lawyer on the East Coast by my side, so I was in the clear. Emily and Gerti stood close by as I made my statement under Daddy's careful direction, while Tyler held my hand for emotional support.

My family members stuck around, and to my surprise, nearly all the partygoers did, too. But I soon learned that they hadn't stayed out of support or concern, they were just nosy. Rumors and speculation had already started to fly through the crowded tent. "When they searched him they found a gun and drugs," one person whispered.

The next sound I heard was my mother's voice echoing through the air as she spoke over the microphone. "Thank you all for coming to celebrate Samantha and Emily's thirtieth birthday," she began, sounding as composed as she always did. "I deeply regret the unfortunate incident that you were subjected to, and I sincerely apologize on behalf of my family for any strain it has caused. The police have assured us that the perpetrators will be prosecuted to the fullest extent of the law."

She went on for another minute or two as she thanked everyone for their contributions to the MS Society and encouraged them to stay and have a good time. As I listened to her speak, she was the picture of calm. I marveled at how eloquently she handled the horrible situation, with dignified grace. She was strong and in control, not erratic and tactless as I had been. It was the first time in my entire life that I ever wanted to be like my mother.

"That was smooth," Tyler said.

I nodded in agreement. "I'm ready to go." I felt terrible and ashamed, and I couldn't stay a minute longer, but I knew there was one thing I had to do first. "I just need to apologize to my mother before we leave."

"Apologize? To your mother?" Tyler said in disbelief. "Excuse me, but what's your name?"

"Yeah, I know, right?" This was the new me, and I was determined to make a change.

Despite Mother's urging for everyone to stay, the crowd quickly dispersed. Now that all the major drama had died down, they wanted to hurry home so they could crank up the gossip mill. Tyler went to bring the car around while I offered Emily a ride home. She actually looked more ready to go than I was. Meanwhile, I braced myself when I saw Mother and Aunt Dorothy approach.

This was one time that I was prepared to acquiesce and accept whatever tongue-lashing Mother was going to dish out. This embarrassing fiasco wasn't Carl's fault, it was mine, for even being associated with him. I needed to claim responsibility for my role in what had happened.

Mother walked up to me and stood close. "How dare you bring shame to this family . . . again!" she hissed in a low voice, looking at me through murderous eyes.

"Calm down, Brenda," Aunt Dorothy cautioned, placing her hand on Mother's shoulder. "Let's go back inside the house and have Gerti make you some tea."

Gerti rolled her eyes at Aunt Dorothy and sucked her teeth in disgust.

I lowered my head. "Mother, I'm sorry for—"

"And you should be," she hissed again. "I spent my time, energy, and money trying to help *you*, and this is the thanks I get?"

"What a bitch," Uncle Ross said under his breath as he looked in Mother's direction.

Mother cut her eyes at Uncle Ross, then continued to speak to me in a low voice, but her tone roared like the rain falling atop the tent. "This is how you repay me for what I've done for you? With embarrassment, humiliation, and shame!"

"I said I was sorry," I pleaded.

"That's the story of your pathetic life! Sorry for getting high in the basement, sorry for the DUI your father had to bail you out of, sorry for having an illegitimate child."

I was trying to apologize, and I wanted to be calm and graceful as she'd been, but her last words set me off because now she'd gone too far. CJ wasn't illegitimate. He was a blessing. The only thing I'd ever done that I was proud of. I put my hand on my hip and shot daggers at Mother with my eyes. "You better slow your roll," I told her.

Slap!

My head went back, then twisted to the side as the palm of Mother's hand came crashing down against the side of my cheek. "How dare you speak to me in that tone," she spat through clenched teeth.

Smack!

I hit her back so hard my hand stung and she staggered backward, falling into Aunt Dorothy's arms before regaining her footing. My head was about to explode. I'd always talked about how I wanted to slap my mother, but never in my life did I think I would actually do it. I lowered my head, feeling the first of an avalanche of tears that had begun to fall. Emily walked over to me, put her arm around my shoulder, and glared at Mother as though she wanted to slap her, too.

Daddy stepped up and gave Mother an icy cold stare. "Dammit, Brenda! This is enough."

His hard tone startled her, and me, too. I had never

heard Daddy speak to her in such a rough manner. Mother's eyes opened wide, as if he'd just stepped on her big toe. Now I wasn't sure who she was angrier with, Daddy or me.

"Ed, how can you stand there and defend what *your* daughter just did," she huffed.

"Because we've all had enough drama for one evening," Daddy huffed right back. He looked over at Emily, then to me. "Come on, ladies, Tyler's waiting for you out front."

After Tyler and I dropped Emily off at her house, we headed home. We didn't exchange many words during the ride back because we were each lost in our own thoughts about everything that had happened. I felt awful that he'd seen the ugly side of me at the party, and now that it was all over and he had time to digest it, I wondered what he was thinking. My only consolation was that he hadn't witnessed the licks that Mother and I had exchanged while he was getting the car.

I was relieved when we walked through my door and into the quiet safety of my home. Tyler and I still hadn't said much to each other. We sat on the couch for a few minutes before I told him that I was going up to take a shower and clear my head. I left him downstairs and hoped he wasn't rethinking our relationship.

Just as I was getting things together, I fucked up again. Poor choices was my middle name. This was like déjà vu, the story of my life, and it made me remember the advice that Gerti had given me at the kitchen table just last weekend.

I peeled out of my little black dress and stepped into the shower. It felt good standing under the stream of warm water as it rained down on my skin. I wished I could wash away my bad decisions and disappointment in myself, but I knew only time and hard work could do that.

After an intensely long and self-reflecting cleanse, I toweled off and walked out to my bedroom. I stood still when I saw Tyler sitting in the middle of the bed holding a cupcake with a single candle in the center.

"Happy birthday to you . . ." Tyler sang the birthday song to me as I stood before him, wrapped in my towel with a smile on my face and puddles of tears in my eyes. It took a hell of a lot to make me cry. Mother had taken me there tonight through anger and hurt, but Tyler was taking me there now, through joy and love. I sat on the bed, made a wish, and blew out the candle.

"What did you wish for?"

I wiped my eyes with the back of my hand. "Like I told CJ tonight . . . that someday I'll deserve this."

Tyler sat the cupcake on the nightstand and then held both of my hands in his. "Sam, I told you, you deserve more than you think. You just need to start believing it."

"How can you say that? You saw how I acted tonight."

"Yeah." He chuckled. "You were talkin' big shit. 'I'ma beat your ass right here in front of all these people,' " he mimicked in a high-pitched voice, rolling his neck from side to side as he mimicked me.

He'd just turned my vulgarity into humor. We both burst into laughter, falling back onto the bed as we roared until our sides hurt. My mind floated back to the conversation that Emily and I had when she asked me if a man had ever made me laugh. That was when it hit me that not only was Tyler my lover, he was my friend, and as Emily had said, he was the kind of man who could reach my heart.

Tyler stroked his hand against my face and spoke to me softly, and gently. "Sam, I love everything about you, baby. I love the good side, the imperfect side, and the crazy wild side. I love it all because it makes you who you are."

I wanted to cry again, but I had bawled enough for one night. I replaced my tears with smiles and my embarrassment with hope. "I love you, too, Tyler." I removed my towel, kissed my man, and thanked God for giving a prodigal child a second chance.

Chapter 24

Brenda . . .

Jealousy Is a Terrible, Terrible Thing

It was shortly after ten when Brenda said good night to her last guest, her sister, Dorothy. If the sight of the police cars that had been parked in front of her house wasn't a dead giveaway that her party had been a complete disaster, the fact that her grand soiree had ended well before midnight definitely was.

"Are you sure you're all right?" Dorothy asked as she stood at Brenda's front door.

"Yes, I'm fine."

"No, you're not. I can stay if you want to talk?"

Brenda tried to paint on a resilient smile. "No, I'll be okay, really."

"Call me tomorrow," Dorothy said as she reluctantly walked to her car.

Brenda shut the door, furious and completely disgusted. After all her hard work, her elegant summer garden party had turned into a triumphant disaster. At the moment, she was thankful for only two things. The first was that Juanita Presley had caught a twenty-four-hour bug and hadn't been able to attend, and the second was that all the guests had dispersed before Samantha had provoked her into a physical confrontation. Just the thought of it all made her head pound.

Brenda walked over to the patio door and looked out into the backyard—the scene of the crime. The large, empty tent was dark and full of disappointment; a stark contrast to the life it had breathed at the beginning of what she thought would be a spectacular evening. Instead, she was humiliated in front of a crowd of the most powerful Who's Who in DC. Every time she thought about her daughter, her head throbbed even harder. She knew that Samantha hated her, but she had no idea how much until tonight. "Samantha ruined everything for me," Brenda fumed, touching the red welt that shined bright on the side of her face.

Samantha had even ruined her chances of securing the prestigious board position she'd been coveting. She was incredulous that her goals had been ripped apart in a matter of minutes. "I was so close," Brenda lamented, thinking about how the chairwoman of Rock Creek Family Support Collaborative had smiled when she heard Emily give loud praise for her kindness and generosity. The disappointment was too much for Brenda to bear, so she headed for the kitchen to claim the bottle of champagne with her name on it. She'd left the bubbly chilling in the refrigerator, a reward to herself in celebration of her fabulous party. But now, it would serve as salve to help ease her wounds.

When she walked into the kitchen she found Gerti standing at the sink, filling the coffeepot with water. Neither of them said a word to each other as Brenda retrieved her bottle of liquid feel-good, ready to go upstairs and drink her troubles away. But both women stopped what they were doing when Ed appeared, looking heated.

"Gerti, there's no need to worry about making me coffee for tomorrow morning," Ed said as he walked toward the back door. He held his keys in one hand and an overnight bag in the other.

"Where are you going at this hour?" Brenda asked, looking at her watch.

"Out, with Ross."

"And that requires your overnight bag?"

"Yes. I won't be back until tomorrow."

"Come again?" Brenda balked, walking toward Ed. She glanced over her shoulder at Gerti, who was still standing at the sink, then lowered her voice. "Ed, let's talk about this in private."

"There's no need for that. Gerti knows the real deal between you and me. I'm leaving now," he said with no emotion.

Brenda drew in a deep breath. "I can't believe you'd leave me all alone in my time of need, especially after all that I've been through tonight."

Ed looked at her and shook his head. "All you think about is yourself. I haven't seen Sam cry since she gashed her knee open when she was learning how to ride her bike. And even then she tried to fight back the tears. But tonight, you, her own mother, slapped her and brought her to tears. It was despicable."

"She was responsible for what happened!"

"And she tried to apologize," Ed shot back. "But you were so full of venom that you didn't even realize she was hurting. I've had it up to here with you." Ed nodded toward Gerti, said good night, and then turned and walked out the back door.

"The nerve," Brenda hissed. "That man doesn't deserve me."

Gerti sucked her teeth and rolled her eyes.

"Do you have something to say?" Brenda glared.

Gerti dumped the water out of the coffeepot and returned it to the counter. "As a matter of fact, I do." She stared at Brenda, not blinking an eye. "There was a time when I used to despise you, just like the rest of them," she said, planting her hands against the counter.

Brenda raised her brow in astonishment and opened her mouth to speak, but the look in Gerti's eyes caused her to back down and remain silent as the woman continued. "I've watched you beat down everybody around you, even your own children, just so you could feel like you were the one on top. But the whole time you were tearing them down, you were standing at the very bottom all by yourself. Once I realized that, I couldn't despise you anymore, and that's when I started to pity you."

"You, of all people, pity *me?"* Brenda scoffed, looking down her nose at Gerti. "Jealousy is a terrible, terrible thing."

"So is being a bitch."

"How dare you speak to me that way."

Gerti rolled her eyes again. "I'm a grown woman and I can speak to you however the hell I like. The only reason I haven't cussed your hateful ass out before now is because I love Sam, Ed, and CJ too much to disrespect you under this roof. I've tried to stay in line so I could protect them from you, and I prayed for years that you'd change, but you haven't. Now I'm through."

Gerti walked away from the sink and over to where Brenda stood at the table. "You've been such a rotten mother to Sam that she doesn't even know how to be a decent one to her own child. She's scared she'll screw up CJ the same way you messed her up," she said, taking a pause.

"I know Sam bears responsibility for the poor decisions she's made over the years and the reckless things she's done, but so do you. She didn't deserve to be slapped across her face," Gerti said, shaking her head again. "But don't worry, Brenda Baldwin, if you think that being embarrassed in front of all your socialite friends was bad, you just wait, 'cause this is only the beginning of your payback. People are sick of your shit and they're not gonna stick around and take it anymore."

Brenda stood with her mouth hanging open as Gerti walked past her toward the back door, giving her one last piece of her mind. "You better be glad I didn't slap you, too. I'm gonna pray for you, Brenda. I really am."

Chapter 25

Ed . . .

I Want You Right Here

I started the engine and heard the sound of freedom. I was leaving home and escaping Brenda. The night had been like something straight out of a novel, only worse because you couldn't make up the kind of drama that had unfolded under my roof. It took everything inside me not to put my hands around Brenda's neck after what she did to Sam, and that was why I knew I had to leave before I ended up beside Carl and his cousin in a holding cell downtown.

It was still pouring rain, and now heavy thunder was clapping loud above, mixing with the lightning that had begun to streak across the sky. I stepped on the gas and headed down the street. I had no intention of hanging out with Ross because I knew he was preoccupied with the attractive woman he'd left the party with. I thought about dropping by Sam's place to make sure she was okay, but I remembered that Tyler was there and he would take care of her, which made my mind rest a little easier. Then naturally, as it always did, my thoughts fell on Emily and the birthday gift I had for her that was tucked away inside my overnight bag. I hit the speaker button on my car phone and dialed her number. She picked up on the third ring.

"Hello."

"Emily, it's Ed."

"I know."

There was a long pause between us before I spoke again. "I want to see you."

"But, Ed . . ."

"Emily, I want to come over." At that moment I didn't want to hear any objections, excuses, or hesitations. All I wanted to do was see her, be with her, and breathe her into my life. "Emily . . . please."

Ten minutes later I walked through Emily's back door. She asked me to park in her garage so I wouldn't have to leave my truck out on the street. I appreciated her discretion, but I really didn't care if anyone knew I was there. She greeted me with a tentative smile as my eyes quickly roamed over her. She had changed out of the beautiful, exotic dress she had worn to the party and was now lounging in a simple cotton T-shirt and a pair of white shorts with the word *pink* written across the perfect roundness of her behind. She looked tantalizing and delicious.

As I walked through her immaculate kitchen and into her cozy living room, I felt a sense of peace, like I was home. We sat on opposite ends of her couch. The room was dimly lit by a small table lamp in the corner and a scented candle, creating an intimate feel. "Thanks for letting me come over," I started.

"The way you asked, did I have a choice?"

"Everyone has a choice."

"Yes, you're right. Everyone does," she said in a whisper.

A calm silence fell across the room as we listened to the rain, which seemed to be coming down even harder since I entered the house. We were beginning the same song and dance that we always found ourselves drowning in, when everything suddenly changed.

Emily slid her body next to mine, then, in one quick motion she straddled my lap and sat on top of me. I looked into her eyes as she placed her hands on my shoulders. "To answer the question you asked me earlier tonight," she said, returning my stare, "yes, Ed. I love you."

She leaned into me and brushed her soft lips against mine, inviting me to taste her sweet tongue. Her mouth was wet, and warm, and I was surprised by the force of her kiss. I had imagined that our first kiss would be slow, innocent, and dainty, like she was. Instead, it was ferocious, hungry, and wanton. I loved every minute of it.

Emily continued to kiss me as her hips began a sultry grind against my crotch. I eased my arms around her waist, pulling her closer to me, enjoying the way her body felt against mine. She managed to unbutton my shirt with remarkable speed as I lifted hers over her head and tossed it to the side of her couch. She wasn't wearing a bra, so I had immediate access. Her breasts were a perfect, supple mouthful, and her dark, round nipples called for me to take a lick. She leaned against me as I sucked her into my mouth, circling my tongue around her soft flesh while I ran my hands down her slender back. She moaned into my ear, "*Mmm.* Oh, Ed."

When I heard her lustfully whisper my name, my erection nearly burst through the zipper of my pants. Emily smiled when she felt my obvious excitement. I slid my hands along the side of her thighs, and then ventured to her soft, round ass that had always made me stand at attention. I continued to suck her breasts while I eased my hands down the elastic waistband of her shorts. My fingers glided against the lacy material of her thong, sending me straight through the roof.

We continued to kiss, and grind, and fondle until neither of us could take it anymore. And again, Emily took the lead. She moved down to the floor and brought me with her. She wiggled out of her shorts and thong and then started unzipping my pants. "Do you want to go upstairs, to your bedroom?" I panted into her ear as I kissed her right below her lobe. Don't ask me why I interrupted the moment with that crazy question. I guess I always envisioned our first time being atop a big, soft bed, with fluffy white sheets. Women weren't the only ones who liked romance.

"I want you right here," Emily panted, kissing me harder and deeper. She was lying on her back, legs spread open, ready for me as I hovered above.

She didn't have to tell me twice. I came out of my pants and boxers, ready to move in for the kill.

"Condoms," she breathed hard, looking up at me. "Do you have condoms?"

Damn! Why hadn't I thought to pick some up on my way over? I'd been so focused on getting here that it didn't cross my mind. I'd hoped that we would do some heavy petting, maybe even a little fondling beneath each other's clothes, but nothing like this. I honestly hadn't anticipated on Emily taking the bull by the balls!

My body was resting on top of hers, in between her luscious brown thighs. It was where I had always wanted to be, and I was literally harder than nails. How could I not be prepared? I rose on my elbows and looked into her eyes. "I don't have any."

I heard a small, disappointed sigh escape Emily's mouth as she turned her head to the side. I thought she was going to tell me that we had to stop, but then she surprised me again.

"Ed, I want you," she whispered. She kissed me and wrapped her arms around the middle of my back as she pressed her chest against mine. Her hips continued to grind below as she opened her legs wider. I could feel her warm wetness against my thigh. Before I knew it I was at the creamy center of what I'd been longing for.

"Oh, Emily," I moaned.

She reached down between our bodies, and when I felt her delicate grip around my swollen manhood, I nearly bit the inside of my jaw. She rubbed her palm up and down the entire length of my thick shaft and smiled. *"Mmm,"* she purred in a seductive voice that made me grow even harder. She jutted her pelvis forward, held me securely in her hand, and then gently nudged the tip of my head inside her. "Ooohhh, Eeeeeeddddd!"

This was magic.

Emily had called all the shots and I followed her lead. But now I needed to take over. I kissed her hard as I plunged inside her with the precise amount of force that I instinctively knew she wanted. She gasped as she took in every inch of me.

"Oh, baby, you feel so good," I moaned into the air as I felt her tight inner walls envelop me like a warm cocoon. I rocked her back and forth until I found her rhythm. Once I did, I stroked her, taking my time, immersing myself in the feel of her soft, naked body against mine and the taste of her salty skin on the tip of my tongue. Damn, I loved this woman.

We moved faster and harder as we kissed, and ground, and moaned our way to the edge of her Persian rug. Sweat poured from my forehead and dripped onto hers before trickling down the side of her beautiful face. I tried to hold back because I wanted the feeling to last all night, but the power of the euphoric sensations running through my body was too great. I felt Emily's warm breath whistle in my ear as she thrashed against me. "Yes! Yes! Ed . . . Ooohhhhh," she moaned.

Emily trembled and slowed her movements, but she continued to engulf me inside her tender warmth. She let out a high-pitched moan as she bucked against me, giving in to a shivering climax that brought an exhausted smile to her lips. I was so turned on that I lost all thought and control. I knew I needed to pull out because I could feel my shaft pulsating with the unmistakable sensation that rises when you're about to come. I was in another world, high on the ecstasy that was surging through my body. "Oooooh, Emily. Oh, baby," I moaned as I unleashed my orgasm in a hot rush until I emptied myself inside her.

We stayed frozen where we were, not moving a muscle. Emily's legs rested against the side of my hips, her arms around my back. She held me like a baby as I lay between her thighs. I tried to ease my body off her and onto my elbows because I didn't want my weight to cause her discomfort. But she wouldn't allow it. She pulled me back onto her sweat-soaked chest and stroked her fingers through my hair, letting her nails graze my scalp. We listened in silence as the rain pelted against the window in sheets. This was heaven, I was sure.

I kissed her collarbone and then found her lips, planting soft, delicate kisses around her mouth. Everything about her felt perfect, and I wanted to live in the moment forever. But reality quickly came rushing back and smacked me hard in my face. I'd been reckless, no better than a horny teenager. We had unprotected sex. "Emily?"

"Yes?"

I spoke into her shoulder. "Are you on the Pill?"

"Yes, Ed. I am." Her voice was a sweet whisper as she spoke. "But I know what you're thinking. We should've used protection." She shifted her head so she could look at me. "I'm sorry."

"For what?"

"I initiated this."

"You weren't in it alone."

"But I had condoms, upstairs in my nightstand," she said, pausing for a second. "But I didn't want to stop. I wanted to make love to you. Still, I knew better."

"So did I." I swept my eyes across her beautiful body, circling my index finger around her firm, right nipple. "Do you regret what we did?"

"No, I don't," she answered, her voice begging to ask me the same question.

"Neither do I."

"Where do we go from here?" she asked softly.

I smiled. "Upstairs to your bedroom."

Chapter 26

Emily . . .

So Powerful, and So All-Consuming

The sun peeked in through the tiny slits of my wooden miniblinds, filling my bedroom with soft rays of light. They say the sun always comes out after a storm, and this morning was proof of that. I looked over at Ed as he slept comfortably beside me. He was lying on his right side, facing me, providing me with the perfect angle to study his face. Before now, I was never able to really look at him with a critical eye, for fear that he or someone else would catch me staring and read my desire. But his slumber mixed with the glorious morning light solved that. Now I could relish him in the privacy of my bedroom.

My eyes took him in. Starting at the top of his head, I studied the way his hairline framed his chiseled face. He was in no danger of receding or balding in the foreseeable future, and his curly pepper-and-salt hair was still full and lush. Moving down, I surveyed his wide brows that perfectly accented his eyes, even with them closed. The bridge of his nose was similar to mine, moderate and slightly narrow, and his lips were just the right size, with just enough hint of pink to make them kissably irresistible. I wanted to run my fingers along the edge of his face and feel his smooth caramel skin against my palm, but I resisted, not wanting to wake him from what looked like peaceful sleep.

I turned on my side and gently nuzzled my body close to his, while he draped his strong arm around my waist, as if it were an involuntary reaction. He pulled me farther into his chest, my bare back freely resting there. "Are you awake?" I asked.

"A little." He kissed me at the nape of my neck as his warm breath grazed my hairline.

I could feel his early-morning erection against my behind, and it took me back to last night.

Samantha and Tyler had dropped me home from what turned out to be a mess of a birthday party. Just as I had suspected, and as Ruben had so accurately predicted, Carl showed up and showed out. The police arrested him and his cousin for trespassing, and I heard a rumor among the partygoers that the officers found a gun and drugs on both of them.

I prayed that once Carl made bail he wouldn't come after Samantha. Ruben's prediction of death was still looming in my mind. But the incident that upset me more than Carl was the way Brenda had treated Samantha. After witnessing her verbally belittle and then physically assault my friend, her own daughter, it was the first time in my life that I had wanted to inflict harm upon another person.

I had been home about an hour when my cell phone rang. My heart raced when I saw Ed's name flash across my screen. I wanted to see him, but I hesitated. *"Please,"* he'd said. Ten minutes later he pulled into my garage and parked his luxury SUV beside Hazel.

We sat at a comfortable distance from each other on my couch, free from the weight of watchful eyes and ears. But we said little. We listened to the rain as it beat against the window, thunder stomping in the sky. Rain. It was a cleansing force, a natural passage. It washed away dirt and grime and left clean new paths in its wake. It breathed life into the earth, and made things grow, and it calmed anxious lovers sitting on a couch, waiting for the inevitable. The rain was my sign. It was my opportunity to wash away my old fears and start living for the first time in my life. No more playing it safe.

In a bold move, I slid over and straddled Ed's lap. And as the saying goes, that was all she wrote.

We made love right there on my living room floor. It was hot, steamy, and passionate. I had wanted him so badly that my emotions led me to reach for what I had desired since that hot August day at Spelman eleven years ago. And while it hadn't unfolded like the idyllic, tender moments I'd envisioned for our first time, it was everything I had hoped it would be, and more.

My only regret was that even though I was on the Pill, we should have used a condom. Pregnancy was one worry, an STD was another. But when I had the only man I had ever wanted in a position I never thought would come, clean medical records had been the last thing on my mind. So after Ed retrieved his overnight bag from his truck and we ventured upstairs to my bedroom, I told him that I had taken an HIV/AIDS test six months ago during a community education drive back home. "I'm negative, and before tonight I haven't been with anyone in eight months," I told him.

Ed looked at me curiously, as if my STD status hadn't

crossed his mind. But in the spirit of mutual disclosure he shared with me that he'd tested negative back in the spring during the citywide HIV/AIDS awareness testing that his organization, 100 Black Men, had sponsored.

After our awkward sharing of medical records, we settled into bed. We were both exhausted, but we were also too excited to close our eyes, wanting to continue our long-awaited moment. We talked for the next two hours about the eleven years of secret desire we'd shared, and laughed about the fact that until I moved here, neither of us had been sure if the other was truly interested. He also admitted that mild jealousy had played a role in his behavior at the restaurant. "I just wanted you so much," he said.

Now, lying next to Ed, snuggled against his warm, naked body, I tingled inside. "Do you want coffee and a bagel?"

"Not this morning. I have everything I need right here."

I loved hearing him say those words.

"How long have you been up?" he asked, stroking the outside of my thigh.

"A while."

"What are you thinking about?"

I smiled. "Last night."

I felt Ed's hand move up to my left breast, cupping it as he planted a soft kiss on the ball of my shoulder. "I love the way you took control," he breathed into my ear, gently tugging on my lobe with his teeth. "But now it's my turn."

With gentle ease, Ed rolled me onto my back, ready to take me on another journey into bliss. I moaned and delighted in the way he sucked my right breast while delicately tweaking the nipple of my left between his thumb and forefinger. He took his time making his way down my body, kissing each exposed inch of my skin until his head rested between my legs. Just as I thought he was going to pleasure me, he paused for a moment, as if studying a map.

"I've been waiting . . . wanting you for so long," he said as he ran his finger over my growing wetness. "So beautiful," he whispered.

My body tensed with excitement when I felt him touch me in the place that until last night I'd only fantasized about. With soft and careful attentiveness, he swept his finger back and forth over my tender opening, watching me as I squirmed beneath his expert touch. Slowly, he spread my lips, slippery and wet, before covering me with his warm mouth.

I could feel his hunger and desire to please me. He perched his mouth at the base of my engorged clit, sucking and softly tugging at it as his tongue probed me. "Oh, yeah," I moaned.

"You taste so good," he breathed, sucking me deep into his mouth.

My hips bucked forward and I arched my lower back as he devoured me—as though taking small bites of an apple. His tongue was skilled, fluid, and precise. He worked with determined concentration, testing different angles of pressure until he found the one that made me cry out so loudly I was sure I could be heard at the coffee shop around the corner. I gripped my fingers at the back of his head and pressed his mouth close against my heated flesh. I loved the sight of him gently lapping between my legs as the morning sun flooded the room.

After he brought me to orgasm with his loving tongue, he moved up, kissed my stomach, journeyed to my breasts, and then found his way to my lips as our bodies moved in unison below. He reached over to the nightstand for a condom, slipped it on, and parted my legs with his knee. He looked into my eyes as he entered me, slowly, and with a hint of restrained force. *"Mmm,"* I moaned.

We both let out soft cries of pleasure as he carefully eased his way farther inside me until I took in every magnificently thick inch of him. He was large, in length and in width, surprisingly more than I'd imagined. Yet, his size felt just right inside me. He filled the empty space that had been waiting just for him, making love to me, purposefully, and without inhibition. "I love you, Emily," he whispered into my ear.

"I love you, too," I panted, engulfed by his soft kiss and smooth strokes.

He increased his rhythm as the next orgasm inside me began to form with a pleasure so great it was nearly indescribable. He must have known what I was feeling because he smiled, then plunged deeper inside me, opening the door to a blessed euphoria I didn't think possible. It was so intense, so powerful, and so all-consuming. I shut my eyes, opened my mouth, and let my body succumb to it. Ed did the same. I felt him bury his head against my collarbone as he made one final thrust before letting out a slow, pleasure-filled moan.

We lay there—still and breathless, completely and blissfully satiated. This was what I had dreamed our first time would be.

We showered together and then returned to my bed. I rested my head on Ed's chest as he stroked my shoulder, applying light pressure for a gentle massage. *"Mmm, that feels good,"* I purred.

"I'm glad."

I looked past the box of Trojans and over to the alarm

clock. It was still early, barely nine o'clock. There was a full day ahead, and it suddenly dawned on me that once Ed walked out of my door he would return to a life that didn't include me. He was in tune with my thoughts, and he could feel my mood turn.

"Emily, what's wrong?"

I mumbled into his chest. "What time do you have to leave? You've been gone since last night and she'll wonder where you are."

Though it wasn't the first time that Brenda had crossed my mind since Ed walked through my door, it was the first she'd come up in our conversation. I hadn't asked any questions last night about how he was going to explain being away from home, or even how he left the house in the first place, I was just happy that he was with me. He had an overnight bag, so I knew he must have given Brenda some kind of explanation for his absence. Now, lying in my bed, on soft, wine-colored sheets, after making beautiful love, I wanted to know. Besides, we had to acknowledge the other side of our paradise, the side that was surely going to raise the hell we had tried to avoid for eleven years.

"I told Brenda that I was going to hang out with Ross, and not to expect me back until today."

"Oh."

Hearing him say her name while lying in my bed sounded like glass shattering on the floor. The thought of what I'd done made me feel ashamed. In just one night I had become one of those women who other women sucked their teeth and rolled their eyes at—a home wrecker, a status I had feared and must now claim. I was the other woman. The *younger* other woman at that. It was a category far worse than all others in the breaking-up-marriages department.

I shouldn't have expected to feel anything different from the guilt that cloaked me. I knew this would be my lot if I had an affair with Ed, so I had to accept it. I took shallow breaths, thinking that after each time we were together I would have to watch him shower away our sex before he returned home to his wife. I thought about the secret phone calls we'd have to make, and the lies we'd have to tell if we wanted to see each other. I thought about the fact that there wouldn't be many occasions, if any more at all, that I would be able to wake up beside him in the morning light.

"Emily, are you okay?"

"No."

He stopped stroking my shoulder and brought me up to his face so he could see mine. "I want to share my life with you."

"But you're married."

"And that can be remedied."

Slowly, I pulled away from him, sat up in my bed, and reached for my robe, which lay on the nightstand at my side. I remembered something that Samantha told me Tyler had said when they were dating. "A woman should never have a serious conversation with a man while she's naked because men will say anything when they've got ass in the palm of their hands."

I knew that Tyler was right, and I wanted Ed to have a clear head when we discussed the future of our relationship. "Let's get dressed and go downstairs so we can talk."

I poured us glasses of orange juice, and then we went into the living room. I purposely sat at a small distance from him on my couch and began to speak. "What's the next step for us?" I asked.

"I think the answer is obvious," he responded in his

always confident tone. "We want to be together, so now it's time to make it happen."

"How do we do that? How can we be together without hurting people?"

"We can't. People will get hurt. That happens in life."

I had to believe that this was the pragmatic lawyer side of him talking, the one driven by facts and rooted in what was tangible and what could be proven. It was a proven fact that people got hurt all the time, but that it would be at my hands was still hard for me to accept.

"Emily," Ed continued. "We avoided this for eleven long years because we knew that people . . . that Brenda and Sam would be affected, so we never acted on our feelings. But in the meantime we suffered, or at least I did," he said, shifting his position on the couch. "I suffered every time I saw you, secretly wanting to be with you but knowing that I couldn't. I suffered every time I heard Sam tell me about a new guy you were dating. I suffered when I saw you at your mother's funeral and I couldn't be the shoulder you cried on. I'm tired of suffering. I'm ready to start living again, and I'm ready to do it with you."

I felt everything he felt, and I told him so. Now it seemed things were simply a matter of logistics.

"I'm going to divorce Brenda," he said. "I know one of the best divorce lawyers on this side of creation. I'll meet with him tomorrow and spend the next week or two getting my ducks in a row before I serve her with papers."

"She'll be devastated."

Ed shook his head. "Not for the reasons you think. She'll get over it."

I didn't want to delve into the complexities that spurred his comment, so I focused on what I understood. "What about Samantha? She'll have a very hard time dealing with this."

"Maybe in the beginning . . ."

"You think she'll accept this . . . us?"

"What other choice does she have? Sam loves both of us, and after she gets over the initial shock she'll be happy for us."

I looked at Ed as if he'd lost his mind. How could he possibly believe what he was saying? Were we talking about the same person? Samantha, the ultimate daddy's girl. His daughter was more territorial of him than Brenda had ever been. She was loyal and protective of him, just like she was of me. He wasn't her father, he was her daddy, and I wasn't her friend, I was her sister. I knew she would see our being together as a serious violation of the bonds she had with us. At that moment, I became more concerned about my potentially shaky relationship with my best friend than I was about being the home-wrecking other woman. "Samantha will freak out," I said. "I just know it."

"Sam's excitable, but she's not unreasonable. She's in a good relationship now, and she's coming into a good place in her life. She can handle it."

"I hope you're right."

Ed moved in closer and took me into his arms. He pulled me on top of his lap and held me in the same position I boldly claimed last night. "What matters now is that I love you, and you love me. The rest is immaterial."

"You think it's that easy?"

"No, but for now I want to enjoy what we have, what we've waited so long to feel."

Gently, we kissed, our tongues darting, circling, and commingling inside each other's hungry mouths. I could feel the moisture between my legs return and the familiar rise of Ed's well-endowed manhood awaken under the weight of my hips. I smiled, slid my knees to the floor, and unzipped his pants. When I took him into my mouth, we both forgot about hurt, divorce papers, and everything else except the feeling we were sharing, right here on my cozy chenille-covered couch.

Chapter 27

Samantha . . .

A Chance at Redemption

Life was throwing me curveballs, and over the past week I'd hit every one of them as I rounded the bases. From my surprise reunion with Tyler, to moving into my new house, to my debacle of a birthday party last night. I had managed to dodge the pitfalls. But even with all the unexpected twists and turns, nothing could have prepared me for the giant fastball that came out of nowhere and hit me square in my head when I woke up this morning and saw my mother's number flash across my cell phone.

Tyler and I were lying in bed when we heard the loud chirping of my phone. I fumbled over to my nightstand and looked at the caller ID. "Oh, shit," I cursed.

"Who is it?" Tyler asked with concern. I knew he was worried that it might be some mess surrounding Carl. Before we fell asleep last night, he told me that he was extending his trip a few extra days, just to make sure I was safe.

"It's my mother," I sighed.

His face looked a little relieved, but only slightly. "Are you going to answer it?"

I paused for a second trying to decide whether I wanted to have my day ruined now, or put it off until later. My life had always been full of bad decisions that resulted from my inability to deal with situations in a mature manner, but now I was working toward being a better me, so I decided to bite the bullet and answer my phone. "Hello, Mother," I said in a flat tone, bracing myself for bullshit.

"Good morning, Samantha . . . um, how are you feeling?" she asked nervously.

Something was wrong. I could feel it. Mother never wanted to know how I was doing and she never sounded nervous, practically jittery, so I proceeded with extreme caution. "Could be better, but I won't complain."

"Listen, I, um . . . I feel bad about what happened last night."

I sat straight up in bed like someone had just thrown ice water on me. Tyler sat up beside me looking alarmed and mouthed, "Is everything okay?" I hunched my shoulders because I didn't know for sure, but I listened as Mother continued.

"Samantha, I spent a lot of time thinking, all night, as a matter of fact. There are moments that make us reassess our lives, and what happened between us last night made me do that."

You mean the way you slapped the shit out of me? I wanted to say, but was too stunned to speak because I couldn't believe my ears. I listened to Mother explain how she regretted the way our relationship had spiraled down to nothing short of hateful contempt. And while she didn't acknowledge responsibility for being one of the major causes of our mother/daughter demise, she said that she wanted us to make amends, starting today. "Can you come over this afternoon?" she asked. "I was hoping we could have a late lunch or early dinner and celebrate your birthday again."

I nearly peed in my panties. "She wants to have lunch," I mouthed to Tyler, who was still looking on with concern. I didn't know what to think. Naturally, I became suspicious of her real intentions. Mother always had an angle for everything she did, and now I had to find out what it was, and because I was a straight shooter, I just put it out there. "I've heard everything you said, but honestly, I don't trust it because I don't trust you. You want me to believe that after thirty years you've all of a sudden had an epiphany? All because you and I had a squabble, which we've been doing all my life?" It was the Sabbath, and I knew God would appreciate me keeping it real, especially since I'd held back the profanity that leapt to my tongue.

Mother let out a loud sigh. "I don't blame you for having reservations. I guess I haven't been as supportive as I could have been. But, Samantha, I tried, in the best way I knew how."

She sounded genuinely hurt, and I'd even go as far as to say remorseful. I thought about what she had said, that she had tried the best way she knew how. It was as if someone had placed a mirror in front of my face and let me listen to my own words. It was the same way I felt about CJ. I had neglected my son in an effort to protect him from *me*. It suddenly dawned on me that maybe all these years my mother had been emotionally unavailable for the same reason.

Mother sniffled, and then paused as if trying to hold back tears. "Please, Samantha. Give me a chance to make things right between us. I don't have another thirty years."

My heart softened. The new me was willing to give her a chance. "Okay, I'll come over this afternoon."

After I hung up the phone, I rehashed our conversation with Tyler.

"Sounds like miracles do happen," he said in amazement.

"Yes, you and I are proof of that. I trust what we have. I know this is real. But my mother . . ."

"At some point you've got to let go of the anger and fear."

"Easier said than done."

"You have another chance, one that many people wish they had. Your mother is still here, and you can turn things around."

"So you think I'm doing the right thing by going?"

Tyler nodded. "Yes, I think you should go see her."

I showered, combed my hair, applied my makeup, and searched through my closet trying to decide what to wear. I was a little nervous about seeing Mother, but I wanted to look good, even if I didn't feel it. Finally, I slipped into my favorite pink dress and fastened the posts of the elegant David Yurman pearl and platinum earrings that Tyler had given me for my birthday. I decided to go bare at the neck, opting to cap off my accessories with a pair of beautiful bone-colored Gucci pumps.

Tyler left to meet Jason for lunch, and we agreed to meet back here this afternoon, and then we would take CJ out for ice cream. I smiled at the thought that I was leading a normal, grown-up life.

I stepped outside, got into my car, and headed for Emily's house. I hit her up on speed dial and told her about my conversation with Mother. Bouncing things off

Tyler was great, but Emily had always been the steadfast, stabilizing force I knew I could count on for sound, logical advice and a mature perspective. She balanced things out for me and always led me in the right direction.

"This sounds major," Emily said.

"Yeah, it is. That's why I want to talk to you about it."

"You know I'm here whenever you need me."

"Great, can I come over now? I'm two minutes away."

"Um . . . sure." She paused.

"Cool, I'll see you in a sec." I knew I could count on my best friend.

Minutes later I rang Emily's bell. She opened the door still wearing her bathrobe. "I can't believe Miss I-get-up-at-the-ass-crack-of-dawn is still lying around the house in her bathrobe at this time of day," I said.

Emily shook her head nervously and laughed. "Yeah, um, come on in."

"Are you okay?"

She coughed, clearing her throat as she pulled her bathrobe tight around her waist. "Just a little tired."

I peered at her closely. "Maybe you're coming down with something. I can come back later."

"No, no," Emily urged. "I want to hear all about your conversation with your mother."

I took a seat on her couch and repeated what Mother had said, almost word for word. I looked into Emily's eyes and could see that she was torn. She usually defended Mother and made excuses for her nasty behavior. But I think after last night, witnessing firsthand how mean-spirited, bitter, and downright vicious my mother could be, it made her jump on the *Brenda is a bitch* bandwagon on which I and everyone else rode.

"So, what do you think?" I asked.

Emily sat back and let out a sigh. "I think you should

take her at her word and approach it with a clear and open mind."

"But you saw how she treated me last night."

"Yes, but today's a new day."

"She's been a bitch for over fifty years. She hasn't changed overnight."

"Maybe not, but everyone deserves a chance at redemption."

"I just have trouble believing that my mother is sincere. She's got to be up to something."

"I don't know, Samantha. Maybe last night was really her wake-up call," Emily said. "One thing's for sure, you'll never know until you talk to her, face-to-face."

"You're right."

"Let go of the past and begin with a clean slate, starting with your visit today." She smiled, then paused. "That's what you're doing with CJ. You're working toward developing a relationship with your child. It just took your mother a little longer."

Emily was right, as usual. After talking with her, I felt more optimistic about the visit and what it could possibly mean for a better understanding between my mother and me. This was what I had always wanted, but now I couldn't understand why I was fighting it so hard. I didn't know if it was fear of disappointment, or the fact that I just flat out didn't trust her. In any event, I knew that as Emily said, the only way to find out the real deal was to meet with Mother and see for myself.

I was about to leave when I noticed a beautiful diamond bracelet dangling from Emily's wrist. "*Ooohhh,* let me see that." I perked up as I reached for her hand. "I know an exquisite piece of jewelry when I see one. And this, my friend, is a genuine prize!"

I recognized it right away. It was the Tiffany & Co. Jazz bracelet set in platinum. I knew this because I had looked at it a few months ago when I treated myself to a shopping spree with the "please forgive me" money that Carl had sent me after one of our big blowouts. I glanced under her coffee table and saw the signature blue box that confirmed it had come from Tiffany. A birthday card sat beside it. I raised my brow and said, "Who gave you a fourteen-thousand-dollar bracelet for your birthday?"

Emily's eyes widened to the size of baseballs. "Fourteen thousand!" she gasped, looking at her wrist as if dynamite was hanging from it.

"Girl, you've got nearly three carats of some of the finest brilliant cut diamonds you can find, all wrapped around your wrist."

"Samantha, are you sure this bracelet cost fourteen thousand dollars?" she asked in awe.

"Hell yeah, I'm sure. You should never doubt my fashion acumen." I smiled proudly. "The question is, who gave it to you and what did you do to get it?" I asked, raising my brow again. I reached for the birthday card, but she quickly took it from my hand and placed it in the gift bag beside the coffee table. "Emily, I can't believe you're holding out on me. You better give up the 411 right now."

I looked around the room to see if I could find any clues and sure enough, I did . . . right there in front of me. "Is he here?" I whispered.

"Who?" Emily asked, looking flustered.

I pointed at the two half-empty glasses that sat on her coffee table. "Whoever was sipping orange juice with you this morning and has you so worn out that you're still in your robe," I said. "Yeah, you're coming down with something all right, a case of dick-itis! Girl, you better give up the info right now."

She looked nervous and embarrassed, and now I knew why she was off-kilter when I walked through her door. I knew my friend, and I knew she couldn't hold out forever. "So, you finally gave in and took the step," I said, nodding.

"I . . . I don't know what you're talking about," she stammered. She was a terrible liar.

"Yes, you do. And Emily, it's all right. I'm not going to judge you for wanting to be with him." I smiled, giving her hand a gentle squeeze. "I know you've been fighting this for a long time. But there comes a point in your life when you have to break your own rules and follow your heart. I think it's great that you're finally doing that."

She looked completely stunned.

"Emily, you act like you've committed a big sin by being with him. Loosen up."

"I can't believe you're okay with this." She blinked.

"Hey, as long as you're happy, I'm happy."

Emily sat in silence, looking down at the floor.

"Oh, for Christ's sake, enjoy the fact that you're in love," I said.

Emily looked up at me with a warm, sincere smile, and took a deep breath as though a load had just been lifted from her shoulders. She spoke softly. "I do love him. I always have."

"I know, and I'm glad you didn't wait until it was too late to finally admit your feelings."

"I just felt so conflicted, and I didn't know how you'd take it, or what you'd think of me."

"See, there you go again, always worrying about everybody except yourself. I love that about you. But honestly, you shouldn't give a damn about what I think, or anyone else. Just as long as it works for you."

A smile covered her face. "Samantha, I'm happier than I've ever been. I'm so glad this is out in the open and that you're really okay with it."

I looked at her and shrugged my shoulders. "Why wouldn't I be? You know I love him to pieces."

"I know. He said you'd be happy for us, and I guess he was right."

"Is he still here?" I asked, looking around again. "I don't want to interrupt anything."

"Um, no . . . he left right before you got here, but he's coming back later tonight."

"Oh, that's right." I nodded with understanding. "I forgot that Bradley has relatives in the city. Is he out visiting them?"

Emily shifted in her seat and started coughing again.

"You okay?"

"Um, yeah. I'm fine," she said, looking self-conscious, like she'd been exposed.

"Listen, I know you said you'd never go back to Bradley, but don't be embarrassed about it. I'm glad you were able to admit that you made a mistake and that you're giving your relationship another try. I guess that's what you meant about everybody needing a chance at redemption." I smiled and ran my finger across her beautiful bracelet for emphasis.

We talked a little longer before I glanced at my watch and realized I only had fifteen minutes to spare before my lunch visit with Mother. So in keeping with my new change of attitude, and not wanting to be late, I gave Emily a big hug and told her that we'd have to look into booking companion flights to Atlanta to see our men, and then headed out the door . . . on my way to set another chain of events into motion.

I was glad when I saw Daddy's Range Rover parked in the garage because if things got funky between Mother and me, he would be around to make sure we didn't hurt each other. After last night, anything was possible.

I walked through the back door and found Mother sitting at the kitchen table. Even though she said she hadn't slept all night, she looked as fresh as the flowers in her garden. Then again, I couldn't remember a time when she didn't look picture perfect. The only blemish on her perfect exterior was the pink mark I'd left on the side of her face from last night.

"I'm glad you came," she said, looking me up and down from head to toe. "That's a lovely ensemble . . . nice pumps."

I wanted to smile, but I held it back along with my guard. "Thanks."

Cautiously, I took a seat across from her and tried to determine what was really going on behind her eyes. She rose from her chair, retrieved two glasses from the cabinet and a bottle of champagne from the fridge. "In the middle of the day?" I asked, looking at the bottle of Perrier-Jouët.

"We're celebrating your birthday, remember?"

Mother poured a glass for me and then one for herself. She sat down and raised her flute to make a toast. "May all your days be filled with nothing but the best. Happy birthday, Samantha."

I raised my glass, tapping it against hers. I sipped slowly as I watched her go back to the refrigerator and return with two plates of food. She sat one in front of me. "Lunch, compliments of last night's leftovers." She smiled sheepishly.

I didn't know what to make of her behavior. Demure and sedated wasn't my mother's style; pushy and extreme was more like it.

"What did Tyler get you for your birthday?" she asked, taking a bite of a tomato wedge.

"The earrings I'm wearing."

She nodded approvingly. "That young man has exceptional taste. I really like him, and I like him for you. I'm so happy that you two are back together."

I couldn't hold my tongue any longer. As optimistic as I wanted to be, I smelled a rat and I was determined to get to the bottom of the real reason why I was sitting across from her, all dressed up, forcing artificial conversation. I put my fork down, wiped my mouth, and looked Mother dead in her eyes. "Let's cut through the niceties and small talk. What's really going on?"

"Samantha, I told you. I want to make amends."

"Yeah, that's what your mouth said."

"Why don't you believe me?"

"Because that's not what you do."

Mother sat ramrod straight in her chair. "Oh, and what *do* I do?"

"Let's see . . . berate people, manipulate situations to your advantage, hurt people's feelings, think solely about yourself, and put on phony airs."

"Is that all you think of me?" she asked in a pitiful voice.

"That's all you've ever shown me."

"Maybe I've changed."

I looked at my watch. "Less than eighteen hours ago I tried to apologize to you, and you stood in the backyard belittling me like you didn't give a damn about my feelings. And then you slapped me. Now you expect me to believe that after thirty years and eighteen hours, you're a changed person."

"How dare you speak to me that way. You have absolutely no right," she huffed.

It was her standard "how dare you" line that I'd heard all my life. The indignant, self-righteous Brenda Baldwin I knew had returned in a flash. I pushed my chair back, reached for my handbag, and started to leave.

"Samantha, please don't go," Mother pleaded.

"Tell me why I should stay."

"Because I need you. I'm about to lose everything I love and I need you."

"What are you talking about?"

She looked down at the half-eaten food on her plate and the empty champagne flute. "I've turned so many people away—even your father chose to stay out with that dreadful Ross Morgan last night rather than be here with me," she sniffled, "and he didn't come home until shortly before you arrived."

"And that concerns me how?"

"It seems everyone hates me. At least that's what Gerti said."

That got my attention. Slowly, I sat back down in my chair. "Gerti said that?"

"Yes, she did . . . among other things."

"Other things like what?"

Mother sniffled again and reached for a silk napkin on the table, dabbing it against an imaginary tear in the corner of her eye. "Hurtful things. Things I'd rather not repeat."

"Were they accurate?"

"No. Actually, nothing she said was true."

"Really?" I said with skepticism. "I've never known Gerti to lie about anything. Aside from Emily, she's the most honest person I know."

Mother smirked with irritation. "Well, you don't know Gerti like I do. The truth is that she's never really cared for me. The only reason I've kept her around all these years is because she does such a good job around this house. But until last night, I never knew that her dislike for me was rooted in pure jealousy."

"Gerti's not jealous of you."

"You didn't hear the things she said to me."

"No, I didn't. But I've never heard Gerti say an unkind word about you, *ever.*"

"You don't know the side of your beloved Gerti that she showed me last night."

I shook my head. First she wanted to make amends with me and now she was bad-mouthing Gerti, the only person in this house who halfway liked her. I didn't know what to make of this bizarre visit that she'd been so desperate for us to have. More than ever, I was convinced that she was up to something. I was pissed that I had allowed myself to get all worked up. And I'll admit, I was a little hopeful that she and I might have a chance to finally put our differences behind us and start working toward a better relationship. But now I could see there was no way that was going to happen. "Mother, I think I better go."

"But we haven't even had dessert."

"I don't want dessert."

"Fine!" Mother laid her fork across the side of her plate and pushed it away. Just then, Daddy came into the room. I looked up at him and he could see there was hot tension in the air.

"Hey, Sam," he said with caution, ignoring Mother completely. "Everything all right?"

"I'm cool."

"Good." Daddy nodded. He walked toward the refrigerator, searching it like he hadn't eaten in days. "Glad you're here. Now I can give you the latest news on Carl."

Mother and I both braced ourselves. "What news?" I asked.

"Carl's in serious trouble, and this time they have enough evidence to finally put him away."

Daddy had called one of his contacts this afternoon and found out the details of the arrest report. As it turned out, not only had Carl been in possession of an unregistered handgun, they'd found a powdery white substance in his Escalade, which had been parked out front. Added to that, they obtained a search warrant for his house early this morning and found evidence that tied him to a new and deadly form of crack cocaine that had appeared on DC streets within the last few months.

Daddy went on to say that the authorities had Carl under tight surveillance for months, which was one of the reasons why they arrived on the scene so quickly last night.

"Bail is off the table," Daddy said. "Flight risk."

I thought about how strangely Carl had been acting, and now this explained why. He was hooked on the new stuff he was selling. I felt relieved that Carl was under tight lock and key for now, preventing him from any further craziness. But a part of me was also sad. He was the father of my child, the man I had shared many experiences with, some bad, but not all. Now he was right where he'd always feared, in a tiny jail cell. I looked at Mother, expecting her to say something rude, nasty, or mean, but she didn't. I think Daddy was surprised by her silence, too.

Finally, she spoke as she fumbled with her napkin. "I'm sorry for what happened last night."

This was the first time she'd apologized since I got here. I immediately became pissed because I knew her contrition was all for Daddy's benefit. I had to get out of the house so I could think about everything that had happened. I walked over to Daddy, gave him a kiss on his cheek, and turned toward the door.

"You headed home?" he asked, claiming the spot where I'd been sitting as he dug into a bowl of pasta salad he'd gotten out of the fridge.

"Yeah, then Tyler and I are going to take CJ out for ice cream."

"That's lovely," Mother said.

Daddy and I both ignored her.

"Oh, and by the way, I have wonderful news," I said

as I looked at Daddy, not wanting Mother to think I was including her in our conversation.

"What's that?" he asked.

I brightened with a big smile. "Emily and Bradley are back together. Isn't that great!"

"Yes, that's wonderful news," Mother cheered. "I'm so happy for her."

I looked at mother and wanted to curse. She had never even met Bradley! Now I was 100 percent sure that she was the same snake that hissed at me during the party last night. So before things turned ugly again I said good-bye to Daddy, walked out the door, and didn't look back.

Chapter 28

Brenda . . .

Her Life in Its Balance

Brenda sat at the kitchen table and watched her husband as he moved his pasta salad around the center of his plate. He was looking at his food in deep concentration. Brenda was livid that Ed had stayed out all night, supposedly with his best friend and universal ladies' man Ross Morgan, whom she despised.

Quietly, Brenda studied Ed as he stared blankly at his mostly untouched food. She knew that he never dallied when he ate a meal, so this was further evidence that something was weighing down his mind. She wanted so badly to tell Ed that she was aware of what he was up to, that she'd found the evidence, but she didn't have all her ammunition or game plan fully in place, so she knew she'd have to bide her time.

Brenda never thought that she and Ed would come to this—divorce! But just as surely as the sun was shining bright in the sky, that's where she knew her marriage was headed. Last night after her confrontation with Gerti, she began to think about the words they exchanged. *People are sick of your shit and they're not gonna stick around to take it anymore,* Gerti had said.

Even though Brenda disliked Gerti, the one thing she had to give the woman credit for was the very comment that Samantha had made—she'd never known Gerti to tell a lie. Brenda's mind raced. She knew that Gerti either sensed something coming or had direct knowledge of changes ahead, and she bet dollars to Prada that it involved her marriage.

She knew that her sex life with Ed had been on the decline for years, but they were still a fabulous-looking couple, living in a fabulous-looking home, driving fabulous-looking vehicles, and making life look just fabulous. She attributed the mundane existence of their marriage to the mere consequence of being with one person for so long. *You can't have it all,* she reasoned. She'd become settled in the notion that she and Ed would simply play out the rest of their lives in forced comfort, putting on a good face in public while privately tolerating each other as they had both learned to do.

But even before Gerti's harsh words, she had begun to notice a definite shift in Ed's behavior. He stopped following what had become their formulated script. Over the last week he'd been spending more time at his office downtown, and when he did finally return home late at night he went straight to his study, falling asleep on the couch by his desk on several occasions.

Her radar was on high alert. And now Gerti's pronouncement had confirmed her worst fears. After Gerti stormed out of the kitchen, Brenda ventured into Ed's study. She knew that he was precise and meticulously diligent in the way he kept his office. So she went through his things one piece of paper at a time, making sure to put each document, pen, folder, and paper clip back where she'd found it.

After an hour of snooping she hadn't uncovered a single thing. She had begun to lose hope when her eyes landed on a business card sticking out from the edge of a thick book that she had somehow overlooked. Her brows shot up to her hairline when she read the cover title: *Domestic Relations Law.* Her hands shook as she opened the pages to where the card had been lodged, and she gasped at the section in bold type that read *Divorce.* She drew in a deep breath, nearly falling out of Ed's chair when she recognized the name on the tiny 3 x 2 inch card that now held her life in its balance.

Brenda stared down at the business card of Anthony L. Longfellow, a well-known and prominent divorce attorney. Her heart beat fast as she thought about what her life would be like without Ed. How would she make it on her own? She knew she was beautiful, talented, and smart, with a certain *je ne sais quoi* that made her stand out in a crowd. But she also realized the hard truth—that she'd never held a job outside the home, not even an internship in college. She started to think about the ways in which her life would change, and what people would say. She sat back in Ed's soft leather chair, knowing she had to approach the situation just as she had every other obstacle in her life—with a well-planned strategy.

She was smart enough to know that unlike when they'd had problems in the past and Ed had threatened to leave her, he would no longer consider staying out of a sense of loyalty, or to keep their family together. Brenda thought about CJ, her little golden goose. Having that boy under her roof over the last year had been the next best thing to diamonds. Ed adored his grandson and was determined to provide a stable home for him. As long as CJ was around, Brenda knew that Ed would stay firmly rooted at home. But now that Samantha had suddenly decided to take a more active role in her son's life, and Emily had moved to town, the dynamics were quickly changing.

Brenda cursed herself for not recognizing the complications earlier on. Now Ed no longer had to worry about being the steady constant in CJ's life because he had help, and that left her in a vulnerable position. Brenda knew she had to find Ed's soft spot and manipulate it in order to keep the perfect life she'd worked so hard to maintain. Then it came to her—Samantha!

For reasons she never understood, Samantha had always been Ed's pride and joy. Brenda snapped her fingers and smiled, knowing that if she could get Samantha on her side, she could keep Ed. Ed had often agonized over their tumultuous mother/daughter relationship, and if she and Samantha could get on a good footing, Brenda knew it would be her new insurance policy. Her closeness with her daughter would bond them and would compel Samantha to help champion her cause to keep her marriage intact.

So Brenda set out to put her plan into action. She called Samantha that morning, ate a small serving of humble pie, and then invited her over for lunch. She even put forth an effort to produce tears to show her sincerity. But during their lunch, no matter how civil she tried to be, Samantha refused to play nice. Even though Brenda wanted to practically shake her ungrateful daughter and be done with her, she remained calm, knowing she had to keep her wits about her and not explode in front of Ed. Somehow, she managed to hold things together until Samantha finally walked out the door.

Now, as she watched Ed while he continued to eat his pasta salad, ignoring her as if she weren't even in the room, a painful realization shot through Brenda's body.

Emotions stirred inside her that she hadn't felt since she had purposely stopped taking her birth control pills thirty-two years ago. What she felt was desperation. And this time she didn't have an obligation to hang over Ed's head.

Ed finished his food, put his plate in the sink, and turned to her. "I'm going upstairs to pack."

"Why? Where are you going now?"

"I'm hanging out with Ross. It's his last night in town," he said flatly. "Besides, I wouldn't want to come in late and ruin your beauty sleep." And without another word, Ed left the room before she could respond.

Brenda had learned long ago that the opposite of love wasn't hate, it was indifference, and that was what Ed had become toward her—indifferent.

Brenda poured herself another glass of bubbly and then went into the den. She kicked off her shoes and curled up on the couch, preparing herself for her regular afternoon nap. She knew that she couldn't afford to operate in panic mode. She had to be smart about the situation and formulate a new plan. So she relaxed herself, not wanting her recent worries and stress to cause any unsightly wrinkles. Within minutes she drifted off to sleep, dreaming about her new strategy.

Chapter 29

Ed . . .

You Learn to Question Everything

I nearly choked on my pasta salad when I heard Sam's news.

"Emily and Bradley are back together!" she announced.

I wanted to ask, when, how? But before I could get any details Sam was out the door. I tried to play it cool, but I had no more appetite for food. All I could do was move my pasta salad around on my plate and think about Emily and Bradley. *Is that why she had the box of condoms in her nightstand?* I wondered. *But she told me that she hadn't been with anyone in eight months.* I was about to become flustered, but then I reminded myself that I needed to gather the facts before I could convict.

I ate in silence while Brenda watched me. I could almost see the wheels turning behind her manipulative eyes. She was up to something, I just didn't know what. A good part of me wanted to lay everything out in the open, but I knew I had to finesse the situation carefully. So I

stood, put my plate in the sink, and told Brenda not to expect me back home tonight. She was pissed at the thought
of me hanging out with Ross again, but I ignored her agitation and headed upstairs.

I stood in my closet and thought about Emily as I put
my brown herringbone suit into my black garment bag.
Sometimes when people waited so long to be together,
the anticipation and excitement could be more fulfilling
than the actual moment. But that was far from the case
with Emily. She was everything I had imagined, desired,
and hoped for.

I'd always loved her quiet sexiness, which I found
much more appealing than the in-your-face boldness that
some women flaunted. There's nothing more alluring and
sensual to a man than a woman who's got it, but doesn't
feel the need to parade it. That was Emily's very style and
definition. It was the subtle things about her that made her
irresistibly sexy in a natural way, like how she could glide
into a room and let the feminine sway of her hips serve as
her calling card, rather than making a boisterous entrance.
It was the way she threw her head back ever so gently
when she laughed. The way she concerned herself with the
well-being of others, and the way she made me feel, alive
and hopeful. Those qualities were a big turn-on for me.

Some people went their entire life without feeling
what I was experiencing now. And that was why I also realized I had to be careful. I'd seen it a million times. Victory could be lost right near the finish line. All it took was
one mistake. I knew I had to watch Brenda. With that
thought in mind, I grabbed my overnight bags and headed
downstairs to my study.

I had suspected that Brenda snooped around in here
from time to time, looking for things that were none of
her concern. And if I knew her as I thought I did, she had
been in here last night. The first thing I noticed was that

my chair was slightly askew, but I waved it off because I couldn't remember if I had forgotten to push it in or not. So I took a seat behind my desk and studied the way I'd left it the day before. I always placed things in a certain spot, and sure enough, I noticed that my pencil holder was sitting at the far corner of my desk instead of the center where I'd left it. "Bingo," I whispered. "She's been in here."

I sat back to see what other evidence I could find, and then it hit me without having to search. My eyes went straight to the law book under my desk. I picked it up and looked at Longfellow's card peeking from inside, marking the divorce section that I had been reading. I knew there was no way that Brenda would've overlooked this. "Shit, she knows," I hissed in a low voice. That explained the easygoing mood she tried to force herself into earlier this afternoon when Sam was here. She knew I was planning to divorce her and she was trying to launch a preemptive strike.

Although I didn't think Brenda deserved honesty, I didn't think she deserved my deceit either. Even when I committed indiscretions in the past, I hated lying to her and sneaking around. And now I hated it even more because this time things were different. Emily was really special to me. More than special. I loved her.

Then my mind landed back to the statement Sam had made before she left. Had Emily and Bradley really reconciled? Had last night been a fling for her? A wild and crazy tryst to bring in her thirtieth birthday? I couldn't believe it, not from Emily. I knew my mind wouldn't rest until I got to the bottom of whatever had given Sam the impression that Bradley was back on the scene. I gathered my things, walked past Brenda, who was sleeping on the sofa, and headed for my truck.

* * *

All I could think about was the box of condoms Emily kept in her nightstand drawer and the comment Sam made about Emily and Bradley's reunion. Then I thought about Ross's question to me from two nights ago. I couldn't say with certainty that Emily wasn't seeing anyone else, and I hadn't asked her directly. Yes, she'd said she loved me and that she wanted to be with me, but that didn't preclude another man from being in the picture.

I didn't want to believe that Emily was that type of woman. I was an excellent judge of character, and when I thought about the sweet, loving, and genuinely good person I knew, I found it difficult to even conceive that Emily would make love to me one night and then go back to Bradley the next day. Hell, Sam had to be mistaken.

But I'd lived long enough to know that anyone, if given certain opportunities or circumstances, was capable of doing just about anything. When you've worked in a profession like mine and seen criminal behavior up close, you come to know that the implausible is possible, and you learn to question everything. It wasn't about what you thought or what you saw, it was about what you could prove, and right now I couldn't prove a damn thing.

But I knew that if Emily and I were going to build a relationship, we had to start with a foundation based on trust. I almost laughed at the irony of my situation. I was a man who was cheating on his wife, and I wanted to build a trusting relationship with my mistress.

I turned down Emily's street and called her, praying she was there, alone. She picked up on the first ring.

"You'll never believe what happened after you left," she said in a rushed voice.

"Are you free? Can I come over?"

"Sure . . . um, is everything all right?" she asked. She could hear the rough edge in my voice.

"Yes, I'm fine. I just want to make sure you're not busy."

"No, I'm not. Ed, what's wrong?"

I didn't want to show how jealous I was, but hell, I loved this woman and there was something about her that rendered me helpless and broke down my machismo. "Sam said that you and Bradley are back together."

"That's what I was trying to tell you . . ."

"So it's true?" I put on my brakes right in the middle of her street.

"Of course not," she said, sounding offended. "Samantha saw the bracelet you gave me this morning and thought it was from Bradley. I couldn't tell her that it was from you, but at the same time I couldn't think of anything else to say, so I let her believe what she wanted."

My heart eased its way up from the pit of my stomach and finally settled back into my chest where it belonged. "Oh," I said. I felt completely foolish.

Honk, honk! The driver in the car behind me laid on his horn, then swerved around me in a frustrated rush.

"Ed, where are you?"

"In the middle of your street."

"Drive around the back, I'll be waiting for you."

A minute later I parked my truck next to Emily's car, just as I did last night. I walked through her back door, only this time I was greeted with a warm hug and a lingering kiss. "It's good to be back," I said, pulling her in close.

She led me by the hand and I followed, glad to climb the stairs on our way to her bedroom. I put down my bags, kicked off my shoes, and reached for Emily, easing her onto the soft comforter. But instead of straddling herself atop my lap as I'd hoped, she sat in the space beside me.

"Ed, we need to talk."

Whenever a woman said those words it couldn't be good. We'd been together for less than twenty-four hours and I was already in the doghouse. "Okay," I said. "What do you want to talk about?"

She looked at me and touched the bracelet around her wrist that I had given her this morning after she'd given me the most outstanding blow job I'd ever had. "I heard the accusatory tone in your voice when you asked about Bradley. I can't believe you thought I was still seeing him."

"I had to ask."

"Do you really think I'd make love to you, tell you that I loved you, and then be with another man?" she asked, releasing a deep sigh. "Ed, I've waited for what has felt like my entire life to be with you. There's no one else for me."

I looked back into Emily's eyes and knew that she was telling me the absolute truth. I felt like shit for doubting her because I could see that my accusation had hurt her. "I'm sorry for jumping to conclusions."

"We need to establish trust."

"Agreed."

Emily crossed her legs, looking like a kid sitting around a camp fire. She was getting comfortable and this could only mean one thing, she wanted to have the "what is our future going to hold" talk. I was actually relieved because although we had covered a lot of bases last night and a few this morning, there were still many important issues we'd yet to touch.

"I want to talk about our future."

I laughed. "I kind of figured that."

She laughed, too, giving me a gentle smile. "Seriously, Ed."

"Okay, you start."

"Well, let's get the toughest one out of the way first . . . Brenda."

I explained to her that Brenda had been snooping in my study and that she more than likely already knew about my plans. "Like I said this morning, after I meet with Longfellow tomorrow I think I'll be ready to serve her with divorce papers within the next few weeks."

"That soon?" she said in an unsure voice.

"I thought you'd be happy. The sooner I'm free, the sooner we can be together."

"And the sooner we'll have to tell Samantha."

"She'll come around. Trust me."

She looked unconvinced but continued on. "Okay, what about children?"

I knew this was going to be next on her list, and honestly, it was number one on mine. It was something I'd given a great deal of thought to, especially over the last couple of days. Emily was in her prime childbearing years, she loved kids, and she'd make a fantastic mother. On the other hand, I was quickly approaching senior citizen status. I had a grown daughter her exact same age and a grandchild who attended the school where she worked. She wanted children. I didn't. Those were the hard cold facts. But I loved this beautiful, soft-spoken woman sitting next to me, and I knew that children were a non-negotiable part of her future.

"You don't want any more children, do you?" she asked as her eyes zeroed in on mine.

"The thought of diapers and sippy cups scares the hell out of me."

"I understand."

"But," I said, taking her hand in mine, "I know you want kids, and you should because you'll make a great mother. Look at the fine job you've done with CJ." She beamed with pride at the mention of her godson. "Emily,

I want us to have a full life together and I don't want you to feel deprived of anything just because you'll be with a man old enough to be your father."

It was the first time our age difference had come up, so now all the big elephants we had skirted were parading around the room.

"Does our age difference bother you?" Emily asked.

"It used to. I felt like a pervert for wanting you. Hell, you could be my daughter."

"But I'm not. I'm a woman who loves you."

I stared at her closely. I knew I was a handsome man and that I looked exceptionally good for my age, but I was also realistic enough to know that when I turned seventy, she'd be younger than I was now, and that was the part I worried about. Not for me, but for her. "Emily, have you thought about what it'll be like to be stuck with an old man?"

She looked down at her hand tucked inside mine. "Of course I've thought about our age difference. It's a bold fact, just like the fact that you're married and that you're my best friend's father. But I love you, Ed, and your age has never stopped my heart from feeling what it does."

"Things are great now. But I'm looking down the road . . . ten, twenty, thirty years even. You're still a young woman. I don't want you to have regrets."

"We don't know what's going to happen down the road. You may have to take care of me, I may have to take care of you. But whatever the case, we'll do it together." She paused and looked at me with intensity. "I'm young enough to be your daughter, but I'm old enough to know what I want, and I want this. I want everything that comes with *us*."

I leaned over and gently laid her down across the bed, settling my body on top of hers. "Damn, I'm one lucky man," I said, kissing her as I ran my hand under her tank top. I loved that she didn't wear a bra around the house. I massaged her breasts as she moaned and spread her legs at the same time. We removed each other's clothes, ready to take another plunge. I reached over to the nightstand for a condom, but then stopped. "If you haven't been seeing anyone, why are you on the Pill and why do you have condoms in your nightstand?"

She laughed. "You're *such* a lawyer!"

"I'm glad you find my question amusing." I laughed, but I was serious.

"I've been on the Pill for years because it regulates my cycle, and I picked up the condoms from CVS last week." She winked. She wiggled out of her aqua-colored panties, flung them to the side, and pulled me back on top of her. "After your visit at the school, I thought I might need them."

I smiled, ripped the condom open, and headed back to paradise.

Chapter 30

Samantha . . .

Because of Who He Is

It was midday, Friday afternoon, and I was sitting on one of the plush sofas in the main lobby area at Mazza Gallerie in the Friendship Heights section of DC. I had just finished eating my Così flatbread sandwich after making a sales call at Neiman Marcus, and I decided to take a few moments to relax before my final appointment at Lord & Taylor around the corner. I was excited just thinking about my late-afternoon flight because I was headed to Atlanta to see Tyler.

It had been seven weeks since Tyler and I reunited, and in that time we'd seen each other every weekend. One weekend he'd fly up here, the next I'd fly down there. I had heard about whirlwind romances; however, I never thought it would happen to me. But Tyler proved me wrong. When I saw him walk into Emily's house that Saturday morning, I knew that my soul mate had just stepped back into my life.

The beautiful part about my relationship with Tyler was that he not only loved me, he also loved my son. And guess what? CJ loved him right back. They instantly bonded, and truth be told, Tyler was better with him than I had ever been. I was still feeling my way into the motherhood role, but I was determined to do right by my son. As a matter of fact, CJ would be moving in with me when the spring term started at his school in a few months. And even though his biological father, who will probably be serving a long sentence in federal prison, was going to miss important events in his life like his graduation from high school and college, CJ would have Tyler and my father in his life to help teach him how to become a good man.

I crossed my long legs and scrolled through the messages on my BlackBerry, thinking about how blessed I was. My life wasn't perfect, but it was just right for me. I was crazy in love, my best friend was crazy in love, and we might be planning a double wedding ceremony in the near future.

Emily and I had shared virtually everything, from the happy beginnings that a birth can bring, to the sad endings that come with death. Now we were both in loving relationships, and it was so ironic because when we married our men, we could still end up in the same city again! It reminded me that I needed to call Bradley this weekend and invite him to join Tyler and me for dinner. I knew that would make Emily's day. She had flown to Atlanta a few weeks ago for a teacher's conference, but I didn't think she'd seen Bradley since then. That's why I knew she'd appreciate me checking in on her man.

I started gathering my things when I remembered something else. I needed to get Tyler a gift because his nonprofit, YFI, had just won an award for its commitment to children and community service. I was so proud of my man! I thought about getting him a nice tie or a new cologne, but those gifts seemed so typical and too practical. I needed to give him something he'd really enjoy, and I knew just the thing. With a smile on my face, I headed back into Neiman and took the escalator up to the lingerie department.

Is that Daddy? I thought as I approached the area lined with feminine intimate apparel. I got closer, and saw that sure enough, it was him. He was talking to a sales associate who was holding an ivory-colored lace teddy in one hand and a sexy red baby doll with a matching silk thong in the other. My first instinct was to walk up and ask him why he was shopping for lingerie in the middle of the afternoon, but the answer was obvious. He was buying it for a woman. Now my brain was in overdrive.

I eased around the side and settled into a space where I could better see and hear what they were saying.

"So, now that we've narrowed it down to these two," the sales associate said, "which one do you like best?"

Daddy tilted his head to the side, like he was thinking.

"Is she more traditional or adventurous?" the saleslady asked.

Daddy placed his hand to his chin and smiled. "She's very delicate, but she's also very sensual. And she's as much adventurous as she is traditional. She's a beautiful combination."

"That's such a lovely thing to say. She's a very lucky woman." The saleslady blushed, looking like she wished he was making the purchase for her. "I think you should get them both."

Daddy nodded. "I think you're right."

"Great, I'll run and get you a medium in both garments and I'll meet you at the register."

I covered my mouth to keep from releasing the loud

gasp that struggled to free itself from the back of my throat as I eased my way out of the lingerie department without being seen. I headed down the escalator and walked outside into the brisk October air, trying to process what I had just witnessed. This was major news and I didn't know how I felt about it. I had always thought that Daddy should leave Mother, but I suddenly felt a slight pang in my stomach knowing that he was cheating on her. Part of my emotions was a result of the new and improved me, and the other part was that I was a woman in love. I would be hurt beyond belief if Tyler bought sexy lingerie for another woman.

I hurried around the corner, crossed the street, and dashed into Lord & Taylor for my last appointment of the day.

A half hour later I emerged from the store, feeling more conflicted than ever about what I had seen. I sat in my car and pulled out my cell. "Are you home yet?" I asked Emily when she answered her phone.

"Yeah, I left work early so I can pick you up and take you to the airport like you asked me to, remember? Are you home now?"

"No, but I'm headed that way as we speak," I said, making a sharp left turn as I sped up the street. "Can you meet me at my place in twenty minutes?"

"You sound like you've just seen a ghost. What's going on?"

"Girl, you're not going to believe it, but I'll tell you when I get there."

Emily sat on the edge of my bed as I pulled clothes from my closet, folded them, and then gently placed them inside my suitcase. "I wish I hadn't seen what I saw," I said. "I mean, who wants to catch their father buying lingerie for his mistress?"

Emily cleared her throat. "How do you know that it wasn't for your mother?"

"Hah!" I laughed. "First of all, Mother would never let her size go up to a medium."

Emily looked down at her thighs and crossed her legs.

"No offense, but you know what I mean," I said. "Anyway, you've seen the way my parents interact. Do they look like anything's going on between their sheets?"

"Um, I can't speculate on that."

"Well, I can." I smirked as I tucked two pairs of stilettos into my shoe bag. "As a matter of fact, the other night when I dropped by the house to spend time with CJ, Gerti told me that they don't even sleep in the same bedroom anymore."

"Really?"

"Really! Daddy's been sleeping in the guest room since our party. I guess the drama that went down that night was the last straw for him. And it's funny because we talk all the time, but he hasn't mentioned anything to me about the tension under their roof."

"Hmm . . ."

"Emily, he's having an affair. This explains why Daddy's been so happy lately. And the way he was describing the woman he was buying lingerie for, he would never talk about Mother in *that* way."

"What way?" she asked with curiosity.

"All romantic like. You should've heard him . . . *She's delicate and sensual,*" I mimicked, deepening my tone as I tried to imitate Daddy's voice.

"He said that?"

"Yes. And you know that doesn't even remotely

sound like my mother. Daddy's never talked about her with that kind of feeling or emotion. I know men, and believe me, he had the look and sound of a man who's passionately into his woman."

Emily smiled wistfully, and then stopped herself.

"I know," I said, nodding in agreement to let her know that I understood. "I'm happy that he's finally happy, too, but . . ." I paused, feeling awkward for what I was about to say. "Do you think it's weird that I'm not too broken up about my father cheating on my mother?"

Emily leaned forward. "It really doesn't bother you?"

"Actually, the more I think about it, it doesn't."

"Do you think it would make a difference if you knew *who* the other woman was?"

"That's a good question," I said, bending down to zip my suitcase. I walked into my bathroom and came out with a few toiletries, and then it hit me. "Oh, shit!" I blurted out as an image suddenly floated in front of my eyes.

"What?"

"I bet Daddy's having an affair with a younger woman."

Emily blinked twice. "What makes you say that?"

I came over and sat down beside her, trying to figure out why that thought had popped into my head. I shrugged. "I don't know, I guess it's just a feeling I get."

"Hmm, that's interesting. There must be something that led you to that particular conclusion," Emily said, patiently waiting for my answer.

This was one of the reasons why I loved bouncing things off Emily. She was a great listener. She never interrupted, which allowed you to complete your thoughts, and she asked follow-up questions that helped you get to the heart of things. Tyler was a lot like that, too. I thought more about my statement, and just like that, I had my answer. "I think the woman he's seeing is younger because of *who* Daddy is."

"What do you mean?"

Emily didn't understand what I was getting at, so I had to break it down to her. "Would you agree that Daddy's handsome?"

"Um, yes. I agree with that."

"And would you agree that he looks much younger than he is?"

"Yes."

"Okay . . . now, I know that you think of him as family. But for a minute, try not to think of him as Daddy," I said. "He's handsome, educated, charismatic, and he's paid. Women from nine to ninety are constantly trying to get with him. Hell, the lingerie saleswoman acted like she wanted to screw him right there in the store." I laughed. "Daddy has good taste, very particular taste I might add, and at this point in his life I can see him going for a hot young thing who'll keep his engine going. And like I said, he can pull it off because of *who* he is."

"Hmm," Emily slightly grunted.

"Yeah, I know what you're thinking, and I'm with you on that. I can't imagine sleeping with a man as old as Daddy."

Emily cleared her throat, visibly disturbed by the image.

"I know, girl. Imagine what it would be like to have a kindergartner and a husband who was on Medicare?"

Emily crossed her legs and sighed. "Well, everyone has to make their own choices and do what makes them happy."

I looked at my friend and shook my head. "Speaking of happy, how are you and Bradley doing? I haven't heard you talk about him lately and I know you haven't been to Atlanta since your conference. Has he been coming here?"

She looked down at her feet. "Samantha, we're not together anymore."

"What? When did this happen?"

"A while ago."

"Emily, why didn't you tell me before now?"

"I guess I'm just trying to move on. But don't worry about me, I *am* moving on," she said, trying to sound convincing.

Emily looked sad and confused all at once. I leaned over and gave her a hug, and that's when she started crying in my arms.

There was one other thing that Emily and I had in common besides our shared birthday, and it was the fact that it took a lot to make us cry. The only times I'd ever seen Emily brought to tears were when CJ was born and when her mother died; two very different kinds of emotions. So now, to see her cry over her breakup with Bradley let me know that she was really hurting, and I could understand why. First she broke up with him, then they got back together, and now they'd broken up again. This year had been rough on her.

I rubbed her back and told her that everything was going to be all right. She was too distraught to talk about the details of what had happened, so I suspected that Bradley had done the breaking up this time.

In all the years that I'd known Emily, men had never broken up with her. Every failed relationship she had was because she'd decided to end it. She was beautiful and kind, and men held on to her like precious metal. She didn't have to tell me how things had gone down because I already knew the deal. Bradley did this out of revenge, just to get back at her for breaking up with him in the first place.

I handed Emily a tissue to dry her tears and tried to get her to laugh by telling her a few jokes about ol' Hazel. "I hope you have an extra can of oil in your trunk so you can make it back from the airport," I teased.

She smiled and tried to act like she was okay, although I knew she wasn't. But that was all right because I was going to make sure she got the last laugh. My focus shifted from my father and his mistress to the well-being of my best friend. I was pissed that Bradley had bought Emily expensive gifts, wined and dined her, and then dumped her like yesterday's news. At least when she broke up with him, she wasn't spiteful as he'd proven himself to be. She had been honest with him from the jump.

The more I thought about Bradley's spineless actions, the madder I became. The new and improved Samantha had been making progress, but right now, it was time for the old me to reach out and touch Mr. Bradley! When I landed in Atlanta, the first thing I planned to do was call him and give him a hard-core piece of my mind.

Chapter 31

Emily . . .

Congratulations

I dropped Samantha off at the airport two hours ago, and now I was lying across my living room couch, trying to sort out all the thoughts that were swirling through my mind. Sometimes people wondered how they landed in certain situations, but I didn't have a moment of question or doubt. I knew exactly what I did to end up where I was now—embroiled in a heated affair with a married man, pregnant with his child.

I remembered the night it all happened, six weeks ago. I had waited eleven long years to be with Ed, and I had wanted him so badly that I threw caution to the wind. We made love on my living room floor, void of a condom or common sense. I was remorseful about my carelessness, and so was he, and after that mistake we made sure that it didn't happen again. We used up my box of condoms and Ed had taken care of our supply ever since.

We were diligent. Careful. The model of responsibility. Not once had I missed a birth control pill. But here I sat, pregnant, living proof that it only took one time, one careless slip, and your whole life could be changed in the time it took to close your eyes.

I had been on the Pill for years and my period usually came like clockwork. But this entire year had been the exception. After my mother died, my cycle became infrequent. One month I'd have it, the next month I wouldn't. I went to see my OB/GYN, and she had told me that even though I was on the Pill, stress could still cause the inconsistency in my cycle. After I moved to DC, the infrequency continued. But I didn't worry until yesterday.

I had looked at the calendar and realized that I was more than two weeks late, which wasn't unusual because I had gone as long as two months without having a period. But I still wasn't particularly worried because even though Ed and I didn't use a condom that first time, according to the information pamphlet stapled to the bag of my birth control pills, if taken as directed they had a 99.7 percent effective rate against conception. I knew I couldn't be *that* unlucky. My mother had died, I had moved to a new city where I only knew a handful of people, I had started sleeping with another woman's husband, I was lying to my best friend, and I was placing undue blame on an innocent man in another state to cover up my deception. Events in my life had taken such a twisted turn, I didn't think they could get any worse.

But, just to be on the safe side, I went to CVS after I left work and bought a pregnancy test. I came home, sat on the toilet, and peed on the white stick. I placed it to the side of the sink and started reading my *Essence* magazine. Several minutes passed before I even remembered to check the test. I looked at it and couldn't remember if the bright pink line staring back at me meant I was pregnant or not, so I reread the instructions for clarification and then proceeded to shit right there on the toilet.

My mouth went dry and my head started to spin. After several deep breaths I quickly removed the other test from the box, believing that the first one had given me a false positive reading. But after taking the second test, the hauntingly pink line appeared again. I wiped myself, grabbed my keys, and headed back to CVS. I purchased two different brands just to be on the safe side, because again, they could read false positive, too. I knew my rationale was a huge stretch, but it was the only hope I had to cling to.

I hurried back home and went straight to my bathroom. After the two tests in the first box verified the results, I didn't bother with the other one. I shoved the unopened package back into the bag and waited for Ed to come over later that evening.

We had settled into a routine of seeing each other every day, even if for only an hour. He had met with his divorce attorney, and upon Longfellow's counsel, he wouldn't serve Brenda with divorce papers for a few more weeks. This would allow everything to be tied up with a neat bow, or as neatly as it could be considering our circumstances.

I had wanted to tell Ed as soon as he walked through the door, but I wasn't sure of how to break the news, especially since I was still in shock and hadn't confirmed it with a doctor. I wanted to be absolutely certain before I gave the man I loved a heart attack, so I decided to wait for a professional medical diagnosis before I opened my mouth.

I woke up this morning and called the doctor that Samantha had referred me to at Georgetown Hospital. Luckily, she had a cancellation at noon, and it worked out perfectly because I had planned to leave work early so I could take Samantha to the airport.

After the preliminary questions, urinalysis, and blood work were complete, Dr. Shepherd smiled at me with her rosy cheeks and said, "Congratulations, Ms. Snow . . ."

I didn't remember the rest. For all I knew she could've been giving me the recipe for homemade cookies. I really couldn't say because I blanked out for a short while. Her words floated over the room but not into my ears. It wasn't until I felt something warm against my skin, looked down, and realized that she was holding my hand that the world came back into focus. This was real. I was pregnant!

I told Dr. Shepherd the first day of my last period, which had ironically been on time, and she estimated that I was about six weeks along. I set up an appointment for my first prenatal visit and then left her office feeling numb. I didn't remember driving home. I just knew I made it by the grace of God. I'd only been in the house for a short time when Samantha called. She sounded extra hyper and edgy, and she wanted me to come over right away. I could hear some sort of devilment brewing in her voice. Normally, I didn't look forward to her drama, but today I needed something to temporarily take my mind off my own troubles, so I jumped into my car and headed to her condo.

After ten minutes of talking with Samantha, I thought I was going to need an oxygen tank and a stiff drink. Hearing her talk about her father's affair was the most uncomfortable conversation I'd ever had in my life. I tried my best not to tell too many direct lies. When she asked what I thought about Ed, I either agreed with her observations or remained silent, being careful not to offer unsolicited comments of my own. When she made the statement about having a kindergartner and a husband on Medicare, I literally felt a small leak in my bladder, so I crossed my legs and tried to remain neutral. And when she asked me about Bradley, I simply told her that we weren't together anymore, which was true. But I was fading fast, and I finally broke down and cried. I wept for all the mistakes I had made and for the consequences that I knew were sure to follow.

I was sitting on the couch when Ed arrived. This weekend was supposed to be special. It was the first time since our trip to Atlanta, when he'd flown down a few weeks ago to join me during my teacher's conference, that we'd be able to spend the entire night together. Brenda had a museum function out of town and would be gone until Monday, leaving us three days to ourselves.

Suddenly, I was nervous and unsure. I didn't know how Ed was going to react to the news. My mind raced to wild and crazy places. Would he fly into a rage? Would he question the baby's paternity, still holding on to the suspicions he had in the beginning of our relationship? Or would he tell me that he was too old for fatherhood and I should handle this on my own?

I didn't move when I heard him walk through the back door. I'd given him a spare key and an extra garage remote a few weeks ago so he could let himself in and out with ease. He strolled into the living room looking painfully handsome in his tailored suit. His overnight bag hung from his right arm while he held a Neiman Marcus bag in one hand and a large box of Godiva chocolates in the other.

He walked over to me, bent down, and kissed me full on my lips. "Hey, beautiful."

"Hey," I offered back in a weak voice.

He handed me the chocolates and set the bags to the side. "Emily, what's wrong?"

I looked down at the gold-colored box of sweets and tried to form a smile. "Thanks."

"Emily, are you okay?"

I leaned into him, buried my head in his chest, and burst into tears. This was only the second time I had cried since my mother's funeral. The first was today with Samantha, and I could only attribute the raw emotions to my budding pregnancy.

Ed held me in his arms and stroked my back just as his daughter had done a few hours ago. "Shh, shh," he whispered in a soothing voice. "What's wrong, baby?"

"Everything," I squeaked out. I wiped my eyes and sucked up my tears. I needed to pull it together and prepare myself before I delivered the news.

Ed looked worried out of his mind. "Emily, baby . . . tell me what's wrong."

I took a deep breath and let it out. "I'm pregnant. I went to the doctor today and confirmed it. I'm about six weeks along." And anticipating his next thoughts, I said, "It was our first time." I sat back and waited for his reaction.

Ed stared at me like I'd just spoken Japanese. I was glad, at least, that he was still breathing and hadn't collapsed to the floor. He was in shock, sitting in silence. After a few moments he ran his hands across his curly black and silver waves of hair, let out a deep breath, and relaxed into the couch. "When are you due?" he asked, staring straight ahead at the pictures fanned out atop my mantel.

It was bad. He couldn't even look at me. "Sometime next June. I have my first prenatal visit in three weeks, that's when my doctor will be able to give me my EDD . . . my estimated delivery date."

He nodded, still staring straight ahead. I was unsure of what else to say, so I simply sat next to him while he continued to concentrate his gaze on the mantel. He sat almost comatose for quite a long time. Even though his shock was understandable, I wanted him to say something. His silence was unbearable. Finally, he spoke as he pointed to the Neiman's bag on the floor. "I got you a surprise, but I guess you've given me a bigger one."

I couldn't discern Ed's mood, and it made me that much more anxious. But regardless of my nerves, I knew I had to tackle this head-on. "Tell me how you feel about this."

For the first time since I broke the news to him, Ed turned and looked at me. "I was studying your pictures on the mantel, wondering if our baby will have your eyes or my mouth. We both have the same nose, so we know that's a done deal."

"You're not upset?"

"No. I'm stunned, but I'm not upset. Are you?"

"Well, yes and no."

Ed reached for my hand. "You don't want to have my child?"

The moment he asked the question a light came on, and everything became crystal clear. My trepidation and fears had been rooted in the moral wrongs I had committed, for which I knew I'd have to pay a price, but they weren't because of my unborn baby. When I thought about the man I loved, and the small pebble of a child growing inside me, my heart felt nothing but pure joy. I smiled, touching my hand to Ed's face. "Thank you for being who you are. I can't wait to have our baby."

Ed pulled me into him and gave me a long, soft kiss. We knew there would be many obstacles in front of us, but for now, we were both happy. "This is a real celebration." He smiled, handing me the Neiman's bag.

"Thank you for my ivory teddy and red baby doll."

Ed looked at me with surprise. "How did you know what I bought?"

"Samantha saw you this afternoon."

I told Ed that Samantha had seen him purchase my gift and overheard his conversation with the saleswoman. He didn't appear to be rattled by it at all. He removed his jacket and tie, kicked off his shoes, and got comfortable. I'd expected him to be as worried as I was, but instead his response was, "I told you she'd be able to deal with it."

"Only because she doesn't know that the woman in question is me," I countered.

"You worry too much." Ed brought me to the seat of his lap, one of our favorite positions. I lifted my skirt and straddled him, looking into his eyes as he held my face in both of his hands. His voice became a soft whisper, filled with intense heat. "I've never loved a woman the way I love you. You mean everything to me, Emily."

Ed traced my mouth with the tip of his finger, gently grazing my lips back and forth. I sucked his index finger, applying gentle pressure as my tongue slid up and down his skin. He moaned, removed my blouse, unhooked my bra, and buried his head in my bare chest. My hips rotated as I felt him harden under me. My skirt came off, then his shirt. He slid my thong down my thighs as I tugged at his zipper, opening his pants as I rubbed my wetness against his satisfying thickness. I rose up from Ed's lap, but he stopped me in midair. "We don't need those anymore." He smiled.

I moved because I automatically thought he was going to retrieve a condom from his overnight bag. But he was right, we no longer needed any barriers. He pulled me back down to his lap, and slowly and happily, I eased my way home.

Chapter 32

Ed . . .

Out in the Open Where It Belonged

I watched Emily as she slept beside me. This was the way I wanted to spend the rest of my life. I thought about tonight, and it was still hard for me to believe that I was going to be a father all over again.

When Emily told me she was pregnant, half of me felt panic, but the other half felt like I was king of the jungle. There's a certain amount of bravado a man feels when he knows that he's planted his seed, and even more so at my age. But aside from my ego's satisfaction, and the initial shock, I could honestly say I was happy that Emily and I were going to have a baby.

We had a long discussion on the subject the night after her birthday. I was a practical, straightforward man. Once I knew the full details of a situation I approached it without second-guessing. My situation with Emily was simple. I wanted her, and having her meant having more children. End of discussion.

My mind drifted to the phone conversation I'd had with Ross several weeks ago.

"So, was it worth the wait?" he'd asked.

I shook my head when I thought about how good it had felt to finally be with Emily. I'd never been the kind of man to kiss and tell, but Ross and I got pretty graphic about things. After a few minutes of mildly scandalous conversation, I laid the heavy guns on him; the part about Emily and me being together and having kids.

"Shit, you're really gonna do this?" Ross asked in disbelief.

"Yeah, man. I love her, and it comes with the territory."

"More power to you, bruh."

"Damn, is that all the advice and wisdom you have to offer?" I was surprised because Ross usually had an answer, rebuttal, or debate ready on the spot. I wanted his insight, and beyond that, a part of me wanted his blessing.

"Listen, man. No matter what I say, you're gonna do what the hell you want anyway."

"Yeah, but honestly, I want to know what you think."

Deep down, Ross was a sensitive guy, and I knew the fact that I wanted his opinion meant a lot to him. "All right," he said as he cleared his throat. "I think you're in for a lot of bullshit and major drama. The situation is fucked up, no matter how you slice it. So you just gotta make sure you keep your head on straight and your money in your wallet so you can survive the storm ahead."

I thought he was finished but he continued. "Ed, even though you're in a situation that I wouldn't wish on Satan . . . I'm happy for you. I saw the passion in your eyes when you talked about Emily, and after meeting her I could see why. She's good for you. She's allowed you to take a chance, step out on faith, and build a new life.

That's a rare opportunity at our age. But you're doing it, and I'm with you all the way, my friend."

"Thanks, Ross."

"You know I got your back."

Ross and I talked constantly since that conversation. I gave him updates while he gave me his typical, straight-no-chaser opinions and advice. So tonight when Emily told me that she was carrying my child, I didn't flinch.

I remembered how I felt when I learned that Brenda was pregnant with our first child. Duty and obligation had dominated my feelings about our upcoming marriage and my impending fatherhood. But when Emily quietly told me her news this evening, my reaction was completely different. In spite of the fact that our relationship and circumstances were far more precarious than the one I was forced into long ago, all I felt was excitement about the baby growing inside Emily's stomach. I wondered if we were having a boy or a girl. Would the baby look like her or me? Would our child want to follow in my footsteps and build a career in law, or go into education like their mother?

Those were questions that would be answered in time, but right now I knew one thing for certain—as soon as Brenda discovered that Emily was pregnant, all hell would break loose. I knew her, so I had to act fast. I planned to call Longfellow first thing Monday morning and inform him that things had changed. I needed to divorce Brenda right away and get everything out in the open where it belonged.

Chapter 33

Samantha . . .

Wow, That's Crazy

My flight to Atlanta was going smoothly, but the thoughts in my head were making for a bumpy ride. I'd just found out that my father was having an affair and that my best friend had been dumped and was now heart-broken. Daddy had found a new love, and Emily had lost one. I didn't know which one had me more on edge, but if I was honest, I'd have to say Emily's situation trumped Daddy's . . . and I'll explain why.

I knew that my father had engaged in affairs in the past, so it really wasn't a surprise. And actually, I was happy for Daddy. As long as his new woman wasn't some gold-digging, hot young thing who was after his money, she and I would get along just fine. But poor Emily. It nearly broke my heart to see her cry. To know that Bradley had used her really pissed me off. When she broke up with him she handled it with class and kindness. Not once did she lead him on or play games. Sure, she accepted his phone calls, but she put the brakes on things by telling him the deal from the jump. She never called him, it was his fingers that dialed her number. And to think that he persuaded me to help him in his plan to woo her back made my blood boil.

What Bradley did was vicious, and it reminded me of some devious shit my mother would pull. He reeled Emily back in so he could make her feel the hurt he had endured. I understood the desire to teach people a lesson, but only if they deserved it—Emily didn't!

I felt awful that I had been a part of bringing him back into Emily's life, because now, he was the reason why she was no doubt sitting alone on her couch at this very minute, crying her eyes out. I couldn't wait until this plane landed. I knew where Bradley lived, and I had his home and cell phone numbers. I was supposed to be making better choices in my life, so I hadn't quite decided what I was going to do, but there was one thing I knew for sure . . . when I finished with his deceitful ass, he was going to be sorry that he ever made my best friend cry. And I meant that!

I grinned like a little kid when I saw Tyler waiting for me at baggage claim. I'd spent the last hour of my flight trying to formulate a plan for the best way to deal with Bradley, so I was fuming when I stomped off the plane. But when I saw my man, all my anger melted away. I ran up to Tyler and planted a long, wet kiss on his soft lips. There was no greater feeling than having someone to love.

After Tyler and I gathered my things we walked out of the terminal and into the dark, cool Georgia night.

Tyler put my bags in the back of his Navigator and headed down Highway 400. "What do you want to eat tonight?" he asked.

"I'll let you decide."

Tyler smiled. "I was hoping you'd say that."

We had eaten at nearly every restaurant in his town and mine. I wasn't a good cook. Hell, who was I fooling? I couldn't and didn't cook at all. I couldn't even make toast without burning it, so restaurants were our saving grace.

It was eight o'clock, and usually when I arrived in town this time of night, we'd head straight to a restaurant and then to Tyler's house afterward. But this time we went directly to his place. I was hungry but I controlled my appetite for food, because hey, he had other things I could munch on, if you know what I mean.

When I walked through Tyler's front door I instantly knew why he didn't want to go out. "Oh, Tyler." I smiled as I looked around the room and saw the romantic setting.

He walked over to the stereo, hit the remote, and let Ledisi serenade us in surround sound. His recessed lights were dimmed low, the dining room table was set with elegant china, and a beautiful bouquet of flowers served as the centerpiece. I inhaled and caught the aroma of what smelled like utopia.

"Let's get you situated so we can eat." Tyler smiled, taking my luggage back to his bedroom.

He'd hired a personal chef to prepare our dinner for the evening. We settled at the table to enjoy a feast of ginger-infused rack of lamb, roasted new potatoes with red pepper relish, a vegetable medley with dill sauce, and for dessert, a scrumptious crème brûlée. It was sinfully delicious. After we finished our meal, we stretched out on the couch, put on a DVD, and opened a bottle of champagne. "To our love and the infinite possibilities," Tyler toasted.

I tapped my glass against his and took a small sip. I watched him as he enjoyed the chilled bubbly, and that was when my heart confirmed what I felt in my spirit the moment I walked through his front door. This was the night that it was going to happen. Tyler was going to ask me to marry him.

A calm, happy feeling spread through my body. A month and a half ago I wouldn't have felt that I deserved to be treated this well, especially not by a man as good as Tyler Jacobs. But he loved me, in spite of myself, and had shown me that I was worthy of good things. His belief in me inspired a change in my life that I never saw coming. I wanted to be a better mother for CJ, I wanted to be a better partner for him, and I wanted to be a better person for me. The love and faith that I saw in Tyler's eyes made me feel like I could do anything.

My good fortune and blessings made me realize that I needed to let go of my ill intentions for Bradley. Creating a scene with him would only set me back on the destructive path I'd walked my entire adult life, and I owed myself more than that.

"What're you thinking about?" Tyler asked, rubbing my shoulder as I lay in his arms.

"How good this feels."

"Yeah, this is nice."

I tilted my head and kissed him softly. "I love you, Tyler."

We ignored the DVD that was playing and kissed for what felt like hours. Finally, Tyler led me by my hand to his bedroom. He removed my clothes, I peeled away his, and we lay across the sheets of his king-sized bed. Tyler kissed my neck, then slid his tongue across my collarbone as he parted my legs with his right hand. I let out a soft moan when I felt two fingers slip inside me. *"Mmm,"* I purred.

"You like that, baby?"

"Oh, yeah, Tyler. I like that."

I ground against his fingers as he kissed me, then he slowly moved his mouth down to my breasts, softly sucking when he found my nipple. The combined sensations he created above and below my waist made me weak. He removed his fingers, licked them, and then eased his way down to my middle. He spread my legs farther apart, giving him full access as he inserted his tongue where his fingers had been, going to work like a soldier. I let out another moan when I felt him gently probing, licking, and sucking me into his mouth. He knew exactly what he was doing, and he took his time showing me.

He devoured me, making sure he ate every inch of me. I could feel my clit about to explode. "I'm gonna come," I panted, nearly out of breath as I continued to grind my pelvis against his face. When I felt him swipe my clit with his tongue and then nibble it with delicate yet steady pressure, I arched my back and let out the mother of all screams.

I was still panting, almost delirious, when I felt Tyler's cheek against mine. He brushed his soft lips close to my ear. "I love you, Sam," he whispered. He reached over to his nightstand to get a condom and I readied myself for what I knew was going to be the very best sex I'd ever had. But instead of a condom, he pulled out a small black box, the one that I knew was coming.

Tyler rested beside me and propped himself up on one elbow. We looked at each other in silence, letting the smiles on our faces speak for what we couldn't get out.

"You do it for me," he finally said, "and I want you to be my wife." He sat up, pulled me to an upright position, and opened the box. The room was dark and I couldn't see the ring very well, but I didn't need to. The size of the stone didn't matter, neither did the other three Cs I would have normally concerned myself with in the past. What mattered to me was that this wonderful man who'd walked back into my life and had given me a second chance at love was telling me that he wanted me, and he was showing me by his actions. "Will you marry me, Sam?"

"Yes, Yes, Yes!" I shouted. I held out my hand as Tyler slipped the ring on my finger. I hugged him tight and lay back on the bed as my fiancé and I made beautiful love.

The next day, Tyler and I slept in, resting from our marathon lovemaking the night before. We didn't venture out until late afternoon when we visited his best friend, Victoria Thornton, and her family, to share our happy news. She eagerly welcomed us into her opulent home, which looked like something straight out of a magazine and could even put Mother's decorating to shame. She introduced me to her handsome, blue-eyed husband and their two adorable, well-mannered children.

Victoria had actually helped Tyler pick out my ring. She was happy for us, which filled me with a great sense of relief. I'd been a little nervous about seeing her again because she knew all the dirty details of my past, and how I had cheated on Tyler in what felt like another lifetime. But she didn't judge me. She was a successful businesswoman, wife, and mother, but she'd also made mistakes of her own. "I know what it's like to fall down," she told me. "The power lies in getting back up." I was grateful for Victoria's approval and support because she was like a sister to Tyler, and her opinion meant a lot to him.

I was also touched that Victoria asked about Emily. Emily had been her daughter's teacher when she lived here in Atlanta. After telling her that Emily was adjusting well to her new life in DC, which was mostly true, the strangest thing happened. Tyler and I were saying our good-byes when Victoria's daughter, Alexandria, walked up to me and put her hand in mine. "Ms. Samantha, I'm sorry about your sister," she said.

I stared at the eleven-year-old girl. "What do you mean, sweetie?"

"Your sister who died," she said, tilting her head to the side as she gave me a sorrowful look. "I'm sorry that your sister died."

I was baffled, and more than a little unnerved by her comment and serious tone. "Alexandria, I don't have a sister."

"Yes, you do . . . your younger sister," she said in a matter-of-fact tone.

Victoria stepped in, apologized for her daughter, and explained that Alexandria had a vivid imagination and often said unusual things. Tyler nodded in agreement, saying that he'd known her to be that way since she was a toddler. We all managed to laugh it off, but there was something in that child's voice that put me a little on edge.

It was raining heavily when we left Victoria's house a few minutes later. We stopped by Barnes & Noble so I could pick up a few bridal magazines, then we were on our way to one of our favorite Thai restaurants. I managed to calm myself and put Alexandria's words out of my mind as I prepared for a good meal. Tyler and I settled into a cozy booth near the window and discussed wedding plans. I decided that I wasn't going to tell Emily or my family until I returned to DC, and we both agreed that we wanted a small but very nice ceremony with all the elegant trimmings.

"We need to make sure we rein in your mother," Tyler said. "She'll probably come up with a guest list the size of a small city."

After all the romance and excitement of last night, I forgot to tell him about the lingerie incident with Daddy. So I dug into my Pad Thai and recounted the entire incident from start to finish.

"Wow, that's crazy," Tyler said in between bites of his chicken in peanut sauce.

"Yeah, you can say that again. We're getting married and my parents are headed for divorce. I'm just glad he's finally going to be happy."

Tyler wasn't too shocked about my nonchalant attitude regarding the state of my parents' marriage. And the fact that I was actually happy that my father was having an affair hadn't been lost on him either. After so many years of working with troubled youth and their dysfunctional families, he had seen it all.

Tyler paid the bill and we were on our way out when a handsome man caught my eye. It was Bradley! He was sitting at a small table, scrolling through his iPhone while he sipped a drink. We had to walk by his table in order to leave, so there was no way I could avoid him.

"Hey, isn't that Bradley?" Tyler said as we headed in his direction.

I hadn't told him about the situation with Emily and Bradley either, so as far as he knew they were still together. I felt a twinge of heat rise inside me when I thought about how he had maliciously set out to hurt my friend. I wanted time to think about how I would handle confronting him, but it was too late, we were at his table.

Bradley looked up as we approached and gave us both a smile. "Hi, Samantha, hi, Tyler." He greeted us with mild awkwardness. "Good to see you." He rose from his seat, gave Tyler a brotherman pound, and then leaned in to give me a light hug. I wasn't good at pretending, so I didn't try to force a smile. But I wanted to show my growth, so I nodded and remained silent as he and Tyler exchanged a few opinions about the Falcons quarterback and the Hawks' new roster for the upcoming season.

I couldn't believe the way Bradley was talking with such ease, like he hadn't done a damn thing! I was starting to get heated just looking at him. "Excuse me, I need to use the ladies' room," I said, feeling I was about to lose it.

Tyler nodded. "Okay, babe. I'll pull the car around so you won't get wet in this nasty rain," he said, then went back to his conversation with the bastard.

I couldn't get to the restroom fast enough. Once inside, I stood in front of the sink and took several deep breaths. I looked into the mirror, proud of myself for having such restraint because it had taken a lot for me not to go the hell off. After one last cleansing breath I walked back out, ready to leave. But what I saw next stopped me dead in my tracks. An attractive woman who could have been Emily's twin came up to Bradley's table, bent over, and gave him a quick kiss on his cheek before taking a seat beside him.

As I got closer, I could see that the woman wasn't as attractive as Emily. She picked up her menu, giggled something into Bradley's ear, and they laughed in that goofy way that new lovers tend to do. I was so pissed I wanted to scream, but I reminded myself that I was bigger than this. I needed to stroll by them, keep my mouth shut, guard my temper, and meet Tyler out front.

When I approached their table on my way out, Bradley stood and walked over to me. I prayed he wouldn't speak, but he did. "Take care of yourself, Samantha." He smiled. Then, after an awkward pause he said, "Um, when you see Emily, please give her my best."

Okay, now that took the damn cake! I couldn't believe that this bastard had the nerve to mention Emily's name after what he'd done. And if that weren't bad enough, he went a step further by having the audacity to stand there and actually look sincere as he did it. Now it was on and poppin'! I glared at him. "You fake-ass, no-good, low-down, dirty rat bastard muthafucker!" I hissed.

Bradley's eyes widened as his mouth dropped open in shock. His date looked stunned, letting her menu fall to the table as she watched just as wide-eyed as he was. Bradley stared at me as if to ask, *What's going on?* His innocent bit made me even madder.

"I can't believe the way your punk ass treated my friend," I continued. "You're a sorry piece of shit! But let me tell you one damn thing, you pathetic son of a bitch, what goes around comes around, and I hope you get yours right up the muthafuckin' ass!" I looked past him in the direction of his date and said, "Good luck with this one, sister!" I turned on my stilettos and walked out the door.

When I buckled myself into the front seat, Tyler could see that I was upset. I filled him in on what Bradley had done to Emily, and told him about the confrontation we'd just had.

"Sam, you've got to control your emotions and your mouth."

I crossed my arms and looked out of the window toward the restaurant. "Did you see how that son of a bitch acted all cavalier?" I said. "He screwed over my best friend!"

"Look at me, Sam," Tyler said, in a tone that was demanding yet calm. I turned and looked at him as he reached for my hand. "Bradley will get his payback, but not from you. Now, I'm serious, you've got to stop shooting off that mouth of yours. You can't fly off the handle just because the mood hits you. I'll help you with some anger management techniques if you want, but something's got to give. Baby, I love your fire and the way you fight for the people you love. But every war doesn't need to be fought. Chill, all right?"

Tyler stroked the back of my hand the entire time he spoke, soothing me with his loving words. This was why I needed him in my life. Other men from my past would've either blown it off or cosigned my madness by jumping in and escalating the drama to another level. But Tyler was responsible and levelheaded, and he balanced me.

"You're right, and I'm sorry," I said, feeling embarrassed. "You sure you still want to marry a drama queen like me?"

"I know what I'm getting myself into." Tyler leaned over and gave me a soft kiss on my lips. "We're all a work in progress."

I knew I was blessed to have such an understanding man. There I was, a foul-mouthed hell raiser, engaged to a man who possessed patience and kindness. And there was Emily, a kind-hearted gem, alone with no romantic prospects. That's not right, is it?

I knew what had to be done, and it was something I should've taken the lead on a long time ago. Once I got back to DC, one of the first things I planned to do was help Emily find a man.

Chapter 34

Brenda . . .

A Strange Knowing

Brenda sat in her first-class seat, consumed with worry. She was on a flight returning home to DC after spending what had started out as a fun-filled weekend in New York, but had ended as a Big Apple disaster. For the first time in her life, Brenda was uncertain about her future and didn't know what to do. She'd always been in control, making the rules that everyone around her had to follow. And even on the rare occasion when things didn't work out the way she envisioned, she always had a backup plan to ensure that she'd still come out smelling like a rose. But now, things had suddenly changed and she was at a loss for what to do.

Her weekend had begun so well on Friday when she arrived at LaGuardia airport. Harry had arranged for a driver to meet her at baggage claim and then whisk her away to a suite at the Carlyle Hotel. He had wanted her to stay at the Four Seasons again, but she felt it would be a bit too risky to return to the place where they first rendezvoused. After all, she was there in the city on legitimate business related to her volunteer activities. She had a meeting the next day with the docent director at the Frick Collection to discuss their consortium program, and then a private dinner party later that evening at the home of a prominent arts patron.

Brenda didn't feel the least bit guilty about having an affair because she knew deep down that her husband was doing the same thing. They hadn't slept in the same bed in over a month, and they barely saw or spoke to each other anymore. It didn't take a genius to figure out that not only was he having an affair, he was etching out a plan for divorce, and Longfellow's card was proof.

Brenda still couldn't believe that Ed was actually making plans to leave her, especially after all the years they'd been together. In the first few days after she realized what he was up to, she began to calculate various ways to save her marriage. But one by one all of her angles proved to be fruitless. Finally, she knew that only one strategy remained. She had to gather concrete evidence to prove that Ed was having an affair.

Initially, she considered hiring a private investigator to follow him, but after carefully thinking it over, Brenda knew she'd be wasting her time and money. Ed was smart and tactical, and he often used private investigators to gather evidence for his clients' cases. He knew the drill all too well and how to cover his tracks. He wouldn't get sloppy, not with so much at stake. They had amassed a small fortune over the years and she knew he would try to hold on to as much of it as he could.

Brenda decided to lay low for a while so she could figure out her next move. She resisted the urge to see

Harry every weekend as she had wanted. Instead, she chose to limit her visits so she could stay close to home and keep an eye on things. But being home depressed her even more. Ed was always gone, Gerti barely spoke to her, and Samantha avoided her. Samantha had even begun to move some of CJ's things into her home and was spending more time with him, so Brenda never saw her grandson either. Emily hadn't been to the house since the night of the party, and even Dorothy seemed too busy lately.

Brenda knew she deserved to be happy and fulfilled, and she was determined to make sure that she enjoyed herself, for at least one weekend. So she agreed to meet Harry for a trip down memory lane.

Once Brenda checked into the hotel, she was delighted to find a large fruit basket, selected pastries, and a bottle of her favorite champagne when she entered her room, again, all compliments of Harry. "This is exactly what I needed," Brenda whispered to herself. She unpacked her bags, put on her silk robe, and settled in while she waited for her lover, whose shift would end in less than an hour. It gave Brenda a charge knowing she was involved with a working-class man, going against the grain of her polished upbringing and the lifestyle to which she was accustomed. But she had to admit, Harry wasn't your average working-class man, and that had been part of his intriguing appeal.

After dozens of phone conversations and three weekends filled with heated passion over the last six weeks, Brenda learned that he held a bachelor's degree in business and had worked in some of the finest restaurants across the country and abroad. He was well versed in food and wine and could speak broadly on topics from politics to current events. She surmised that he made a comfortable salary. However, she wasn't too impressed because it was miniscule in comparison to the money Ed pulled in. But despite the fact that she knew Harry wasn't in her league, he was still a delicious distraction that she could use to alleviate her stress.

After Harry left work he came straight to Brenda's room. He was right on time as he'd promised and he filled her evening with enough heat, lust, and salacious moans to make her forget about her problems at home.

The next day, Brenda attended her meeting at the museum and then made a brief appearance at the director's dinner party that evening. She left early so she and Harry could continue where they'd left off under the sheets. Brenda loved the way Harry handled her in the bedroom, and she wanted to hold on to him while still maintaining her marriage to Ed. She was a woman who was used to having it all, and after her weekend romp was over, she intended to devise a new plan that would net her both.

It wasn't until her final evening in the city that everything began to crumble in front of Brenda's eyes. She and Harry had spent the day in bed, enjoying a variety of positions that had rendered them exhausted. When evening came, Harry made a suggestion that caused the entire deck of cards to come tumbling down.

Because all of their time together had been spent within the confines of hotel rooms, Harry wanted to take Brenda out for the evening. He made reservations at an intimate restaurant not too far from her hotel and suggested that they cap off the evening by listening to jazz at one of his favorite nightspots. He knew the best and most discreet places in town, and he wanted to show Brenda a good time. But almost as soon as he made the offer, she forcefully objected, making it clear that she didn't want to be seen out in public—with him!

"Brenda, this restaurant is very private. I wouldn't have suggested it otherwise," Harry said, trying to persuade her.

"There are always eyes around," she countered. "I can't run the risk of being seen out with *you*."

Harry stood, pulling his boxers up the length of his lean legs. "If someone happens to see us, you can just say we're having a business dinner."

"On a Sunday night?" Brenda scoffed, shaking her head at the ridiculous thought. She looked Harry up and down as he stood beside the bed. "You don't even look like someone I'd be doing business with."

"What's that supposed to mean?"

Brenda could hear the tension in Harry's voice. Her time with him was supposed to be fun and free of hassles. Now he was acting as though he wanted more than what she was willing to offer, and she didn't like it. "Harry, must you get so testy? I just meant that you're not the business executive type . . . that's all."

Harry smirked. "Neither are you, so what's the big deal?"

"I beg your pardon?"

"You're an attractive, well-kept housewife who volunteers with museums and charities to make yourself feel good. You shop all day and drink all night. I may be wrong, but that's a far cry from a high-powered business executive."

Brenda sat up in bed, completely beside herself with indignation. "You have some nerve talking to me that way. You don't know a thing about me!"

Harry laughed and gave Brenda a sly smile. "I know you a lot better than you think."

This time the tone in Harry's voice unnerved Brenda

because it matched a strange knowing in his eyes. A knowing that sent a slight chill through her body.

Harry dressed quietly, pulling on his shirt with care.

"Oh, Harry, come back to bed," Brenda purred. "Let's not spend our last night together squabbling over silliness."

To Brenda's dismay, he ignored her. Harry continued to dress in silence, and once he was finished he turned and spoke. "You don't remember me, but I remember you."

The chill that Brenda had felt a moment ago suddenly returned. She didn't know how she knew it, but she was sure that Harry was going to tell her something devastating . . . and she was right!

"Think back in time. Way back," Harry said. "Martha's Vineyard. The summer of 1973. Tuesday nights at the cove beyond the beach. The country boy from Ocean View Restaurant with the high-top Chuck Taylors. Any of that ring a bell?"

Brenda drew in a sharp breath. Her past had just walked into her present. She had experimented with several boys when she was a budding teenager during her summers on the Vineyard. Those days had been an easy way for her to test the sexual waters without damaging her reputation back home. She had a good time practicing techniques that had prepared her for womanhood, and particularly for Edward Baldwin, whom she'd wanted since she was twelve years old. As Brenda's mind raced back in time, she formed a memory of the lone boy who had stood out from the rest. *"Henry?"* she gasped in astonishment.

She remembered the mysterious, dark, sinewy boy who worked in the kitchen at Ocean View Restaurant. He'd boasted baby-smooth skin, a bright smile, and an almost mystical allure that had made even the grown women on the beach take notice. He wore T-shirts and jeans every single day, and he somehow managed to keep his white high-top Chuck Taylor Converse sneakers immaculate, as if he'd just picked them off the shelf at the shoe store. He hadn't been her first, but he had definitely been her best.

Over the years, she'd pushed the memories of those summers to a secret place she no longer had use for. Now, as she peered into Harry's intense brown eyes and studied his face, a sliver of recognition began to form, placing him back on the Vineyard, to those steamy nights of young passion.

"Yes, Brenda, it's me." Harry nodded. "You always called me *Henry,* instead of my real name. But after two or three times, I just stopped correcting you."

Brenda was so flustered she gathered the bedsheet up to her neck, as if a Peeping Tom were lurking at the window. "How . . . how did you know it was me? And why didn't you say anything before now?"

As Brenda sat with her mouth slightly agape, Harry went on to tell her that when he had initially spoken with her over the phone, he thought she was merely a disgruntled guest voicing her dissatisfaction with the hotel's room service. But as he listened to her speak, there was something strangely familiar about her voice, prompting him to deliver her meal himself, which was something he rarely did.

When she opened the door, he immediately recognized her as his secret love from the special summer of his past, even though nearly four decades had gone by since he'd last seen her. He revealed that he'd often wondered what had become of her.

"You were the prettiest girl I'd ever seen," Harry said,

"and more sophisticated than anyone I'd ever met. After that summer I wanted to contact you, but I didn't know your last name, or your real first name, for that matter."

Brenda covered her mouth and shook her head, remembering she'd told her summer lovers that her name was Betty, and that she and her family were from Boston, not Washington, DC. She continued to sit in astonished shock as Harry spoke.

"I knew right away that you had no clue who I was, and I didn't tell you because I wanted to see if our connection would naturally click as it had in the past . . . and it did." He smiled. "I can't offer you the grandeur of the life that you now lead, but what I can give you is happiness, laughter, and love."

Brenda blinked back her confusion. "I don't understand."

"I care about you, Brenda. You haven't talked about your marriage, but I know you're not happy. If you were, you wouldn't be here with me."

"My marriage doesn't concern you."

Harry's mouth formed into a frown. "Since I'm the man you're having an affair with, I think it does."

"Well, we can fix that rather quickly," Brenda said, her voice turning icy like the winter wind. "Get out!"

"What?"

"You heard me. Leave! And if you don't, I'll have you escorted out by security."

Harry looked at the coldness behind Brenda's eyes, realization sinking in. "I guess I didn't know the real you. I've been holding on to the fantasy of my youth."

"Get out, Harry!" she hissed. "And as I said, if you don't leave, I'll call security."

Harry shook his head calmly. "No, Brenda, you're not going to do that."

"Give me one reason why I'm not."

"I'll give you two."

The chill returned to Brenda's body as she held her breath, bracing herself for what Harry was going to say next.

"For one, you don't want to bring that kind of unseemly attention to yourself. And two, you don't want Ed or Samantha to find out about us, now do you?"

Brenda couldn't think straight. "How—"

"It's the Internet age," Harry interrupted. "When you stayed at the Four Seasons, I got your information from the hotel computer and did a little research."

"What are you going to do, blackmail me?"

"I'm not sure yet. But once I decide, you'll be the first to know," Harry said, then put one freshly polished wingtip in front of the other and walked out of the room.

Brenda sat in bed, completely dazed. But unbeknownst to her, she had little to fear from her smooth, ebony-hued lover because once Harry reached the elevator, he lowered his head with disappointment. Brenda didn't know that Harry had hoped that after so many years she would've grown beyond the spoiled little rich girl who had captured his heart. She was a dream he'd fallen in love with, one that couldn't hold up to the reality of who she really was.

Sitting in her room, trembling with fear, Brenda never saw Harry as he stepped inside the elevator feeling torn about his hint of blackmail. He wasn't a malicious person, so he felt remorseful about what he'd said, but not enough to give Brenda the relief of lifting the threat he'd loomed over her head. He decided to make her squirm a bit before letting her off the hook, thinking it was the least a country boy like himself could do.

As Brenda's flight began its descent into National

Airport, she felt as though her world was coming apart at the seams. One minute she was in control, ready to orchestrate a new plan that would set her life back on its proper course, and the next, she was falling in a nosedive, headed straight for the ground without a parachute.

Chapter 35

Emily . . .

Don't Let Nothing Steal Your Joy

Ed and I were both early risers, even on weekends. We usually greeted the sun on our way out the door, but this morning we lay in bed a little longer than usual. It was Monday, a teacher workday at school, and I was happy to have the day off. Since Ed didn't have any early-morning meetings, he decided to lie next to me after he made a call to attorney Longfellow. Brenda wasn't returning until sometime this afternoon, and even though she and Ed didn't see much of each other these days, the absence of her physical presence took a great amount of pressure off both our minds.

It felt good lying beside Ed. I nestled in his arms as I watched his right eyelid gently flutter while he continued to sleep. My heart was overwhelmed with joy, knowing that my child would have a strong, loving, and genuinely good father. I couldn't help but smile with nothing less than humble gratitude. As improbable as it seemed, our complicated situation was going to bring forth new hope and new life.

When Ed and I discussed raising our child, he was concerned about his age, and frankly, I was, too. It was a reality we had to face. When our son or daughter graduated from high school, Ed would be in his early seventies. I'd lived most of my life without my father in it, so naturally I needed to talk my feelings through the delicate subject. But in the end, we both agreed that no one's future was promised, and we couldn't predict what would happen to either of us. All we could do was live the best life God blessed us to have and shower our child with as much love as we could.

Noon was approaching, so Ed and I finally rolled out of bed, showered, and got dressed. I fixed him a cup of coffee and a toasted bagel. It was funny how some things in life dramatically changed, while others remained steadfastly the same. I sipped my herbal tea as Ed finished his coffee, smiling at me across the table in my bright, sun-filled dining room.

Ed was headed to work, and ironically, I was headed to his house. I was going there to pick up CJ. He'd been looking forward to us spending this day together for the last two weeks. And because Samantha was becoming more involved in his life, I thought it would be nice to include her. After I picked him up, I planned to drive to the airport to pick up Samantha, who was returning from her trip in Atlanta. Afterward, the three of us were going to spend the rest of the day together.

I didn't want to run into Brenda, so I asked Ed, "Um, what time will Brenda be arriving home this afternoon?"

He put down the *Washington Post* and looked at me. "She's already there."

"What!" My eyes bucked and my throat went dry.

"Remember, I told you that she always takes the first flight out when she travels."

He was right, he had mentioned it Friday night. But I'd been so worked up over the pregnancy news and him getting caught by Samantha at Neiman that I hadn't thought twice about it. I removed his plate and coffee cup, placing them in the sink as I cursed my bad memory and bad luck. "She doesn't get out of bed until close to noon most days, but she prefers early-morning flights? I just don't understand," I pondered as I shook my head.

"I know, it's the damndest thing. Don't get me started." Ed scowled.

Lately, the mere mention of Brenda frustrated him. Ed rose from his chair and slipped his charcoal gray jacket over his French-blue shirt. "But don't worry, you won't run into her. The first thing she does when she comes home from an early-morning flight is head straight to bed. After that, she won't be seen until the sun goes down, then she'll rise again."

His description reminded me of a vampire, conjuring up images of Brenda ascending from a silk-and-lace-draped coffin. I tried to put her out of my mind as I gathered my purse, put my scarf around my neck, and grabbed my keys. "I'm headed over there now."

Ed looked out the window of my back door, staring at our vehicles parked beside each other. "Baby, I've been meaning to ask you . . . we need to go shopping for a car soon."

He wasn't asking me, he was telling me that ol' Hazel just wasn't cutting it. I had to admit that Hazel hadn't held up well since the long road trip here. I should have shipped her, which would have given her a few extra months of life. But now she was on her last leg, and with a baby coming I knew I needed reliable transportation. I nodded, acknowledging agreement.

Ed smiled. "I know what Hazel means to you. We can keep her garaged, but we need to get you into something that won't leave you stranded. I worry about you every time you get on the road."

I walked over to the door and looked out at my old jalopy, parked snugly beside his luxury SUV. It was like looking at the two of us. Even though we might not match on the surface, we fit perfectly together where it counted.

Ed looked at me, smiling the way he does when we're in bed making love. He walked over to me and planted one hand on my behind, the other firmly on the small of my back. He drew me into him, giving me the last taste of his coffee. His java tongue melted in my mouth the way my body always did in his arms. After a long, sensuous kiss, he looked into my eyes and calmed my fears. "Emily, everything's gonna be all right."

I thought back to my first day in DC. Those were the same words Samantha had said to me. I smiled, knowing this was a sign. A very good sign.

I was nervous as I parked my car in front of Ed's house. It was a simple exercise I'd done so many times in the past, but now things were very different. And despite what Ed had told me, I was still worried that I'd run into Brenda. What I was doing with her husband was morally wrong at best, and I knew I couldn't look her in the eye. I hadn't seen her since the night of the party, and I wanted to keep it that way. I took a deep breath and rang the doorbell.

"It's so good to see you. Come on in." Ms. Gerti beamed, hugging me into her chest.

I missed Ms. Gerti. I saw her every now and then when she picked up CJ from school on the days that Samantha's schedule wouldn't allow, but we never had a chance to talk. I planned to set aside some time to spend with her in the coming weeks.

CJ was still upstairs playing with his games, so I joined Ms. Gerti at the kitchen table for a quick chat. Thank goodness Ed had been right, Brenda was nowhere in sight. I breathed a little easier as I sat back in my chair. "So tell me, how've you been?" I asked.

"Oh, you know me. I'm just fine." She smiled. "How're you doin', sugar?"

I smiled back, unable to hide my love high. "Actually, I'm great."

Ms. Gerti put her hand on top of mine. "I'm real happy for you, sugar. You've got that glow."

I peered at her, wondering if she sensed my pregnancy.

"I can see the joy in you. The emptiness you used to carry in your eyes is gone."

I nodded, knowing what she meant, relieved that my happiness was all that she could see.

Ms. Gerti paused for a moment, and then looked at me as she squeezed my hand. "I'm happy for you *both*."

"Thank you, Ms. Gerti. He's happy, too," I said, careful not to say too much. Brenda was sleeping upstairs and I didn't want to be completely disrespectful.

"These days I only see Ed in the mornings, but I've noticed a peaceful look about him. I've never seen him this happy in all the years I've been with this family, and I know you're to thank for that."

Her words encouraged me, but I also felt a modicum of shame. I was now an official home wrecker. I lowered my head. "I'm sorry that people will get hurt at the expense of my happiness." I looked away from her and kept my voice low. "But I don't want to give him up. I love him."

This time when Ms. Gerti spoke she kept her voice low, too. "Emily, people get what's coming to them in life. Happiness is what you deserve and you're finally getting it. But others," she paused, looking up to the ceiling, toward Brenda's bedroom above, "they get what they deserve, too, and sometimes it ain't all that happy. But that's not your cross to bear. You're a good person, so don't beat yourself up and don't let nothing steal your joy, you hear me?"

I rose from my chair and hugged Ms. Gerti with all my might. Even though I knew the road ahead was going to be difficult, as Ms. Marabelle had predicted, Ms. Gerti's words gave me the strength to face anything that was coming my way.

CJ and I stood in front of the baggage claim carousel at the airport, waiting for Samantha. He was telling me about the new dog he wanted Ed to get him for Christmas, which I couldn't believe was just a month and a half away. I'd just pulled out a stick of sugar-free gum for him when I spotted Samantha. "Here comes your mother." I smiled, excited to see my friend.

But my smile quickly dropped when I saw the visible disturbance on Samantha's face. She was practically stomping as she walked toward us. The scowl around her mouth was deep, and her body language screamed of discomfort. She looked as if someone had just cleaned out her bank account. I took a deep breath because a second later I realized why she was all out of sorts. Brenda was trailing close on her heels!

"Heeeyyyy!" CJ grinned as he ran up to Samantha and her mother, giving both of them big hugs.

I was unable to move my feet. My entire body tensed. How could this be? I thought Brenda had been upstairs in her bedroom, lying in a dead sleep when CJ and I left. Then again, Ms. Gerti never said that Brenda was upstairs. I had just assumed that because I hadn't seen her, she must've been in her room as Ed had said she'd be.

Samantha walked up to me and wrapped my body in a stilted hug. "Look whose flight landed at the same time as mine," she said into my ear, rolling her eyes toward her mother, who was standing behind her.

"Hello, Emily dear." Brenda smiled. She glided past Samantha, reached for me, and gave me two air-kisses without ever embracing me. This was one time that I was thankful for Brenda's reserve toward human contact. "How have you been?" she asked. "I haven't seen you in ages, since the party."

Samantha shot her a nasty look. "I'm headed over there to wait for my bags," she said, taking CJ by the hand as she walked away. My heart dropped. I was left standing alone beside the woman whose husband I had just made love to up against my kitchen sink before leaving my house two hours ago. I was about to crumble when Samantha turned in midstride and asked, "Emily, you comin'?"

"Excuse me, Brenda." I took off like I was being chased, glad to get away from her.

"It's just my shitty luck for that heifer to rain on my parade," Samantha ranted, glaring over in her mother's direction.

I pulled out CJ's video game from my overstuffed bag and handed it to him. "Sweet Pea, why don't you sit over there and play with your game, where your mommy and I can see you," I said, pointing to the set of metal chairs over to the side. He gladly took the game and was soon drawn into another world. I turned to Samantha. "I know you're upset, but, Samantha, you've got to start watching what you say around CJ."

"You're right, but you don't understand how she can kill a person's joy. I was happy as hell until I stepped off the plane and saw her walking my way," Samantha huffed. "She always takes the first flight out when she travels. But *noooo,* she just had to bring her ass home this afternoon. She claims that her business meetings had her so stressed out that she was too tired to make it to the airport in time for her flight. Hell, I think she flew in late just so she could funk up my groove and spoil my good news."

I shook my head. "I've discovered that your mother is capable of many things, but I doubt she switched flights just so she could run into you." In truth, Brenda was probably as perturbed about seeing Samantha as Samantha was about seeing her.

"Girl, like I've always told you, you don't know her like I do. She can ruin a wet dream."

"Well, anyway, tell me the good news she spoiled."

Samantha looked over to where Brenda was waiting for her bags at a separate carousel, making sure she wasn't watching us. She reached into her large designer handbag, retrieved a small box, and pulled out a beautiful engagement ring. "Tyler asked me to marry him!" she said in a low, jubilant squeal.

"Oh, Samantha! It's beautiful!" I said as I hugged her. "Why aren't you wearing this gorgeous rock on your finger?"

"I don't want Mother to know about my engagement just yet, so I pulled it off as soon as I saw her walking my way."

It was sad that she didn't want to share this monumental step with her mother, but I understood. "Girl, you know I'm so happy for you and Tyler. God is good!"

Samantha and I talked while we waited for her bags. She told me that Tyler's best friend, Victoria Thornton, had asked about me, and that she'd met Victoria's family. "Alexandria is so beautiful to be so young," she said, and then paused, "but she says the strangest things."

"I know," I agreed, feeling a cold sensation creep up on my arms. Just as I was about to ask her what Alexandria had said, Brenda walked up to us, pulling her large roller bag behind her.

"Looks like you two are in deep conversation," Brenda said.

Samantha looked as though she had an ugly comment on the tip of her tongue, but she held it. Thankfully, her bag came around just in time. After she gathered her things and we collected CJ from his chair, we all walked outside the terminal in silence.

"Emily, dear," Brenda said, turning her back to Samantha as she spoke to me. "Do you mind if I ride back with you?"

Samantha's eyes widened. "Mother, Emily's car is small and—"

"I've seen Emily's car, and it will accommodate all of us just fine." Brenda smiled, looking at me.

For the life of me, I couldn't figure out why Brenda wanted to ride home with us, especially considering the fashion in which she'd be traveling. Hazel was no match for the kind of luxury to which she was accustomed. Lord knows I didn't want to drive my lover's wife home, but I couldn't think of a way to tell her no.

After we put all the luggage into my trunk, we were off. I briefly looked at Brenda in my rearview mirror and saw a look on her face that resembled the expression one would have if inhaling an unpleasant odor. Even though it was a cool fifty degrees outside, it felt like an inferno to me. As I drove toward the airport exit, Brenda sat in the backseat, unusually chatty. For our own separate reasons, Samantha and I rode in silence. CJ was so into his video game that he was completely unaware that at any moment, something hostile could erupt.

"Emily, how have things been going?" Brenda asked.

I cleared my throat. "Um, pretty well."

"That's wonderful, dear. Are you dating anyone? You know this city is teeming with eligible young bachelors."

I looked straight ahead as I drove, keeping my guilt-ridden eyes on the road. Samantha put her hand on my shoulder. "It's all right."

"Oh, did I touch upon a sensitive subject?" Brenda asked, almost with a strange delight.

Samantha turned around and faced her mother. "Yes, you obviously touched upon a sensitive subject. Why don't you just sit back there and ride."

Brenda furrowed her brow and was about to say something in response when I turned up the volume on my stereo. An uncomfortable thirty minutes later we were at Brenda's front door. I pulled the lever beside my seat to open the trunk.

"Well, whatever's going on in your life, if you ever need to talk you know you can always come to me," Brenda smiled, reaching for her bags. "My marriage hasn't always been perfect, but it's strong and lasting."

I looked down at my feet. "I'll keep that in mind."

"Ed and I have had our ups and downs, but we always manage to get through them. Time, patience, and having a good plan. Those are the keys to a successful relationship, my dear."

I continued to look down at my feet, then toward the house. "I better get going."

"Thank you for the ride." She smiled. "And dear, you might want to get an upgrade soon." She frowned, looking at Hazel.

I watched Brenda as she strode to her front door, and I thought about what she'd just said about her and Ed. I wondered who she was trying to fool, me or herself.

Chapter 36

Samantha . . .

My Mouth Dropped Open

As Gerti would say, I was fit to be tied! Mother had hijacked my happiness once again. When I saw her walking toward me with that fake smile of hers, all the joy I'd felt over the past three days instantly vanished. Instead of greeting me with, "Hi, Samantha, good running into you here. How was your trip?" she looked up at the arrival board, noting that I had just come in from Atlanta, and said, "I take it that you and Tyler haven't broken up yet."

I had planned to tell her about our engagement after I told everyone else who truly mattered in my life, but now I was just going to let her find out through the grapevine. I'd hoped that one day Mother and I would be able to form some semblance of a relationship, but now I realized that was damn near impossible. At this point I had to stay away from her. I couldn't allow her negative energy to impede my progress as a mother or my happiness as a woman on a mission of growth.

Since I was a little girl I'd always wondered why Mother was so hateful and coldhearted, selfish and manipulative. And why she had never shown me motherly affection, or even told me that she loved me. But ever since my birthday party, I'd come to realize that she was a damaged person who had deep-rooted issues that had nothing to do with me, but everything to do with who she was inside. Gerti once told me, "Sam, there are some people who walk this earth with a rotten spirit through and through." Mother was one of them.

I used to promise myself that when I grew up I wouldn't be anything like my mother, but in some ways I failed because I was almost as bad a parent to my child as she'd been to me. Almost. But I was working to turn that around.

We had just dropped Mother off, and I didn't know who was happier to get her out of the car, Emily or me. She'd hit a nerve by pressing Emily about her love life, as if she really cared. I saw the look in Emily's eyes, almost like she was horrified. I knew that breaking up with Bradley really hurt her because not only had he played with her emotions, he'd dumped her and had already moved on. But I got him good, and I was going to let my friend know. Maybe that would give her a little vindication. "Emily," I said, "about Bradley . . ."

"I don't want to talk about him."

"But . . ."

Emily took her eyes off the road for a split second so she could look at me. "I really don't want to talk about Bradley or the situation between us." She sighed, turning her focus back to the road. "What we had ended long ago. Can we just drop it, please?"

She sounded tired, and a pained look flashed through her eyes. She'd probably been lying in bed, crying into her pillow all weekend and didn't want any reminders of the man who'd broken her heart. Emily and I had been through a lot of heartaches together, most of them mine, so I could relate to what she felt, and I let it go.

After we unloaded my luggage we headed for Chuck E. Cheese. Emily and I laughed and played games with CJ. It was clear that he didn't feel the natural bond or comfort toward me that he did for Emily, but I was okay with that because I understood. As I watched them interact, I saw the concern in Emily's eyes, the caring tone in her voice, and the sincere love on her face that she had for my son. I prayed that one day I'd be as good with him as she was.

By the time we dropped CJ off at my parents' house it was nearing his bedtime, and he was worn out. I stood at the bottom of the staircase and kissed him good night. "I'll see you in the morning when I come to pick you up for school," I told him as Gerti and Emily stood nearby.

CJ smiled at me. "I like it when you take me to school in the morning."

"You do?" I asked with surprise.

"Yeah, you're fun and we listen to good music!"

My heart swelled. Upon the suggestion of my parenting skills group leader, I had purchased a CD by the Mosiac Project, which teaches young children how to express empathy, resolve conflict, and embrace diversity while they sing along to music. I was so overjoyed that I was finally doing something good and something right for my child.

On our ride back to my place, Emily smiled at me. "Samantha, I'm so proud of you."

Her words warmed me. "Thanks, but I have a long way to go."

We parked in front of my condo with the engine running. "You don't have as long as you think. The natural mother in you is coming out. You just have to embrace it."

"You think?"

"I know."

"Thanks, Emily, but I'm not a *natural* at it like you. You're so good with kids."

"I better be, I work with the little rugrats every day." She laughed.

"You're going to make a great mother some day," I said. I didn't know if it was because of the fun we had today or because of the heartfelt emotion she experienced at seeing CJ and me together, but Emily had a special glow that I hadn't noticed before, and the more I stared the more she seemed to practically beam.

"Why are you looking at me with that weird expression?" she asked.

"You have a glow that's almost . . . radiant."

Emily blushed. "Maybe it's my new moisturizer."

"Girl, if I didn't know any better I'd say you had that pregnancy glow."

Emily coughed and braced herself against her steering wheel.

"You okay?"

"Uh, yeah, my throat's a little dry, that's all." She coughed again. "Well, I guess I better go home so I can prepare for class tomorrow."

We hugged good night, and I headed upstairs. After unpacking my bags and taking a nice long shower, I settled into bed and called Tyler. We talked until my eyes started to feel heavy. After I hung up, I nestled my head into my fluffy pillow and thought about my day. Notwithstanding my mother, it had been one of the best days I'd had in a very long time. I started it off by making love to my new fiancé, then spent time with my son and my best friend, and now I was lying in my comfortable bed, feeling happy. But then I thought about Emily and remem-

bered my promise to myself. I was going to help her find
a good man to go along with her amazing glow.

A week later, I sat at the computer in my home office,
reviewing my sales chart analysis when my cell phone
rang. I looked at the number and frowned. It was Bradley.
I couldn't imagine what that low-down snake in the grass
wanted. At first I was going to ignore his call, but the fact
that he had the balls to even dial my number made me
pick up—purely for the purpose of giving him the rest of
the tongue-lashing I'd held back on at the restaurant. I
was changing, but there were some situations that required me to bring the thunder, and when you messed
with someone I loved, it was on! "Speak, asshole," I said
into the phone.

"Whoa, Samantha," Bradley said in his crisp and
proper diction. "Why are you so hostile toward me, and
what did I do to deserve the way you talked to me last
weekend?"

"Is that why you're calling me?"

"Of course that's why I'm calling you. I'm a man of
honor, and I want to clear the air and find out what made
you say the things you did. I didn't deserve that."

I had to give it to homeboy, he was good. He actually
sounded as hurt and sincere as he did at the restaurant that
night. "You've got to be kidding me," I shot back.

"No, I'm not. I don't know what I did to cause your
reaction, but I want you to know that you ruined my date.
The young woman I was with won't even return my
phone calls."

"Good, maybe that'll teach you not to fuck with people's feelings."

"I have no idea what you're talking about. And as a
side note, I could do without the vulgarity."

I pictured Bradley sitting behind his desk in his perfectly starched shirt and conservative tie, looking indignant. "You should be ashamed of yourself. The way you took advantage of Emily was just downright—"

"Took advantage of her? What are you talking about?"

"You know what the hell I'm talking about. First you give her a fourteen-thousand-dollar bracelet, then you break up with her and start screwing someone else."

"Samantha, I have no idea what you're talking about. I didn't give Emily a fourteen-thousand-dollar bracelet!"

"Don't lie, Bradley. I saw the bracelet with my own eyes, and the birthday card you gave her."

"I sent Emily an e-card to wish her happy birthday, but that was it. I haven't even spoken to her since I flew up there to DC to help her move in, upon your encouragement, I might add."

"Why would she say that you gave her that gift if you didn't? She was even crying her eyes out over you last weekend."

Bradley sighed deeply into the phone. "Listen, I don't know what's going on with Emily, but there's some kind of mix-up. Why would I buy a fourteen-thousand-dollar bracelet for a woman who broke up with me—twice! I don't know who gave her that gift, but it wasn't me. Maybe the guy who gave it to her is the reason why she doesn't want to be with me."

I sat in silence, not knowing what to believe. Bradley sounded so sincere, and I could hear the shock and questioning in his voice. But I knew how deceitful men could be. Carl was the king of dirt and deception, and had taught me that people were capable of just about anything.

On one hand, I had my girl who had been true blue since the day we met, who had been by my side through thick and thin, who was loving and honest to a fault. Then I had this smooth talker on the line who was romancing another woman the same night that my best friend was nursing a broken heart that he had caused. I couldn't believe that I even questioned who was in the wrong. Bradley was slicker than I had ever given him credit for. I was pissed that he called me to play games.

I won't go into the foul-mouthed, four-letter vulgar cursing that I put on Bradley's ass . . . 'cause I was trying to do better. But let's just say that after he hung up on me, I was confident he'd never ring my phone again.

As I sat at my desk and replayed the call, my first inclination was to tell Emily about our conversation, particularly about the lies he'd told, but then I decided against it. I remembered how she looked yesterday when I dropped by her classroom while I was picking CJ up from school. She looked peaceful, and the glow on her face was even more luminous than it was last week. I knew that telling her about a crazy conversation I'd just had with her ex would resurrect a kind of pain she didn't deserve, so I decided to keep it to myself. Meanwhile, I scrolled through my address book and started contacting a few of my handsome cousins, on my quest to hook Emily up with a good man.

Two weeks later, the day before Thanksgiving, it was early evening and I was headed to the airport to pick up Tyler. Time had flown by like a whirlwind riding a roller coaster. Between putting in long hours at work, spending as much time as I could with CJ, and trying to maintain a long-distance relationship while planning a summer wedding, I was asleep most nights before my eyes closed. I was *sooooo* not a morning person, but I was learning to become one. I was known for being late, but now I was mastering time management. And I was notorious for cursing out someone in a flash, but lately I was learning how to control my tongue.

Gone were the carefree days when I lived in my trendy Tribeca apartment and swept into town every now and then on the weekends to party with Carl and pay my son a brief visit. That life seemed so long ago. It had been replaced by schedules, deadlines, and compromise. But I was happier now than I'd ever been. It had been challenging, especially for a girl like me. But I was growing. I was smarter. I was becoming more patient. And it was all because of love. My husband-to-be was a good man, and he had integrated himself into my son's life so smoothly it blew me away.

Who would've believed that I, Samantha Elise Baldwin, a wild, free-spirited hell raiser, would be a settled wife and mother? I never pictured it, and I certainly never wanted a traditional life. Yet that was all I thought about these days. I wanted the white picket fence, and I even thought about having another child. I know, it's crazy, right?

I made a right onto the airport exit, excited about seeing Tyler. I walked into the terminal with an extra spring in my stylish Louboutins, but the moment I saw my man, I immediately knew that something was wrong. His skin looked flushed and his eyes appeared heavy and tired. His sexy swagger was lagging and as he descended down the escalator to where I was waiting, I could see the fatigue in his body. He tried to paint on a smile when he saw the concern on my face. "Tyler, what's wrong?"

He wrapped his arms around me and gave me a kiss on my right cheek. When his face brushed against mine, his skin was cool and clammy. "Hey, babe," he greeted me.

"Tyler, you don't look so good."

"I'm coming down with a lil somethin'. No biggie," he said, trying to smile again. "It just hit me when I woke up this morning."

"Oh, baby. Maybe you shouldn't have traveled."

"And miss Thanksgiving with the family? Not on your pretty life."

He already thought of my family as his own. "Yeah, but you're not well."

"I'm okay. Nothing a little rest and a whole lot of TLC can't cure."

Tyler was always on the move and had more energy than anyone I knew. So when he walked through my door, curled up on my couch, and reached for the warm blanket lying beside it, I knew he was sick. I took his bags upstairs, then went into the kitchen and poured him the last of the orange juice left in the container. "Here, drink this," I said, handing him the glass.

He sipped slowly. "Babe, do you have any Tylenol, maybe even some Theraflu?"

"You feel that bad?" He never took medicine, and the only pills I'd ever seen him swallow were his vitamins.

"Yeah, I gotta kick this bug before tomorrow. I want to be well enough to throw down on Gerti's food."

"Tyler, I'm not sure you'll be up to it."

"I will be if you nurse me back to health." He winked, drawing me down to his chest for a light kiss.

"I can't believe you want to get it on right now."

He chuckled. "I don't, I just wanted a kiss. What I really need is some cold medicine."

I felt his forehead and he was hot to the touch. I didn't know a thing about nursing anyone who was sick. Hell, I didn't even own a bottle of aspirin.

"I think I'm running a temp. Can you get me something from the drugstore?"

"Sure, baby." I nodded. "I'll pick up some chicken soup, too."

Tyler pulled the blanket up to his neck and closed his eyes. "Thanks, babe. I think I'll just rest until you get back."

I went to CVS and picked up throat lozenges, cold medicine, orange juice, and a few cans of chicken noodle soup. As I headed back home, I drove down Emily's street and saw that her lights downstairs were on. She was probably up baking her scrumptious apple crisp for tomorrow's Thanksgiving meal at my parents' house. I knew she kept a cabinet full of all kinds of homeopathic teas and herbs, so I decided to pop in, get something for Tyler, and then go home and nurse him back to health. Besides, I wanted to chat with her for a minute to see if she had called my cousin's friend who was interested in going out with her.

I found a space on Emily's street that was close to her house and parked my car in the spot. I didn't like showing up at people's doors completely unannounced, so I dialed her cell.

"Hey, Samantha," she said, sounding happy and relaxed.

"Are you busy?"

"No, I'm just lounging on my couch. Why?"

"I'm getting out of my car and walking to your door, so open up." I grinned.

"You're where?"

"I'm at your door," I said, then rang her bell as I laughed. "Girl, open this door. It's cold out here."

After a minute or two, Emily opened the door slowly. As with Tyler, I could see that something was wrong with her. She didn't look sick, but it was apparent that she wasn't altogether right. "What's wrong with you?" I asked.

"Um, nothing, I just wasn't expecting anyone."

"You act like I'm company or something," I said as I walked over toward her couch. I took a deep breath and inhaled a wonderful aroma. "Mmm, I knew you were baking your apple crisp."

"I just put it in the oven twenty minutes ago."

"I can't wait to dig into it tomorrow." I grinned.

Emily glanced at her watch. "What's going on? Do you need something?"

"I thought you said you weren't expecting anyone."

"I'm not. What makes you say that?"

"Because you're acting all nervous and looking at your watch."

I took a seat on her couch and looked at her closely, wondering what was going on. I could see that Emily was very uncomfortable, like she wanted to be alone. Then it hit me. This was her first family holiday without Ms. Lucille. How insensitive of me to forget what my girl must be going through right now. I knew I needed to cut my visit short and give her the quiet time she needed. I relaxed my tone. "I'm not going to stay long, I just dropped by to borrow some herbal tea for Tyler. He caught a cold and he's not feeling well."

"Oh, no," Emily sighed, running her fingers through her hair, which was growing like she'd been fertilizing it.

She came over to the coach to sit down beside me and that's when I noticed the thick book lying on the sofa cushion. I looked at her and my mouth dropped open. "You're pregnant!" I said, holding up the book, *The Mocha Manual to a Fabulous Pregnancy.*

Chapter 37

Emily . . .

The Real World Kicked Back In

I was nearing my tenth week of pregnancy, and so far so good. After my initial shock of finding out that I was going to have a baby, the worry began to sink in. So the first thing I did was go online to find out everything I could. What I discovered sent me into a minor tailspin. Knowing that 15 to 20 percent of all known pregnancies ended in miscarriage, and that 80 percent of those occurred in the first twelve weeks, made me want to put myself on bed rest. I was terrified, and I didn't think I could take another loss.

"Emily, you're going to worry yourself into bad health if you don't stop," Ed told me one evening after I had rattled off another horrifying statistic I'd read about miscarriages. He rubbed my still-flat stomach and spoke gently. "You're going to be fine and our baby's going to be born healthy."

His words comforted me, and I knew he was right. I

couldn't sit around worrying about something that was out of my control. If it was meant for us to have this baby, we would, and if not, we'd pick up the pieces and accept what God put in front of us. But there was one thing I knew for sure: Whatever the outcome, Ed and I were going to go through it together. Still, the vulnerable, human side of me wanted more assurance, so I invited Ruben over for tea two nights ago.

We'd both been so busy that we hadn't seen each other in weeks. But as soon as he walked in and gave me a hug, he knew. Ruben released me from his soft embrace, looked at me, and smiled wide. *"Oh, E-mi-leee,* you're going to have a bambino!"

We sat on my couch nibbling on organic brown sugar cookies. Ruben oohed and ahhed over baby names and color schemes for the nursery. "Ruben," I said, not wanting him to get too carried away. "Am I going to have this baby? I mean, am I going to carry to full term?"

Ruben gave me a gentle smile. "When I hugged you, I saw your daughter as plain as day. She had pink ribbons tied around long ponytails, and a smile just like yours."

I nearly broke into tears as I reached out and hugged him again. My life was finally bringing me happiness. After so many disappointments and heartache, good fortune was coming my way. A few weeks ago, Ed and his lawyer had resolved the issues that were necessary to move forward with serving Brenda divorce papers. She threw a small fit, but then seemed to acquiesce, almost overnight. She had a very good attorney representing her, but she wasn't putting up the fight that Ed thought she would. Her only request was that they hold off on announcing their divorce until after the holidays. "I deserve that courtesy for being a good wife to you and mother to our children," Brenda had told him.

Ed conceded to her wishes. He also agreed to relinquish their home, two of his many rental properties, and a generous amount of cash that would allow her to live comfortably. Longfellow had balked, saying they should have started off low instead of putting so much on the table for their initial offer. But Ed didn't take his suggestion. He felt he was doing the right thing. He said that at the end of the day, regardless of his feelings toward her, Brenda would always be the mother of his children, and he wanted to honor that.

Meanwhile, he moved most of his clothes and personal items into a studio apartment in one of the rental units he owned downtown. I hadn't realized the extent of his wealth, which was substantial. And even though it looked like theirs was going to be a fairly clean divorce, Ed still believed that Brenda was up to something because she hadn't pushed for more material possessions than he'd offered. I was just glad that it would be over soon.

Now it was the day before Thanksgiving and I was feeling a wee bit melancholy. Samantha and I always celebrated our birthday together, but the holidays were reserved for Mom and me. I had to keep reminding myself that she wouldn't have wanted me to be sad during this time of thanks and that instead, she'd want me to celebrate my blessings. So I decided to honor her by enjoying this time that I'd been given.

I put my signature apple crisp in the oven, a recipe that was handed down to me from my mother and also happened to be one of Samantha's favorite desserts. I was baking it for the Baldwin family feast tomorrow. But honestly, I didn't want to go. There was no way I could sit across the table from Brenda knowing that I was carrying her husband's child. There was something inherently wrong about that. I may have been a Jezebel, but I wasn't a complete heathen. I planned to drop off the apple crisp and then excuse myself. I'd tell them that I wasn't feeling well, and then I'd come home and wait for Ed. He told me that he understood, and I think he was actually a little relieved about my decision.

I inhaled the buttery-sweet aroma of the apple crisp floating through the house and felt warm all over. After I poured myself a cup of juice, I stretched across my couch and started reading my favorite new book, *The Mocha Manual to a Fabulous Pregnancy,* while I waited for Ed to come home. I was learning about the physical changes in store for me during my second trimester when my cell phone rang. It was Samantha, so I answered with enthusiasm. But I soon panicked when she told me that she was walking up the steps to my front door. Under any other circumstances I would've just moseyed on over and let her in. But my mind immediately went to Ed. I didn't know when he'd be back, and it was possible that he could walk through the door at any minute.

I couldn't say that I was busy because I'd just told her that I was lounging on my couch. I felt trapped and I didn't know what to do. "Girl, open this door. It's cold out here." Samantha laughed into the phone.

I knew I had no other choice, so I took baby steps toward the door and let her in. She entered with inspecting eyes, and she could see that I wasn't myself. She asked if I was okay, and I brushed off her question, telling her I was fine. Samantha can spot a lie, especially on me, and she gave me a look that said, *Okay, if that's your story . . .*

Her mind shifted when she smelled the apple crisp baking in the oven. The enticing aroma seemed to calm her for a moment as she began to tell me how much she was looking forward to the dessert tomorrow. I glanced down at my watch, noting the time. Ed could come walking through my back door an hour from now, or at any minute. I didn't know which, but I had to find a way to get Samantha out of my living room before he came back.

"I thought you said you weren't expecting anyone," Samantha said with a quizzical look.

She caught me peering at my watch and she told me that I looked nervous. She was right, but what was I to do? I tried to shrug off her comment, but then she took a seat on my couch and I thought my knees were going to collapse right out from under me. *Oh, Lord!* She looked like she was trying to make herself comfortable and stay a while. Now I really started to panic, and a queasy feeling in my stomach told me that the dominos were about to tumble around my feet.

Just as I felt the axe about to fall, Samantha softened her eyes and told me that she wasn't going to stay long because she had to get back home to Tyler. He'd caught a cold and she simply wanted to stop by so she could borrow some herbal tea.

I was about to go into the kitchen for a box of echinacea when I noticed that I had left my pregnancy book on the sofa, mere inches away from where Samantha was sitting. Small beads of sweat popped on my forehead. "Oh, no," I sighed, nervously running my fingers through my hair. I walked over to the sofa to try to hide the book before she saw it, but I was too late.

"You're pregnant!" Samantha shouted, holding up my book.

My ears started to ring and my stomach jumped. There was no way I could get out of telling her the truth. I gathered myself and looked into Samantha's eyes. "Yes, I'm going to have a baby," I said, taking a seat next to her on the couch.

She shook her head, her mouth still hanging open.

"Oh my God!" she screamed. "That's why you have that glow! You're pregnant!"

A look of happiness mixed with confusion filled her face. I could see the shock and flurry of questions bubbling behind her eyes.

"I was planning to tell you when the time was right," I said.

"Emily, I can't believe you kept something this important from me," she said, looking slightly hurt.

"I'm sorry. I just didn't know how to tell you. Everything's so complicated . . ."

"You know I'm the last person to judge. After all the shit I've done and the countless times you've been there to help me clean it up." She sighed, looking at me through sincere eyes. "You know there's nothing you can't tell me, Emily. Nothing."

"Samantha, it's more complicated than you know." Her mind was still racing, so I answered the question that I knew was next. "Bradley's not the father."

She sat back and rubbed her right temple. "Now it all makes sense. He was telling the truth after all."

I watched Samantha's chest rise and fall at rapid speed as she quickly told me about her encounter with Bradley during one of her trips to Atlanta, and the phone conversation they'd had two weeks ago.

I lowered my head, because now I understood what real shame felt like. All the emotions I'd experienced before were merely a mixture of guilt, anxiety, and my own fear. But sitting on my couch, looking into the fiercely loyal eyes of my best friend who had defended my honor not knowing that I was undeserving of such a gesture, a blanket of hot shame cloaked my entire body. I couldn't even look at her. "I never meant to hurt Bradley," I said quietly.

Samantha sat in silence for a long moment before she spoke. "When I think about it, every time I mentioned Bradley's name, you never confirmed or denied a thing." The wheels turned inside her mind as she spoke, almost in a whisper. "That's a courtroom technique that Daddy's talked about many times . . ." she said, her voice trailing off.

A fresh wave of panic and queasiness gripped my stomach. Samantha stared at me with a look that let me know she was slowly sorting out the pieces of the puzzle, connecting them one by one until they slid into place to form the true picture of what had been happening right under her nose. And then, as if things couldn't possibly get any worse, I heard the back door open and a set of heavy keys clank against the granite countertop where Ed had just tossed them.

"Emily, baby, I'm home," he yelled out as I heard the door shut behind him. *"Mmm,* that apple crisp smells delicious. I'm ready to have a little dessert of my own," he said, lust coating his voice as he walked through the kitchen and into the living room.

I closed my eyes, took a deep breath, and held it for a moment. For that brief second in time everything was dark, quiet, and calm. But when I opened them again, the real world kicked back in.

Ed stood in silence at the edge of the living room, holding a cautious but calm look on his face. Unlike his daughter, he was a very rational and controlled person, so it didn't surprise me that he was seemingly relaxed. Maybe a small part of him was even relieved that everything was finally out in the open.

Samantha stood up and looked from Ed to me, shaking her head. "She's who you were buying lingerie for?"

she asked, still speaking barely above a whisper, still processing the whole situation.

I sat glued to my seat on the couch as Ed spoke. "Sam, we wanted to tell you, but we had to wait until the timing was right."

Samantha drew in a deep breath, still shaking her head. "How long has this been going on?"

"I've loved Emily for a very long time."

"How long?" she demanded.

"Since I first met her."

Samantha took a few steps toward him. "You've been fucking my best friend since we were in college?" Her voice was beginning to rise.

"I'm still your father, so watch your language and your tone when you speak to me," Ed cautioned.

Samantha backed down, but I could see the fire in her eyes. "Okay, *Father*," she said with bold sarcasm. "How long have you and Emily been—"

"Emily and I didn't start seeing each other until after she moved here. After the birthday party."

I noticed that the entire time that Samantha and Ed had been talking, neither of them had looked in my direction. They were throwing my name around the room as though I weren't even there. I needed to say something, so I rose from the couch and started to speak. "Samantha, it's true. We didn't start seeing each other until after I moved here. That's why I told you it was complicated."

Samantha turned her head toward me, her long, sandy blond locks flying through the air. "Oh, shit!" she gasped. "Daddy's the father, isn't he?"

Things had been tense and highly uncomfortable up to this point, but now I knew the situation was about to explode.

Samantha huffed and stomped over to where I stood. She came to within a few inches of me and stopped. She looked down at my pregnancy book, then over toward Ed, before casting her eyes back on me. "I believed in you. I loved you. I had faith in you. I defended you!" she said as tears began to stream down her cheeks. "You were the best person I knew, honest and decent and kind, but it was all an act. Eleven years of fucking deceit!"

"I'm so sorry," I cried. I reached out to touch her but she recoiled and stepped away. I had to explain so she would understand. "Samantha, you've got to know that this was hard for me. I've loved Ed for so long, but I had to keep it bottled up inside." I sobbed and panted. "I never meant to hurt you. I love you like a sister. You're my family."

"Family, my ass! If we're family, sisters as you say, why did you screw our father?"

"I've never looked at Ed that way. I've always loved him. From the very beginning. Lord knows I didn't want to have these feelings because I knew where they would lead. But I couldn't help it." I could taste the salty tears running down into my mouth, but I swallowed them and continued. "I've loved, and I've lost, and I've lived most of my life with an emptiness that I didn't think would ever be filled. But being with Ed has changed all that." I took a step toward her. "Samantha, I love your father. I'm finally happy, and I'm not going to apologize for it."

Samantha looked down to the floor as she spoke. "Of all the people in the world, I would've never thought that the two of you would be capable of something like this." She shook her head, reached over me like I wasn't even there, and grabbed her handbag off the couch.

"Samantha, wait!" I said in a desperate cry as she walked toward the door.

She didn't curse or scream. She didn't throw any objects. She didn't do any of the things I knew she was capable of, or that I thought she would do. She didn't even slam the door when she walked out without looking back or saying a single word.

I stood still, like petrified wood. I felt Ed's strong, protective arms wrap around me, followed by an intensely sharp pain in my lower abdomen. I looked up at him, not wanting to accept what I could feel coming. "Take me to the hospital."

Chapter 38

Samantha . . .

It Was Really Her All Along

I walked through my door with tears in my eyes. I went over to the couch where Tyler was lying and sat down beside him.

"Sam, what's wrong?" Tyler asked as he sat up. He was tired and weak, and I could hear the congestion in his voice as he spoke. "Baby, why're you crying?"

I looked at him, my red eyes matching his as I began to sob even harder. "They lied to me. They tricked me. They deceived me," I cried as I leaned forward, resting my head in my hands.

"Sam, baby, what're you talking about? Who lied to you?" Tyler asked through his own sniffles.

At that moment, I realized that the cold medicine, soup, and juice I had gotten for him were still sitting in the trunk of my car. I'd left an hour ago in search of relief for my man, but what I found instead was chaos. "I left your medicine in the car," I said as tears rolled into my mouth.

Tyler looked at me with alarm. "Forget the medicine. Tell me what happened."

I gasped between sobs as I told Tyler what I had just witnessed at Emily's house. I told him how I saw the pregnancy book on her couch, and how my father walked through her back door so casually, as if they lived together. I told him about the affair they'd been having, the lies they'd told, secrets they'd kept, and games they'd played. "They did it all while smiling in my face, pretending we were a loving family," I said with outrage. "The fourteen-thousand-dollar bracelet, the lingerie. It was all him and her. I defended Emily and even cursed out Bradley—twice!"

"Damn," Tyler said, slowly shaking his head.

"Can you believe what they did?"

Tyler looked at me with bewilderment. "Wow, this is one that I, um . . . I don't even know what to say."

The fact that Tyler was so shocked that he couldn't get words out made me cry even harder. I was numb when I walked out of Emily's house. Emotions coursed through my body that I didn't know where to place, while my mind fought to rationalize what I had just seen. My father and my best friend. Lovers! It was something I'd never imagined, not even in my wildest, most bizarre dreams. I was confused, angry, and hurt.

Now, as I sat on my couch with Tyler holding my hand, I thought about the friend who had been there for me through thick and thin, who had always encouraged me to make good choices and do the right things. Then I thought about my father, the man who had always been there for me, too, and who had taught me the importance of respect, honor, and forthrightness. I couldn't believe they were the same two people who had lied and deceived me at the highest level.

I grew angry all over again as I thought about my so-called best friend. Emily had led me to believe that Bradley was the conniving, deceitful one, when it was really her all along. Then, in a flash, my mind returned to that day in Neiman. I dropped Tyler's hand, jumped up from the couch, and started pacing the room as I spoke. "I can't believe her!" I screamed. "All this time Emily's been having an affair with my father and lying about it. And him . . . he listened to me talk about Emily and Bradley getting back together and he was fucking her the whole time!"

"Sam, I know you're upset. But try to calm down," Tyler urged as he walked toward me.

My hair was all over the place, I was sweating like it was a hundred degrees, and my face was so hot and red it burned almost as badly as my teary eyes. I was hysterical, but I didn't care.

"Baby, please calm down," Tyler said in a soothing voice.

I ignored him. "Emily had the balls to sit on my bed while I told her how I caught my father buying lingerie for his mistress, all the while knowing that he was buying it for her! She let me go on and on about how I suspected that he was having an affair, and she even had the nerve to question me about it, pretending to be surprised," I huffed. "That's some low-down, cunning, deceitful shit I'd expect from my mother. Come to think of it, maybe that's why they've always gotten along so well . . . two fucking peas in a pod!" I screamed as tears raced down my cheeks.

I would've never put Emily and my mother in the same category, but there they sat, side by side. I felt like I'd been carved out by a knife and left hollow. My tears

stopped falling and the numbness I felt when I left
Emily's house returned.

When I opened my eyes the next morning they felt as
though they were still shut. My lids had turned into puffy
folds of swollen skin from all the tears I had shed last
night, and I could barely see the morning sun that was
shining into my bedroom.

"Here, drink this," Tyler said as he handed me a cup
of orange juice.

"Where'd you . . ."

He blew his nose with a tissue. "I got it out of the
bags you left in your car last night," he said as he coughed
and blew his nose again.

It was the first time in my entire life that I'd cried myself to sleep. After I rehashed everything with Tyler, he'd
calmed me down enough for me to take a shower and
crawl into bed. But as I lay under my warm comforter, all
I could think about was my so-called best friend and my
father. Each time I tried to fall asleep my mind hit me
with a new vision, them hugged up together when he gave
her the expensive Tiffany bracelet, her modeling the lingerie he'd bought her, him listening with a straight face as
I told him about how happy Emily had been after the
weekend she'd supposedly spent with Bradley when she
went to Atlanta for her teacher's conference. They'd both
played me for a fool.

Beep, beep, beep, my phone rang. Tyler looked at me
and sighed. "You need to answer that, you know it's your
father again."

He'd called three times last night, but left only one
message, which I immediately deleted. I reached for my
phone and looked at the caller ID. *DADDY* appeared
across the screen. I let it roll into voice mail again, just

like all of his other calls. A minute later I heard the familiar buzz signal that a message had been left. I punched in my code to retrieve it, then deleted it without even listening to what his lying mouth had to say.

"Sam, don't you think you should at least talk to him?" Tyler asked as he lifted the comforter and crawled into bed beside me. "I know you're hurt, but you love them both, and despite how things went down, they love you, too. Baby, everybody makes mistakes."

"I don't want to talk about him or her. I just want to put them out of my mind right now."

"Sam, you need to call him back . . ."

My voice was hoarse from all my crying, but it was strong enough to speak the words my heart meant. "I'm putting both of them out of my mind."

Chapter 39

Emily . . .

I Don't Know

I listened to Ed as he left Samantha another message, telling her the sad news we had just received an hour ago. Then he called Ms. Gerti and repeated the same heartbreaking details he'd left for his daughter in a voice message that she was unlikely to retrieve. I knew my friend.

I watched Ed closely as he spoke to Ms. Gerti in a whisper, his posture slumping a bit. He looked out the window of my hospital room and breathed a heavy sigh as he ended the call. The only other time I'd ever seen him look so tired was the day he helped me move. But even then he didn't look the way he did now because on that day, his fatigue had been born of a hope-filled promise for a long-awaited love. The weary exhaustion that covered his eyes this morning was steeped in a hurt and sadness that was hard to put into words.

"You're up." Ed smiled as he came over from the

window and sat on the edge of my bed, careful to avoid my IV drip.

"Did you manage to get any sleep?" I asked, looking into his bloodshot eyes.

He hunched his shoulders and smiled, which told me he hadn't. "How do you feel?"

I shook my head. "I don't know."

Last night had been the worst night of my life. I remembered my ten-year-old self, and how sad I'd been when I stood over my father's casket as he was lowered into the ground. Then I thought about the heart-wrenching pain I felt when I looked into my mother's quiet face one last time before the funeral director closed her coffin, separating our worlds. Those losses had been nearly unbearable, but I managed to go on because although I knew my parents would never walk this earth again, my faith gave me comfort that we would be together one day in paradise, and in the meantime, their spirits would still live with me.

But the loss that engulfed me today was different. It still walked around. Still breathed air. Still lived life. Yet it felt as dead as the two people I had loved and buried.

When Samantha came over to my house last night, I knew right away that there was going to be trouble. I knew the minute she saw my pregnancy book that the truth would slowly come to light. I knew she would discover all the secrets I'd been keeping as soon as Ed came walking through my back door. And I knew the instant she and I locked eyes and exchanged heated words that things would never be the same. But what I didn't know, what I was still unsure of as I lay in my blue and white hospital gown, was what would happen next.

After Samantha turned on her heels and walked out my door, I wondered if the back of her head would be the last image I saw of the best friend who I had loved, and yet betrayed.

"I don't know how I feel," I repeated to Ed.

"Try to get some rest, you've been through so much."

I looked into Ed's steadfast eyes and saw his anguish and pain. He was frantic when we parked in front of the emergency room entrance last night. After we got settled into my room it became a game of watch and wait. Our baby was still holding on. He called Samantha and left her a message, but she didn't call back. The medicine they gave me helped me to rest a little, but Ed paced the floor all night with worry. Then an hour ago, the monitor I'd been hooked up to went flat. Our baby was gone.

I had been thinking about my loss, but now I thought about his, too. He'd lost two children in one night, one who he had loved for over thirty years and another who he had loved for just a few short weeks.

I raised my hand to his cheek and looked into his eyes, letting him know that I felt his heartbreak, too. "I'm so sorry, Ed," I whispered.

He kissed my hand and rubbed my empty stomach as a small tear trickled down the side of his face. "Don't be sorry. We still have each other, and I know that everything's gonna be all right."

Chapter 40

Samantha . . .

A Long Way to Go

Seven months later

Time heals all wounds.

I had always believed that saying, and now more than ever, I desperately wanted it to be true. It was two weeks from my wedding day, and as I stood in the bridal shop for my final fitting, with Gerti by my side, I couldn't help but think about Emily. This was the first big occasion in my adult life that I was going to experience without her.

Fall had turned into winter, winter rolled into spring, and spring quickly crept into summer. But the changing seasons hadn't mended a friendship and love that had been ripped apart. In the weeks that followed my discovery of Emily and my father's affair, there were so many days that I wanted to sit down with both of them and just ask, why? I wished they had been straight up with me from the beginning. Yes, I would have no doubt been pissed and shocked, but at least I would've known the truth and we would have all been honest with each other.

As I stood patiently while the seamstress pinned my gown around my waist, I tried to keep my mind focused on my wedding day. But it was hard to concentrate on anything other than the emptiness I felt knowing that Emily and my father wouldn't be there to share the special day with me.

"You look so pretty, Sam." Gerti smiled. "Sure would be nice to have Emily in your wedding. You know you need to call her."

I knew that Gerti was right. I missed Emily. My heart had ached for her when I found out about the loss of her baby. No one should have to suffer that kind of pain. After Gerti told me the news, I mailed Emily a card, but that was as far as my olive branch had reached. She called me several times, and e-mailed and texted me, too. But I avoided her messages because I didn't know what to say other than angry words. There were several occasions when I had wanted to pick up the phone and talk to her, but every time I thought about how my friend had smiled in my face while secretly sleeping with my father, I felt sick to my stomach.

I wanted to be a bigger person. After all, I knew better than anyone what it was like to mess up. My father had always been there for me, loving and encouraging me through all of my mistakes. And Emily had been a rock-solid friend who I could depend on, and had even raised my child when I couldn't. I wanted to forgive, and I wanted to embrace them again. I had done a lot of growing, but I still had a long way to go because I couldn't get past the image I saw that night: Emily looking nervous, trying to get rid of me before my father arrived.

I stepped out of my handmade silk gown after the seamstress tucked the final pin into place, and waited for her to leave the fitting room before I spoke. "I know, Gerti. But I just need time," I said quietly.

I looked in the mirror, my white satin slip hanging on my thin frame. I thought about my wedding gown and the careful alterations that would provide the perfect fit. I hoped that one day my relationship with Emily and my father could be mended as nicely. I wanted us to be whole again, but getting there was going to take time.

"All right, Sam," Gerti said, taking a deep breath. "I understand your hurt, but don't take too much time. Life is short and you might not get another chance to make things right."

Chapter 41

Emily . . .

Finally Had to Let It Go

"How was your day?" Ed asked as he came through the back door. He kissed me on my cheek and sat beside me on the couch.

"It was good," I said, smiling back at him. "Everything went well."

I had just completed my first full week back on the job. My coworkers thought I was crazy for returning with only a few weeks left in the school year, but I knew it was time to get back on track, regardless of where the starting line began. I'd been out since last fall after taking an indefinite leave of absence. I needed the time to recover.

After my miscarriage I was so distraught that I could barely function. I wanted to be strong for Ed because he had suffered, too, but the culmination of loss was too great. My dreams were dashed in one swift, crushing blow. And poor Ed. He was just as devastated. That first night home from the hospital we held each other in bed, shutting out the world as we tried to heal.

Thankfully, Ed was able to move on much quicker than I had. I was a wreck back then. I lay around the house for three weeks before I attempted to call Samantha. She had sent me a beautiful sympathy card, but when I tried to reach out to her she wouldn't answer my calls or respond to the e-mails and texts I sent. I missed her.

I knew that my best friend was an integral part of my life, but I hadn't realized how much until she was absent from it. Normally, if something happened to me, good or bad, Samantha was there to share the occasion. Now she was gone, and it was all because of the incredibly bad choices I had made. I should have come forward with the truth from the very beginning, no matter how hard it would have been for all of us to swallow. I realized now that dreading something was far worse than doing it.

Ed missed Samantha, too. I would see a glimpse of sadness cross his eyes from time to time, and I knew it was because of his broken relationship with his daughter. He and I went back and forth, blaming ourselves for the way things had fallen apart. But after months of unreturned phone calls and unanswered mail, we finally had to let it go and start living again.

"I'm going to order dinner. Are you in the mood for Japanese or Italian?" Ed asked as he rose from the couch and headed toward the cabinet in search of a take-out menu.

"Ms. Gerti's fried chicken." I smiled, following him into the kitchen. "It's in the fridge. She dropped it off at school this afternoon when she picked up CJ."

"Nothing hits the spot like Gerti's fried chicken." Ed grinned as he set two plates on the counter.

"Tomorrow is Samantha's big day," I said. I wanted to sound upbeat, but how could I?

I was supposed to be her maid of honor and Ed was supposed to walk her down the aisle. Instead, others who had never shared in her most heartfelt joys or painful sorrows would be doing the honors. I had hoped and prayed that by some stroke of divine intervention, Samantha would have a change of heart. I envisioned her ringing my phone and asking Ed and me to celebrate with her. But with less than twenty-four hours before she was set to say *I do,* I had to embrace the reality that like my lost child, it was another crushed dream.

Ed walked over to me and wrapped his arms around my waist, pulling me in close. "I know," he said. "But don't be sad, because we have a lot to celebrate, and although it might not seem like it now, time heals all wounds. Sam is going to come around."

"You think?"

"Emily, I don't think, I know. And just as surely as she's going to marry Tyler tomorrow, and I'm going to make you my wife in two weeks, we'll all be celebrating together one day. You'll see."

I looked into the steadfast eyes of the man who I knew I would love until my dying day, and for the first time in a long time, I shed a tear.

Chapter 42

Gerti . . .

Three Years Later

It's Thanksgiving day, and I'm as happy as I can be. I started cooking yesterday to make sure I'd have everything ready by this afternoon. All that's left to do now is put the yeast rolls in the oven before everyone gets here. Out of all the holidays, this one is my favorite. It's a time for family and a time to give thanks for all of God's grace, all of his mercy, and all of his blessings. It's a time to celebrate with the people you love. I've done some living on this here earth, and I learned a long time ago that family has nothing to do with blood, but love has everything to do with forgiveness.

As I walk through the kitchen and place a freshly baked sweet potato pie on the sideboard with the rest of the desserts, I smile, thinking about the feast we're going to devour when everyone arrives.

I look at my watch. I still have a half hour before my

doorbell will start ringing and a small herd of people who I love most in this world will come bursting in, ready to eat, laugh, and enjoy each other as we celebrate and give thanks for our blessings. I walk into the living room and sit for a moment to reflect on this day and the magnitude of what it means.

It's hard to believe that just three years ago, this day was a living nightmare. I'll never forget when I picked up the phone that morning and heard Tyler's voice on the other end. "Um, Gerti . . . Sam and I aren't going to make it for dinner," he'd said, sounding congested and stuffy.

The boy had gone and caught a cold, but that wasn't the reason why they weren't coming to the house for Thanksgiving dinner. He told me everything that had happened the night before, how Sam had learned the truth about Emily and her father, and about the baby they were expecting. Hell, that last part took me by surprise and added a whole new dimension to things. A baby was normally a blessing, but in that already sensitive situation, it was like igniting a powder keg.

I remember sitting down and feeling a heavy burden in my heart that day. The phone rang a few minutes later and I instantly knew that the call was going to bring more bad news, and it did. It was Ed. I let him know that Tyler had just called and told me everything. Ed listened in silence and then piled tragic news on top of bad. Emily had lost the baby.

The holidays that year were something awful. But I made sure that CJ wasn't affected too badly. We still had a hearty Thanksgiving dinner, and a big tree in the living room the next month for Christmas. I skirted around his questions when he asked why his Auntie Emee didn't come around anymore and why his papa hadn't lived in the house in months. I tell you, it was a rough time around here.

That summer, Sam and Tyler got married. She made the perfect June bride, Tyler was the model of a proud, handsome groom, and CJ was the cutest little ring bearer in his black tuxedo. And Brenda, she took the cake. She looked good, dressed as sharp as ever, but she was mad as hell because Sam had requested that the ushers seat me right beside her on the pew reserved for the mother of the bride. She looked like she was sucking on a lemon throughout the entire service. But as usual, I didn't pay her one bit of attention, 'cause that day wasn't about her.

Sam wore a long, traditional white gown. Even though everybody in the church, including me, thought that white was a *big* stretch for her, it was what she wanted. It was a beautiful wedding full of love, but at the same time the ceremony carried a sense of sadness. Although it was touching that her favorite cousin, Parker, walked her down the aisle, I knew she wished that her father had given her hand away in marriage. And while her cousin, Claudette, made a nice maid of honor, I knew with all my heart that she wished it had been Emily standing beside her, holding her bouquet while she repeated her vows.

Two weeks later I went to the courthouse downtown for a less extravagant wedding. Ed and Emily exchanged vows in a simple ceremony within one of the judge's chambers. She was radiant. Just as beautiful as she could be in an ivory-colored silk dress that flowed around her body. And Ed looked dashing in his dark gray suit and ivory shirt and tie. Emily's neighbor, Ruben, stood by her side, while Ed's best friend, Ross, stood by his.

After the ceremony, Emily asked me about Sam's wedding. "It was grand, and she looked so pretty," I told her. "But it was missing the two people she loves dearly."

"She won't return my phone calls or e-mails," Emily said.

"Don't you get sad on me," I coaxed. "This is a happy

day, so you enjoy it. Sam will come around. Just give her some time."

Emily nodded and walked over to a bag she'd placed in one of the chairs. She pulled out a card and a beautifully wrapped box. "From Ed and me, for Samantha and Tyler," she said. "Tell her that I wish her happiness, and nothing but the best."

Ding, ding, dong. The sound of the ringing doorbell draws me from the past and back to where I'm so happy to be at this present moment. I walk to the front door and smile. "Happy Thanksgiving, Gerti!" Sam screams. That child is still loud as hell, and ain't never gonna change. But that's why I love her. She wraps her long arms around me for a big hug.

She looks good, and most of all, happy. Her long weave has been replaced by a sophisticated chin-length bob that suits her slim features. She doesn't paint her face up like she used to, now it's just a little blush on her cheeks and some tinted lip gloss. She's still long and skinny, but she has a strong, healthy glow that let's me know she's living right.

"Hey, Gerti!" Tyler says, giving me a kiss on my cheek. He looks the same, with the exception of a few gray hairs at his temple, which I knew would happen being married to Sam and running after two very active little boys.

"Chase, come back here," Samantha says as their sandy-haired two-year-old zips past me and dashes straight toward the kitchen.

"I'll get him," CJ says as he gives me a quick kiss on my cheek and then runs after his little brother.

I smile as we all walk into the living room. CJ is tall and lanky, just like his mother, and Chase is compact and lean, like his father. They're great kids, and Sam's a big part of why. She's turned into a fine mother and I couldn't be more proud.

After they settle in, the doorbell rings again. "I'll be right back," I say, heading to the front door.

"Hey, Ms. Gerti!" Emily smiles, giving me a hug so warm and tight you'd think she hadn't seen me in years instead of just yesterday afternoon when she came by to pick up Elise, her two-year-old daughter.

Losing her first baby nearly crippled Emily. She grieved hard because she didn't just lose a child that night, she lost her best friend, too. Ed took care of things so she could take a long leave of absence from her job. In the weeks that followed she cried and prayed, and then cried and prayed some more until she finally started to heal. Marrying Ed helped her to recover, and when they found out she was pregnant again, the light came back into her eyes.

"Nana Gerrrreeee!" Elise says, grinning in her father's arms. I thought it was nice that Emily gave her daughter her best friend's middle name.

I lean over and kiss Elise on her soft cheek. Emily and Ed have the most adorable little girl in the world, with pink bows tied around long ponytails that hang to her shoulders, a smile just like her mother's, and eyes so big and brown you can drown in them. She has a sweet, gentle nature just like Emily, and a strong-willed, confident side like Ed. He drops her off in the morning and Emily picks her up in the afternoon. Elise and I go for long walks in the quiet neighborhood where I purchased my very own home. All those years of not having to pay rent when I worked for the Baldwins came in real handy.

"What do you say to Nana Gerti?" Ed smiles at Elise, holding his little girl like she's his most prized possession.

"Appy tanksgibin." She grins wide as she claps her little hands together.

"Awww, ain't that sweet." I smile. "Y'all come on in, everyone's almost here."

As soon as Emily and Sam see each other, they embrace. "Girl, you look so good!" Sam says to Emily.

"Just tryin' to keep up with you." Emily smiles back, hugging her friend.

Looking at these two girls makes my whole day!

After I gave Sam the wedding gift that Emily and Ed bought her, she still didn't make an effort to reach out to them. It was the last traces of her childish stubbornness, mixed with a little hurt. Then a few months later, they both called me with news that they were pregnant. At that point I told Sam point-blank that it was time for the silliness to end.

It's amazing how children can change things. A week after I spoke to Sam, she called Emily. It wasn't easy for her, but slowly she let her guard down and opened up her heart.

"Hey, Sam." Ed smiles as he walks over to give her a kiss. "How's my girl."

"Daddy!" Samantha says, bursting into another big smile. She wraps her arms around her father, who is still holding Elise, and gives them both kisses on their cheeks. "Look at my lil sis, all cute in her pink ribbons and ponytails," Samantha coos. She pauses a minute. "It's still weird that my sister and my son are the same age."

I smile and nod. "That's life."

"And I wouldn't have it any other way," she says with sincerity, looking over to Emily. "I really mean that."

Ding, ding, dong. The doorbell sounds again. I know who it is, and I'm glad he's finally here.

"Happy Thanksgiving, Gerti," my tall, dark and

handsome cousin greets me. He is holding a bottle of wine to go along with his beaming smile.

"Harry, it's so good to see you. Come on in."

My cousin, Harry Winston, is a small but very important part of why this day is even able to happen. A few years ago, right before all hell broke loose, he unknowingly became involved with the woman I worked for.

I'll never forget the night he called me. Harry and I had lost touch once we graduated from high school and moved away from our small town. We'd vaguely kept up with each other through a distant aunt we shared, so when I heard from him out of the blue, questioning me about Brenda, I nearly dropped the phone.

Harry told me that a miracle had happened and that he'd reconnected with the woman of his dreams. When we were teenagers, his father's friend was able to get Harry a summer job in Oak Bluffs on Martha's Vineyard. It was a big deal for us country folk from Alabama. After the summer ended, Harry returned home completely love-struck. He'd met a girl named Betty whose wealthy family had vacationed there. She had his nose wide open, and over the years, Harry never forgot about the girl he'd met that summer, the one he called the woman of his dreams.

All I could do was shake my head at the thought that Brenda had given him a false name. She'd been sneaky, even as a teenager—some things never change. When Harry saw her at the hotel, he remembered her right away. He looked her up in the hotel registry and found all of her information. He knew I was living in DC, working for a well-to-do family, so he took a chance and called our great-aunt Mary to get my phone number.

I found out about their affair the night of Emily and Samantha's big birthday party. Harry's nose was still open after all those years. I told him the real deal about Brenda, but he wouldn't believe me. He had a fantasy in his mind that had never left him. Well, you can't argue with grown folk. So I shut my mouth, sat back, and let him find out for himself.

Harry called me right after a big blowout they'd had. When he told me how he struck the fear of God in Brenda by pretending he was going to blackmail her, I encouraged him to string her along and keep her on edge for as long as he could. I know everybody gets what's coming to them, but sometimes people need a little help along the way!

Knowing she had dirt hanging over her head kept Brenda from fighting Ed on the divorce and causing all kinds of hell. I had sat back and watched her ruin lives for too long. Emily and Ed deserved a shot at happiness, and so did Sam. Brenda needed to either let them be happy or stay out of the way, which turned out to be one and the same.

By the time Brenda learned the truth about Emily and Ed, the divorce papers had already been finalized and the two of them were living together. Boy oh boy, was she furious! I knew she could be sneaky and vindictive, but even I had underestimated her ability to act a plumb fool. She stalked Emily, made harassing phone calls to her house day and night, and tried to run her over one day when she was leaving the grocery store. But what took the cake was when she showed up at Ed's office and threatened to cut off his privates and shove them down his throat . . . but only after she killed him first! But the humiliation of her public arrest after the outburst finally quieted her down. Today, she still lives in her big fancy house on the Gold Coast, but she has no one to share it with.

Harry walks into the living room and greets everyone, introducing himself to people who don't know how much gratitude they really owe him.

"You need me to help with anything?" Bill asks, coming around the corner from my bedroom.

Bill Harris is my *friend*. We met two and a half years ago when I moved to this neighborhood. He's a retired accountant and die-hard Redskins fan. He lost his wife ten years ago and hadn't dated much since. One day he saw me working in my front yard and told me that a lady as pretty as me shouldn't be down on my knees, digging in the dirt. I laughed and told him that where I was from, that's all we used to do. Turns out he's from the South, too. We hit it off over coffee and my sweet potato pie, and he's been sitting his feet under my table ever since.

I smile and look up at him. "As a matter of fact, I know how you can help me." I wink, motioning for him to come over and give me the kind of sugar that don't go in no cake!

I never thought I'd find love fifty years after I lost it, but I have. God surely is good because I have a wonderful man, children who love me, and grandchildren to spoil. I didn't come by my family the traditional way that most folks do, but they're mine just as surely as if I'd breathed life into each one of them. In the end, things always work out like they're supposed to. I've learned that you just have to play the hand you're dealt.

Don't miss Trice Hickman's latest novel in
the Unexpected Love series,

When Trouble Finds You

On sale in August 2014!

"How can two small words cause so much trouble?" Victoria whispered aloud as she stared at the name flashing across her cell phone screen. Her back stiffened against the soft fabric of her high-back office chair as she bit down on her ruby-colored lower lip, a nervous habit she'd developed when she was a teenager. The name "Parker Brightwood" flashed at her like a warning light, and she knew that a call from him was something for which she needed to brace herself.

She sat forward, propped one elbow on top of her large mahogany desk, and debated whether she should answer his call or let it roll into her voice mailbox. She knew she'd have to talk to him sooner or later, so rather than avoid and ignore him—a costly mistake she'd made in the past—she hit the talk button.

"Hello Parker."

"Are you okay?"

"Yes, I'm fine. Why do you ask?"

"Because you sound so formal. Not like your usual self."

She wanted to ask him how he could possibly know

what she usually sounded like. After all, it wasn't as if they talked on a regular basis. Those days had ended many years ago. But she also knew that as much as her life and circumstances had changed in that long span of time, a few delicate, if not complicated things hadn't, and Parker was one of them.

"You sure you're okay?" he repeated.

"I'm sure. Now how can I help you?"

He chuckled. "There you go again, talking to me like a greeter in a department store."

"I have to keep things on a business level with you."

"Oh, and why is that?"

She took a deep breath. "Because you don't know how to act."

"Well, since you're the consummate purveyor of proper etiquette, maybe you can give me a few lessons. I'm a very good student and I catch on pretty quick, but you already know that, don't you?"

She smiled on the other end, despite not wanting to.

They were both quiet for a short pause. Victoria could hear him breathing through the silence on the other end, and she imagined the sly grin that was no doubt spread across his lusciously soft lips that carried a perfect tint of pink. She was almost pulled in for a moment, but she quickly regained her focus. "I don't have all day, Parker. What do you want?"

"Victoria, I think you're losing that gracious southern charm that always made you so lovable, and I might add, irresistible."

"Get to the point or I'm hanging up."

"Okay, okay. I want to know if I can add two more guests to the list for the reception?"

Victoria reached for her silver plated writing pen and softly tapped it against the top of her desk as she let out a small sigh. She knew that Parker's question was nothing more than an excuse to talk to her. When he'd called last month asking her the very same thing, she'd told him then, that according to the guest list which she'd spent hours meticulously creating, there was room for up to 5 additional guests he could invite, all in preparation for the final headcount for his son's and her daughter's wedding next month.

Ever since that bright, sunny afternoon one year ago when her daughter, Alexandria, happily told her that she'd reconnected with PJ, her childhood best friend, who happened to be Dr. Parker Brightwood Sr's son, Victoria had known that trouble was waiting to find her.

A storm cloud of memories had rushed back into her life that day, but unlike her encounters with Parker from the past, she now knew she'd have to handle him, and their dealings, in a very different way.

Rather than rehashing the fact that she'd already answered his question last month, and pointing out that his phone call was basically a rouse to engage her in conversation, she simply went along with the flow. "Yes Parker, that's fine. You can bring two more people. Anything else?"

He chuckled again, this time in a slow, seductive tone. "Damn, that was easy. If I'd known you were going to be so accommodating I would've asked for more . . . much more."

His smooth, deep and sexy voice hadn't changed over the years. And even though his words were laced with dangerous innuendo, coming from his mouth, they sounded as good and as sweet as apple pie. Silky seduction was part of his undeniable charm, and it had worked on her more times than she cared to remember. Victoria knew she couldn't be lulled in by his sexiness or the natural chemistry they'd always shared. She had to use her head and shut things down before they had an inkling of a chance to get started.

"I know exactly what you're hinting at, Parker. And I'm not having it. We're too old to play these ridiculous cat and mouse games."

"Who's old and who's playing games?"

Victoria pressed her hand against her left temple. "Bring whoever you want, just make sure you all show up on time."

"Are you upset?"

"No, I'm irritated."

"Have you been having a rough day?"

"Not until you called me with this foolishness." Now she couldn't hold back any longer. "You knew full well when you dialed my number that you could invite more guests because we discussed this last month when we talked. You didn't have to call me today."

Parker cleared his throat. "Victoria, I have a hectic schedule and a very busy practice at two hospitals. Sometimes it's hard to keep everything straight. I know we've talked about this before, but I honestly wasn't sure if I'd reached the headcount you gave me, so I wanted to check with you before extending an invitation to two of my colleagues.

"Uh huh, right . . ."

"It's true."

"Sure, Parker. Whatever you say."

"Listen, I'm being straight with you. I have no reason at all to lie. You know I don't play games."

"Sure you don't."

"Damn, I don't remember you being this cold."

"Put on a jacket and get used to it."

Parker laughed, then lowered his voice. "You're really something else."

"Are you finished?"

"No, I have one more question.

Victoria sighed, not sure she wanted to hear what he had to say, much less answer it. "Go ahead."

"I want to know what's wrong with me calling you? We're going to be in-laws . . . family, in a manner of speaking. A phone call is much more personal than an email. I can get personal with you, can't I?"

Victoria squirmed in her chair. "Get personal? What's that supposed to mean?"

"Anything you want it to."

"Parker, I don't have time for this. Like I said, bring whoever the hell you want to bring, and as I told you at the beginning of this conversation, don't call me again with any more foolishness."

Parker's deep voice took on an even deeper tone. "Our children's wedding day isn't foolishness."

"You know what I meant."

"I know what you just said."

Victoria stood up and walked over to her office window, pacing back and forth in her black patent leather peep-toe heels. "Of course the wedding isn't foolishness. It's going to be the single biggest day of Alexandria's and PJ's lives, and I know without a doubt that it will be the start of a happy future for them both. What I'm talking about is the way you're always dropping hints and alluding to things . . ."

"Alluding?" Parker interrupted her in a surprised voice. "Victoria, we go way back, and you know me. I don't allude, I take action. I might flirt, but I don't drop hints. I'm direct and I say what I mean."

"Then why are you calling me during the middle of the day with this?"

"I thought I already explained that."

Victoria took a deep breath, continuing to pace back and forth.

"I hear you taking those deep breaths," Parker said. "Just calm down and stop pacing back and forth in front of your window. Relax."

Victoria stopped in her tracks. He knew her too well, even after all these years. She walked back to her desk and sat down. "You're right. We're going to be in-laws soon. We'll be seeing each other at the holidays and other occasions as the years go on, so I want to get something straight right now."

"Okay, I'm listening."

"I'm happily married. Our children are getting ready to be happily married. And from what I hear, hopefully, you will be happily married, too. So please stop this flirting or whatever you want to call it. This isn't right and it needs to end right now on this call."

Parker cleared his throat and let out a small laugh. "That's really interesting. I don't know who you've been talking to, but I can assure you that marriage isn't on the table for me. However, I couldn't agree with you more about PJ and Alexandria, and I wish them nothing but the very best. I love Alexandria like the daughter I never had, and I have no doubt that she and my son will enjoy many years of happiness."

Victoria wasn't about to tell him that PJ had been the source of her information, or that he wasn't a fan of his father's significant other, and now she regretted making the comment. "I'm happy to hear that, Parker, and I'm glad we understand each other."

"I think we always have."

"Okay, well, you take care and I'll see you at the wedding."

She didn't give him a chance to respond. She hit the end button and leaned back against her chair as she let out a deep breath. She thought about the wise saying that Alexandria told her Grandma Allene had whispered to her one evening. *You can never go wrong doing right.* Victoria knew that Parker was anything but right, and if she wasn't careful with him she could find herself going in the wrong direction.

Parker had broken her heart in what seemed like another lifetime, and the poor choices she'd made with him years later had nearly cost her the happy marriage she'd talked about moments ago. "This time I'm going to do the right thing. I'm not going to make the same mistake a third time."

But even as Victoria spoke those words, a small voice told her to hold on tight for the bumpy road ahead.

The Hottest African American Fiction
from
Dafina Books